So, there was or

Valentine Odey, wh   )

know that. One day a Big Envelope fell on his ...   o

work. The fact that it landed flat on HIS head seemed indicative of something, so Valentine took it to his office and opened it up. Inside the envelope there was a large manuscript which he read from cover to cover. And when he was done, he sighed. Not that it was exciting, certainly not, but it was good. Valentine set the envelope down on his desk. He didn't know what to do with it. He was already a poet but he wasn't sure if he was good at it. With caution he looked at the front of the envelope again. "For the attention of **VICK PREY, PRIVATE INVESTIGATOR.**" He tried to imagine the scandal it would cause if he wrote that on his own door. He looked around his office, how everything was in business order except for his own reading interests which were hopelessly piled up on his desk. The clock on his wall said 7:30 am with its red hands on a white bed. Valentine was already tired and thought he should rest before everyone came to see him. So, he sat down in his chair which hardly fit into his office where he'd piled up all his mysteries and treatises about philosophical differences and put his head on this new addition, which barely fit into the rest of it. Soon there was a knock at his door. But it was at a different door, as he was already asleep on The Envelope. Valentine Odey, middle manager at Nike in a complicated world. The last thing he expected was to be read.

2.11-23

For Claire,
Best Regards!

~ *(signature)*

This is a book of entertainment. It's
nicely spaced, and at times it's
vaguely helpful.

THIS IS FOR MY MOM AND DAD__
WHO LOVED TO SKATE ON THE
ROUGE RIVER

A Loosely Wrapped Bundle

A Loosely Wrapped Bundle is a work of fiction, although some of it is true. My thanks to my wife, Linda, who is my genuine muse, whose paintings and moods have sustained me. All rights are reserved with regard to this book. For permission to use any part of it, in any format, please write to Eight Dog Corner Press at 120 Bruce Hill Rd., Spencer, NY 14883, or to 8dog@lightlink.com. Just so you know how this works. In this story The Envelope was a labor of generations, PORTFIRO came about quickly, and the rest of it came about with trepidation. I hope you enjoy it.

Printed In The United States Of America

Eight Dog Corner Press

Far from being a sentinel for the Nike Corporation, Valentine Odey is a middle manager. But on occasion when he falls asleep in his office he becomes a sentinel and is whisked out of his office and flown away. Nothing really grande ever happens to him, but in his dreams at least it gets rearranged.

Part One

The Envelope,
And The Unlikely Choice
of Valentine Odey

For Patrick & Joyce

I

The Way To Floss
In Which The Role Of Vick Prey
Is Thrust Upon Valentine Odey

1.
The Knock At My Door

~ I was just settling in to, *Eighty Dollars To Stamford,* a wonderful pulp novel by Lucille Fletcher, when there was a knock at my door. I couldn't imagine who that was. At the same time I oddly found myself doing a mental checklist which was unfamiliar to me: Rent, Tara's Cleaning, New York Licensing Board, Permits, possibly another government agency I didn't know about, Tara. And then I noticed a stencil leaning against a wall of my office with, 'NO CHANGE,' made up on it in big letters and fresh orange paint dripping liberally from it. Egads, what was that about? Further complicating matters there was a stuffed moose in the corner with his big head looking down benevolently on me, a pair of slippers with bells on them were waiting at my feet, and a cape draped over my coat rack with blood upon it. I don't ever remember my office looking like this before.

And THEN there was another knock, similar in metre to the first. In truth it was a quiet knock, not one of those enthusiastic ones which always makes me nervous, but just a nice knock like maybe I was expecting it. Still, you never know, the mind can be faulty, so, I said, "Who is it?" which I don't think you can fault me for doing.

The person at my door said, "My name is Ray Lin and I would like to speak to the Private Investigator, Mr. Vick Prey." She said this with such a soft and confident voice that I stopped working on my entry to the San Diego Poetry Magazine and hoped she was talking about me.

"Well, I'm Vick Prey!" I said, wondering if I really could be mistaken for him.

"Oh, good!" she said. "Because I would like to employ your services."

"You would!"

"Yes, I'm sure of it."

Now I was beside myself. I had a feeling the Envelope had something to do with this, but I don't know what I did with it. Maybe this person at my door knows where it is.

"Would you like to come in."

"Yes, I really would," she said.

1

Something in the back of my mind, which might be where The Envelope went, was pulsing MADLY, like it was trying to tell me that this was a very important part that was in it. I looked around my office, again, at the stencil, the stuffed moose in my corner, the slippers with bells on them at my feet, and the cape on my coat rack with blood upon it. Then I chose peril and said,

"Well, then, you should!"

2.

A Rock In A Field Is A Star In A Bin

~ Beneath my office there's a car wash. I'm not sure Nike is aware of this. She came in during the Laser Spin Dry. She was blonde. It's possible they all are in here. I was about to say, "I assume you're Ray Lin," but I was pretty sure she knew that. She stood in the doorway and I could hear a new car coming into the bay. The baby blue wall behind her looked like the heaven she came out of. I got up to greet her and we stood on either side of my Sears and Roebuck card table. I had a nice maple desk once and I wished I had it now, but I had a feeling this wasn't that first impression you read about, and that Ms. Lin already knew a lot about me. We just couldn't stand there all day.

"Can I get you a chair Ms. Lin."

"Do you have one?"

I'm thinking of Maisy and Lennon singing "You be the King, I'll be the People." I'm also thinking about the unusual possibility that I only have one chair.

"Mr. Prey."

"I'm sorry, Ms. Lin. I was just thinking of something."

"I know."

"You do?"

Ms. Lin is wearing a long leopard print dress, with wide mascara eyes, and hair that flows like a burning candle. Her face is like a painting by Renoir with faintly colored lips, which I almost fell into when I leaned over my table to look at them. The truth is, I slipped, possibly on my new slippers, and went flying toward her which may have alarmed her. The linoleum tiles on my floor passed slowly beneath me like farmland, neatly laid out in squares that could have been Italian. I was descending in the middle of them as well as in the middle of all my books. My stacks of mysteries and philosophy fluttered in the chaos and a number of pages turned before me, parts of which were, "Her eyes had cargo and transport written all over them."

I got a hold of myself. The manuscript seemed like a dream to me now. Call me Ismael, if you want, for I looked disconsolately into her sea. I felt a little foolish. But Ms. Lin in turn smiled at me.

"Don't you have another office, maybe a little larger one!"

Well, I did, but I don't know what happened to it. To make up for it, I remembered from the manuscript that I had a Winnebago Warrior out in the parking lot.

"Is that the one I saw in the drive-thru!"

I said it probably was unless an ungrateful crew had pushed it out of the way. I asked her if it had a bold green stripe on the outside. She said, "It did!" I also knew it had a lot of room and a wonderful radio on the inside. In the end that's where we decided to go. I hated to abandon my books and my office by the bay so soon. I had wanted to show her around a bit. But something new had clicked into 'Play' in my environment and I was going with it. Ms. Lin turned in the fluorescent light and allowed me to come around to her side. We both had an air of confidence and motors that could jump. Her heady fragrance was pulling me toward a cliff. We'd be lucky if we got out of this alive. The rope hanging from the transom above my door gave me an idea I hadn't had before. I grabbed Ray Lin by the waist and drew her to me. She was as soft as her hair. But, I knew I couldn't stop here and go on about her texture, not now. Someone in *Rebel Without a Cause* on the little tv set in my corner was already flapping her high school jacket and leaping wildly in the air. The throbbing undercurrent of our engines had changed into a crazy Stravinsky charge. Our headlights were coming into the transom. There was no time. With her in one hand and an invoice in the other I yelled to her, "PULL IT!" She did and as we walked down the hall to the sound of tin, I told her, "You know, a rock in a field is a star in a bin."

3.
Something Else You May Not Be Aware Of

~ At The Plant

At the plant where they make floss
a watchman by the name of Ross
bought a spool of fishing line
and gave it to his boss.
At the plant where they make floss
the boss, who liked to be called Hoss,

thought the fishing line was
something new they had in mind
and sawed his jaw in half.

~ Something else you may not be aware of, in time we'll come to Ross's Guard Shack. Ross's Guard Shack is in a small municipality called Floss. Specifically, it's just inside the gate at Floss, Inc., which is also in Floss. Ross and Hoss are the watchmen who work there. In the manuscript we go to Floss, so that's what we're doing. Hoss didn't really saw his jaw in half, I'm quite sure of that. Poets can take a lot of liberties with their thoughts, and I gave a lot of thought to this one. I'm sure Ross and Hoss get along together very well. It might appear from this poem that Hoss is a fool, but we won't know that for sure until we get to the second part of this adventure. And we won't really know for sure until we get to the third part of this adventure. And that's a very long ways away.

"Is there a secret to this!"

Ms. Lin was having difficulty lashing herself to The Warrior. Of course, I was only too happy to reach over and help. She seemed to be excited about our transition from the office. I don't think she'd ever been in a Winnebago before so I wasn't taken back by her state. But soon I thought it was time we signaled our intentions, so I asked Ms. Lin if she wouldn't mind sticking her hand out the window and wiggling it.

"Like this!" she said.

It would be hard to describe what I saw. Her hand was like a delicate flag in the Spanish American War, surrendering to one and all, including noncombatants. All wars would be over, or would only be started if there was a promise of just such a sight as this at the end of them. I told Ms. Lin she was doing a good job and that it would certainly gain the attention of everyone in the final rinse cycle so they wouldn't run over us as we pulled away. But this only made her go back to it even more vociferously. I wondered if I was missing something. It was becoming clear to me that Ms. Lin was more complicated than I thought. I couldn't rule out anything. In truth, she may be a spy. I know they like them to be beautiful and resourceful.

In the hummingbird heart of the car wash someone was playing a song. It sounded very much like Corinne Bailey Rae, and she was singing a song about relationships. I was taken by it and wondered if it was possible in a flash to know everything there is to know about somebody because you got lined up perfectly, or if you always had to work at it. I leaned back with my elbow out the window of The Warrior and watched Ms. Lin waving broadly to the line of cars waiting to enter the car wash, with the long boom in the automatic car wash bay whirling and Corinne Bailey Rae singing. We certainly did seem to be lined up for something.

Ms. Lin turned to me and smiled, and as she brushed her hair from the left side of her face I could see she had a small mole by the line of her jawbone. I read somewhere that such a thing was a sign of beauty. I wondered if it made sense to be asking someone who was born under that sign to let you know if the coast was clear. It seemed so small to ask that. On the other hand, without my doing so we might be stuck in this drive-thru forever. I waited to see if she would brush her hair away again before I broke the ice.

(Ms. Lin, I want to ask you about your mole.)

"Ms. Lin, I think it's time we peek in the wings and see if any consorts have made it back stage."

"What do they look like."

"In this area they are disguised. You may see one in tights who dons an Elizabethan garb and carries a loose pouch of gold. That's Gerald. I wouldn't in the least be afraid of him. But he is a good example. Otherwise, Ms. Lin, your assignment is to observe if anyone now, at all, is in our moat or in any way impedes us as the Shared W is ignited."

"Well, I really don't see that anyone is in our way!" she said.

"Perfect, Ms. Lin! You are a Master Rigger! I doubt there is any wind you could not re-route us on that blows upon our sea. Climb down from your spire and take your rightful place beside me in our palanquin. Not even Vernet can expose us."

"Can I turn the radio on."

"Of course, you can."

4.

Dave Thompson On The Radio

~ Dave Thompson had just been introduced on 90.1 FM Different Radio. "Thank you. It's nice to be back here in Central New York!"

So that's where we were.

Resounding applause, which included whistles and cheers, something which sounded like gargling and the sound of cans opening, came across very well on the radio.

"Thank you, Central NY!!! I got my daughter, Dia, with me again, and her back-up girls, The Demures. Our song is called, "Tasha, Hook Me Up." It's about a revolution in the economy. If we have any Tashas out there you're a big part. So, I hope you like it."

There were shouts of approval in the grandstands as Dave pulled his guitar strap over his shoulder. "Let's get ready to appreciate a story of suspense. Ya Ready."

...Dave

"Every time I get a loan
I feel that I have grown."

Dia and The Demures

"Tasha, Hook Me Up
Tasha, Hook Me Up."

Back to Dave

"It doesn't matter if the platter's
got a record goin on."

"Tasha, Hook me Up
Tasha, Hook Me Up."

"You can lead a horse to water
but you gotta turn it on."

"Hey Tasha,
Tasha, Hook Me Up
Hey Tasha."

"My friends come around
they call me Mr. Joan,
say, that boy's got the magic
he can get along."

"Extreme Tasha,
Tasha, Hook Me Up
Will you, Tasha."

I looked over at Ms. Lin to see how this was going with her.

"You can turn them down if you want, Ms. Lin. They're probably not done yet. Dave, in particular, tends to go on."

"I think they're great!"

"Then, I do too, Ms. Lin!"

5.

We're On Our Way

~ We're slogging on a medieval road which the Ingenious Don Quixote de La Mancha will soon cross. He's a wonderful figure in literature, tilting at Windmills in Spain in the 1500's, imagining them to be Giants. He was also infatuated with Dulcinea del Toboso, a local girl who must have lived in his neighborhood. The years went by, they lost touch, and Don Quixote became an old man who had a cat. Dulcinea, however, remained his inspiration/obsession. As the magnificent Miguel de Cervantes, the author, wrote about him, our Unsettled Squire resided in a modest home in the suburbs of Madrid and was considered quite odd. Sometimes he put a kitchen pot on his head when he went tilting in his backyard, believing it to be an elegant helmet. Don Quixote had stacks and stacks of books piled up all around him in his reading room. They were mostly about Chivalry, and Knights riding off to save citizens in distress and generally to right wrongs in the world. I always have him in mind. Don had difficulty with the immediate past but anything long ago came right to his mind. Then he would raise his sword up in his chair and swear to avenge those who were last. All this, of course, alarmed his cat, who stayed with him, nonetheless, and rode with Don Quixote on his lap. Don Quixote had a barn horse whom he imagined to be a great horse, who was fit for him to ride and go off to save the world on. One day Don Quixote decided to do just that, to go off on a long quest, to tilt at windmills and to look once again for the beautiful Dulcinea del Toboso. There was a farm worker in the neighborhood who Don Quixote convinced to go off with him as his aide, also. His name was Sancho. And the horse's name was Rozinante.

You have to imagine our ill-suited Squire sallying thru his yard into his field out back in a rapture of joy to begin his adventure. In our case between the garbage cans and the vacuum stanchions and over the spots reserved for our successful neighbors. We were off on our adventure. "L.A. Woman, Motel Madness," surged out of car radios all around us, but Dave was still going strong on ours. The push-pull of eternal forces was clearly aligned in our favor and I only had time to take one more peek at Ms. Lin to make sure I wasn't dreaming before the Dashing Dimension, which is another name I have for Our Beloved Warrior, pulled out of the car wash.

We're on our way and I instinctively look in my rearview mirror to see if anything fell off. Nothing has which I take to be a good sign. I also had been rewarded with Ms. Lin showing up.

"Are you comfortable."

"Oh, very!"

"This is a straight back seat. You can't get them anymore on a normal American car."

"Where did you find it."

"What?"

"The seat!"

"Oh, actually it came with the Shared W. I don't know where they got it."

It appeared Ms. Lin was comfortable with our new arrangement.

Behind us now the early morning sun has discovered a paper bag in a Maple tree. Ms. Lin, for her part, was on an exploration all her own. She opened my glove compartment and stirred thru a big pile of Beemans gum wrappers, unfolded them and smelled them. I really thought she was going to lick them. There was a big map under the pile, but she seemed to decidedly avoid that, for now, for some reason, and went on to brush her hands mysteriously over a slew of Marble Memo Pads which were filled with unruly handwriting and big, looping letters which appalled me. Then she looked at my expense sheets, which were empty. And THEN she put on my Winchester Sunglasses.

"How do I look!"

I told her she looked like a movie star, or at the very least a singer of some importance. Ms. Lin closed the glove compartment.

Apparently, there was another pressing thing which she wanted to get on to.

"Is Vick Prey your real name?"

"What!"

"I was just wondering if Vick Prey is your real name."

"Of course not!"

"Well, what is it?"

"I can't tell you that. It would ruin everything."

"Oh, Mr. Prey."

"Even that dulls it!"

"I'll try to be more careful."

After a short delay I said, "I adjusted it a little bit to sound Dangerous, that's all. I thought it might help. I'm sure the other one will surface at some point, but for now I have cards made up, 'VICK PREY, PRIVATE EYE.' I drew a big eye on them and I typed in the word, 'PRIVATE,' under that. I also put my address on them."
"Did you end up with a lot of clients?"
"A small number, probably. But they're all very interesting."

"Do you know what I like now!" she said.
I was soon discovering that Ms. Lin could be a little taxing. I wasn't sure how many guesses I got. There really wasn't much in here.
"I like all these CDs which you have piled up on your beautiful dash. But it looks like they're all Rock 'n Roll. Oh, here's Portland's Quality Bop Incorporated, and Duffy, and King Tubby!"
"Misfortune happens on many stages, Ms. Lin. I have to be ready. You can put one on if you want, but if it's Tom Waits we may have to pull over."
She laughed. But, with Dave still serenading us, I knew she would hold off to pick one later. For now, she cupped Tom Waits in her hands, and giggled, every now and then.

6.
Floss

~ Subject Matters

Working on the Thruway
Maurice had a border issue.

~ The municipality of Floss lies in between Victor Victoria and Steve McQueen. Floss, Inc., which is important to the story, is located in the middle of Floss. A lot of people who live in Floss also work at Floss, Inc., so it's commonly called Floss, also. I have a pleasant interaction with the employees at Floss, in which I undertake a little sport with them, setting them to music, which I hear. The music, of course, is my poems. Sometimes I refer to them as my paintings. I hope you don't get confused by that. I don't think my subjects mind at all and often they ask to see them. You've already seen some. I'm a little inconsistent with the form, but, in general, it keeps me sharp. Then

I go back to my office and check everything for spelling. And then I look for a good book.

In the middle of Floss, Inc. is The Great Spool. I'm told that it's endless. It's also complicated. There will probably be more on that later.

Floss is against war, and this is commonly known. For my part I'm more interested in the forces at work on a more personal level, ever since I discovered Guy de Maupassant and the poet, Shelley. Oh, also Bishop Sheen. I still don't know what happened to him. He may be working at a fair. But these three are always on my mind, as is Mr. Quixote.

"Is there anywhere to go to the bathroom?"

That was Ms. Lin.

"Ms. Lin, I'm not sure if they do that in movies, or in books either for that matter."

"But we're in a Winnebago!"

"Oh. Right."

Now that we're alone my gears seem to be ramming up. A lot of clicking is going on in my head which is mildly uncomfortable. The role of The Private Investigator With The Unfortunate Name (In Truth He Would Like To Be A Poet. I added that.) has been more fully thrust upon me.

Floss has a lot of signs. Whichever way you want to go there's usually a sign with an arrow on it going that way. It's very affirming. When you get lost it's probably because you've followed a sign with no arrow. I regard those as gifts from outer space. My favorite place to hang out at Floss, Inc. is Ross's Guard Shack where I'm always working on a report or reading to him from Verlaine. There are all sorts of notes on the wall. I haven't read all of them yet. I'm sure one of them says, 'Read These Notes.' It's also possible that one of them says, 'Beware of Vick Prey.' Ms. Lin has returned.

"Did I miss anything!"

"No, just a billboard. With way too much on it to remember, at 30 mph. I hope I didn't rock you."

"No, not at all. You have a very comfortable seat back there. What is it."

"It's a horse collar."

I wasn't quite ready to tell her, yet, that the horse was Rozinante.

7.
Our Merry Band Expands

~ Her golden eyes, the makeup of the sun, sought refuge out her side of The Warrior. In truth, she looked wistful. It had warmed up and my client could roll her window down now but she doesn't wish to. I think she liked the glass. Maybe she felt comfortable with it that way, for some reason. Security. I don't really know. For a moment I wondered if she had been a cashier or a receptionist at some point, at which time there was glass for her to sit behind. She was listening to Dave, again, on the radio. He was imploring Tasha to give him a loan, which I assume is 'The Revolution In The Economy.' He says to her, *"Taha, look here, baby, this your Honeycomb."*

Ms. Lin asks me, "What's a honeycomb."
I told her, "In this case I believe it's a term of endearment."
"That's nice," she said.

But, at last she did roll her window down. Her hair opened and closed in the wash of cars going by like the aperture of a 35mm camera. In another setting she might have been a Spokane Indian calling her salmon up the waves. But in this one she waited patiently on her gray surface, for destiny.

Then "STOP!!!" she very suddenly yelled, at the top of her lungs.

"WHY!!!" I yelled at the top of mine.

"Because he might be going the wrong way!" she said.

"WHO?" I said.

When out of the corner of my eye I espied a young man in a mariner sweater on the other side of the road. He had an instrument case with him. No doubt, a guitar. We both laughed and The Warrior, who had apparently decided to take Ms. Lin's side all along, began the long process of pulling over from 30 mph. At that time, I also couldn't help but notice that the

11

fortuneteller's house on the left was vacant. That was unfortunate. I had taken up a habit of promoting her activity as I was always hopeful of a good reading. But now the wonderful OPEN sign was gone, as was the one on the side which said, READINGS & ADVICE – DON'T SIGN ANYTHING UNTIL YOU TALK TO ME.

"And he might have something important to say!"

Somehow, I felt that Ms. Lin was fumbling her lines, or at the very least, offering me the chance to make a right decision. But we did stop and it turned out that this person had a dog, also, which I think was a given. As we waited for our new band members to make it over to us I could tell that Ms. Lin was enjoying this. Her beautiful hair was illuminated in the early morning sun like a harbor light at the mouth of a sea. I was sure she couldn't help but be seen.

8.
Chaos In Our Theatre

~ "I wonder what's taking them so long."

"Apart from the possibility of pulling luggage out from behind trees, maybe a country buffet has sprung up and captivated our landmarks. Do you see a stack of trays and a poor soul with a rubber apron on standing before an ash mountain of pots and pans."

"Nothing like that."

"Ms. Lin, I am running out of likely scenarios. Why don't you just give a hoot and see if anything comes running. If we were in the heart of Floss I wouldn't suggest such a thing as it might set off a general alarm, but out here in Belleville we're probably safe. Are you ready."

As it turned out she didn't have to be.
"There they are!"

I know this is where you're supposed to have a pause which allows the scene to develop, but the thought of unintended consequences has always made me nervous. Yet, I didn't know how to insert myself in these as I was wedged behind the wheel. I would have to rely upon Ms. Lin to relay the information I needed. So I thought, just how do I promote her to do that when I am without any information about her. I don't know how long this can go on, this game of cat & mouse, which she is so skillfully perpetrating. I've used up so many words to this point that I'm starting to lose a clear sense of what they mean. I have to think. Could I have prevented this. No, it's not likely. Ms. Lin holds all the cards. I'll just wait here for her to return with our Native Sons, and act surprised.

"They were looking at the moon!"

"I was coming to that."

Our tranquility was broken by a clang of armour in the kitchen. In addition to that, something large and clumsy was skittering along our aluminum runway. It seemed like the choice we had made was about to engulf us. I was right.

"Sa gou boy!"

"Ms. Lin, are you ok?"

"I'm quite ok," she said, giggling, as she surveyed a large tag on a large dog. "And so's, 'Leonard.' You know what, Leonard, this is Mr. Prey!"

We looked at each other awkwardly. His companion soon arrived.

I feel I'm obligated to describe our new companions to you, as they may turn out to be important to the story. I hope this helps. The person we had first seen on the side of the road was tall, a weightless looking boy of indescribable age wearing a tattered tangerine sweater, with brown trousers. A faded yellow sash was pulled thru the belt loops of these trousers, and thereafter was tied loosely and allowed to drop down a good foot. And it was indeed a guitar which he had with him, in a blue case. His companion was a rebel of sorts. He wore no clothes. Of the two he was the happiest to see us, probably because of our warm accommodations. He had irregular angles which spread out in all directions, certainly not according to any plan which I knew about, and around his neck he a had a collar made of yellow hemp, and on that collar there was a tag which said 'L E O N A R D' in big block letters.

"I'm sorry about that pot you had hanging up in the kitchen. I hope Leonard didn't surprise you too much. He's a love bug."

Ms. Lin couldn't stop beaming at them. Eventually the young mariner extended his hand to me.

"I'm Piedmont Red," he said, as though he was clarifying his position on a color wheel.

"Piedmont Red?" I said, incredulously. "Don't you have to be a little older to have a name like that."

He laughed. "You can call me Hew if you want! A lot of other people do. It seems to depend on what Schedule you're on."

I didn't know what schedule I was on. Nevertheless, Hew, went on.

"You've met Leonard!   He's also known by other names. Chopper, The Chop Doctor, Chop, Chop City, Chop City The Hustler, Hus, Jus Hus, Grand Hus, Doc, The Doctor of Love. All will get equal responses, but you can just stick with Leonard. We're trying to uncomplicate things." "My name is Ray Lin," Ms. Lin then said, unusually demonstratively, I thought. "And this is Vick Prey. He's a Private Investigator. He has another name which I'm sure is also quite nice, but he seems to prefer this one."

This carousel of names was beginning to unnerve me.
"What kind of dog is Leonard," I said.
"He's half American Pit Bull, and half Greyhound," Hew said. "His father was a Blue Tick Hound Dog!"
While I was left to untangle that mess Hew told Ms. Lin about his escapades with Leonard, how they had crisscrossed the country together, apparently by boxcar, which Hew described to Ms. Lin as, "Mirages in the American Desert with graffiti written all over them!" She bubbled to hear him tell of it and of all the places they'd been.
"Mr. Prey, do you know what the motto of Montana is?"
"No, I don't."
"'Oro y Plata!'" Ms. Lin said, and smiled. "Hmmm," I said.

I don't know if I told you, yet, that Leonard looks like Batman. Well, he does. His ears look like two I. M. Pei Pyramids in the Louvre Courtyard, and his eyes, which are somewhat sad, fit into a small mask and look out at you. I suppose Hew could resemble Robin, but he doesn't. In this case Leonard is quite alone. It's probably an earlier comic. I'm trying to remember if Batman flies. I hope that Leonard is not about to do that. He doesn't look like he is. He looks like he's in the last frames of a very long story in which he's tried to be helpful.

But, right now Leonard is not helpful as he's draped over Ms. Lin and occupies most of the front seat after hardly paying attention to my suggestions that he get in the back. In one of the pyramids in the Louvre Courtyard Ms. Lin took up my case and finally Leonard leaped over us. Now that I could see her again, I asked if she knew what happened to the ignition key, which seems to have disengaged. I didn't think Leonard had anything to do with that.

"You haven't moved."

"I know that," I said, "but it appears to have disappeared."

When it became clear after a while that the Shared W wasn't about to reveal the whereabouts, just yet, of our key, I decided it was up to Ms. Lin to figure this one out.

"Maybe we should have a picnic!" she said

We all decided that that was a good idea.

9.

The Eucalyptus Tree

~ Anglena's Fortunes

I went to see my Fortune Teller today.
The first thing I had to do was sit in her parlor
Where it's very warm and comforting
And there's a lot of colors
And peculiar things.
Anglena asked me what I wanted.
I asked her what was available.
She said that a reading was $35.00
There was something else for $40.00
And the Tarot was $50.00.
I told her I only had $53.00.
She said, "Well, then, it's the cards!"

~ Now I'm worried that Leonard will be confused with all of us getting off after they had just gotten on. I'm afraid he will feel unwanted. Nothing could be further from the truth, of course. So, I felt I should address him. "Grand Hus!" I said, which got his attention right away, "We're going to have a picnic, and you're coming with us. In fact, you can be the first one out the door. It's possible Peter Qualtere-Burcher will appear on a rise to sweeten the moment. He plays the saxophone so you can't miss him. But the Miller Gang might show up, also. They appeared in the movie, *High Noon,* and opposed Gary Cooper, who was the Marshal. I saw the movie four times and Gary always came out on top, but I still worry about them as they may, even now, be riding under the moonlight of our peers, drumming on the road behind us, Long Riders, over centuries, contrary to goodness. I hope you can watch out for them."

I thought it was important that I got all that in. Leonard cocked his head at me. I didn't know if I should repeat anything. We really didn't have time. Ms. Lin and Hew were already waiting for us in the Pantry. Soon I was in position to point out the order of things. Things I'd stored from A-Z, although I really did end with Tangerines. I couldn't think of anything after that. But it was all a hit and we loaded up our arms and followed Leonard out into the sunlight.

When we got there we discovered that The Warrior had wedged under a Eucalyptus tree, barely leaving room for our picnic. But with some unusual maneuvering we managed to get our lawn chairs and a small table down from the top of The Warrior and made ourselves comfortable. Hew sat next to me, Ms. Lin sat across from us, and Leonard sat beside us and looked over expectantly. There were so many containers of take-out I forgot where I got it all; sweet peas and potato salad, white rice, water chestnuts, cold salmon, cooked beans of all sort, fortune cookies, pesto and pine nuts.

I thought about my hero and the concerns he had on his journey. Of course, I'm speaking of the Incomparable Don Quixote de La Mancha, who appeared in several editions, also. In the beginning he put on his armour, buckled his ill-contrived helmet, seized his lance and exited the back gate of his yard in a rapture of joy. I remember how he had doubts, too, because he had never been knighted, and therefore according to the Laws of Chivalry could not enter the Lists. The Lists were the centerpiece of Medieval Events, in which knights pointed their lances and galloped headlong at each other. Meanwhile, Our Hero also knew that even if he had been knighted and received that mark of distinction, that he was obligated to wear white which signified a new knight and ride without any device upon his shield until such time as he was entitled to it.

I grew tired. While Ms. Lin and Hew continued to laugh and talk about things which confused me, I decided to sit under the Eucalyptus tree. I heard them say something about 'The Bar in the Deep Blue Sea,' and drifted off. The branches of the Eucalyptus tree pulled me down into the earth where its water coursed and its roots ran free. In that environment I found a haiku resting against a rock.

The sound of a train
The men and women upon them
Nothing is settled.

I was trying to let that settle upon me when I also heard the sound of scampering coming down the hole next to me. It was Sancho, who apparently mistook me for his boss, The Love Struck Squire, and he engaged me immediately.

"Sire, you're injured!"

"Sancho, it's good to see you. I may have dropped off my horse. I've had some difficulty staying focused, lately."

"But Dulcinea awaits you."

"You're kidding!"

"No, I'm not. In fact, she says that you've captured her heart. Here, let me be of hand."

"Thanks, Sancho. You're very kind to me. Did she say anything else?"

"Yes, she also said you had a good sense of humor."

"I think that's very good!! We should get me up on Rozinante and go see her immediately. I'll grab a hold of Rozinante's halter. Red and White? Whoever thought of that."

"I think you did, Your Grace."

"That's possible. Where are your hands, Sancho. You know what, Sancho, this armour weighs a ton. I can't imagine that any dispute has ever been settled in here. Where are your hands, anyway?"

"They're under your feet, Your Grace."

"Oh, brother, now I've done it. I think my visor's stuck again, and my feet hurt. You would think this stuff could come in aluminum."

"I could push you up, My Lord."

"No, that's alright. Ah, my faithful Sancho, I hate to have you see me like this. I don't suppose we have a ladder, or a step stool with us. Do we?"

"No, we don't."

"Then I am beside myself."

Just then a peasant walked by in a wonderful collection of layers. He was smoking an electronic cigarette, which I don't recommend at all, and his thoughts were sifting through the steam, the dung, and the sun. In his own way he's thinking about the balance of three things. It's always three things.

"Sancho, ask him if he has a ladder."

"Mr. Prey, Mr. Prey!"

The Eucalyptus tree, which appears to have grown, released me from her grip. Ms. Lin said, "We should go now."

We packed up our table and lawn chairs and got back in The Warrior. The key was magically back in the ignition, and, I thought I would sit in the back with Leonard. I was very tired from my nap.

10.
The Mystery Of Ms. Lin

~ We rounded a corner and lost the signal from Dave. He was saying to Tasha,

*"I must be wrong.
How can a pretty voice like this
be ready to go on!"*

I assume he was sweet talking Tasha.   Ms. Lin does not ask for an explanation about this.

From my perspective in the back I notice that my Femme has a tattoo of a falcon on the back of her left shoulder. I don't know why I didn't notice that before. All these things seem to be noticed when they're supposed to. In our little cocoon I asked Ms. Lin where she got it. She said, "Key West." I thought that's what she said. Just then a truck went by with a big sign on it, 'CARAVAGGIO IS INNOCENT.' It just so happens that Caravaggio is one of my most favorite painters. He lived in the 16th and 17th Centuries. He painted huge paintings with very dramatic flourishes. He used a lot of red paint. Apparently he also got in a lot of trouble. I thought I would entertain Leonard by telling him how the Florida Keys got their name. Of course I would make it all up. But Leonard seemed like the kind who wouldn't mind that at all. He seemed very forgiving. So, with Leonard nestled into The Warrior beside me I began to provide my explanation how the Florida Keys got their name. I told him that originally they were called the Florida Extensions by a developer who had very little imagination. "Luckily, Leonard," I said, "This developer got into weightlifting and won a contest in Indiana, so he moved up there. What happened next was, a tattoo artist by the name of Paris tattooed three household keys over the heart of a very pretty girl who lived in the West Extensions. She went clubbing a lot and pretty soon she became known as The Three Keys. A map maker from Rand McNally became sweet on her, this was before Google, and so to immortalize her, he said, 'Oh, what the heck,' and he slipped her and that whole part of Florida on the map as The Three Keys, which he then abbreviated to The Keys so he could keep her to himself." Just then I noticed the truck had come back and a big sign on the other side of it said, 'NO HE'S NOT.' Leonard has fallen asleep against the open window and I'm left to myself.

I feel like I'm going off on a tangent, even on the rails of this manuscript. I hope that's not what working outside the office is like. It's just that this isn't going the way I thought it would. I'm sure Ms. Lin is supposed to tell me what she wants by now. I think she's supposed to tell me that right away. She remains a mystery, let alone whatever it is she wanted. It's like she decided even before she met me that I was her man. For the life of me I can't imagine how she came to that conclusion, or how she even knew where I was. I know I like to sit by my window and sing the craziest things that come into my head. But I'm sure that can only travel so far. Maybe she saw one of my posters. I numbered them. I'm sure that's it. And she was impressed by my design. Sometimes there's a simplicity to things which seem to be a mystery. You just have to wait them out.

11.
The Crossroads

~ A Time To Be Bold.

~ We've come a long way. Now we stop at a trestle in the woods which has a lawn in front of it. A man came out of that woods and approached us.

"Where are we, and why is that man approaching us," I said.
"Why, we're at the Crossroads, Mr. Prey. It's really very beautiful."
And with that Hew was dismounting and Ms. Lin was out also. Leonard seemed content to stay behind. He didn't seem to be into adventure at this point. I don't know why. I told him I would bring him something to eat when we got back and closed the door to the camper.
In no time I joined our ensemble. On one side of this lawn there was a fence. On the other side of the fence there was a beautifully painted half-wolf, half-coyote on a spring. This mysterious cut-out peered over the fence at us and bobbed and weaved to a light patter of music, whose source I had no knowledge of. On the other side of the lawn there was a small tree which was slumped over. Its pointed branches which were naked now of any fruit it once had reached out to a small path that was worn to it. The man who approached us walked between these two aspects. I set my eyes on him and shifted my belt. He was a wiry man, with wiry hair, a wiry smile, and his wiry hat said, *'The Rev. Chicory D. Possum, Pastor of the Handy Man, God Almighty, Never Enough, Dig Down In That Purse, Again, A Little Bit Deeper This Time, Lily, Church.'*

He exclaimed, "Piedmont! Gimme some love!"

I had a feeling this meeting was not unexpected. The easy display of handclasps and chest bumps between Hew and The Reverend mesmerized me. But they were too convoluted for even my imagination to follow. So when it came my turn to say hello I merely shook The Reverend's hand. But I also said, "That's a very interesting hat you're wearing, Mr. Possum. I don't suppose I could get one."

The Reverend Chicory D. Possum laughed like a bowlful of jelly. I couldn't imagine how he did that, a man of his physique. Hew and Ms. Lin laughed, also. Then The Reverend looked at Ms. Lin, like she had grown up somehow and he couldn't believe his eyes. The only thing that was missing in our ceremony was Leonard. Though I noticed that the children who had been behind us had disappeared, also. The Reverend asked if we were staying for the festivities. He hoped we were and he'd see about getting me a hat, too. All this happened in about a minute. I was amazed that a chapter called The Crossroads could happen so quick.

The Miller Gang came to my mind. I don't know why they bother me so. I was worried if we stopped here for too long they would be emboldened. Now my head was swimming with the possibilities where the gang might tie up. The fence, the tree. Then there was Ms. Lin. And behind The Reverend I now saw there was a whole building to account for. Apparently, The Reverend Chicory D. Possum could sense these things and he dismissed them for me.

"The trees we have here they can't find, Vick. Don't worry about it. The door's opening up. Ya Ready!"

I felt I was drawn in by circumstance. Plus, I really wanted that hat.

12.
The Church Service

~ "That's Nothing." Paula Putting On Her Makeup

Paula looked into the mirror on the
4th floor in accounting at Floss, Inc.
Darnelle was beside her
telling her about spending the weekend
at a Lou Rawls Concert
in Sheboygan, Wisconsin,
how he was, 'Talking The Song.'
"That's Nothing," Paula said.

When I was traveling, I went over to
Janis Joplin's house in Port Arthur, TX
where she grew up, and it looked just
like my house where I grew up in Detroit.
So I went over to
her elementary school where
she went to school and
it looked just like my
old elementary school,
so I started to sing,
and I sounded
just like Janis Joplin.

~ In the building in question a person at the door was watching Peter, Paul and Mary on a small black and white television set. They were singing, "The Times They Are A-Changin'," and Mary, who I was always fond of, was striking her fist in the air like she really meant business. A lot of yellow pine and yellow light spilled out upon us, and The Reverend winked at me as we happily went trooping in. Our haven looked like a gym. The wooden bleachers on either side were filled with bright conversations and occasional manly laughter, and when our presence became known we were greeted with a tremendous roar of approval and I was sorry Leonard was not there to hear it. We waved to the congregation and followed Mr. Possum, who led us to a stage at the far end while shaking hands with a number of ladies along the way. Behind a curtain a small set of stairs was painted with stars and small yellow pears. The Reverend said, "Be careful, or you'll fall from one, and trample the other!" Of course, we were all very careful upon hearing that. But we did make it up on the stage and all saw a sign in the back of it that said, 'Chicory D. Possum, Heating and Plumbing, Leave a Message.' A small notebook and pencil for that purpose was on a stand next to it. The Reverend, however, didn't check on that today. Instead he went over to hug the drummer and bass violin player who were setting up their instruments. The drummer was wearing a long black kimono which looked perfect on him, and the bass violin player was dressed in a brilliant yellow vest and spinning his bass violin upon a pin. The Reverend took the microphone off the stand with a whip of his hand, and said, "Aren't these guys somethin!"

I could hardly wait to ask Ms. Lin what she knew of this place. She whispered that Hew said it was a good idea to bring a lot of change with you! I would soon see why as a pretty girl in an Orange Sarong went up into the bleachers with a big Green Basket with handles on. When it could hold no more money or valuables she smiled and placed it back on stage on an apparatus which appeared to be a railroad scale.

"Is that a railroad scale!" I said to Hew.

"Yes, it is," he said.

Now I knew that Mary really did mean business.

"Welcome to the Day the Lord made, and what a wonderful day it is!" The Reverend Chicory D. Possum exploded into the microphone.

Someone in the bleachers yelled, "Nail it, Chic."

I asked Ms. Lin if that was allowable.

She said it was. I wondered if I should think of something myself.

But at that time the gymnasium erupted into song, which was apparently directed at the appearance of The Pastor, actually.

"The Plumber is a drummer
from nine to five,
our boy is back
and he's really alive

Knock down cymbas
Bim, Bam, Boom,
he can make sound dance
across the room

You can read him like a comic
in the afternoon,
you and The Phantom
and the drums of Khartoum

Deep in the jungle
the panting of the herd,
hoboes tip their cap
to the train you just heard

Disorder in the court
Boom
take off your hat
Boom

listen to the choir
Boom
take it to the mat!"
Boom Boom

And all the ladies flung their arms up at that and started singing and shaking all about. I thought a rocket was going to take off.

13.
"ON YOUR FEET"

~ Now what. A thundering roar, much bigger than all the rest, rippled thru the bleachers as the children who had disappeared earlier returned and a figure who was familiar to me was amongst them. It was Leonard!! He looked like a King!!! I couldn't imagine what that was about, or how he got out. But, he seemed to accept it all with aplomb, like he'd been thru it before. I wondered if others had come thru this way for reasons like mine. What are my reasons? I'm getting lightheaded. I just want Ms. Lin to tell me what she wants. A beautiful white blanket is draped over Leonard's back. There's a crest on either side, of a tree in winter with crows on all the branches, and red lettering which appears to be in Ojibwe all around it. The lettering is very beautiful. The whole thing is very noble, and Leonard looks very noble. I look around like this is a magic place. The windows are painted over with beautiful scenes of people at work and crows, a lot of crows, and wolves, and tobacco, and Cadillac Eldorados, and canes, and big frigate looking ships. The young drummer, whose name was Ricky, was playing like Mary, like he really meant business. The Reverend did a little soft shoe to go with him. An odd combination. The older Bass man, whose name I learned was Emerald, was pulling on the strings of his bass violin. They reminded me of the cables on the Toledo Bridge which I am always foolishly afraid are going to pop when I'm under them. They didn't pop here, either, and Emerald got our heads bobbin, our lips pursin, our shoulders tippin. Bass man. Leonard, meanwhile, was out amongst the children, letting them ride on his back like he was a strong horse. It really was quite magic for me. It's all quite magic for me. I don't normally get soft like that. Probably the lighting. But, that's how Leonard got on stage and sat amongst us.

14.
The Reverend Tells Us A Parable To
Send Us Off, And I Get Knighted

~ The Reverend beamed.

"This is a special day. You know that! Our visitors are about to embark on a great adventure. So I think I'm going to tell them a parable to send them off in good hands. Might be scary, but they got to look out. This is about a place not far from here. Probably not far away from any of us. Ya Ready!"

The Rev Chicory D. Possum got out a tall notebook, not the small notebook, as this one was bigger and was full of long handwritten entries, some poems of his, and Kate Newmann, and articles from a newspaper or magazine, or pages from a book which he's copied on a machine in his office, covers too, and pictures of kites. He had written dates on each page, like, 'Tuesday, December 18,' like that. The notebook looked old and was coming apart. The Pastor put this collection on the music stand and hummed as he looked through it for his parable. He even started singing and whistling as the days went on. I didn't know if he'd ever get to it but this seemed to be part of the reading, actually.

"Ok, here we are. Tuesday, June 3. 'The Adjustment Café.'"

Ricky did a little silver whisk on his cymbals, which the Rev smiled at.

"Ok. Here's the Parable. Here it is! 'In The Adjustment Cafe I saw a man once drop a spoon on a floor which was parquet. The menu consisted of Trout, Trout, and Trout. It wasn't so much when you came in, as when you went out.'"

He closed his notebook with a thump. I asked Ms. Lin if she got it. The Reverend said, "You think about that."

"Ok, do we have any requests or concerns before we go eat our cake."

"I have one, Reverend."

"Why, Beautiful Ray, whatever would that be!"

"Mr. Prey would like to be knighted!"

"Oh, he would, would he."

I don't recall mentioning that to Ms. Lin, but she may have inferred it from several of the veiled allusions I made to Mr. La Mancha. Obviously, I hadn't been as subtle as I thought. But I didn't see what The Reverend could do about it as he didn't even have a sword, which you're supposed to have for knighting purposes.

The Reverend said, "Emerald, let me have that bow of yours a minute. Mr. Prey, come on over here to the microphone."

I hope he gets my name right. I can't believe that this has any validity. I hate to go forward with an incorrect dubbing. I should probably say something.

"My name is Valentine Odey."

"That's all right. I'm going to give you something to go with it."

"I can't imagine what that would be."

"Sure you can."

And before I knew it something shiny had whacked me right in the middle of my forehead.

SPAT!

15.

I Manage To Send A Letter To Dulcinea

~ It seemed like I was laying in a Baltic Summer, as warm as I could be. I was fit into something perfectly. I was hoping it was my office. It might have been. But somehow it had relocated to the top of a tower in Romania. Before me was a copy of *The Necklace* in which Guy de Maupassant was undoubtedly telling me about Dulcinea. "She was one of those pretty and charming girls, who, as if by mistake of destiny, are born in a family of employees. She had no dowry, no expectations, no means of becoming known, understood, loved, wedded by any rich and distinguished man; and so she let herself be married to a petty clerk in the Bureau of Public Instruction."

I was surprised to find these instructions laid out so clearly before me, and I wrote to her right away.

Darling Girl,

I want you to know that I have received my appointment as a Knight. I won't trouble you with the circumstances, but suffice that I can now come to your aid legally, according to the laws of Chivalry, and what wonderful colors I have, Red and White. I want you to look for them and whistle when you see me so I won't keep going. If you are successful in detaining me you might have to help me off my horse, also. I've had some difficulty lately. I can't tell you, right now, what my plans are for you, and in fact they may change by the time I get there, but they're incidental to my real quest, which is to find you in the first place. This is the beginning of a swell time for us, and I, personally, can't wait. The reason for all our troubles up to now will be hashed over in the hour in which I arrive. I hope you can hold on.

P.S. I'm having trouble with my visor, so you may have to throw a rock at me, too.

Vick

And then I went to my window and summoned Factorus, The Crow, who normally catches peanuts at my window in my real office. Immediately, I tied my letter to his leg, and told him,

"Factorus!"

"I want you to take this to the girl in this chapter. I know it may be difficult as the story was written a hundred years ago, but it was included in the collection, *Contes du jour et de la nuit,* and was well publicized. I want you to find her before all else. Before the morning at least as I may be moved. Don't ask Poe for directions or he'll go on and on about his own work, and besides you'll find envy there, a Raven, who cannot contend with your own beauty. Avoid him and that loose cannon. Fly higher, look for Keats and Swinburne amongst the fairy works sewing indelicate lines in the hearts of clouds. Then swoop thru the cur of night, to a Ball where I believe you'll find her in a purchased dress. Turn into a Prince, as I know you can, and dance with her to the delight of the crowd and her. Then hand her this letter, and bowing to all, exit upon this stage for home. Report to me, and we will call Rozinante and fulfill my promise. Anon, Factorus. Fly like the wind and let the night sky envelop you like a star."

The sight of Factorus jumping off my window sill and flying in the right direction made me feel better.

16.
I Try To Get Used To Who I Am Now

~ "Who's Rosy."

I opened my eyes.
"Rosy?"

A heady fragrance and the strain of a familiar motor was of comfort to me. I looked around and saw that I was in the backseat back in The Warrior, with my bandaged head in Ms. Lin's lap.

"Yes, Rosy. You were telling 'Rosy' to get ready."
I responded as best I could.
"Oh, that. I think I was involved in a dream in which I might have been a fool."
"I doubt it was as bad as that!" she said. "You just have to get used to who you are now."
"Will it take very long."
"Probably not."
"Will it always be like this."
"You mean, with your head in my lap."
"Yeah. That's what I was wondering."
"I don't think so."
"I was afraid of that. Well, I may have information about the object of my affection who I adopted earlier. The waters could be muddy, however. She may already be married."
"Dulcinea!"
"You know her!!!?"
"No, but I can't wait to meet her."
"Thank you. That means a lot to me. Factorus is checking on things right now."
"Is he the one you were talking to."
"Yes. He's a crow. He's also very beautiful."
"I can't wait to meet him, either!"
The Warrior rolled on. Leonard and Hew were piloting us as though nothing had happened. It had, of course. I had a feeling it didn't matter if I pointed it out to them. It was like they were on to a new chapter which they were well aware of, and I wasn't.

17.
The Disappointment In My Hat

~ "How's your head, Mr. Prey."
"I feel like I fell down a mine."
Ms. Lin laughed. She said I was close.

Hew adjusted my wonderful rearview mirror so that he could smile at me as I had now managed to sit up.

"I bet you're wondering what happened."

"You mean, how I was assaulted," I feigned, but in truth I couldn't wait to hear what happened.

Ms. Lin filled me in. She said that in the ceremony that Emerald had a gold bar on the end of his bow which The Reverend didn't know about. And that The Reverend did not tap me lightly on each shoulder, which I think you're supposed to do, but instead swung mightily, at which time the bar flew off into my forehead. "Then it ricocheted off you and fell in the Basket. Mr. Possum said that was the most provident sign he'd ever seen. After you didn't get up The Congregation carried you out on a bleacher and put you in The Warrior, and now you woke up. The Reverend said to tell you that you were a good sport and you're welcome back anytime. The Rev also said it was a very good knighting and something amazing was sure to some of it."

"Well, I'm sorry I missed it."

My head was still swimming. But between Hew's head and Leonard's ears I noticed a hat sitting up on my dash. My goodness! So, The Rev had remembered his promise to me, after all. I forgave him immediately for everything. I looked closer at my new hat. It said, *'Terrell's Falafels.'* Egads! What was that about. I had no idea what The Reverend was thinking. Maybe this is just what he had handy. I was reluctant to express my disappointment to Ms. Lin or Hew. But as soon as I get Leonard alone I'm going to give him an earful. I had been hoping for something a little more fearsome. Like, *'Welcome To Lake Erie,'* or possibly, *'Luna Pier.'* *Terrell's Falafels.* Who wears a hat like that.

18.
"Let's Hear It," By Deniece Williams

~ So much has transpired since Ms. Lin came to get me that it's like a new lifetime has taken over. I don't think I've done anything to prepare for it, other than my extensive reading which has been implied, I'm sure. I think it's more that I got up the nerve to answer when Ms. Lin knocked. She really made quite an impression on me, and her request seemed sincere, although a lot of it she hasn't disclosed to me yet. And then there's the circumstance with Piedmont and Leonard happening to be by the side of the road. Maybe they were there all along and I've just not had anyone with me to point them out before. I'm glad Ms. Lin raised such a fuss about it. I really think if I had not stopped she would have left, evaporated, just like that. Poof. I'm glad I gave in to her. Initially I had some suspicions. But, as it turns out Hew and Leonard haven't been a bother at all. I've grown quite fond of Leonard. He reminds me of the monk I met at Mount Saviour who ran the bookshop. I think it was St. Jerome. That's funny, I mean Brother Jerome, of course. But I didn't think to ask him about that. I'm feeling stronger. A dozen times so from my difficulty earlier. I wonder if I should say I'm Inspector Clouseau, now. Ms. Lin can be my Kato. She can test me. She can jump on me from behind a curtain when I return home from work. I will scream, "Ms. Lin!" "Ms. Lin!" and she will scream, "Mr. Prey!" "Mr. Prey!" I don't know what Leonard will think of that. I doubt if he'll take sides. I'm anxious to hear him bark. Hew is sorting out our supplies. He's really taken over a lot of the stocking duties which used to take up a lot of my time. I notice he's blocked a lot of my heavier items against the interior walls of The Warrior. I don't know what that's about. He goes in and comes out with things, humming, "Let's Hear It," by Deniece Williams all the while. He seems very industrious for a hobo. I was surprised by that. It's just that you don't think of them that way.

The Warrior is putting on War Paint. Long curls of it, which change with the clouds and the jet streams. My favorite is cinnamon. Ahead of us we must look like a circus to anyone who's looking. If Hoss has his long glass out he's probably saying to Ross right now, "Gypsies!"

The Warrior has stopped and Ms. Lin and I are practicing parrying in preparation for the dangers ahead, but I soon gave out. I literally couldn't engage any more. Ms. Lin was advancing and retreating like we were dancing a tango, but I wasn't. I sat and watched her unfold her hands and twist them and step back in warning. Crossed in front of her they were a barrier to her opponent which he would be wise to walk around. She pointed them in the direction of his meek escape and let them come to rest in front of her. Then she exhaled, and smiled at me. I had a feeling that Ms. Lin could be a handful.

19.
WILLSEYVILLE

~ Where The Warrior had come to a halt on the edge of a bluff over Floss, the Mt. Saviour Monastery, which I recently mentioned, lay in the valley below us. We're not going to stop there, not after stopping at The Retreat, as that might be redundant. Their sign says, *'Down in The Valley, Down in The Camp, Where The Monks of Mount Saviour Sing and Chant.'* I stayed there once to see what it was all about, which is when I met Brother Jerome in the bookstore. It didn't seem to be about anything and I left after one of the Hours. Shortly thereafter a wave of mysterious depths came upon me and I had an urge to go back. Immediately. But it was a half strength, and the other half said, "Oh, go on for now." But that was a long time ago.

From our vantage point The Floss Drive-In on the other side of the road from the monastery was showing a movie, a matinee, which according to the manuscript I'd seen 14 times before. We decided to watch from our new location and all rushed back to the kitchen to get some popcorn. I had labeled it under, 'C,' which temporarily delayed us, and then we rushed back to our balcony to get ready.

"What do you know of this movie, Mr. Prey," Ms. Lin asked, innocently enough, while she was applying a large amount of butter to her bowl.

I looked suspiciously at Ms. Lin, as I wondered if she had seen this one before. Somehow, I think she's seen everything before.

"Well, it starts off as a simple misdemeanor, but ends up with Larry and Colleen going to Port Radium in the Northwest Territories, which is in Canada, where Colleen gets sung to by Larry and involved with the Northern Lights, then saved from a pack of wolves by E. F. Kiseljak, and then, finding out she's pregnant, comes back to Willseyville in a modular home and the charges get dropped."

"Well! Thank you for telling us that."
It appears Ms. Lin has not seen this movie before.

"Who's E. F. Kiseljak?"

Upon the screen below us the title of the movie appeared in wonderful capital italic letters, *WILLSEYVILLE.* Just like that, posted on the front of a post office. Then an Introduction appeared on the screen, in the form of a page of a letter which had whipped open in the wind, *'Colleen Sandra Day O'Connor Has Been Charged With Having No Clothes On.'* I knew, because I'd seen the movie 14 times, that Colleen was just checking on something. But apparently because she was in public view, once again the judge said she was guilty of some offence and gave her a week to get ready before he would impose his harsh punishment. Now her boyfriend, Larry, was on his way to the courthouse to save her.

"What."

"Who's E. F. Kiseljak?"

"Ms. Lin, you'll just have to wait. I feel that I may have revealed too much already."

Larry pulled up in front of the courthouse in his 1972 Plymouth Duster, where Colleen was waiting inside for him.

"Larry, where have you been. I don't imagine Rozinante is out in the parking lot."

Colleen had been reading Don Quixote on her breaks and had aspirations for Larry. Larry picked her up and kissed her, which is what everybody was waiting for. Myrr, an out of towner with no agenda that anybody knew of, took their picture, and Harlan, who was sweet on Colleen, and who worked part time for the Tioga County Sheriff and Camelot Modular Homes the rest of the time, said he had to go move a house, anyway.

Now the camera focused on the Duster in its cyber green cloak travelling northwest toward Port Radium in the Northwest Territories. We're never told why they're going that way. They just are. We see Colleen get a miniature calendar from a take-out in Owen Sound in the Bruce Peninsula, Ontario Province, Canada, and tape it to the dash of the Duster. It has all the signs of the zodiac on it and Colleen has drawn a circle around the seven days ahead which were in Scorpio, and today was already crossed off. She hopes it will take 3 1/2 days to get to Port Radium. But it takes longer than that, which adds to her unrest. Colleen gets sullen, breaks down, looks out the window. Larry holds her hand. She tells him you're supposed to have two hands on the wheel. So, he puts two hands on the wheel, and lays his head on her shoulder. That breaks the ice. Small, ziggy crack. "Ok, one hand," she says.

A string of towns whoosh by them, Blind River, Neepawa, Peace River, Rae, Wha Ti. They remind Colleen of starting out at the restaurant when she was eight. Her jumping up and down to see what kind of pie they had on the pie shelf. That's how she got her nickname, 'Bounce,' which became a term of affection after that, like, "Hey, Bounce!!" if you hadn't seen her in a while. Now all these towns were in front of her, on her level, and she didn't know who to bring them to. Snow had been falling seriously and even they were getting covered up. She put her head on Larry's shoulder, moved his hat over, and fell asleep.

Colleen dreamed of a blue house in the middle of a desert. Its windows were shut and its curtains were drawn. But the music coming out of it couldn't be kept in. People came from miles around to listen to the music. There was no describing it. It appealed to all the faiths, and all the animals, and all the politicians. There were no tickets. Nobody to collect tickets. It didn't seem to work that way. A FedEx man came and opened the door. He listened to the music for a while and looked around. Then he said, "Will anyone sign for this package I have," and Colleen came racing down.

"Colleen, wake up. We're here."

20.
Port Radium

~ It's daylight, vast, and cold. Larry and Colleen get out of their car. There isn't anything that says, 'Welcome To Port Radium.' There's just a sign that says, 'THE ELDORADO URANIUM MINE.' Someone had written, "I'm Gonna Find Me A Reckless Man," on it, in big red letters. Larry and Colleen looked at each other in disbelief. That was their song. That's the thing about a movie. You can go a thousand miles, and there's your cat. Then they turned and looked out over a big calamity of spirit. There was no town at all. A ghost of one. A ghost with leg irons worse than anything Scrooge had ever seen in his bedroom at Christmas. A cabin with the words RCMP on it, for the Royal Canadian Mounted Police, was all that was standing. This is where they would stay. They didn't know it at first, but a man was watching them. A tall man in a lavender coat, with lumberjack spurs on his feet. His name was Landline. And his dog's name was E. F. Kiseljak.

At that moment another letter opened in the wind and plastered itself to THE ELDORADO URANIUM MINE sign just above the admonition about finding a reckless man. It said,

~ That's Landline. He's a ghost, really. Him and E. F. Kiseljak. E. F. is a beautiful German Shepherd, part Husky, with coal black eyes and a big heart, which I'm sure Leonard already figured out. E. F. stands for, "Escaped From," Kiseljak, Croatia. Landline was a Ranger with Canadian Special Forces in the Bosnia Croatia Conflict and E. F. was assigned to him. I don't want you to be alarmed by this, but they both got blown up, survived, and came back to Port Radium. The kids loved Kiseljak, as all dogs should be loved. Landline stayed back. Probably because half his face was blown off, but the kids loved him, too. He's a ghost, really. The natives still say if he looks at you it's good luck. He doesn't involve himself in conflict anymore. E. F. doesn't, either, for that *matter. They just seemed to wander. Show up places. And this turns out to be important, in a minute!* ~

We all looked at Leonard for an explanation but got none.

"What's the purpose of this movie, Mr. Prey?"
"I have no idea what it has to do with our quest."
"But you've seen it 14 times! It must have something to do with it."
Ms. Lin is my instructor, asking me to think about it.

21.
The Aurora Borealis

~ Night came and Larry and Colleen bundled up and sat on the porch of the Mountie's cabin. The sky started to waver like it was breaking apart. Gorgeous colors broke into each other and danced by the side of the moon. Wolves howled also.
"What's that!" Colleen said.
"Wolves."
"No, THAT!"
"That's pretty."
"I know that, Larry, but what is it."
"I think it's the Aurora Borealis, Colleen, or the Northern Lights. You have to be pretty far north to see them, and we're pretty far north. Some people say it has a sound to it, but that might be personal."

It sounded like fission.
The wolves sounded like they were on alert.
Colleen was bathing in it like it was all healing.
They slept the warmest sleep and dreamed in color.

The next day Colleen suggested they have a campfire by the lake, a big one. So, together they brought down more of Port Radium and stacked it up, got their Hudson Bay blankets and Larry's guitar, and down to the water they went. Night fell again. It just falls on you like a hammer up there. Soon the fire was roaring, and Larry announced he had a song just for Colleen, but you'll have to go see the movie to find out about that. Then Colleen told Larry that she wanted to dance for him, so he turned his guitar over and started thumping on the back of it. Colleen proceeded to take all her clothes off which brought Larry to a halt. But Colleen says, "No, I want to do this." The drums start up again and Colleen is prancing and swooping before the Aurora Borealis and this big bonfire. Stretching her arms up and out, extending herself. The wind picks up, wolves start howling. Closely. Colleen is pursing her lips, pulling out all the stops, twirling, her bare feet barely touching the ground, her blonde hair whipping in the cold air, she extends her arms out now to the Lights, beckoning them to dance with her. The green and blue and red are like a Toreador holding out his cape to her, his unending, beautiful, irresistible cape and she swishes thru it, feeling his pass, his breath, his lancet to her heart

"larry,"

THE WOLVES WERE UPON HER, tearing at her flesh. Larry is up, swinging at them, grabbing them, shouting to Colleen. A figure appears on the slope above them. He growls like a bear and leaps down in them. E. F. Kiseljak, ripping, tearing apart the wolves' circle, standing in front of Colleen and warning their leader one last time that he'll have none of this. They leave. Kiseljak goes over to Colleen, Colleen on the ground bleeding, he lays down next to her and licks her wounds. From over the hill there's a cry like an Indian trill. Kiseljak gets up and walks away.

Larry holding Colleen in the blankets now, unsure what to do. Suddenly, new lights in the air, focused lights, and they land on the lake beside them. A door opens up at the end of an Eldorado pier. A face comes out.

"Need help!?"

22.
The Stanton Territorial Hospital In Yellowknife

~ Ms. Lin turns to me in apprehension.
"I hope this turns out alright."
"It does."
It's late October in Port Radium. Great Bear Lake is settling into its hibernation, disturbed only by the sudden splash of Jerry Hiniker's seaplane. Now Larry is sitting in the lobby of the Stanton Territorial Hospital in Yellowknife with his guitar on his lap. Jerry's gone. A bush pilot back on his way to Deline. "I'm sure everything will be fine, Larry, once Colleen sees how

she fits in, now, in the Galaxy. And there might be more to this. Your kids might meet on that porch someday to talk about you. Take care of Colleen!"

"Larry?"

An attractive woman in a white coat.

"Yes."
"I'm Doctor Ziegler. I'd like to talk to you about Colleen."
"Right." Dr. Ziegler sits down next to Larry.
"Jerry told me what happened. E. F. jumping in on the pack. Him going over Great Bear Lake and Landline getting him on one of those ancient lines he taps into. Colleen's going to be ok." "Can I see her." "We're getting there!"
"Colleen lost a lot of blood even though Jerry broke a record getting her here. We closed all the wounds. There might be a scarring issue with some of them but we can address that later. There's another issue. Colleen's pregnant, which has been on her mind. She said if it didn't have anything to do with cars or guitars you probably didn't know about it."
"What?"
"I guess she was right."
"So, here's what's happening. Colleen's not going anywhere for a few days. And after that she's not going anywhere unless there's a bed in it. Now we can go see Colleen!"

Larry and Dr. Ziegler step behind a curtain and go up a small set of stairs.

23.
Chekhov's Rooms

~ This movie is like a play by Chekhov. Except for what happened in Chapter 21, it doesn't have a lot of action in it. Mostly just people talking to each other in the confines of small rooms.

On the third day after Colleen had been admitted a Camelot modular home on a flatbed truck pulled up to the front entrance of the Stanton Territorial Hospital. Not a normal experience. Harlan was driving and Myrr was poking a long pole out his window, moving wires, and they were escorted by four members of the Royal Canadian Mounted Police. And they were on horseback.

"Colleen. You have a visitor."

"Harlan?" **"Harlan!!!"**

"Hey, Bounce!!"

You have to hear some affection here.

"Can I come in!"

Colleen wipes away new tears. She hugs Harlan, who's gone over to her.
"How did you know where we were, Harlan?"
"Larry called the Tioga County Sheriff, let them know you weren't missing, that sort of thing."
"So you come here to arrest me."
"I come here to take you home."

"In what!!"

"In a nice Cape Cod, with a Cantilevered Bay Window off the kitchen, Polished Stone Fireplace, Hardwood Floors, and Two Baths."
Colleen is laughing now. This is unexpected.
"Where do they think it is!"
"Getting detailed."
Larry smiles at Harlan, goes over to the window. He sees Myrr standing by the flatbed explaining the lot model's features to a crowd.
"Myrr's here, too. He's my pole man."
Larry says, "It's really there, Colleen. And it looks comfortable."
"It is. And we have a bed set up in the living room by the fire and a load of wood."
"I have to ask Dr. Ziegler if I can go, first."
Dr. Ziegler stuck her head in the door.
"You can go. Remember everything we talked about, Colleen." Then she looked at Harlan, and smiled at his daring. "You made good time, I'm glad!"
Harlan looked sheepish, but nobody looked sad. Now it was time for everyone to sweep out of the room into the cherry orchard.

"We better go before Myrr starts letting people in. You don't have to worry about those charges when we get back, Colleen. The judge reconsidered, with this new information."

Harlan has a blue house at the end of Willseyville Square. That's important.

"You and Larry can both stay at my house when we get back, if you want. Myrr wants me to drive him out to Colorado to pick up a couple of friends of his. He's not sure exactly what day we'll be back but you can stay on after that, too."

We watch all the scurrying about, the goodbyes, the paperwork, Colleen coming out in a wheelchair to the front door, Larry carrying her into the house, Harlan and Myrr getting into the cab of the truck.

A light snow is falling. The flatbed is going south out of Yellowknife with the Duster hitched behind it. Hillside, pine trees, smoke coming out of the lot model's chimney. Colleen gets up and looks out the bay window in the kitchen.

"Larry!! Look!!!"

And both of them saw Landline and E. F. Kiseljak at the same time.

The End.

24.
I Resume Command

~ I resumed command of the Shared W for our entry into Floss. Ms. Lin was beside me, and our companions were again in the back. I was also wearing my new hat.

"That was some movie, wasn't it!"
"Yes, it was, Ms. Lin. We were fortunate how that went. No fog."
"Is fog a problem around here in the afternoon."
"No, why?"
"Nothing."
"Now, Ms. Lin, you're not going to turn into Colleen on me, are you, looking out the window like that!"

I might not mind that, actually. On the 15th try I grew quite fond of her.

Ms. Lin smiled. "No. I was just thinking of her going home. It will be such a long way."

"Well, I'm sure everything was fine. I don't know if there was a sequel, so we don't know for sure, but it looked ok to me."

That was resolved and we were quiet for a while. But soon I couldn't help but notice a small grin spreading across Ms. Lin's face, and her and Hew's eyes flitting between them. I wondered if they were communicating with each other in a way I didn't know about. Then Ms. Lin's grin burst wide open.

"Valentine Odey!!!"

"It wasn't my fault!"

And so we crossed over the boundary of Floss laughing at ourselves. The Warrior was blazing down the hill, Erika Wennerstrom's beautiful primal voice enveloping our machine, her guitarists electrifying us. In the distance I could almost see The Great Spool topping off the yard at the plant, at Floss, Incorporated. What wonders waited us there, and in Floss, itself.

I told Ms. Lin I couldn't wait.

"I can't either, Mr. Prey!"

II

The Signs By The Corral
In Which The Warrior Gets Boarded
And Valentine Is Examined In The Desert Grove

1.
Where we Left Off

~ I placed The Warrior into D1 to slow our descent. You will recall we had just finished watching, *WILLSEYVILLE*, and were now on our way to meet the winding road that would take us the rest of the way into Floss. It wasn't long before we found it, lodged between the Monastery and the Drive-In. There were signs on either side of the road, pointing in opposite directions, and each one said, 'Floss, This Way.' I distinctly heard Ms. Lin say, "Oops." Now I had three things to consider, but Ms. Lin rescued me, and herself, from all of them, "Why don't we stop at that take-out and get something to eat before we get there."

"What take-out?" I said.

"Right there!"

"That's funny, I don't recall that before."

"But, I think it's a good idea."

"Well, Ok," I said, "If it will make you happy," and I pulled The Warrior up a narrow drive to a small building with a small window, which said, 'Convenient Quick Serve.'

"What do they serve here, Vick."

"I'm not familiar with this place at all," I said. Hew didn't seem to mind what I said. I began to think it was just a question he wanted me to think about, not necessarily give him an answer to.

At that point Leonard sat up and looked at the window and seemed to be relieved, almost as if he was thinking, "At last." I assumed he was starving.

Suddenly, the window, which now looked like a roller from a medium sized desk, rolled up, and a head poked out.

"How Many," it said, very demonstrative like.

I was taken by surprise.

"Well, what is it you serve," I said, politely. But this person could only repeat, "How Many."

Ms. Lin said, "You should ask her what they are."

I thought I had already done that.

"It appears we've alarmed her for some reason, Ms. Lin."

39

"Well, see if you can barter with her," she said, which drew a smile from Hew.

"I'll try."

"Madame, we don't have a lot of change left. It would be difficult to explain how that happened. It has to do with a green basket in the woods. Also, a Pastor who is a little underweight. But you can have the rest if you will just tell us what it is you have back there."

This seemed to really anger her, now, for she grew quite agitated and began to yell loudly,

"How Many, How Many, How Many."

Both Ms. Lin and Hew laughed quite disrespectfully at that, and Leonard looked at them like they were children. This whole thing was going off the rails. Our attendant was now blowing her bangs off her forehead with large whaling gusts directed upward by her bottom lip, which created the most violent gale, and began bucking her heels out behind her like a horse. And then, and then she S-C-R-E-A-M-E-D at the top of her lungs,

"HOW MANY"

"HOW MANY"

"HOW

MANY" "HOW MANY"

I was about to tell Ms. Lin I didn't think we had prepared for this in Part One when she said, "Tell her, four."

I said, "Excuse me, Madame, I hope this isn't inconvenient, but we'll take four."

And with that the window was slammed shut and we could hear a great deal of rummaging behind its square. It also sounded like our attendant was muttering to herself about us being late. Suddenly the window flew back open and four bags, which were stapled at the top, were chucked into our lap.

"Thank you," I said. And we drove off.

2.
We Enter The Gate

~ **"Who goes there!"** came out of a metal structure by the side of the road.

"Who goes there! Why, what do you mean by that!"

"I mean, you have to state your business."

"Well, that's silly. We are simply entering Floss. Besides, is that you, Hoss!"

"Yes, it is. You look familiar."

"I should! It's me, Hoss. Vick Prey, The Private Investigator With The Unfortunate Name. I've spent a considerable amount of time entertaining you in the Guard Shack."

"I never knew what you were doing in there. I thought you were under arrest."

"Well, I certainly wasn't! At any rate, there are four occupants in this emissary of peace. And, for heaven's sake, you can turn that flashlight off. It's probably time for the Little Hour of None at the very latest, and I can't imagine what good it's doing you."

"Hi, I'm Ray Lin, and Piedmont Red and Leonard are in the back."

"Which one's Leonard."

"He's the one on the right."

"He's a dog."

"Hoss, what are we doing talking to you, and why do you have a Guard Shack on the edge of Floss, anyway?"

"I only do what I'm told."

"I bet you've wandered into a shed and can't help yourself. There's no such thing as a gate to get into Floss."

"Says you. The Department of Public Works says otherwise. Also, they declared this a walking day. I forgot to mention that."

"That's preposterous! We will not leave The Warrior behind. The last time we did that I may have left the door open. I was also grievously assaulted."

"I heard about that."

"You did!!"

"Mr. Prey, I don't mind walking and I'm sure Leonard and Piedmont don't either."

"I'm in, Vick. Put my hands in my pocket, tip my hat back, listen for some music. I'm sure Leonard is on that side, too."

"Very Well. Ok, Hoss, but we will need to secure the Shared W in a safe environment, and have his valves checked while we are away, which hopefully will not be long. Do you have a solution for that."

"I know just the place."

Why do I feel these people are all in this together. I feel like I'm a pinball in a machine in which the bumpers are working hard to keep me going. And now Hoss has pulled the lever back and is really going to really let it go.

3.
The Valet And His Page

~ "Buster, I have a party here who needs their van boarded."

We had arrived at a place with no sign at all. Like it was just a curb in the universe which had been overlooked by the Planning Board.

"The Warrior is not a van, specifically, and he's not a dog, either. No offense to you, Leonard."

Leonard didn't seem to be offended.

Everyone's attention turned to Buster as he got up from his seat and leisurely walked around The Warrior. "Sure, no problem. I can make room."

I knew I had to return to work on my case and would have to leave the The Warrior with this caregiver or not go back at all. But I really didn't want to leave. I wanted to explain how the pedals worked. Buster seemed to be a matter of fact fellow. Possibly one of the *Clans Of The Alphane Moon.* Head down, worker type. I really have to find that book for Ms. Lin. I promised her I would. Buster looked quickly at Ms. Lin. Maybe he thought she had the keys. She just smiled and said nothing. It was just the Valet and me. We were in the middle of the stage.

"I'm sure you found no damage to our chariot in your inspection, if that's what you were doing," I said, rather boldly. "We've recently come out of a cloud and are on an important mission. The Warrior has been our base of operations. I can't tell you more or you might have me sign something."

"What's the charge, Hoss! You still got, 'This side up,' tatted on the top of your haid!"

A new actor has burst upon our scene, which turned my attention. Hoss blushed, if that's possible.

"Hello. My name is Vick Prey," I said to this lightning bolt.

"That's a very unusual name, sir. Do we have to fear you. 'Hombre of Fear!'"

42

"I hadn't thought of that. I'm sorry if I intimidate you, Miss..."

"Rio Margie Marie. Nice to make your acquaintance, Mr. Man of Fear. Me and Buster, we work this service. Are you the guy they speak about."

"What?"

"You know, like the one that's coming."

"We have to park our mobile home. That's all. It appears it has to be with you."

"Don't worry. This place that me and Buster have, this is a pretty good place. I think the worse has not yet come."

"Ms. Lin, don't you think we should go out and come back in again. I feel like we've fallen into a warp of some sort."

"Oh, Mr. Prey. You do let your sensibilities get in the way of you. These seem like very nice people and I think The Warrior has taken a liking to them."

"You do."

"Yes, I do."

"Hew. Can you help me out here."

"Does Floss have a leash law."

"That's a good question. I'm afraid to ask Hoss. Miss Marie, assuming we accept your offer, would you have any kind of braid we could borrow, in case we're stopped in Floss."

"You mean for the beautiful one."

"If you're speaking of Leonard, yes."

"I have a lariat. But you should put it on your belt. 'Man With Lariat.' That would be better."

"Well, I guess we've covered everything. If you need to get in touch with us you can leave a message in the Guard Shack at Floss. We'll probably stop by there at some point. Until we get our bearings we bid you adieu. Who knows, this may be the last homely house we come to. So early. But you have been kind to us. Goodbye."

4.

Porchfest

~ "Do you know what I like the best so far!"

I was looking back in the direction of the Valet Service and almost missed what Ms. Lin said. There were Maple trees on this block. I looked high in the branches for a paper bag but saw none. It was a new day, in a way.

"I like all the porches. I haven't lived where you could just have a porch outside in a while. I almost forgot what it's like to sit outside. Whenever you want, I mean."

We were on an outer spoke of Floss.

"If you're trying to make me nostalgic, you're succeeding, Ms. Lin. They are likeable. In this part of Floss they are very common. It's amazing how much people take to them, after all that trouble to build a house. So, where have you lived?"

"What!"

Of course something would have to come up to save her. And it did. We ran into an event called Porchfest, and Ms. Lin visibly smiled. The neighborhood we had come to was alive with the sound of bands. From jazz, to rock 'n roll, horns, and a tall fellow singing to his daughter, "Take your protein pills and put your helmet on!"

Hew commandeered a porch and began to sing "The Wanderer," and drew a pretty good crowd for his first time around. Everywhere was a festive air. I asked Ms. Lin if she'd like to dance, and we whirled around the street. While others sang and drank in peace, all we did was lift our feet. Gone was the worry of taking tests, of lessons, of being best. A Poet stood upon a stoop and read his poem to a very large group.

-Springtime waiting by a naked stream
Playing the game praying to the queen,
Following down to the path
Out across the blue clay
Hoof prints pass,
She'll make you whistle like a blade of grass
In a game of traps without a map
To place upon the looking glass.

Camp coffee in a cup of tin
Any day something might sink in,
Mornings clearest at the brim
With bird song right where they've always been,
She'll write to you on the wind
As you hike out toward where things begin.

Lone day to gaze into the star filled egg
Green rivers running thru the shade,
Shifting gears where the rocks give way

Tell me again how things get made-

Ms. Lin clung to my arm, and whispered fast. "Out across the blue clay hoof prints pass."

I thought about our picnic and our provisions, how it was all a hit then, and how we loaded up our arms and followed Leonard out into the sunlight. Now a new direction was pushing us, and we were full again. People waved to us, a horn sounded in the background. We bounded up a hill and over a crest, far from the porches which Ms. Lin liked best.

5.
The London Bridge

~ I'm thinking of the Gentleman of La Mancha, once more, who took upon himself to redress the world of the abuses which had taken over. Who scarce was clear of his home, and set out to address these wrongs, when he realized he had to be knighted first in order to enter into the Lists. In The Book he returned home and started over. We're much too far along for that. Plus, I've already been knighted. I don't have a device for my shield, yet.

"You should practice your lariat!"
"I almost forgot I had it. I've watched Hoss twirl these things. I hope I'm not mistaken for him."
"What do you want to throw it at."
"I don't know if I'm capable of throwing it at all, Ms. Lin. I've barely opened up this present. There are probably instructions somewhere."

"C'mon, Mr. Prey!"
"Very well. If I remember right you're supposed to let a trail amount lay loose in one of your hands and flap the other end over your head in some kind of rhythm until it takes the shape of a galaxy. Seems silly."
"It's not."
"Was that a statement or are you lending me support!"
"Both!"
"Ok. I'll try."
And so with Ms. Lin and Piedmont and Leonard looking on I began to spin a galaxy in its infancy. I was surprised, it really didn't take that long. But

soon it started to wobble and then it collapsed. I was sure that was to be expected. I thought I was terrible at it, but Ms. Lin said it was a good start. She always seems so encouraging. I fastened my lariat to my belt and we went on.

Soon we came to a bridge to take us into Downtown Floss, upon which a little girl in a railroad conductor's uniform greeted us. "Kalo Mina!," she said. I felt this was a pleasant greeting and Ms. Lin said it was. I didn't recognize this bridge but as The Warrior and I are always zooming over these things it's hard to remember all of them. At this time Hew said, "Maybe we should open our bags now." I forgot about them. I never really thought they had any food in them as Leonard paid little attention to his when it landed in the back seat. And then I was so relieved to be away from that figure of confusion that I forgot about it. I really don't know why we stopped at that store in the first place. I didn't think we were that hungry. But now we have come to a bridge whose name I can't remember at all.

"Why, it's The London Bridge, Mr. Prey. It says right there, 'The London Bridge.'"

"Huh." I was surprised Floss was that creative. It was also smaller than I thought.

The little girl smiled at us, and waited patiently. "Your tokens, please. May I have your tokens, please."

Hew opened his bag and pulled out a beautiful token, which was six sided and sparkled in the air.

I looked in my bag, and there was one in there, too. Only, mine had five sides and one of the sides was sharp. And Ms. Lin's was seven sided and hers were very smooth.

And Leonard's had twelve sides and looked like the wheel of a great locomotive.

The little girl said, "Thank you," and put our tokens in her pocket. We started to walk across. I looked back and she was gone.

6.
We Stop To Rest

~ The Sobbing Girl

The Sobbing Girl outside the Floss Free Library drew my attention. "But you said things," she said. She held her hair and spoke into a flip phone, and pressed her lips against it. She hung up, but almost immediately dialed back.

She turned her head toward the library window, and almost looked directly at me thru the glass. I got up and moved back to give her some privacy. She sobbed deeply, and gestured again toward the phone. She smoothed her face with her hands, and pressed her wet palms against her hair. Her shoulders jolted, and jolted again, like a transmission being interrupted. I was afraid she was going to go out.

~ We sat down on a bench in the middle of The London Bridge. Some seagulls flapped around us. Ms. Lin said they probably came up from the K-Mart parking lot. I turned and looked at her. More and more this conversation seems to be turning her way. On the far side from us, across the water, there was a rampart and a boy and girl were pretending they were the subjects of Sargent's painting, *Capri*, in which they were playing a tambourine and dancing. Ms. Lin and Hew looked at them intently. It could have been the colors they were interested in, mostly. Orange, like in Charles Sheeler's, *The Mandarin*, but lighter, and greys, and pink. "That's the south side of Floss," I said. "It's really very gay and festive. But, we may not be going that way, today."

The rampart and water also looked like bread and wine which hadn't been transformed yet. I didn't know if there was a priest around who was powerful enough to get all that in. Ourselves, we were left with the quietest of multitudes and a huge freighter coming down from Port Huron. Nothing could lap at our feet as we were high in the air. Leonard put his head thru the slats and Ms. Lin said, "Get back here!" Both her and Hew laughed at that. The past was breaking away, sloughing off some iceberg in Antarctica and we didn't even know it. If we waited here long enough it would come bouncing by. A wave of new knights trotted by us with their attendants, their family crests bobbing up and down on their T-shirts. One said the House of Harlan. Ms. Lin looked at me and made her eyes very big. Actually, we both did! The House of Pete Plain, another house, but one which had apparently fallen in the water, barely made it under the bridge and the singing inside it heartened us. A girl in a black leather miniskirt came by and read a statement from the President. "These men and women will never die, they will be forever walking to their capsule and leading us to the dawn of a new age." Ms. Lin began to cry. This was unexpected. I wanted to put my arm around her and tell her that if that happened, I would go with her, and I wondered if that was what I should write about. I would begin, 'Just in case we all get crated up, and shipped to outer space...' I missed the car wash. I missed my office. It occurred to me that Ms. Lin missed something, too.

7.
We Get To The Other Side

~ When we got to the other side, the girl in the black miniskirt was waiting and pinned my token to my chest. She said, "This is de-vice." A lot of people applauded. I thought it would be too difficult to figure out how she got it, so I just accepted the honor. Now I was complete. We turned around and Downtown Floss was before us.

I wasn't sure what we should do first. I was going to say we should get out of the street, but then I remembered it was a walking day.

I decided as my first act of responsibility I would ask Ms. Lin if she'd like to visit a dress shop.

"Maybe that's a good way to start!" I said.

Ms. Lin stepped back and looked at me in surprise. I may have made a bad assumption. She looked at me for a full minute, and then, satisfied about something, my intentions, I don't really know what, she smiled softly, and came back to my side.

The streets of Floss are made of brick which look like pieces of cayenne. Thanks to the Public Works Department you can walk on them as well as the sidewalk. And I'm sure that's what a lot of people did at night, in the amber streetlight.

I'm worried now more than ever that I'm lost. I know this is a terrible way to start, now that we are here. But I can't help it. I don't seem to be any closer to the truth than I was this morning. That is a long time, right? Maybe I'm being unrealistic. I think Ms. Lin has a plan. I just don't know what it is. I don't know why Hew and Leonard aren't as annoyed as I am about it. It all seems to be clouded by Ms. Lin.

"Wasn't that a little abrupt how I got the device for my shield," I said.

"No."

"It wasn't."

"You earned it."

"I did?"

She didn't seem to want to talk any more about it. It gleamed from my chest, my lariat at my side, my dented forehead covered by my advertisement for *Terrell's Falafels.*

I was ready for the lists.

8.
I Look For An Adversary

~ Testing 1-2-3
A Conversation At 6 AM

Kerry
Do you like the dress
What
My dress, do you like it
It's nice
I know but do you like it
It's ok

Do you think I should put it on
What
My dress! Do you think I should put it on
Do you want to
Yeah, I do. But do you think I should
Hey, go ahead

What do you think
I think you look very nice
Do you like it
I like it even more now
What time do you have to go in
I have to think about that.

~ A man on a wooden stilt came by and I eyed him warily. Ms. Lin laughed, "No, not that way!"

That wasn't a good start. In the end, I couldn't think of anyone else to challenge.

We walked all around downtown. I forgot about my preoccupation with finding somebody to joust with. I just enjoyed the antics of my friends. "Let's go in here!" A common refrain. I couldn't deny them. I mean, we had been cooped up for a while. Ms. Lin and Hew never purchased things. I think they thought that these little shops were just the way that Floss displayed itself. It didn't seem to occur to them that maybe they were expected to take something with them when they left. In and out the shops we went. Korik the Tailor leaned out his window on one end of The Common Way, and John the Tailor on the other. Between them they watched us sew all the shops together. The ones that stood out had free samples. It's hard to beat that. Vinegar and oil, cream cheese and olives, roasted garlic from Crane Hill Garlic on the Circus Truck, jelly beans and chocolate. Leonard got a plate full, except for the chocolate. In other stores Hew tried on belts just to amuse himself, and Ms. Lin held fabric up in front of herself in a mirror until she found something complementary. She closed her eyes. I thought she was trying to lock it in. Time release. Kodak film. I didn't have the heart to tell her they went out of business. "What do you think" "I think you look very nice" "Do you like it" "I like it even more now" "What time do you have to go in" "I have to think about that." Ms. Lin laughed, and I felt very sorry when she put it back.

9.
We Accept A Ride

~ Not having found an adversary here, I noticed a float going by. Ms. Lin said, "Let's get on it!"

I knew where we were going, of course. We were on our way to Floss. The other one, with the employees. And, to be sure, it was they who provided this merry van. Leonard easily jumped on, then Hew, then Ms. Lin, who seemed to wish herself aboard. But I was on alert after my recent investiture and temporarily could only see Giants before me who were throwing garlands to the crowd. I was about to say, "Aha! So there you are," but then I heard Hew call out, "Jump, Vick," so I put one hand on my badge to keep it from flying off and the other on the float and hoped that my momentum carried me with it. I didn't quite make it, when one of the Giants picked me up and said, "C'mere little man." I was sure I had been foolish to trust a hobo. But the Giant put me down as gentle as that, and I could tell he was just trying to get all of me on to begin with. I thanked him and told him he would have my fealty, at least until the end of this ride. And then I bowed and took my hat off to him, also. And that was the end of my first real confrontation. At least it was something. I thought about The Book, again, *The Adventures Of Don Quixote de La Mancha*. I don't mean to keep doing that. It's like a small anchor that keeps pulling me back into place. "Thrice happy and fortunate was that age which produced the most audacious knight, Don Quixote de La Mancha."

Alas, it may be too soon for this age to be aware of ME. I also didn't see that anybody else was watching. But I was thankful for this beginning, and relieved for all the effort I put into it. I couldn't wait to tell Ms. Lin about it.

They have all wandered away to the front to wait for me. I felt like a rural Prince who has stepped out of his castle to see what's going on. There's a lass not far from me, sitting on a bench with headphones on and a white cord is winding its way to a small box in her hands. She looks like a listening post and a good place to start. I approach and sit down next to her.

10.
Riding Thru Newark Valley

~ The Valentine

At the plant where they make floss
a Watchman by the name of Ross
got assigned to watch Compartment C
where they added up time lost.
At the plant where they make floss
Ross saw Cindy thru the gloss
with a stack of hours that hadn't been filled
and heard her make a little cough.
At the plant where they make floss
Ross bought a Valentine for Cindy
and put it in her window
and threw her counting off.

~ "DO YOU KNOW HOW TO TURN THIS DOWN."

I jumped. This is not what I expected. I guess I just thought my listening post would turn to me and say, "Hello."

I didn't think anything I said could get through those jelly rolls on her ears. She looked like a Russian Cosmonaut. They never did look very jolly in those newsreels. Maybe she had to listen to John Denver all the way down and she couldn't stand it anymore. I really couldn't blame her, and I frowned at her to let her know how much I understood. She looked back at me like I was from Mars. We may have been connecting and I just didn't know it. I threw my hands up and she thought that was great. And then everybody was doing it. I reached over and turned the volume down on her console. She seemed greatly relieved. "Thank you, Mister." This might be easier than I thought. I wished her well. I wished that all the jangled wiring in her set were smooth again, and bid her adieu.

The next person was walking on a fine line which I couldn't see. I don't think he could either because he kept falling off and then he'd go back to the beginning and try again. People were walking around him and not paying any attention to whether they were walking on his line or not. I found a curling broom and went along in front of him vigorously sweeping it off. Finally, he got to the other end, and hugged me profusely.

A man was singing a tribute to Leonard Lively on a banjo. Something about an uncloudy day. *"Oh they tell me of a home far beyond the skies, Oh they tell me of a home far away, Oh they tell me of a home where no storm clouds rise, Oh they tell me of an uncloudy day."* A lot of people gathered at his feet to listen. The sky, itself, was everywhere and bright as it could be. I wondered in any way if this has to do with our Leonard, too. I like to think it does.

A woman was dressed like a teapot and her husband was dressed like a gown. I'm a tempest in a teapot she said, and he ran around and around.

A man was having breakfast, which consisted of Rice Krispies and white chardonnay. I asked him why he was having breakfast, and he said, would you please go away.

So far I think I have two right.

A man who was an acrobat on the float was asked by an interviewer from Channel 3 News what he liked to do in his spare time. He said he liked to play miniature golf. The interviewer asked him what there was about miniature golf that interested him. He didn't know. He said he liked The Windmill, and that he was very good on that hole. The interviewer saw nothing interesting in this man and quickly moved away.

There was a space carved out on one side of the float. A road went thru it, and there were minicars you could ride down the road in. I got in one. The sign for the ride said, 'Riding Thru Newark Valley.' Halfway thru the ride I saw two old dogs in a yard, one barking inside the ear of the other. I thought that was great and I recommended the ride to everyone.

There was a woman with two children on the other side of Newark Valley. She said she was protesting drilling practices on her property. I asked her how she got into that mess in the first place. She blamed it on fine print and shifty salesmen. I asked her how many she talked to. She said, "One, but they're all like that." I almost ran into her with my minicar. I never want to be a salesman.

A man was dying on the side of the road. I asked him what I could do for him. He said, "Nothing." That this was just meant to be. I made a note that it's not all peaches and cream on a float.

I saw children who were hungry, and tired, and dressed poorly. I thought of the poet, Marina Tsvetaeva, who lived poorly herself. I wondered what she would say about this. Then I thought I should say something myself, but they got up and walked away before I could compose it.

I saw people in love who had certificates to prove it. I saw other people protesting that they wanted a certificate, too. It occurred to me that I had no certificate. I didn't know if my Dulcinea had one either.

I saw a sign that said, *'Berkshire. Knight Dreams This Way,'* and I insisted that we find it. But my cart was going another way, and I had to be reassured, oh, several times, that there were enough of them behind it.

I saw a man cheat another man and walk away with a smug look on his face. I was hoping he just had a part in a play. The problem was, he did.

I watched the fireworks rise over the crowd. It was really by their illumination that I found the others, at all. At first, they didn't say anything but just looked at me to see if I'd changed. Soon, we were talking animatedly with each other and I showed them my receipt for The Ride Thru Newark Valley. A bitter rain came up. Our conveyance moved further and further off, and a loudspeaker blared to every street we crossed, "This is the Float that goes to Floss, This is the Float that goes to Floss."

11.
We Arrive At Floss Inc., And The Greeting That Occurred
There

~ When, at last, we got to Floss, Inc., the gate opened wide and Ross leaned out the Guard Shack and blew a trumpet. Hoss, who was back, was jumping up and down in the yard like a maniac. Apparently he was also in charge. "Out you go, Amigo!" And all of us funneled off like we had arrived at boot camp. Ms. Lin, of course, hammed it up, asking Hoss if he would please help her down. Hoss blushed and put a lei around her neck and welcomed her to Floss. "Welcome to the birthplace of the grin, Ms. Lin. Also the shenanigan, the purse that let the devil in, and a lot of other things I can't remember. Usually I'm pretty good at it."

Hoss recovered and launched into a litany of Floss's accomplishments, which he did remember, the last of which was, "We were also the first to get the lead out."

Hoss waited for the laughter. But, it was very quiet.

"Ok, did you hear the one about the cashier and the cat." I was surprised that half the group raised their hands. So was Hoss. Enough of that.

Back in the Guard Shack, Ross was watching the woman from the end of Newark Valley who had a complaint. She told her two children to go over and punch him. Things were definitely getting out of hand. I thought this was a good time to lead my companions away.

"Would you like to see the Guard Shack," I said.

"Would I!!!" exclaimed Ms. Lin.

Ross greeted us warmly. Hew shook his hand like they were in league together and Ms. Lin kissed him. I wondered if I should introduce them after that. I looked out the window and saw that Hoss was drawing a line in the sand with a golf club he had borrowed from the acrobat and was daring anyone to cross it.

'Being in the guard shack has advantages to it. Everybody has to come to you. You're set up and they're not.' A parade of Hoss's favorite episodes of, "Burn Notice," was on the little tv set in his corner. 'Spies aren't trained to fight fair. Spies are trained to win. Spies are trained to use whatever resources are around them.' "Does Hoss watch a lot of this stuff?" "24-7. Also, The Simpsons, and anything with Jessica Simpson in it. I think he's trying to master the art of being subtle." 'When you hide in water, fire is your friend. It illuminates the surface and camouflages you as well. In high security areas uniforms are for show. Like a wedding, an armed extraction requires a lot of planning. In close quarters, use an armoured car.' "It doesn't sound like there's a lot of subtle stuff going on here." "Everything is subtle to Hoss." 'The lone spy who works alone is a myth. They always keep a special set of friends near them. It's never clear who they are.'

Dust blew in the window and settled on the desk. Hew drew a circle and made a smudge with his thumb inside it. Ross smiled at him. Leonard laid down in the corner with his head between his feet, and made some kind of settling noise. It was warm, like being in The Warrior. I hope he's being taken care of like they said. Buster and Rio Margie Marie. They seemed like very sweet people. I wonder how they met. I wonder if they're living in The Warrior.

To my pleasant surprise Ross has hung some of my paintings of the Plant on the wall. I saw they had little poke holes in them, and on Hoss's desk I

noticed he had an open box of darts. Ms. Lin walked between them like she
was in a museum.

Steve

Steve has a heart of gold
and works in the zoo.
Then he comes over to the Plant
and works there, too.

Washington

Washington works in Shipping, and boxes in
the Golden Gloves. The only thing he can't pick up
is what his manager is thinking of. "We're going to
the Big Time, Washington, just bring him a little shove,"
because Washington is thinking about Century
how she looks so good in gloves.

New Rules At The Gate

When they instituted badges
Ross realized it was new,
but he didn't see the sense in identifying
everybody he already knew.
Hoss said, "Suppose somebody slips by,
did you ever think of that."
He had thought it was all over Hoss's head,
but after he said that
Ross put on his badge
and put the issue to bed.

Hoss

It's Slam Poetry Night at the Wolverine.
Hoss is standing in front of the Stuffed Moose.

It's his turn.

"Ok. Ya Ready!" "Here I go."

"When Merle Haggard says, Convicts,
The blocks roll off his tongue
You can feel them piling up
One by one.
When Merle Haggard says, Convicts,
It's for certain they exist
Just like after working out
You want a Sierra Mist.
When Merle Haggard says, Convicts,
The warden comes to call
And one more block is carried away
But the building never falls.
When Merle Haggard says, Convicts,
You think, well, there's three meals and some sun
But at night you lay awake
Under a hefty sum.
When Merle Haggard says, CONVICTS,
And you think that you are one
Just remember how he said it,
Because none of it is fun."

"Thank you very much, and I hope you vote for me."

I notice this last one has been spared the wrath of Hoss's darts.

Outside the window I could see our tourists had Hoss down on the ground and were pummeling him. I expressed my concern to Ross. "He'll get out of it. He always does." I looked out the other window and could see the crown of The Great Spool illuminated in the long afternoon light. Ms. Lin saw it, too. We both looked at it for a long time. It was dazzling, and was the real reason for the tour. It looked like an exotic animal being adjusted by a mechanical apparatus which flung loops of new thread over it in a frantic effort to keep it in. The natural draw, of course, was if it got out. A Chief of the Coeur d'Alene tribe was sitting next to The Great Spool smacking his drum. 'BOOM BOOM BOOM.' 'BOOM BOOM BOOM.' He was part of the attraction, really. He was the Old Harmony. The workers called him Lennie.

He didn't seem to mind as long as they kept the tobacco coming. 'BOOM BOOM BOOM.' 'BOOM BOOM BOOM.' Danger sells and Floss couldn't make enough of it.

Our segregationists have stopped pummeling Hoss to listen to Lennie. And Hoss got up and ran for it. "See!"

Ross was right.

12.
A Clash of Civilizations

~ Some teens on the lot got in a galley exhibit and started pushing the oars back and forth. One of them had a T-shirt on that said, *'Make It Up To Darlene.'* Above us soft voices wafted down to our aisle. The monks of Mt. Saviour were at it again. Their melodious singing of the Gospel threatening to compromise Lennie. A clash of civilizations. The Great Spool tried to wriggle free of both of them. There must be some area of compromise. I looked at Ms. Lin but she was busy writing something in the guest register. I hoped it was good comments about my paintings. I may never know because she then said something to Ross who immediately folded them all up and put them in her bag along with the register. Ms. Lin smiled at me. I felt honored and didn't know why.
    The girl with the T-shirt got off the boat and walked around our set holding up a placard. I halfway expected it to say, 'Round Three,' but instead it said, 'And Now, The Shuttle Bus.' Sure enough, Lucy, who drove the Shuttle Bus, pulled up and let the air brakes off. Hoss had returned to the set and was genteelly ushering everyone on board. "No hard feelings, eh." The woman with the complaint asked if they allowed drilling here. Hoss said, "No, ma'am, we don't." "Two by two, now," Hoss said, and the seats began to fill up and the tires began to go down.
    "Do you think we should get on," I said to Ross. "No, I think you're expected elsewhere, Vick, at least today."
    I looked at The Great Spool tied up in the West and tried to remember its name.

13.
The Story In The Passageway

~ I'm dissolvin
Somebody call Colvin
Tell him I'm dissolvin.

~ Ross led us to a Passageway in the back of the Guard Shack. I always thought it was the bathroom. But apparently it wasn't. I hoped one wasn't too far away.

It felt like we had entered a modern underground railroad and I couldn't imagine what would be at the end of this one. The Passageway was cramped and we kept bumping into each other. I don't know why Ross shooed us in here.

Ms. Lin is leading us now, but with a different temperament. Gone was her dress, and replaced with a foresty looking ensemble, and soft red shoes. She also had a quiver with three arrows, and her hair was pulled back in a ponytail. The light I had to see all that by was coming from somewhere. I hoped it wasn't from a hole in the Lonely Mountain. That's where Smaug, The Dragon, is. I've fallen behind with Leonard. He seems to be tired. This has been a long quest. I asked him if he wanted to sit down for a minute. It would be on the ground, of course, but Leonard is used to that. So, we stopped, and listened to the patter of Ms. Lin and Hew going steadily away from us. We were alone. Leonard's eyes seemed grey. I think he's having a hard time with all this. I hoped I wasn't the cause of it. Somehow our missions have gotten tangled up together. I put my hand up to his crown, which really was as dazzling to me as the Spool's. I wondered what was in his. Something exotic there, too, I'm sure! Maybe even a danger, to somebody. What a wise companion. He looked at me without blinking. Dogs do that.

"Let's see if you have something in your bag you can eat," I said. I didn't think there was before, but now of course there was. It was a bowl of dumplings with broth and a biscuit for afterwards. Leonard ate deliberately. When he was done he held his head in the air before me and then rested it in my lap. "I'm sure you'd like some water. I don't think there's any in the bag. We can only ask so much of it. When we get to wherever we're going I'll make sure you get a large bowlful."

The dark was heavy but not distressing. I leaned back against a pillar. Strange place. The floor all beaten down. Nothing on the walls. People in a hurry. My badge with its sharp edge gleamed in the dark. It occurred to me that I haven't used it yet. Maybe this is not that kind of quest. Maybe it just represented where I'm at so far. Down in the hollow of the tunnel I can hear Ms. Lin singing a Woody Guthrie song, in the way Woody wrote it, *"This land is your land, This land is my land, from California to the New York island. From the red wood forest, to the Gulf Stream waters, This land was made for you and Me."* Sounds like we're late. Still, Leonard is tired. I notice a small book, almost like an old log, in his bag. What's this? *GIM and the High Fashion.* Whoa. Doesn't sound like a dog's tale to me, but what do I know. There's a picture of an unusual rocket ship on it, tilted in a starry void, as they all are, and a small flame coming out the back of it. On the first page somebody wrote in the margin, *'Time Is A Queen.'* I decided to read it out loud. I alerted Leonard. "Leonard, Ya Ready!" Leonard's pyramids lit up. He was alert and tuned in. "Ok. Here I go!"

~ GIM and I had been in Deep S[pace] for over a year. A year in human terms but longer in Starling terms, or to be more precise, for those of us in Jump School. Today was Free Exercise Day which we all looked forward to. A welcome relief from classes. GIM and I let go and the High Fashion dropped 20,000 feet. Get a rush going! Then we locked into a cosmic drift and let it carry us over to The Path of Orion's Kings, see our third sunset of the day. GIM said, "Isn't that one Beautiful. That's the best one yet!" To which I responded, "Yeah, and it might be your last one, you don't miss that 'roid." "Yeoww! Where'd that come from?" It came from speed, of course, and GIM knew it. Normally the Fashion will pick them up and easily curve around them, as she's very adept at doing that. I think she ignored this one out of jealousy! She's very possessive of her Captain's affection. She had a strike on her core drive that said, 'Admire ME.' Nobody knew how it got there, but it's what sold GIM on her on Mating Day. The High Fashion was GIM's Jumper. 'Beautiful, indeed,' flashed on the monitor. GIM and I laughed, and the hum overtook us. We were riding. ~

Leonard was asleep. With all the cacophony going on at the end of the tunnel I was surprised he could sleep at all. The Beam from there seems to change. First, it's a brilliant yellow, like the bleachers spilling out on us at The Retreat, then green like the Rev's wonderful Basket, then red like the beautiful lettering on Leonard's blanket. Maybe there's a huge Projector and they're catching up, up there. This whole existence thing seems to precariously balance on successfully remembering the past, otherwise we'd wake up every morning screaming, "WHERE AM I!!!" I think about the car wash. People lining up in the alleyway to get to it. I think about people lining up at my door to get change and me sitting at my card table wondering what that change might be. I think about all the cacophony going on in Lucy's Shuttle Bus right now. This is a different kind of past, which also piles up quickly even though you're not on the bus. I hope The Warrior doesn't think I've abandoned him, or turned him in for a float. Maybe he's being prepared for a mission himself, at this very minute, and I don't know about that, either. It's been a special day. I have all the accoutrements of a Knight now, but I'm in a dark hole. I'll have to re-read how our role model vanquished such a thing. Thank goodness I have Leonard to help me. I wonder if Leonard thinks we're pack. I hope he does. I don't think we would do very well in the L.A. Canine Patrol. Pack for some other reason.

I'm worried about my name. I don't think I'm getting the play out of it I thought I would. People just look at me dumbfounded. Not Ms. Lin, of course, or Hew, or Leonard. Ms. Lin asked me about my new name but I think she just wanted to clarify it to see if she had the spelling right. Now I wonder if I got it wrong. Vick Prey doesn't have the ring of "Don Quixote de la Mancha." Maybe I should have remembered, "Billy Fade, The Poet Of Copacabana." That might be better. I could have written a thriller. - Emerging from the shadows Billy Fade put his hand on his knee. His limp from being shot there was hardly noticeable anymore, or he hid it well. Billy took his place at his usual table in the Copacabana Café looking out over the Florida Keys and watched closely as three figures disappeared into the Orange Sunset. "Well, that's the end of that," he said, as he straightened his tie and pulled up his chair. "What'll it be, Mr. Fade." "Rum and Coke, Jimmie." "You know that Coke's bad for you, Mr. Fade." "I know that, Jimmie." -   Billy Fade. He seems easier to understand.

I finished reading the story of GIM and wondered who she was. She seemed very adventuresome. In the end, though, she got terribly lost, somehow. I assumed there was a sequel in which she was found but it wasn't in the bag. I tried to think if Leonard was a complete soul. He seemed to be that way. I tried to remember his token. I couldn't remember if there was a beautiful stone in the middle of his or if it was missing. I can only remember the sides which seemed very symmetrical. Sometimes his eyes seem sad which I think I mentioned before. Otherwise he seems very regal and wise. The beam at the end of the tunnel has flipped to white, like the snow E. F. Kiseljak is bounding over to save Colleen. Finally, there's applause. It's hard to escape the past. And just when you think you did it sweetly calls down the path, *"Mr. Prey, where are you,"* and you come to grips with it at last.

14.
The Angelica Theatre

~ Leonard and I made up ground and came upon what looked like a rip in a fence. I've never trusted those things. A lot of the elementary debris of life are usually behind them. Like scrub brush and old bricks, shattered glass, bits of paper, cigarette packs with pictures of camels and mosques, of all things, and empty Falstaff beer bottles sticking out of the sand. Generally, a good place for a murder. And also the source of our light. I was worried the Miller Gang might be on the other side of this one, just waiting for me to emerge. I was explaining my concern to Leonard when a hand reached thru the fence and nabbed me.

"Gotcha!"

"Ms. Lin!! I was about to deploy Leonard in my defense, you frightened me so."

"But you didn't, Mr. Prey. Your confidence is growing!"

"I was just glad to see you, that's all. My Goodness, where are we."

"The Angelica Theatre!"

"How do you know that."

"It says so, right there, 'Welcome to the Angelica Theatre.'"

"Well, I've never heard of this place and I don't remember Hoss talking about it. We should probably keep going."

"We will. But first you have to take a part. There are several available. I'm The Archer."

More names!!! When will this end! "Ms. Lin, I don't know if you are familiar with the Salvo Montalbano compact disc series but pronouncing the character's names alone takes up half the book. I hope that's not the case here."

"Of course not. You can choose a short name if you'd like. Would you like to be, 'Top.'"

"Hmmm. Well, I don't want to be in charge."

"You won't."

"Ok, I'll be Top."

I was given a uniform which had no medals on it, or rank, either. Some people started saluting me immediately which made me feel uncomfortable. I couldn't wait to complain to Ms. Lin. But she had gone to a large stage on which a target with a heart in the middle was placed 50 yards from her. She pulled back her bow and let a beautiful arrow go. It had duck feathers on it and swam toward the target, missing the heart by about two feet.

Hew was standing at the top of the key with a basketball in his hands. He was apparently 'Larry Bird.' Larry was concentrating on the basket. A clock in the corner with a huge hand on it was going down to seconds. Hew jumped in his green shorts and arced the ball toward the hoop. When it fell thru everybody in the theatre shouted with glee. A trophy was brought on stage and Hew was paraded up and down. Leonard howled at the top of his lungs, which had grown weaker in our ordeal but still had plenty left. Ms. Lin smiled. She took out her second arrow.

I sat down in a theatre chair. I thought about Bob Toski. I always wanted to play golf well and I didn't know if he could help me. I looked over my shoulder to be sure but he wasn't there. I was hoping this was some kind of fulfillment facility, as Hew was winning and Ms. Lin had two shots left. But I was alone. I remember before when I asked Ms. Lin if she'd be around when I had to figure things out myself, and she said, "Oh, no, you'll be quite alone." Somehow, I never felt it would be quite that way, but I wasn't going to tell Ms. Lin that.

Meanwhile there seemed to be a play going on in front of us, which itself was in front of a movie. In the movie hordes of marauding warriors were thundering over the Russian Steppes, brandishing their arsenal and screaming, "Get out of our way." They went on forever, apparently covering thousands of miles. Everyone got out of their way and then they turned around and rode back again. When they got back the director said they had to do it again and the head warrior said, "I don't think so." Of course, I thought about Our Warrior, how he would hide the key to a scene on me, sometimes, also. I was surprised at the similarity.

Ms. Lin drew back her bow and let the second arrow go. There were eagle feathers on this one and it swooped down on the target at tremendous speed. It missed the heart by one foot. I went and got a big bowl of water for Leonard, who had come over and laid down next to me in the audience. I was on the aisle.

In the theatre part of this, the play was going on full blast. Basically, it seemed to be a line of knights approaching a balcony. They were all dressed in mid-twelfth century garb and an attendant beside them carried their armour and displayed it to the audience. There was no pretense of being on horses. My complaint is they all seemed to be fresh so I don't think they came a long distance which is the way I remember it's supposed to be done. Nonetheless I applauded all of them loudly and got shushed for it. Soon the window to the balcony opened and the Queen and her daughter, the Princess Maureen, came out to greet the knights. To one side of them there was a rampart upon which there were roses, big red ones, and a fellow in a one piece gown holding a Proclamation Pad. He smiled at the Queen and waited for the horn section to give their big blast and then he unfurled his Proclamation Pad and proclaimed,

"THE CASTLE OF MAUREEN"

You could tell the Knights were nervous as all of them had done well in the lists. The problem was one of math, really. In the Tournament it wasn't supposed to happen but there were five of them left. It was a matter of division. The Princess would just have to pick one of them and be done with it.

Meanwhile Ms. Lin drew back her third and final arrow. The falcon which was tattooed on the back of her left shoulder was stretched so far it almost took off with it. This one had crow feathers on it which seemed like an odd choice for so important a task. Really, they were surprised to be going that fast. More suited to conversation were they, than winning a contest. Sailing thru the trees and over the wires they were accustomed to, you could almost hear them singing, "Wheeeeeee!" not caring what it was all about. Rather to listen to one of their great orators bellow in the trees, *"As fair as the air has been..."*

Mischievous, intelligent fellows. They were probably as surprised as anyone when they hit the heart.

Finally, everyone was in place and the fellow in the one piece gown with the Proclamation Pad had some bad news for the knights.

"With Regard To Maureen...," he cautioningly said,

"Each of you has challenged for her,
And hoped that you'd be seen.
You aimed your lances for her heart
And rode upon the Green.

But, to be honest, boys, your lances thud on metal.
Yet you got the attention of the Queen
Who brought her daughter out to see you
Parade upon The Green.

In times before Maureen has stood before you

And gratefully surveyed your scene
And sometimes dropped a handkerchief
The handkerchief of Maureen.

But, of course, there's more to it,

As there's something to be learned
By people in your craft
That even the hearts of Princesses,
Are like the Copernicus of Glass.

In fact, as she watched you jab her linen, then,
And look up for more to pass
She wondered what she would mean to you
If linen wouldn't last.

For that reason, and others that have to do with youth, and gas,
At least for now
While she is young
And the wind is at her back

We're closing the Royal Window
And Maureen is sneaking out the back,
Because she has picked the Jester, not just because he loved,
But because he made her laugh."

15.
We Cross Over To Steve McQueen

~ And so, in The Angelica Theater we found out that you can have any name
that you want, and that conversation and laughter are the way to the heart.
These things are important, but I wanted to complain how the knights were
treated, also. "And I know for a fact that Copernicus came 300 years later," I
said. Ms. Lin laughed. She said that that was about alliteration and that we
have to keep our eye on the prize.
    "What does that mean?"
    Ms. Lin was silent.

Filing out of the theatre the line was too long to go to the bathroom.

That was too bad.

But now we're on our way to Steve McQueen. He was a famous actor. To some extent he lived in the desert, even in his roles, which I'm sure were well planned out. But he just had the element of wander, and heat about him. I'm sure if he found out a town was named for him he'd be on his Husqvarna there today to check it out. Well, we may have crossed over already as the smell of gas fumes was in the air. I knew being here that there would be camaraderie and fast cars, and of course motorcycles: Indians and Harleys and Husqvarnas. Zip, Zip. They were already flying around us. Ms. Lin was twirling like Colleen and shouting to them. Hew and Leonard were amazed. Well, Hew was. It's hard to amaze Leonard. Maybe he thinks he's faster. I'd bet on Leonard. By surprise, one of them stopped in front of us and the operator asked Ms. Lin if she'd like to ride. He had a long beard and red goggles and his hair was pulled back in a ponytail, also. He said his name was, Pecos Bill.

Ms. Lin turned to me and asked if I wouldn't mind.

"Well, just for a minute," I said.

The Zip, Zip started anew. Ms. Lin's peal of laughter and their two ponytails were fluffing in the wind as Pecos Bill zoomed up and down dales and around until they finally drew up before us again.

"Pecos Bill wants me to ride with him to the Desert Grove. He says it's not far. We'll meet you there!" And off they went.

"I hope that's not the last we see of Ms. Lin," I said.

"I doubt that it is, Vick. The Desert Grove is only a mile or so away. I think there's a train track that goes by the back of it. I'm sure I've seen it before. I may have forgotten to mention that."

I'm constantly surprised.

We walked for what seemed like hours. Of course, it wasn't that long. I thought about the relationship of Steve McQueen to Floss. One simmering and one smiling. And so close to the border their change. The Warrior and I had only come to Steve McQueen on one other occasion, to get a tire fixed. They had this huge lift which made The Warrior frightened. He was sure I was going to leave him up there. I had to sing to him for days after that.

I looked around for wild horses. They're supposed to be here, too. I've heard that if they feel you're reliable, that you're not a danger to them, that they'll protect you. The kids said Steve McQueen was real. I wondered if he was ever protected by wild horses.

The three of us, now, trudged on. My prospects of finding Dulcinea seeming to dwindle. I brushed off my badge and straightened my hat. Hew started to whistle which may have been to make up for Ms. Lin's absence. I was never very good at that. I thought about Walt Whitman whistling down the lane with his hat cocked to one side. I never imagined myself to be of the same cut of cloth as that Roughneck. More often I like poetry which is even more common than his, unless it's the Romantics, whom I adored.

Hew may have overheard my disclaimer about Walt Whitman. He got out his harmonica and I wondered what was on the way and how long it would be. He said, "This is, "The Ballad Of Tom Hammer!"" It was very long. It had to do with the roofing industry, and boys working on the tops of houses in 103 degrees, modern day roughnecks. Tom Hammer was 'The Roofin Man.' "Catch a ladder, watch your hand, step back in the pack, here comes the roofin man!" The ballad was very catchy, free, and bold and I enjoyed it very much. In the end I even said, *"Diggity,"* with genuine gusto and Hew and I draped our arms over each other's shoulders and started skipping.

When the Desert Grove was within sight I could see Ms. Lin out front, smiling, and waving broadly. When we finally got there she ran up and gave me a kiss.

"What took you so long!"

I told her I had been learning how "Song of Myself " fits in neatly. And that I was feeling bolder than ever.

I think she said, "Well, that's good. You might need it." But, in fact, I was still lost in the fog of her lips upon mine. This happens to Inspector Montalbano all the time, but I was surprised it happened to me at all.

Ms. Lin hardly gave me time to recover. She reminded me of my new vows and my feeling rough and pointed to the narrow opening to The Desert Grove and said that I had to go in by myself.

"Where'd Pecos Bill go," I asked, still thinking of her.

"To get gas."

"Will anybody else in there know me."

"I don't think so."

"Do they have a bathroom."

"I'm not sure. You'll have to find out."

"Will you be here when I get back."

Ms. Lin quickly looked at Hew.

"Yes, we'll be here when you get back."

Ms. Lin made sure my badge was pinned tight to my chest. I told her to watch out for the sharp edge. Then she turned the bill of my hat around to the back and tightened my lariat. She said I looked very nice and hoped I enjoyed myself. I really wasn't sure what I was looking at. It just seemed like a grove of palm trees and a lot of motorcycles parked outside. There certainly was no door. "Is this a biker's bar," I said. "Yes, it is" replied Ms. Lin. "But, I don't have a bike." "They don't know that."

I asked Ms. Lin if she was sure I had to go in alone. She said she was.

16.
The Desert Grove

~ Like a willing Time Traveler, I stood within the oddest place. And yet I felt at home here. All manner of activity was before me. The head of refreshments winked at me in a strange manner and whisked his towel around like a scorpion's plume. I raised my eyebrows at him and he smiled at me and slapped the top of the bar, KABOOM! In the corner a platform of sorts had been set up and a line of people were going up with guitars, and lutes, all kinds of instruments, and whatever voice God gave them. It was probably Karaoke Night, or was always Karaoke Night, and the contestants had their name badges on and were having fun with it. A fellow holding a long neck bottle of Lone Star Beer was working the room. The front of his T Shirt said, 'The Fridge,' and the back of it said, 'I can fix it.' He was singing something by Noel Evans and every woman in the tent was cooing up to him. Then 'Robin' got up to address the other side of the room. She said, "Look out," and sang, "These boots are made for walkin. Walkin all over you," and the boys were loving it, while I was wondering what size boot she had. Then 'Tim' got up with his guitar and was reading a diagram for a muffler installation. Somebody said, "What the heck is this," and somebody else said, "Shut up, I'm interested in this." The tent was rolling precariously.

In their pandemonium I tried to make myself invisible behind a small palm. But I was soon discovered by a rather large person.
"D'you have a Salem."
"Of course not," I said, emphatically. "Smoking's bad for you. You'd be better off chewing it, if you had any teeth."

I hoped I hadn't been too lousy with my choice of words. I could have turned things differently if I had more time. To make matters worse it appeared we'd been overheard.

"Hey Carlos, you got any teeth!" came a shout from across this calliope den. I looked back over my shoulder. Ms. Lin was lining up on her tippy toes to see what was going on. I was about to yell out to her that things had not started off well when suddenly my hulking maniac changed his tune.

"Hey, where'd yu get that hat."
"Oh, that," I said. "It's just a kitchen pot. I forgot where I put it. I got it from a wiseman and I certainly won't part with it. He also gave me a parable and I won't part with that, either, even though I don't understand it." Then I said that I had several other members of my band outside, and a very big dog, and that we were on a secret mission. "We've stopped here for some reason which hasn't been explained to me. A lot of what we do has to do with a text."
All of this seemed to fit in exactly with what he thought as he said, "You're alright!" And he led me to a pillow in the middle of the "room."

I soon watched Carlos go about, talking to men who were playing cards, women, too, and pointing in my direction. What he was telling them seemed to take a long time, not like he was announcing me, but like he was telling them he was pretty sure about something. I also overheard him say, "Pecos Bill," to one of them. Before long a line of desperados descended upon me. Their robes whooshed as they sat by me, and a woman, whose name I learned was Dara, said, "Make way, ya big fish," and sat amongst them. They all looked me over, from my lariat, to my badge, to my hat, and stayed put. I thought that was a good sign. Then one of them, who may have been appointed to do this because he was French, started off the questioning.

"Excuse me, Monsieur, but what is your name."
I felt no need to be circumspect with these people.
"My name is Valentine Odey," I told him.
He said, "I know, but we have heard of another name."
"Oh, that one," I went on. "Well, I'm not sure that that one is working out."
"But we are at your pillow, Monsieur," he said almost plaintively. "So there must be something to it, don't you think."
"That could be true."
"So, why don't we start over."
"Ok."
"Excuse me, Monsieur,"
"Yes."
"No! You have to wait until I ask you the question!"

"Oh, sorry."
"That's ok. You are nervous. But, you don't have to be."
"Ok."
"Excuse me, Monsieur, but what is your name."
"My name is Vick Prey."
A man at the sandbar said, "Yeah, right."
But the rest of them defended me.

I knew that I was in.

17.
The Further Discussion That Took Place In The Desert
Grove

~ A loftier Argo cleaves the main,
Fraught with a later prize;
Another Orpheus sings again,
And loves, and weeps, and dies.

- P. Shelley

The Dowager Princess Cixi restored the Summer Palace Gardens with funds embezzled from the Imperial Navy. She got a lot of flak for it.

~ I was hoping we could get something to eat before the quiz began. Other than our picnic, and the popcorn at our drive-in, it seems like eating is a missing element in this story. Inspector Montalbano would be appalled.

So, I used the time while the regulars were putting on their own name badges to ask the head of refreshments if a tray of triangle sandwiches could be brought to my pillow. And some milk, too. "A pitcher of milk?" "With ice in it." "You want toothpicks in the sandwiches." "I think that's a good idea."

I wondered if this was going to be a grueling test. I was surprised Ms. Lin wouldn't want to be by my side. I'll have to remember to tell her all about it, just like all the things I have to remember to tell The Warrior about. I hope I'm not reaching capacity. It does seem like I have a lot on my mind. As I look around my pillow I can't believe we've evolved in so many directions. With their name tags on now I feel like I have my bearings but still I have a lot to learn. Itchy & Scratchy, who looked like angels in their robes, looked at the pitcher of milk and then at each other. They were inseparable. Carlos was complaining to Dago about the weight of oil. Dago suggested putting some Jack Daniels in it, laughed at himself, and slapped Carlos heartily. Raif was lighting a candle on his side of the circle and said we should turn the lights out (?). Mad Dog, who I felt sorry for, asked about Bonnie but no one had seen her. Chechi was shuffling a deck of cards over and over until he got them all face up. John B. sat alone with his thoughts and they were very hard to see. Dara cocked her head at me like she was trying to figure me out. "What kind of Chopper do you have?" she said. My eyes misted up, which brought their activities to a halt. Say what you want, at their core this was a sensitive bunch. Again, it was the sweet mannered man, whose name I now knew to be Claude, who led them off in their questioning. The sandwiches had arrived.

"Monsieur, could you tell us about Courage."

Well, that was quick. I didn't think I could tell them about Ms. Lin and I picking up Hew and Leonard, not knowing if they would sack us. I think more was expected, although that worked for me. I tried to remember if Ms. Lin had prepared me for this. In a way I think she had. After all, she's been with me up to now. This is what I said.

"Courage is like a chain which runs in the same direction, day after day. And then, for some reason we do not know why, one day it catches, and with great effort reverses itself." "But, Monsieur, after all that isn't the chain just going the other way." "That could be true, Claude, but it took courage to do it."

Itchy and Scratchy looked at me and of one mind asked me to tell them about Friendship. First, I took a bite of my sandwich, and thought about it.

"You are an example of friendship without limiting it by describing it," I said. "Friendship is like a hummingbird and a flower. One will always look for the other. It's possible that one will fly and one will not. But the flight path is always between them. Even when the nectar is poor they will look for each other." And then I took a sip of milk.

Dago asked me about Good Times. I told him that good times were like soft Velcro. That they can come undone and run away from us. I told him it's a good idea to have a shoelace, too.

Carlos asked me about faulty Transmissions. I told him about the sobbing girl outside the library who almost went out. I told him that jolting is a sign that something warm is missing, or broken.

And so, it went on. I parried their odd questions with deft returns. I did feel right about it. It's just that nobody ever asked me before.

Mad Dog asked me to explain Loss. I asked him if it was irreparable. He said it was. I told him that loss is tied to sorrow, and that they will always try to acquit each other but he should be prepared for a long haul. He nodded his head and wept, and I thought I should tell him more. I told him that loss is like the petal of a flower which someone put in a book for safekeeping. I told him to read books because he may open to that page again.

Chechi asked me about the Faces of Cards. I told him he was always looking for his face but the odds were against him.

Raif asked me about the Light of Candles. I told him that Darkness is wary of even the Smallest Light, because it is sincere.

John B. didn't ask me anything.

Dara asked me about Love.

When the pitcher of milk was gone, I read to them from Socrates. From, "The Apology," just in case.

But my companions of the pillow warmly surrounded me and clapped me so hard on my back I thought that chicken feathers might come out.

My questioning was over.

Apparently I passed, as they told me I could go on.

18.
I Tell Ms. Lin What Happened

~ "How'd it go!"

"Pretty good. I think they found me to be reliable. I only missed one question."

"What was that."

"It was Dara's. I don't think I got it right. But I was really starting to get tired."

"Or, Maybe you have to work on that!"

And so our quartet was back together. I felt like I was on top of the world. Somewhat behind us outside the Desert Grove my new councilors were lifting their glasses in our direction and singing, "All Hail The King, All Hail The King," like they had almost forgotten something. Leonard turned to look at them. I really thought they were going overboard. I said, "Well, I'm glad they got that out of their system." Ms. Lin said, "So, am I." But she said it like we had passed a marker and I was as confused as ever.

From here on, Ms. Lin, in particular, seemed fidgety. Hew and Leonard seemed willing to take things as they come, but Ms. Lin seemed anxious. She didn't seem willing to abandon herself to tomorrow. She seemed worried about it. I thought maybe I could have done a better job showing them around Floss. No, it was something that was ahead that was bothering her, not behind. All of us were strangely quiet. I couldn't think of anything to lighten the mood. And it was starting to get dark. Maybe she was worried where we would stay. That's probably it. I assured her there would always be a motel court we could stay at on the Lincoln Highway, if we got that far. She looked at me and smiled.

At a certain point, further down this road, it became clear to me that I couldn't put off my bathroom break any longer. I don't know how my Three Sherpas have managed it but I just had to go. Luckily there was a porta-potty on the side of the road. What's the chance of that. I told my comrades I'd be right back and hopped in. My fear that it may be just an old phone booth was allayed. I was so relieved that I started to sing, "Delta Dawn," at the top of my lungs. When I was done I flung the door of the porta-potty open and boasted,

"I'M DONNNE!"

But my comrades were nowhere to be found.

"Ms. Lin?"

"Leonard?"

"Hew?"

"Where are you guys???"

19.
Now My Loss Is On The Table

~ I wonder where the Dalai Lama is tonight
In his clean sheets

And his case of Diet Sprite

~ The thing is, there were very few trees to look behind. Ms. Lin, Leonard, and Hew were gone. Simply gone. I looked as far down the road as I could, trying to imagine how far they could have gone. I called out loudly, **"MS. LIN, LEONARD, HEW."** But it was to no avail. I wondered if I should retrace our steps to the Desert Grove. Perhaps they returned there for some reason I do not know. But there was a long ways in that and surely I could see them going there if they were. I couldn't think of any other direction to look in. They had simply vanished. A vanishing point had begun, or ended here. I was left to scramble around the canvas to see if a brushstroke may have covered them. If they're under one of Lucien Freud's I'm done for. His thick, luscious gobs of oil cocooning everything.

After some time I was sure they had been kidnapped. Yes, a robber band had happened upon them while they were waiting so patiently for me to finish my song. They were probably gagged and tied up by now. Perhaps slung across pack mules and quickly carried away. But why hadn't the kidnappers waited for me. Surely, I must have some value. Now, I felt my temperature rising. I had been robbed and slighted at the same time. I could stand it no more.

"BRIGANDS, BRIGANDS," I shouted loudly. "You who have stolen my precious. You who have stolen every ring from my hand. You who have left my hand lighter but my heart heavier, release them. I'll give you to the count of 10 and then I'm coming looking, and you'll be sorry." But everything was quiet. Pawnee quiet. And quietly I said to myself, Brigands, brigands, and sat down upon the road. I hadn't realized until then how uncomfortable it would be without them. I mean, really, without them. Was I to be a wolf in a newsreel wandering alone looking for my pack? The fact that it might be shown on PBS was of little comfort to me. I was alone. I wondered if this was another of those big moments which Ms. Lin is always talking about when she says, "Oh, no, you'll be quite alone," because I didn't like this one at all.

20.
The Other Past Catches Up With Me

~ "I'd like to report a disappearance."
I had gone to the nearest police office. A puffy man who looked like he had just gotten off a bicycle was on the desk.

"Hold on. I have to tuck in my shirt."

"I'll wait."

"Ok."

"How do I look."

"You look like Dennis Franz."

"That's good. How can I help you."

"I'd like to report a disappearance."

"Usually we like to wait 24 hours. Has it been 24 hours."

"I don't think we have 24 hours. I'm sure that what's going to happen to me will be tonight. We don't have Jack Bauer's luxury in this case, I'm afraid."

"Ok. What's your name."

"My name is Vick Prey."

"That's an unfortunate name."

"I know that."

"Tell me about the disappeared."

"Actually, there are three."

"Three!" .

And I went on to describe my pack in as clear a terms as possible. When I was done the officer said, "So, we're looking for a woman with no history, a hobo, and a dog."

"That's about it."

"And why were you together in the first place."

"Well, it seems to be a mystery. For myself, I was clearly in pursuit of the beautiful Dulcinea del Toboso."

"Is she Puerto Rican."

"I think she's from Spain."

I could tell Mr. Franz was getting exasperated. And he was a very messy writer. He kept flipping the pages of his notepad and writing bigger and bigger. Eventually he threw the whole thing down and screamed,

"Mister, are you from Victor Victoria."

I left the station in disarray. I didn't even keep a copy of the report. I felt gangly and beaten, with very little humanity left in me. I walked for what seemed like days. Elena Garro's distinction between illusion and reality was constantly on my mind. I was fraying at the edges. I just wanted to ride in somebody's car and look at the stars.

Not far out of Steve McQueen a line of cars popped up out of nowhere and went by me slowly with their brights on, in which these signs were lit up in the night,

. . .

My Dangerous Darling

Don't you see

That love is never

Unaccompanied

It doesn't matter who you are, the clothes you wear, or the name of your star

My Dangerous Darling

Don't you see

that love opens up like

a

DeLorean

I had my hopes up immediately. I was thirsty and I drank from this. I looked around like Gollum for "My Precious," but there were only these bright signs with no arrows on them. I wondered if they really were just a row of Burma Shave signs, or if, according to one of my irrational theories, they were gifts from outer space. Then the cars passed and it was dark again. At the end of the street there was a corral. It was empty. I didn't like the looks of it. The ground was trampled from the escape of wild horses.

I looked up, and Frank Miller was right in front of me.

"Evening Val. Or, is it, Vick, now."

The Miller Gang had found me.

21.

In The End, An Unlikely Escape, But I Take It

~ The Englishman
Who wanted to be rough
Challenged him to a duel
With cuffs
And cuffs.

~ Ever since I'd seen *High Noon* four times I was dreading this moment. I tried to tell Hew that, and Ms. Lin, but I don't think they understood me. I can't imagine how the gang tracked me. I mean, who goes to Floss, anyway. But here they were. Frank, and Ben Miller, Jack Colby, and Jim Pierce, and half of Kansas behind them. Everything had been leading up to this. I looked up at Frank and the swarm of harm he represented. I could never figure out what I'd done. I just went to see the movie, ok, four times. But not nearly as much as, *WILLSEYVILLE.* There were the business cards, and the posters. But it must be something deeper than that. Some glump of guilt which I could never get rid of, which had finally caught up with me. Frank was just a hired gun. He had a job to do. I could tell him that Caravaggio was innocent but he'd just look at me like I was from Texas. I'm sure my badge already infuriated him. He was anxious to get to it. His gang drew out their 22's, their long rifles from their saddle bags, and their ranch horses whinnied. "Looks like you're alone, Val," Frank said.

But I could hear the Screaming of Throttles. The Thunder of Wild Horses. And what looked like a refrigerator delivery truck racing in my direction.

"Maybe not, Frank."

LIGHTS SPLATTERED IN THE CORRAL! Pecos Bill rolled in with all my friends from the Desert Grove, and they were swirling up the dust inside the corral and swinging their pole axes. Good God, pole axes! And Dara and John B were screeching in some kind of waddled nomadic Berber tongue that scared the pants off me. Frank and his gang pulled back just enough that the refrigerator delivery truck could get between me and them. But it wasn't a refrigerator delivery truck at all. *IT WAS THE WARRIOR!* The Warrior painted in his finest cinnamon swirls and bursting with energy, with Buster at the wheel and Rio Margie Marie banging away on top of him. Pop, Pop, Thud, Thud, Spoot, Spoot. All Hell was breaking loose. Not to mention the Wild Horses. I felt like my guilt was being assuaged. Suddenly, an object appeared. It appeared to float down from the sky, with lights gleaming out of portholes. The Display on its brow said, 'IT'S NOT HERE.' Then the front of it dropped open like the mouth of a whale, and three figures in the most wonderful light waved at me. One of them yelled, "JUMP, VICK!" Then I heard another voice behind me, which I remembered from before, but which was sweeter this time, say, "Look in the bag, first." I was surprised it was still with me and looked in immediately. I found a cape which looked very much like a Toreador's. There was blood on it, and the smell of a cub jet. I pinned it to my shoulders but nothing happened. Rio Margie Marie was still banging away on top of The Warrior. I had the strongest urge to just run and get in him. Now the maw of this great object in the air was going up. Something was ending and something was beginning. I had to make my choice. I knew what it was. I just didn't know how to get there. Then I heard The Demures, their smooth back-up on the side of the stage,

"The Lariat, The Lariat, The Lariat, The Lariat."

Oh, right! I drew my lariat from my waist and started its swing. And, "YOU CAN DO IT, VICK," rang out from the light as I swung and swung and let it fling.

Pop, Pop, Thud, Thud, Spoot, Spoot.

....ZING

III

Only A Poet Can Find Me
In Which The Reason For Ms. Lin's Visit Is Mentioned
And Valentine Addresses The Rotation

1.
Again, Where We Left Off

~ At the end of Part Two I had snagged the front of a spaceship. I'm sure you were as surprised as I was. I hope your surprise wasn't about my ability to do it. After all I had been practicing. But there I was flying off into space with a firestorm beneath me. It was as if I was being propelled by it. Like all its flame was actually coming out of my back end. Then growing smaller and smaller and eventually fading away in the west, somewhere over the car wash.

I had no idea where I was going or why. I knew The Warrior wasn't going with me and that made me sad. I hope he's ok. I hope the Indian won this one. But he's very forgiving. For all I know he could be piloting Frank Miller on some adventure over the Great Plains at this very minute. I didn't feel that guilty. I'm sure if he could see me as far up as I am now he'd cock his grill and say, "How do you do that?"

The canopy above me looked like a trattoria in Inspector Montalbano's brain. A moveable feast. It also looked like a new world order in which a thousand menorahs were lit up in windows of wonderful mosaic design after all the trouble between them. Both things made me hopeful. I was also perfectly happy to be on my own as I tied my lasso, which was caught on the object above me, firmly around my waist and I even created a little sling to sit in in this inferno. My cape fluttered behind me, and my hat. Egads!!! My hat. There it was, having become unhinged, now floating aimlessly down the pike, letting gravity and the solar wind determine its destiny. Perhaps a new novitiate will find it and put it on, and my hulk will say to him, "Where'd ju get that hat." And he or she will be off on their adventure. I miss my questioners from the desert. I wonder if the answers I gave them stayed with them. I don't know if they were really answers, more like quick responses when I was put on the spot. I don't know exactly where the waters of that fountain came from. I did feel confident about it, though. I wish Ms. Lin were here so I could ask her how that happened. The zeppelin like creature above me, meanwhile, is floating along under some power I am not aware of. I'm sure it has something to do with photons, advanced physics, a mission, that sort of thing. But why had it come to Floss, which below me seemed indistinguishable even at this height. Maybe honing devices had something to do with it. I have to trust they were good ones. Well, they had their souvenir, but I don't even know if they knew they had me. I looked at my Device, which Ms. Lin had soundly pinned to me. Its sharp edge seemed to be getting smoother, like it had been filed. I don't remember doing that. It could just be my imagination, as I was trying very hard to imagine a resolution to all this. But a more satisfying place than right now I don't know if I could ever dream of. Flying along with delightful climate control under the stars of heaven and the bill having not been brought to my table yet. Maybe it never will be. Maybe I've entered a billless society. If so I can't imagine at all what they do with their time. Star gazing, I guess. But that never seemed to be a full-time occupation that I remember. This must be some kind of interim I'm in. If that's true it's very beautiful. My memory of Floss is at a disadvantage in this new kind of timelessness. I missed Floss, but I wasn't sad, either, when suddenly it occurred to me that I was being reeled in at last by whoever had that job in the object above me. After everything I'd read, I was disappointed there was no tractor beam, or blue ray, tootling me aboard. It just sounded like a crank was winding up my lariat. I hoped that would be the last of my disappointments.

2.
My First Encounter In The New World

~ Ordinance No. 9

Any parcel
Left undeveloped
To a friend
Shall be
A crime.

~ "I gotcha."

"Well I have to get my leg up there. This thing isn't going to close on us, is it. I'm all tangled up in my sling. I think I've done it now. Could you please stop that winch. You're winding me up like a ball of yarn. That's not the intent, is it. I hope I'm not going to be somebody's hat after I've just lost my own. Could you please stop all that racket. Is this a zoo."

The "person" who had me was very young, obviously not used to something as large as me and my cape. At last everything came to rest and I tumbled to the "floor."

"Goodness, are you all right???"

"Well, it appears that I am. No thanks to you."

I wasn't prepared for the crocodile tears that welled up in my workman's eyes. I felt terrible about my statement. I was just about to say, "There, there," when he popped out of it.

"I'm sorry for my emotions, sir. I'm just so glad we found you. Can I help you get up."

"Am I on the floor."

"The floor???"

"Yeah, the thing that you stand on."

"Oh, that. I was told you might ask that."

"Well, what did "They" tell you to tell "Me.""

"That you were, indeed, on the floor. In our briefing Princess TALIM said you liked to be reassured a lot."

"Oh boy. I may have to get used to this. Okay, you can help me up. Don't step on my cape."

"Who's Princess Talim?"

3.

I Get Processed

~ One Of The Seven Stories Of Creation

In the Gun Turrets in my new home, which had been converted into Observation Balls, you could sit there and look out. Usually, unusually wavy music was piped in. But on this occasion a person who sounded very much like Lucinda Williams was doing a reading of one of the Seven Stories of Creation which my new community had loaned her to think about.

"'One Night God was out
and he was flying his kite.
It was a box kite.
It was Blue and it had a sherbet of
ribbons tied to it by hand.
But the kite got away and

80

fell. God looked everywhere
for it but he couldn't find it.
So he wept to be alone again with
all his might and his tears rained down
for forty years.
When he looked at
what he had done, that his tears
had sparked the Seas
and given the pieces Life,
he said, That's Ok, and then
he went home and hid
in order to avoid the limelight.'"

. . .

But Lucinda figured out where he was.
So, she sang to him
in her favorite tone
which bounced across the Roads of Rome,
"Are You Alright."

~ When Ms. Lin disappeared I tried very hard to imagine her in a car in a line of traffic in front of me. She would be fumbling with her hair in a mesmerizing way. Smoothing it with her delicate fingers, picking at it, bunching it, smelling it, letting it go. I would catch up to her and she would get in The Warrior with me. Dave Thompson would still be on our radio, singing his hit, "Tasha, Hook Me Up." He would be at the part where he goes off on a tangent, **"E D D D D i e get in trouble, his pur momma moan."** This line just out of the blue, and wavy, and the auditorium is up on it and holding their fists up high, and shaking their bodies about to accompany Dave's sudden rhythm. Supposedly, Momma comes back at Dave, like, *"What I gone do, Davy, if my Eddie can't come home."* And Dave gets out his Blackberry and pretends he's calling Tasha, again, to see if he can get a loan to bail Eddie out. He tells the crowd, "We gotta watch out now cause she's got that Caller ID, which we all know is the enemy!" And the crowd loves it. Dave gets Tasha on the phone and right away she says, *"Is this Mr. Joan, is this Mr. Joan, lookin for a loan."* And Dave says, *"Taha, look here, baby, this your Honeycomb!"* Then Tasha says, *"Didn't you already call today."* And Dave says, in a sweet voice, *"Baby, this is not about me, this is a emergency."* He lets her think about that. Then he says, *"You see, it's about this."* And he tells her about Eddie's situation, how it was *"probably a little situation, a difference was shown. But, I got his*

Momma on the other line and she sure wants him to come home." Tasha isn't responding. The auditorium is quiet. Dave decides to throw down his ace for Tasha to think about. He says, *"Baby, look, when your keys are on the table and your face in Kodachrome you gotta have a angel can give a boy a loan."* Then Dave takes his guitar off and steps to the side with Dia, like he's giving Tasha space to think about it. Evidently, Tasha is doing that. Quiet. Pause. Too much to bear. The crowd starts shouting, ***"GIVE HIM THE MONEY!"*** Tasha done thinkin. Gets back on the phone, says to Dave, *"Come on over lion and you're ready to roam."* The crowd goes viral. Dave throws his guitar strap back over his shoulder with a flourish, says to Momma. *"Don't Worry, Momma."* Bump, Bump. *"I say, Don't Worry, Momma."* Bump, Bump. *"I say, Don't Worry, Momma, Don't Worry, Momma. Don't worry, Momma, Your boy's comin home!"* Bump, Bump.

I look over at Ms. Lin in my dream and she smiles, and says, "Well, that was something!"

But now Eddie and Momma are gone, and I have to concentrate on the delicate manservant in front of me. He's the only thing that has any dimension in my processing area. Everything else is perfectly white, Valspar flat ceiling white, and on the walls white, and the "floor" which still seemed translucent to me, white. He introduced himself as JIM.

I thought about that. It seemed a little highbrow to me, and I hadn't even seen him write it yet. I proposed a solution.

"Did anyone ever call you Jimmie."

"Ooouuuu, I like that."

"Then Jimmie it is."

I could see we were going to get along very well.

"Now what's this stuff about Princess Talim and where are we, anyway."

Jimmie looked at me and I swore his head started to shift with his stomach, and his legs with his arms. It was like he was detaching and reassembling at the same time. I took this for thinking.

"One thing at a time, eh! Ok, where are we?"

"Why we're aboard, The Bar In The Deep Blue Sea, of course!"

Where had I heard that before. "Isn't that rather long."

"You're right. It was TIM's idea! GLIM said we should call it, The Night Train To Georgia. Of course, they were both right, but Princess TALIM liked, The Bar In The Deep Blue Sea, so it stuck. It's actually a very long ship."

"What's the abbreviated name."

"I don't think there is one."

"Well, Jimmie, what do we do now."

"I have to read you the Pythagorean Theorem and then offer you our clothing."

"Sounds about right. But, I have to keep the badge, and the lariat if you could unwind it."

Jimmie outfitted me in a lovely white kaftan and looped my lariat around me. He folded up my cape and put it in the corner. "You may have to get that dry cleaned." Then he put slippers on my feet which had curly toes pointed up at the tips, with bells on them. They seemed familiar.

"I look very quiet," I told him.

"Wait til you walk," Jimmie said, and he started to laugh uncontrollably. I asked him why he didn't have bells on the tips of his slippers and he seemed to be puzzled by that.

"That's a good question," he said, and began laughing again. I was soon to find out that I was the only one who had bells.

"Ok, Jimmie, now level with me. Who's Princess Talim, and while we're at it, who's Tim, and Glim."

Just then a beautiful face with lips like Renoir and hair that flowed like a burning candle popped through a line in the "door."

"Are you decent!"

4.
I Experience Weightlessness

~ It was Ms. Lin. I ran to her and pressed myself to her, and tears rolled down my cheeks. She was lovelier than I had ever fantasized. I couldn't get over her. All I could think of was the motto of Montana, 'Oro y Plata.' She looked like a real mine to me. A gold and silver one, of course. I wanted to hold her and pan her at the same time. I decided to hold her. She said that I looked very much the part of a space pirate and asked me if I had come to carry her away on my rope to my ship. I told her that Ozymandias awaited her nearby. She thought that was great and I smudged Renoir's best work with my own lips, paying little attention to the card which was neatly typed up beside her, *'Do Not Touch The Artwork.'*

"Where did you go," I said, imploringly, at last, not thinking thru what I said. Ray Lin looked at me and said sweetly, "Home."

So that's where we were. As simple as that.

Jimmie had disappeared. I was to learn that disappearing was the same as leaving a room. It's how it was done. No trace. Just Poof. I was starting to see how my amigos had slipped away from me so easily. But I was entranced with Ms. Lin. I held her tight so she couldn't disappear, at least not without taking me with her. But she showed no sign of wanting to leave. I asked her if she had any furniture around here and she laughed at that. Immediately an ensemble scrambled. "You do like red don't you." I drew her to me. So, our lives had funneled to here. Not even my 1952 Vincent Motorcycle (I forgot to tell you about that) was more beautiful than Ms. Lin, and that's saying a lot. The ensemble disappeared and when the set was clear we floated entwined like an image in a mirror. "What can you hear." "Only the beating of you who are near." "What can you taste." "Only the oil of your lips out of place!" "What can you feel." "Only the wave of you against me." "What can you see." "Your Amazing Circuitry!"

"That's really good, Mr. Prey!"

We collapsed to the "floor" and I realized I was still in training.

I was probably more disappointed than you are.

5.

Something Philosophical

~ This time I was even further away than Montana. I doubt very much there are bears up here. Where would they hibernate. Then I'll probably find out there's a whole planet of them and the sun disappears from their view for 6 months out of the year behind a very big asteroid. I like bears. If I was in trouble I'd like a bear to come to my rescue, or E. F. Kiseljak, who can growl like a bear. There's nothing like a bear for a friend. "Oh, I see you got your bear with you, Mr. Prey. Everything's on the house. We have a Tortellini Alfresco with marinara sauce which will melt in your mouth. And for your friend, also, I could put some honey in it. Sit anywhere you want, Mr. Prey. It's a pleasure you came by." And kids want to pet the bear. "Watch out, he bites."

We brushed ourselves off. I straightened out the loops of my lariat and looked fully at Ms. Lin. This time I could see all of her. In, *The Terra-Cotta Dog*, Inspector Montalbano is intrigued to find a cave within a cave. In the second cave he finds the skeletal remains of two young lovers who were sealed up with their love a long time ago. They lay serenely together with their arms around each other, as if they were waiting for someone to take their picture. That's precisely what the forensic team did, of course, from many angles. For Inspector Montalbano the smell of the second cave reminded him of a tomb he visited once in Cairo. Thick, almost moist with honey. Now, in our circumstance, who were lovers here waiting for. Was it death. Was it Vick. Our rocket ship is almost like a cave within a cave. There were no skeletal remains here that Vick knew of (you can see how my experience of weightlessness has suddenly temporarily affected the vantage point from which I'm telling this story), as Time, here, has just begun for him. But there was a smell of honey. And everyone in this cave seemed to be waiting for him. Inspector Montalbano got down on his belly and crawled thru the passageway out of the second cave. Vick had no intention to do that.

6.
Princess TALIM

~ "Did you see the signs."
"The ones by the corral!"
"Yes."
"I was hoping they were from you. I was also wondering if you were up to something."
"You're not mad at me are you."
"Of course not. I don't think that's possible. But, I'm curious, was everyone in on it?"
"Pretty much."
"Are they all angels."
"I'm not sure in what sense you mean that. But, yes, they're all angels."
"Even Hoss?"
"No. Hoss is a Lama."
I laughed out loud. I would have been disappointed to learn that Hoss was only an angel.
"So, now, who are you."
"I'm Ms. Lin."
"I know that. But who does everyone HERE think you are."
"Oh, that. I wanted to tell you before but I was afraid it would ruin everything."
"So, you asked Jimmie to tell me before you came in."
"Oh, Vick, I just had to get you here."
Of course, we flew into each other's arms, again. If there were a transom over the "door," I would have lowered it to protect our privacy. This time Ms. Lin was softer than her hair which cascaded about me.

7.
The Black Pond

~ So, briefly, I play the part of a Rogue Private Eye. I don't think it will extend beyond this alabaster unit, for now at least, unless some editor gets a hold of the manuscript and says, "There, There, we need to develop that, right There." In unison Ms. Lin and I will say, "What." Because we have to maintain order as we see it and carry our case to its conclusion. Still, this was a brave new world we were in, in which intimacy was like hope. Cut off from anything solid it took the place of it. It wasn't like we were flying randomly here anymore than we were on Earth, but here we really knew it.

When at last we were ready to go on, as we must, Ms. Lin tied my lariat back around me and brushed her hand in front of her. The line which I had earlier interpreted as a "door," separated, and we slipped unceremoniously into the next room.

This unit was rouge and had soft music in it, which I immediately recognized as Mountain Man. The walls were liquid crystal and you could slide your fingers over them and change the scene, like a Smart Phone. Ms. Lin simply blew a breath and we were several exchanges away, in Zambia. Mountain Man was singing over a murmuration of starlings which were separating and reforming over a Black Pond. Immediately this seemed like a room where wishes were made. I wished I knew where I was. Ms. Lin smiled.

"You're on a transport ship."

"What does it transport."

"You."

I thought that almost sounded logical.

"But, I thought these things were supposed to be rigid."

"Normally it is. Right now it's breathing."

"Well, why doesn't it just take a deep breath and hold it."

"It just did."

I wondered what she meant by that.

Jimmie reappeared with paperwork which I had to sign. "There, and There, and There." He didn't look like an editor, but you never know. I would certainly keep my eye on him. Jimmie "left."

We sat beside the Black Pond.

8.
Just Talking

~ Overheard In Anne's Pancakes

You know what used to be good around here.
   A Laundromat.

   ~ "Will we ever go back."
   "You mean to Floss."
   "Yeah."
   "We might."
   "Will it be the same."
   "You mean, will Hoss be there, and The Warrior. That sort of thing."
   "Yeah."
   "I don't know. Time is different here. And there are different Schedules.
It's hard to say if we'll be on theirs, again."

   "Did you see the way Rio Margie Marie swiveled her holsters!"
   "That was amazing."
   "And Buster at the wheel."
   "That was something."
   "I hope they're alright."
   "I bet they are."
   "I'm worried about The Warrior."
   "I wouldn't be. I'm sure he's alright."
   "Where's Leonard."
   "He's resting right now. We'll go see him soon."

   "That was some shootout, wasn't it."
   "Yes, it was."
   "I really am worried about The Warrior. I think I heard some thuds."
   "I'm sure The Warrior is ok."
   "Did you see him winking at me."
   "Actually, I did!"
   "I only called him the Shared W because he was a Republican."
   "Oh!"

   "Weren't the Riders from the Desert Grove great, including Dara."
   "They were cool."

"I'm glad Pecos Bill went to get gas."
"So am I."
"Where's Hew."
"He's preparing the Report To The Rotation. Leonard asked him to."
"Oh?"

"The Miller Gang can't get up here, can they."
"We have lookouts."

The Black Pond shimmered, like it was clearing away some debris. I really wanted to throw a stick in it. Ms. Lin laughed. I asked her what she was laughing at. She put her head on my shoulder, and I wondered if we were on our way to Port Radium.

9.
GLIM & TIM

~ "Would you like to meet GLIM."
"He won't break the spell, will he."
"I don't think so. I think you'll find him very dear."
"Then we should do it!"
On some crossroad in my mind I was thinking, "And tell them he's a horse. And a very fine horse at that." It occurred to me that I hadn't been on a tangent in a while. I'm always drawn to that. "Rozinante, my faithful friend, look at what's come of us. Riding without ground to pound upon. Without you, I doubt that this is real but I have recently been given good reason by Ms. Lin to believe that it is. I hope you're being fed well. You might check with Buster and Rio Margie Marie. They have prepared a stall for The Warrior and they may have room for you, too. Oh, Factorus, where are you now. If you're still flying over Romania, I have misled you. I'm no longer in the van, as I have taken a ride in a festive balloon. If you have word you need to share with me, keep it locked up in your beautiful bill until we can meet again to discuss it. Anon, I miss all of you. I think I especially miss my office where I would be writing of all of you this minute. Farewell. This might take a while."
"Mr. Prey?"
"I'm sorry, Ms. Lin, I was somewhat distracted with my thoughts."
"I know!"
We both got up and left the Black Pond to itself. Ms. Lin blew and it went out.

"Can we come in!"

We seemed to be on the doorstep of a library.

"Of course you can, TALIM. Hello, Mr. Prey!"

"Leonard???"

I don't know if I told you, yet, that Leonard looks like Batman. Well, he does. His ears look like two I. M. Pei Pyramids in the Louvre Courtyard, and his eyes, which are somewhat sad, fit into a small mask and look out at you. I suppose Hew could resemble Robin, but he doesn't. In this case Leonard is quite alone. It's probably an earlier comic. I'm trying to remember if Batman flies. I hope that Leonard is not about to do that. He doesn't look like he is. He looks like he's in the last frames of a very long story in which he's tried to be helpful.

"Leonard?"

"It's me!"

"But, I mean, you have Leonard's ears."

"And I have all the rest of him, too, Vick! I hope you don't mind if I call you that. I think we grew quite attached, don't you. Have you been by the Black Pond, yet."

"We've just come from there, Father."

"Good, so that's out of the way. You're one of us now, Vick. This calls for a celebration. TALIM, you should tell TIM that Mr. Prey is here."

Ms. Lin pirouetted and smiled at me on the way out. She actually walked out.

"Isn't she a sweetheart."

"I'm not sure what to say."

"Or what to think, eh! Don't worry about that little trick we do, Vick. It's like a radio, it's not always on. Do you people still use radios?"

"I have a wonderful one in The Warrior."

"Oh yes, I remember that. How'd that work out for Eddie. Did he get out?"

"I think he's about to."

"Well, that's good."

Somehow, I had to slow this down.

"Ignoring the improbability of this situation, which on a scale of 1 - 10 I'm leaning toward 10, do I call you Leonard, or Glim?"

"Leonard is fine! I actually liked it."

"Ok. Well, if Talim is the Princess. Then,"

"I'm the King.! Isn't that a hoot. You actually guessed it back at the Church. We were all a little nervous about that. The rest of the manuscript had to play out, you know. You probably didn't notice how quickly you forgot about it."

"So, I probably can't pet you."

"You can do that. Who said you can't!"

"Vick!!!"

"Hew!"

My Merry Band was coming out of the trees.

I found that my affection for Hew had grown, not diminished. I wasn't even upset about his part in leaving me in the field. First, it had been prophesied by Ms. Lin that I would be alone at some point, and second, if that's all she meant it turned out alright. What I wasn't ready for was the huge bear hug he gave me, which reminded me of George "The Animal" Steele, a favorite character of mine when I could get wrestling on the little tv in my office.

While Leonard was showing everyone how he could howl Ms. Lin whispered to me that this was a ship of refugees, wandering in the desert. Immediately I thought I'd come upon another grove, or that the first one I came upon had something to do with this one. But now I wasn't being asked things. I was being told.

10.
Rembrandt's Eyes

~ The celebration with my band was just the fill I needed. My battery compartment was bustling with energy and for me walking away with Ms. Lin under the Bar's beautiful Dome, it was like we were back in the front seat of The Warrior, again, with the whole world in front of us. There were no Maple trees, no real ones, that is. But there were drawings of them overhead and I looked up for a bag in their catacombs. In fact, my own had floated up there somehow and was caught on a "branch." It was a new day.

Ms. Lin turned to me as we were walking.

"I'm glad you get along with 'Jimmie.'"

"Why are you glad I get along with Jimmie."

"Because he wants to be your footman. Sometimes his rotation is off, but he's really very sweet."

"Well, I'm not sure I've accepted him yet. He really has to have credentials. Does he have any of those things?"

"He knows his way around The Deep Blue Sea as well as anyone."

"That's it. That's his credentials!"

"Ok, he's also worked for several Emperors, a few Prime Ministers, a Prophet, and a Lieutenant Colonel in the American Revolutionary War, and he was a printer's apprentice in Paris."

For a minute I thought Ms. Lin was putting me on, but she said these things so easily it was hard not to believe her.

"Well, ok, if it will make you happy!" I said.

Today I'm reading a large book which I got out of Glim's library. I'll never get thru it. I just like to keep these things around. It has to do with how Rembrandt saw things. I'm always thinking that Ms. Lin sees things differently. I go along with it. I'd do anything to be a part of her canvas. And what harm is there to seeing things differently. Look at the size of this book. Well, you can imagine that it's very big.

I like to watch Ms. Lin walk about the ship. It's been two days since Ms. Lin took me to see Glim and Tim. She's taken me to all her favorite places. The long line of carrels at the end of the library are most intriguing. It's apparently a span where difficult questions are addressed. The carrels went on and on. I never realized how many things hadn't been resolved yet. I was led to believe that most of them had and it was just a matter of control. I saw a very determined man in a short grey waistcoat hunched over his carrel with a long pen in his hand. He was working fervently. "Who's that," I asked Ms. Lin. "That's Dostoevsky," she said. "He's revising, *Crime and Punishment.*" "How's he doing." "He's having a hard time keeping up because of all the cyber stuff." Thomas Merton, the monk, was in the next carrel, doodling, and making faces at Dostoevsky. Apart from the past I wondered if the carrels were also possibly a vague retreat for great living artists. I looked around for all the people who had appeared recently in *Art in America.* They weren't there. But a number of artists who looked familiar to me were. It seemed odd that they all ended up here, tending to The Bar In The Deep Blue Sea. Now Ms. Lin has left me alone. Probably so I could make up my own mind about what's going on. Good luck with that. I prefer to just sit on the bench and watch her walk about the ship. Or disappear from one section and appear in another. She calls that, "jumping ship." It makes me laugh.

I'm sure I'll revisit the carrels, later.

11.
My Sleeping Accommodations

~ All men dream but not equally. Those who dream
by night in the dusty recesses of their minds
wake in the day to find that it was vanity: but
the dreamers of the day are dangerous men, for
they may act their dream with open eyes, to
make it possible.

- T. E. Lawrence

~ "How do you expect me to sleep in that," I had said the first night, when I
was assigned a bed with a plush pink pillow, a stuffed dragon, and an
elephant.

"You'll get used to it," Hew said. "TALIM did."

I noticed the one across from it had a nice green pillow, a scary snake,
and a ...

"What's the matter with that one."

"Nothing. ...It's mine!"

"Will I be sharing my secrets with you in this nursery!"

"No! I have The Midnight Room now. I think TALIM sleeps in a falcon's
nest. She's hard to locate after dark."

"It's always dark up here."

I thought about Larry and Colleen with the days growing shorter in Port
Radium, sitting out on the porch. It seemed like they had such a wide expanse
before them, which would soon be covered entirely with snow and darkness
and a spectacle of light. In the end they didn't stay there that long. I think if
they had, they would have been transformed into a work of art. Two figures in
a wavy universe which had been gessoed white. Plenty of time to think about
what to do with it. When they dreamed, the Aurora Borealis probably
conducted madly on their canvas, and when they woke up, they were probably
always surprised it was white. If they ever go back, I'm sure they'll look for
that porch, again.

The porch here is an old gun turret, which I mentioned before. There are
several of them spaced around the ship. There must have been some huge
battle at one point. My porch is right outside my sleeping quarters so I can
dream during the day as well as the night. Afterward, the dreams I have
during the day I spread around the ship as I have learned to detect a slight
beep indicating someone's listening to me.

I dreamed the owner of the car wash said, "What are you doing here. Your rent is due." I told him he would just have to wait as I was on an important mission, and I started telling him about the Valet Service, and Ms. Lin, and the Knights of the Desert Grove. He cupped his ears and said, "ENOUGH. My God are you nuts!" I was offended by this and told him I wouldn't be paying my rent now no matter what he said. I was glad I set him straight as he went running off in the direction of an alley. "Good," I said. When I went walking around the ship with that in my head, everyone looked at me and said, "Ooooohhhh!" I wondered if they thought that I could really make things possible. Or if I was to be feared.

12.
The Graffiti

~ On a day in which the sunsets of Saturn kept me busy for an hour I went looking for Jimmie. In the corridor ahead there was some commotion. My God, an error in space? This could be serious. But it wasn't an error at all. Apparently, someone had decorated a grey post with orange graffiti. I can't imagine who would have done that. *'I REGARD ALL FAME AS FALSE COMPROMISE TO MY QUEST.'* It was done with a bold flourish. I looked over my shoulder as I passed to see what kind of attention it was getting. Several onlookers were disassembling and reassembling trying to get a better look at it. The morning was going rather well.

Ms. Lin was standing by a tube of some sort. Possibly for mail.

"Have you seen Jimmie."
Ms. Lin turned with a feigned start. "Why Mr. Prey, have you heard about the graffiti!"

"Yes, I hope it doesn't delay us."
"It won't. Everybody likes it!"
"They do! Still, I hope you reprimand whoever is responsible."
"Do you think it was Jimmie?"
"Of course not."
Ms. Lin smiled.
"Truth be in the Heart, and the Heart be in it."
"What!??"
"That was the last graffiti we had. We look forward to it."

"And what happened to that sojourner."

"She's here."

I now imagined that there was a whole recess of remarks left by my predecessors, lying somewhere in this labyrinth. A Monument Avenue. There is probably also heavy equipment which is used to pry these things off their moorings. My God, I am flying in a ship of fillings. I'm surprised this thing holds together at all. If I had my notebooks with me it would surely be the end of it.

At last I saw Jimmie and bid Ms. Lin adieu. A large machine was busy sawing off the post and loading it on a conveyor. It went through a compartment which looked like a luggage carousel at a terminal and I never saw it again.

13.

Jimmie

~ By the time I got up to Jimmie I was thirsty. I told him right away he could be my footman. He seemed to be relieved about that.

"Would you like some evanesced water oyster crystals," he said.

"What I'd like is a Lone Star Beer, if you have one."

Jimmie blushed, "Ooouuuuu, that sounds yummie!"

I was off to a good start with my footman.

"Jimmie, I have to ask you some tough questions. To begin with, what's going on around here."

"Why, whatever do you mean, Sir?"

"I mean, why am I here, for example. Generally, in the first two hours of a case I'm told what's going on but in this one I haven't been told anything and there doesn't seem to be any end to it."

"Oh my, how long has this been going on."

"At least two days."

"Well, if it's a relief to you, Sir, sometimes it can go on a lot longer than that."

"Is that because of the difference in Schedules."

"I think it is. I'm never quite told, specifically."

I learned from Inspector Montalbano that sometimes the best way to get to the bottom of an issue is to throw the conversation off.

"Jimmie, have you ever read a story in a passageway."
"Maybe."
"Is Gim the Queen."

At this point Jimmie started flying apart, his eyes spun like a slot machine, and the rest of him was crisscrossing in the air like a juggler had said, "Here, let me show you how I do that." I may have gone too far.
"Jimmie, snap out of it. For God's sake, keep yourself together."
Jimmie went the opposite direction. It looked like he was going to melt, entirely. No longer the explosive look, but the Pure Michigan look, and in this case a raging Michigan brook behind it.
"Sir, we were attacked by someone from a different Schedule. I think it was Thun. He was looking for a Dressmaker and we had one. She was the best one, of course. GLIM was wounded badly in the attack. So was TIM. Ms. Lin, as you call her, was asleep and knew nothing about it. That has haunted her. There were no demands. We didn't see the Dressmaker after that. The name of their ship was, the Scroll. They got her and got away. We're all very sad. The Dressmaker is GIM. I can't help it, Sir. It's GIM. To me she was always, Denise, from, *The Paradise*, on Masterpiece Theatre. But, It's GIM. You have to find her, Sir. It's GIM."
"And is Gim, Talim's birth mother."
"Yes."
"How about Tim."
"No, he was adopted."
"Another admirable thing, Jimmie!"
I had taken a shot in the dark. And the sky which had been clouded by Ms. Lin was clearing. Why Ms. Lin didn't blurt all this out in the first place was beyond me. Maybe she wanted to see if I made it this far. Well, I had. I told Jimmie that we might need some horses if we were to go further.
"We don't have any. Somebody let them out, along with all the other animals. It's a little lonely without them."
"That's ok, Jimmie," I told him, softly. "We'll make up for it. We'll fill up this tub before we're through. We'll find Gim, and reconnect you with the animals, and the birds, and possibly the whales, and treats for all of them."
"I hope we have room for all that."

"We'll make room, Jimmie. And I will tell you about Rozinante. I don't imagine you've read about him in, *The Adventures of Don Quixote de La Mancha,* have you?"

"I think Cervantes is in the Carrels."

"Good. We may consult with him."

"Don't you think you should talk to the others first."

"You're right! They may have already overheard us, but it's best to be polite."

"I'm sorry we don't have any Lone Star Beer."

"Don't worry, Jimmie," I said. "We'll add it to the list!" And I thrust my arm in the air like I'd seen Don Quixote do in the Tobias Smollett Edition.

14.
Things That Are Pulled Out Of A Hat

~ My band's intelligence had already alerted them to what I was up to, and by the time Jimmie and I got to Glim's library they seemed to be relieved.

"Good!!!" said Glim. "The box is open. A scene well played by you and your footman. So now you know, Vick, that we need your help to find GIM. I'm sure you're wondering why we couldn't have told you all this to begin with. But would you have believed us. Would you have believed that you were talking to a Princess from another Planet. Would you have agreed to have a conversation with a dog, other than the ones you kept having! Would you have volunteered to blast off into outer space with a hat, a lariat, and a token from a little girl at a bridge. And would you have believed you could do what we needed you to do without the revelations about yourself being revealed to you."

Glim had a point. There is a limit to what I will believe. But after this I think it's pretty far out there.

Glim, who really seemed to be filling his role now, went on.

"Our real Home, Mr. Prey, is covered in myth, and legend, and fact. It's pretty well covered up, but we just call it M. We actually picked that letter out of a hat! M is at the top of the Schedules, and it has a very special fabric. The Scroll, a false scroll, has always tried to fool, cajole, and brew, to get into M. The first thing they would do, of course, is tear the fabric, and that would be a bad thing. We lost at battle, which eventually came, and were driven out. But not before GIM cloaked M behind us. The Scroll didn't know what happened to it. We settled here in The Bar In The Deep Blue Sea and the Scroll left us alone while they buzzed around looking for M."

96

"I felt remorse for letting the animals out," Glim continued. "Yes, JIM, it was I who did that. I didn't think it was fair to them to confine them to our capsule for so long, so I let them out. I think most of them are living on Jupiter. There really is water there. GIM understood my remorse and she made it possible for me to become, 'Leonard,' and switch back and forth. It's an odd thing, called, 'Exchanging.' I got it from my mom, she got it from her mom. We all have it. But you have to have an 'Exchanger' to show you how to do it, and that's where GIM fits in, besides the fact that she knows how to cloak."

"I don't mean to interrupt, but how many of them are there."

"About 25, but they're all spread out."

Ms. Lin looked at me.

"Anyway, as Leonard I would wander around the ship. I became some kind of phantom, which everyone talked about. A writer in the carrels tried to hook me up to a sled one day. I think it was Jack London. I knew I had to be careful after that. So, I made sure I was just a connection to the past that no one could put their finger on. Except the children, of course. But Thun was always monitoring things. I think he saw me jump over a "river" one day. He put two and two together, and figured out what had happened, to me, and to M, and who did it. And the Scroll came back for GIM."

Ms. Lin went over to Glim and put her arm around him. At that moment, I really wanted to call her Talim. I could see how much thought he'd put into it. But mostly I could see that he was sad. This time, like he had let everyone down. I could also see that Talim was angry. I didn't think for a minute that her anger was directed at him. But now I had one question to go, and I asked it.

"Why me? Was I picked out of a hat?"

"No. You were a lure that fit perfectly at the end of a perfect line."

"And what was this fishing line?"

– "ONLY A POET CAN FIND ME." –

"It was the last thing GIM said as they pulled her out the door."

Of course, I was quite floored. I felt like L. S. Lowry in Leather Lane, surprised that anyone would like my little figures which are so plain. And yet I have a Champion, and a Queen at that. Damn right we'll find her!

It was like my friends jumped out of a box to "Pop Goes The Weasel."
They all vied to speak, as obviously they had been listening to what I was
thinking. "But I implore you, each of you," I said. "Where do you think she is,
anyway."

I realized immediately that that was not very stirring, and I vowed to make
up for. It was Jimmie, possibly the closest of all to Gim, who came to my
rescue.

"Are we going to go after them, Sir," he loudly cried.

"Yes, Jimmie," I said, to his bouncing green and blue eyes. "We're going
to go after them."

15.
I Address The Rotation

~ Now our plans would be more broadly known. Hew was scheduled to
Report to The Rotation. I wondered if others had been brought here to help,
and it just didn't work out. Maybe an earlier note from Gim had said that only
a plumber could find her, or a carpenter, or an electrician. I thought of the
Rev. Chicory D. Possum. He was a plumber. Somehow I felt he had a hand in
this, even now. What was his parable, again, 'I saw a man once drop a spoon
on a floor which was parquet. The menu consisted of Trout, Trout, and Trout.
It wasn't so much when you came in, as when you went out.' What have I
gotten myself into. Still, I am myself exhilarated. I want to catch fire with the
masses. I want to be their Mary, to assure them that I really mean business.

In the hall on the day of The Report I noticed that my poems, which you'll
remember I sometimes refer to as my paintings, were tacked up on the walls
and everyone was looking at them. Of course, I was very puffed up by that. I
wanted to mingle with the crowd and see which one bowled them over. But
then a bell chimed and we all had to sit down

For some time Hew talked about the financial health of the Cooperative,
that new observation balls were planned for the coming year, and that the
population has grown by 23, not to mention The Carrels. Enclosed as they
were the discussion about Climate Control was mainly about the increasing
threat of space junk. What really stuck out in my mind was the absence of an
offering basket. In a way I missed it. There was a rhythm to that as well which
I had come to appreciate. But now Hew rocketed back to the microphone like
The Reverend and veritably yelped,

"THE TRAIN THRU FLOSS RIDES EVERY DAY!"

My God, you would have thought that not a single part of this clan's body was actually connected. Parts were flying everywhere. It must be very liberating to always be this detached. No matter how many times I saw this it was remarkable. When it came time for Hew to introduce me, I looked at Ms. Lin like an incandescent light bulb had reached its short life in my head and popped. All the ideas I thought I had, had evaporated. Ms. Lin smiled, as if to say I wouldn't need them. She has such confidence in me. I grabbed the microphone with a flourish which The Reverend would also have been proud of. Somewhere a great chain was about to go the other way. And I yelled loudly,

"THE TRAIN THRU FLOSS RIDES EVERY DAY!"

Then I stuck my fist out like Mary. It occurred to me that this was a moment I was meant to fill in. I was going to excel at this.

I was ready.

I told them about Dave. I told them how life is a loan, and that I was one, too. I explained how Tasha was the loan giver in his case, but nonetheless we had to have a good reason to get one in ours. I told them that Saving GIM was a good reason.

I told them that things had turned out well on another float I was on.

I told them that I never tired of seeing *High Noon* and *WILLSEYVILLE*.

I told them how E. F. Kiseljak had saved Colleen.

I told them I was armed with a parable even though I didn't understand it.

I told them that somehow I came up with answers in another bar I was in, which was a surprise to me there, too, but nonetheless I had experience.

I told them Princess TALIM came to see me in the car wash.

I told them their King was a dog.

I told them I didn't know if Love needed another favor, but I would do my best.

I told them The Warrior had the scent of something only he knew about.

When I was done, they all stayed completely intact. I was sure that I had failed. But Ms. Lin looked at me and when I looked at her, her rivulets of tears contradicted that.

16.
My Meeting With Miguel de Cervantes

~ In the late afternoon edition, the news in the Bar Gazette was all about Glim being a dog. "THE KING IS A DOG!" Soon thereafter I saw Hew entertaining a group of elementary school age children in the corridor. He had their rapt attention.

"Your King and I were on this train and we were coming up on Dead Man's Curve, which was shaped like a W, and if we got in there and continued to swerve, we would pull down everything that was on its way to the Alamogordo Naval Reserve. So, I said, 'Leonard you got to get off quick and somehow tell the Engineer about the ticklish situation we got back here.' So, he jumped off and started to run, and there were about a hundred cars and we were number 101. I yelled, 'Leonard, you got to get down low!' but the only speed he knows is Go, and go he did. And you know what, your King caught that engine and managed to explain and that Engineer pulled up with the wheels a smokin and the tracks aflame..."

Over in the corner, under a "tree," Leonard, as Leonard, sat blissfully.

Further down the corridor several little M's were at a table drawing lines with colored pencils on a large map. I stopped and asked them if the red ones were the interstates. They giggled, and a little girl in a blue bonnet said, "I don't know," which set them off in fits, again. Along with the menorahs and mosaic patterns reforming together in the heavens they made me feel hopeful, also.

At last I reached Glim's Library and I knew there was something here I had to do.

"I'd like to see Miguel de Cervantes. I believe you have him in solitary."

Soon I was led to a tower above the carrels. A sign with big letters said, 'The Patriot Lounge,' and before me sat the Masked Man of Infinity, a pot upon his head, a sword resting across his lap, a lance in the corner, and a cat. I was surprised about the cat. I thought I had made that up. "Who's the cat," I said to the caretaker. "That's Keith Richards. I don't know how he got in here." "But that is Cervantes?" "Oh, Yes. He thinks he's Don Quixote now. We have to keep him away from the others. He asked me if you were from the Bar Gazette. It's probably best that you say you are. He wants his story to be told, but you only have five minutes."

...

"Do I have the pleasure of speaking with The Illustrious Don Quixote de La Mancha."

Feeble, crazed looking almond eyes looked up at mine and pored thru me, looking for the truth.

"I am."
My worries melted, just to think of him again! I knew everything would be alright.
"Fair Sir, my name is Valentine Odey. The Odeys even have a Coat of Arms. I don't know if you're familiar with that."
"There are too many anymore to ask me to keep up. I'll take your word for it."
"May I sit down."
"Sure, bring that mortar over here. I don't think it's armed as nothing here seems to be. What did you say your name was, again."
"Valentine Odey."
"That's unfortunate. I was hoping it was Vick Prey. I read in the Gazette that he's coming here today to find GIM. You don't have a horse, do you?"
"Um, you mean in my mind, or in fact."
Mr. La Mancha roared, and stomped his feet, and clapped me on my back. Having gone deeper into the onion of his mind I knew that I was in.
"Kind Sir, may I ask what you found in the world in your adventure to be everlasting."
"Hmmm. Well, Sancho and I were always looking for a place to stay or something to eat, for ourselves, or for Rozinante. Otherwise, bad teeth, hurt feelings, the unfortunate lapse in memory, those sorts of things we found, along with Injustice with its jagged keel abusing our beautiful sea. We also found that very little was as it seemed to me. I was always being corrected. Are you from the Gazette."
I could not lie to him. I brought out my notebook and a pencil and hoped he would make an association which was not real either, but he would be comfortable with that.
"Do you mind if I write this down."
"I think that's what you're supposed to do."
"Why did you think that windmills were Giants."
"I turned my kaleidoscope before my eyes, Val, and there were Giants. Don't you have one, too!"
Much like with Hew, I thought this a question he just wanted me to think about, not give him an answer to. He went on to expand on this logic.

"I would like to have seen one of those new windmills your age has. A man by the name of Ricardo here, who I believe is French Canadian, said their blades go 300 mph. But, Rozinante and I would have engaged them. It was all about Rozinante, really. Half the time my visor fell down and I couldn't see a thing. But he would paw the earth and gauge their revolution. Then we were off like a bullet. So jumbled was I upon him."

"How did you hold on."

"By chance, Val. I had no commission. In the end, we were propelled by Chivalry."

"Did you ever have one true enemy."

"Yes, the appointment of Reason for all things. If I had succumbed to that I would never have made it to here."

"But now you're in solitary."

"That's their choice, not mine."

"But can't you see that you wear them out with your fantasy."

"A point that my beleaguered Sancho often made to me. I try to avoid these discussions of liability. The problem is Harm, Valentine, not me."

"Where are Sancho and Rozinante now."

"They're looking for an open door. As soon as they find one we will leave here and continue our quest. It's far from complete, you know."

"Will it be complete when you find Dulcinea."

"Ah, Dulcinea. Valentine, you've brought her up! These things are a mystery. It's possible she may no longer exist for me, you know. But like a boy jumping off a barn in spring, when you go, you go. You can't turn back in air. So, I'll continue. But, yes, if I found her I would consider my quest ended. I hope that doesn't bother the publishers."

We continued talking about everything I had in my outline. My five minutes were up. The caretaker stood in the doorway and motioned for me to come out. I got up and extended my hand.

"Is that the one you write with."

"No. It's the other one."

"Then give me that one."

And he took it with both of his.

"Say something nice about me in the Gazette. I'll be looking for it. You don't want a cat, do you."

I looked at Keith Richards, who nestled against his old warrior and purred.

"No, that's alright. But that was nice of you."

I furthermore looked back upon my leaving. Don Quixote had risen and was wagging his sword at a fan with Keith Richards hanging on for dear life.

I wondered if I was looking at my future.

17.
The Dressmaker's Studio, And Other Things

~ "Ms. Lin, wait up!"

I was almost out of breath as I had run the length of the ship. I wanted to tell her about my conversation with Miguel. But I had gone over it so many times in my mind so I wouldn't forget it that she already had it down.

"No, we can't take him with us."

"But why. Give me one good reason."

"It's not allowed."

"What's not allowed. You do everything else here strangely. Why not let him come, also."

"Those who are in the carrels are Treasures Of The Schedule. We would have to give him back if it were found out. Besides, he's a little exasperating to put up with."

"Well, I think that's silly."

"But I'm not Hoss, and he's not coming. If you want to leave him clues where we're going, that's your business. How you leave them is also up to you. But we have a lot of preparations to be made, starting now. I hope you don't find me curt, Mr. Prey, but the lamp is lit and we must move within its flame."

Egads. What was that all about. I stepped back and looked closely at Ms. Lin.

"You cut your hair!"

I tried to remember if Mary had ever done that. My first concern was that we had to start over. Then I realized that Ms. Lin was simply preparing to go to work. Still I missed her hair, which if you will recall, cascaded like a burning candle. Now I could see her ears which were pointed at the top like her father. Not exactly like him, not like Pyramids in the Louvre Courtyard, more like the tips of Dairy Queen ice cream cones when perfectly poured. I don't know why I hadn't seen that before. I guess I would have been overly intrigued if I had. Her eyes now, maybe because of this, seemed bigger, like De Kooning's eyes of children in his earlier work. Pale orbs with shadelike pupils. My God, this must be nasty business we're getting in. Kidnapping.

"Do you like it."

"I think it's perfect."

The last of our preparations were being made. Beyond the maps there were all sorts of things to be thought of. Machines which calculated distances, and pumps, and tubes, and tall chairs with little wheels on the bottom of them which went "Wheee," and musical instruments of all kinds. "You guys really have a thing about music, don't you!" There was also a strange book on the cart, *What Would You Do If It Happened To You.* The bookmark was on Chapter 4, "What Did You Forget." Jimmie helped Ms. Lin and I assemble everything, which he took away and whistled to in a tone that sounded Hungarian. Then he broke out in song, "We will live in tubes and pay for air in genubes/gelubes," then back to whistling in Hungarian. I was concerned about our welfare. It seemed to me that what we were packing wasn't enough and that we should go back and read Chapter 4, again.

Ms. Lin smiled.

"The ship which is waiting for you is equipped with everything else. It's been equipped for some time. All it was missing was you."

In the middle of The Bar In The Deep Blue Sea there was a room. I'd passed it many times and never seen anyone going in or out. "This is GIM's Studio," Ray Lin said, softly. After a small hesitation, she turned the knob on the door, which I noticed was shaped like the shell of a turtle. I let my eyes adjust to the darkness. The light there was, was by reflection from the corridor which we had just left, and from a large round window cut into the "wall" directly across from us, thru which the grey night of the universe poured in. A comet shot by and illuminated everything better, and I could see that bolts of cloth were piled up on either side of us as we entered, like soft pillars. Immediately I felt warm, and I was sure they were flannel, which is my favorite.

Ms. Lin hesitated, again, and then resumed her mission, which apparently was to outfit me for the next part of our adventure. She went over to a box in the middle of the room and pulled out a pair of puffy riding pants and held them up to me. "You've got to be kidding," I said. "No! I think you'll look very nice in them, and look how big the pockets are." She had a point. I like to keep things arranged, even in my pockets. "Well, okay," I said. Then she found a long sleeve flannel shirt, which was the lightest of grey, with cute little curly red flaps over the pockets, and white pearl snap buttons, and a ochre tackle vest to go over all of that, with big pockets in that, too. Then a pair of black work boots with safety toes on them, and finally, a hat. This she gave to me proudly. "I sewed the letters on myself! I hope you like it."

It said, **VP**, on the blue crown in big black letters. I told Ray Lin it was almost as cool as the comet. "So, how do I look?" "You look like a bounty hunter." "I do!" "Yes, I'd give up immediately, if you were looking for me." I held out my slippers with the bells on them. "We have to give these back to Jimmie. Where is he, anyway." "I'm right here." I jumped. "Will you stop doing that! From now on you have to announce yourself." Jimmie offered to help me put on my new clothes. I told him to check if there were any pins. Then Ms. Lin fastened my badge to my new tackle vest and tied my lariat to my belt. Despite Ms. Lin's reassurances, I was sure I looked like a Ringmaster who liked to go fishing. I was convinced I wasn't going to scare anybody.

Ms. Lin then said it was time for us to go to the hangar. That Tim and Glim were waiting for us there.

"We should go there now."

Suddenly I was overtaken by melancholy. I was sure that what was there would take us away from here. I had grown fond of The Bar In The Deep Blue Sea. I had my routines and now they were to be interrupted again.

"How about if I meet you guys there. It's the one with the grey door. Right?"

18.
My Period Of Detection

~ Left alone in Gim's Studio I sat upon a blue chair and looked around. On every bench were the rinds of Gim's work. There were snippings of paper patterns everywhere. It looked like she never picked anything up. I wondered what she was doing in here. If she was making clothes, she sure was making a lot of them. A quick survey took me to a spot over her cutting table where she had tacked two lines upon the wall. 'There is a crack in everything. That's how the light gets in.' Another fan of Leonard Cohen. I remembered how Factorus was a fan of Leonard Cohen, too. Although you rarely see a crow on a wire. And now, about our kidnappers. I'm sure they searched the room. The Scroll would leave nothing untouched. I wonder if they searched it for a long time. So long, in fact, that Gim had time to leave a clue, a wonderful clue, to where they were going. Now what would that be.
There are many detective styles. It's possible mine is not as colorful as the Ingenious Squire's. He had his kaleidoscope. I have my periscope. You see, I

turned my gaze like I was viewing the surface of a sea from its vantage point. Everything seemed flat to me and wavy, of course, but I expected that. I looked at the dressers, and the drawers. I wondered what was in them. That didn't seem to be part of my style. My style has a lot of mystery to it. I lowered my periscope and looked at the snippings. Boy, what a mess. I settled on a book on one of Gim's shelves, *Dangerous Women*, edited by Otto Penzler. I wonder if the kidnappers saw that one. It's possible there are no pictures in it and to their peril they moved on.

I'm coming to the end of my revolution around the room. Not a thing out of place. But, I'm sure I'm missing something. There is always a clue. There is always a clue. I thought about what Our Resourceful Nobleman would do. "I turned my kaleidoscope before my eyes, Val, and there were Giants. Don't you have one, too." I needed to find something big! I lowered my periscope carefully to the waterline, and let my Reason go. The snippings! They floated closer to me and I could see a constellation of stars, cut up at the last moment, coming together for me.

19.
Ms. Lin & I Leave Behind The Bar In The Deep Blue Sea

~ "I KNOW WHERE SHE IS!!!"

But before I could tell them more, as if this wasn't the whole reason for my visit, I saw they were gathered around a wounded animal. Immediately I took their side and set down my clue which was curling up in the air behind me.

"My God, what's that."
"It's the High Fashion."
"It looks a little beat up."

"It is. She tried to defend GIM. They came thru here. It's the only open door on the ship."

The High Fashion, Gim's Jumper, was straining against the cables which had been applied to keep her upright in her bay. She reminded me very much of The Great Spool in the heart of Floss, straining against its restraints. There being a danger, of an unexpected nature, if it ever got out. The danger here would be to whoever took Gim. But for the High Fashion to leave in this shape on a voyage of this magnitude would be a mistake. She'd never get there. I don't know how many more days of rest she'll require. I just knew we didn't have the time to wait.

"So I won't be taking this one."

"I'm afraid not, Vick." Glim said. "But we have one for you from the same class. The Elvis Velvet. Actually, it's mine!"

The Jumper beside the High Fashion was blue. It hummed in the hangar like a refrigerator delivery truck from an old era in the South. Immediately I took a liking to it.

"I'll take it!" I said to Glim.

Then I laid out our clue on the drawing table for everyone to see.

"What are all these pins?" asked Hew.

Jimmie looked up, wondering if he had missed them.

"I had to put everything back together. This is where Gim is. She's in there!" And I pointed to an area of seven major stars. I looked at Glim. "I think you know where they are."

Glim looked at me, his eyes glistening. "Yes, I do. You and TALIM take Elvis, Vick. TIM and I will follow in GIM's if we can. I think everything is ready for you now. Don't you."

For a minute I looked around. I knew we wouldn't return to here, either. It was sad. But at least when we were here we found out what Ms. Lin wanted. I know that's been on everybody's mind for a long time. But just to be sure I turned to her as we were leaving and said, "Is this what you wanted?" and she said, "Pretty much."

We climbed aboard the Elvis Velvet. Jimmie clamored in behind us. Glim looked at Ms. Lin and did some silent talking. I reached out my hand to Hew who took it, along with an envelope I gave him. "Take this letter to the Gazette without delay, will you."

"I will."

And the hatch closed on Ms. Lin, and Jimmie, and me.

IV

The Path Of Kings
In Which Valentine's Dream Draws To An End,
At Least For Now

1.
Where We Left Off. But This Is For The Last Time

~ "My God, How do you turn this thing on."

The Elvis Velvet had fallen out of the Bar and appeared to be plummeting. As I couldn't be sure it was to Earth we were falling, and that wouldn't be good, either, from this height, I repeated myself, "HOW DO YOU TURN THIS THING ON!" And then I added a few more notes to be sure I was heard. "Does it have a key? Aren't we supposed to go up!"

My appeals went unnoticed. I didn't know how as I also began flailing about in my seat and screaming, "What have I done." I was perfectly content to be in The Bar In The Deep Blue Sea, and now I was sure I had prematurely recommended that we leave it. "Ms. Lin, do you have your headset on. I'm trying to get your attention. And Jimmie, are you in here. This is a disappointment and we haven't even gotten anywhere yet."

"Oh, Mr. Prey, you do let your sensibilities get in the way of you." Where had I heard that before. "We're perfectly fine. The Elvis Velvet is simply showing off."

"You mean like he's just taking a dip in the pool?"

"Something like that. It's also possible we may be out of gas."

"Gas!! What kind of rocketship is this!"

"It's GLIM's. He's never been very fussy about those things. But you said we had to get going. So, we'll just have to make do."

"Ms. Lin, you're letting the air out of all my expectations about space travel."

"Well, it gets better!"

"I hope so."

I was having a hard time adjusting to my headset and I was relieved that Ms. Lin could hear me. I've never heard so much racket in my life. I honestly think somebody could have thrown us to our destination easier than the way we're going about it. But even in crisis situations the most unusual thoughts creep in. For example, I think the most beautiful girls in the world are from

Lebanon, but now it doesn't look like we'll be going there, either. Ms. Lin turned to me and smiled. I thought I should address the matter of the gas.

"Is there a refueling station we could dock at soon, just to relieve my fears. Somehow I think that's the least of what should be my fears, but right now it's bothering me."

"We don't go out that much, Mr. Prey. Don't you remember. Going to find you was a big deal. We'll just have to see what happens."

Just then there was a big CALUMP, and the Velvet leveled off.

Jimmie fixed it.

2.
My Notebook

~ Take that way
It goes to the brazen wood.
What about the other way.
Nothing good will come of that.
    I wouldn't.

~ Now that we had leveled off I felt a whole lot better. I couldn't wait for Jimmie to appear, to congratulate him. Whatever it was he did. Ms. Lin seemed relieved, too. I wondered how long we had to keep our headsets on. The thought of losing Ms. Lin's frequency and having to write everything down and hold it up in front of her crossed my mind. So, I kept saying, "Can you hear me. Can you hear me." Finally, she took her headset off and said, "Of course!" It was little things like that which made the transition to our new situation a pleasant one.

I looked around at all the vinyl records hung on our interior. Evidently every one which the real Elvis made was considered platinum to Glim and was displayed, the collection concluding with his possession of, "Heartbreak Hotel." I assumed that was the one he put up when Gim disappeared.

I noticed that Ms. Lin didn't even nod at that thought. There were several controls in front of her and I'm sure she was preoccupied.

To Glim, Elvis was probably a strange character. I tried to imagine Glim bellowing like a hound dog. It seemed out of character. Then I remembered a recent example where that was exactly the case, and that as Leonard his father was a hound dog, so maybe it wasn't. At any rate I'm sure it was Glim that picked out the name for this ship. I don't think that Elvis was ever meant to go to war. I didn't see any catapults, or torpedo tubes, or smoking gun turrets, or knobs with warning signs over them. I also didn't see any drawing tables upon which we could triangulate a course. We might have to hope that the scent the Elvis had was the right one. Ms. Lin looked at me and said it was. Still, I couldn't wait to fiddle with things and have occasional stern looks as we passed by asteroids.

"You mean the Velvet is aware of our course?"

"He shares our ability. You know!"

"Oh, that."

I'm surrounded. I got out my notebook and made a note of it.

"I hope it won't take 3 1/2 days to get there. It is Orion we're heading for. You knew that, too, didn't you."

"Not until you figured it out! We were all flummoxed. That's why we needed you, Vick. We've gone over that."

"So, it's Vick, now!"

"Occasionally. I hope that's alright."

"I don't mind. I think it's a natural development. You can even call me Valentine if you want. He seems to be the one who's always getting in trouble. But, where's Jimmie."

"I'm right here, sir!"

But Jimmie wasn't "right here." He was on the screen in front of us.

"Where, exactly, are you," I said, and fiddled with a control I knew nothing about.

"I'm in the bulkhead. We're going to need some gas. We also had a leak which accounted for our wobble. I fixed it."

"That was it?"

"Pretty much."

"Still, Jimmie, you are to be commended. How soon can you get here so Ms. Lin can give you a hug."

Jimmie blushed, on screen, and faded out.

The Velvet was humming along. Ms. Lin was sorting out papers, which I'm sure were important. I was thinking about my office, and wondered if I left the window open.

3.

CYL

~ Leaping like a greyhound with one yard to go the Elvis Velvet was cutting through space like nobody's business. The thin element of surprise would NOT be our calling card. The triumphant charge of the masses would be. I began walking up and down the aisle of our transportation and mimicking freedom. Ms. Lin laughed and Jimmie made big eyes like saucers at my antics. Gone was Floss with her captains of industry presenting goods at my court. I was away from them and I was expanding at tremendous speed. "Power in a few can never replace the strength in many," I yelled loudly, hoping I could meld with the fluff of the universe. "But there are only three of us," exclaimed Ms. Lin, who had recovered her composure but was nonetheless laughing. I looked around and saw that that was true.

The three of us have settled into a routine which consists of checking reports, and fiddling with the controls, which I've mentioned before. The latter never has any effect, really, as the Velvet is on course. But sometimes I spin them wildly and holler, "Look out." And then I sit back and admire what I have done, and the vast greyness that slowly recedes behind us. I was waiting for something to happen as I knew it would. I was sure we wouldn't just get to where we were going. So, when Ms. Lin said, "Look at that!" I knew she wasn't just pointing at something for no reason and that it would be a part of our quest. It was a gas station. I quickly typed onto my keyboard, "Stop at the gas station." The Velvet considered my request and slowed and we landed upon a blinking pad with a big X on it, next to a sign of a horse with red wings.

"I hope they have Ethel," I said. "That's very good gas."

Ms. Lin thought that was hilarious. It's possible they have a different kind of gas here. I did see piles and piles of cylinders, far larger than the Co2 ones I put in the back end of my balsa wood cars when I was young. That was a dangerous sport, having to carve them.

"Can we get out." That sounded like a logical question to me, without spacesuits and tethers. "I mean, can we?"

"Of course we can, Vick. We can do anything we want!" And with that Ms. Lin was out, just like at the Retreat. I was sure something was in store for us. Jimmie jumped out, too, and we all looked at a cylinder with a bow tie on, which I thought was a cylinder with a bow tie on.

"Hi, CYL!" Jimmie said, and ran over to meet him, or her. "Boy, it's good to see you!"

"Ah, JIM. Where have you been. The route has so few travelers these days. And is that Princess TALIM?! Come here you pretty thing and give me a kiss."

"Oh, CYL. How I've missed you!"

"Ummmmmmm mmppfff!"

"Now WHO is this," the bow tie said, after they untangled.

"It's Mr. Prey, CYL. You know, like the one that's coming. Only he's here now!"

"Oohhh, I like him!"

"Well, you can't have him! We're on a very important mission, which you know all about."

"Well, maybe when you're done with that..."

"CYL, don't be so explosive!"

And then there was another round of kisses.

Soon, we sat down to eat around a very small table. I couldn't imagine that much stuff could be placed upon it, but several things were and then more things were, and it seemed like we were building a very large castle of food, indeed. I was soon to find out that we had a great deal to discuss. Over our shoulders while we were engaged, CYL had Little Peggy March, who I always liked, cranked up on the camp radio. Peggy was singing, "I Will Follow Him," which was about Peggy's boyfriend, not me. But it was quite loud. CYL noticed my concern about the volume. She, or he, said, "Darling, it has to do with spies who may be about. We don't want to be too clear with them, now, do we." I looked around and imagined all sorts of masqueraded appliances and poles.

We began and over a wonderful bowl of iceberg lettuce with Ken's Italian Dressing & Marinade Ms. Lin asked CYL if Thun's spies HAD been about.

"They come. I overcharge them. Tell them all sorts of cockeyed things. About rumors. They love rumors. The one that's bothering them, of course, is that someone has been found who will defeat them. I tell them I know nothing of this, and, indeed, until now, I really didn't. Are you a Supreme Poet, Mr. Prey?"

I was caught with a Super Basic Burrito from Viva Taqueria in my mouth, but, nonetheless, I managed to mumble, "What?"

"A Supreme Poet. I am aware of GIM's profession, that only a poet can find her. But we all know that only a Supreme Poet will do. Find her, and free her. Are you that person, Mr. Prey?"

Jimmie passed the pepper to Ms. Lin who held it over her lovely Quiche, with its savory filling of Top's Wicked Cheddar Cheese.

"I don't know. I hope I am. Do I have to know what I'm doing?"

"Do you mean, do you have to understand what you're getting at when you're writing?"

"Yeah, I was thinking of that."

"Well, I think you have to have some idea what you're getting at. You do, don't you!"

Now I was completely jammed up with pitted olives from the Deli Section, and put my finger up like I needed a time out. Jimmie reached in the stack and pulled out a plum, and said, "Oh, good!" which set us all laughing, and gave me time to think about the question.

"No, I don't."

CYL smiled at Ms. Lin.

"I think you have him! Wizardry will not defeat Thun, nor the fruits of the Hour of Compline alone, but honesty might."

Ms. Lin and Jimmie nodded in agreement. I, personally, was surprised that that was all there was to it. Then I realized that it might actually be very complicated.

"I was hoping we could look at The Map, CYL," said Ms. Lin, and she looked at me sincerely like I couldn't be expected to do everything.

"Of course!" CYL said.

4.
The Map

~ The Cashier And The Cat

I like your nails
Thanks
What color is that
It's teal
Nice. Who's the cat
That's Elizabeth
(bending down to get a bag)
Actually, I think it's aqua marine
I try an do 'em once a week.

~ Now we were getting down to business. The food disappeared. Actually, we had finished all of it. CYL spread The Map out on our table. If there were spies about, CYL must feel we had worn them out by now.

"This is the Universe, Mr. Prey, or as much of it as you are aware. Now, where did you say GIM was, again?"

I pointed at the Constellation of Orion.

CYL gasped. "The Path of Kings. A Very Dangerous Path. Are you sure of this, Mr. Prey!"

I wanted to tell CYL (I thought a minute about the nature of that gasp. It wasn't a giveaway at all) how I figured it out. I wasn't sure how to explain my detective style or how I pieced together the clue. But Jimmie jumped to my defense, and explained about the pins, how I used them to my advantage. CYL said that he or she never doubted it.

I glanced furtively at The Map, which looked like a sheet of music. There was an astounding array of beads on it, slung and swung in all directions. CYL quietly let me look at the beauty and complexity of it. I had no idea how to look at it in a logical way. It wasn't like the map I have in the glove compartment of The Warrior. That one has Montana on it. This one appeared to be a hologram. A light field in which everything in front of us was in three dimension, but even more than that, could present any time lapse we wanted. Ms. Lin wanted to see a day in the space of five seconds. CYL made that happen. I don't know how. I made a note to watch his or her hands closer next time. Of course, we could zoom in or zoom out. Old hat. This was new in that everything we saw WAS happening, in real time, and with a twist of a knob, which said, "Tease me," we could get a hint of things to come.

"Does Thun have this," I naively asked.

CYL said, "Darling, there's only one. And you're going to take it with you."

I considered the responsibility. I was starting to get loaded down with effects, what with my badge, my lariat, my hat, and now this.

"Where will I put it."

"You can easily put it in one of your pockets. You have quite a few!"

"That was Ms. Lin's idea," I said, in defense of my own concept of style, even though I wasn't sure I had one.

CYL laughed. "But it does appear you have room."

We all hovered over The Map after that.

"Rook to Knight Five," Jimmie said.

"Ordinarily, but in this case Five is protected by Thun's armies," CYL replied calmly.

I saw that my three companions were in a different trance than I was. Indeed, they seemed to take on new countenances as they were together again and flying over a terrain that was clearly familiar to them, in a game they'd played before. For Ms. Lin's part, her hair became even shorter and her fingers were now like spikes, with rakes of silver rings, and upon one of them the amulet of a turtle. She also had copper tattoos on her knuckles. I'd heard that prisoners do that, tattoo themselves on their knuckles. Usually in blue ink, but these were definitely copper. One hand said, FAIN. The other said, LOVE. I wondered whose prison she'd been in. I went on to inspect Ms. Lin's eyes. They were constellations themselves. Not a reflection of constellations from The Map but constellations themselves, of Virgo, and Pisces, Taurus, Aquarius, and Cancer, Aries and others unnamed, all whirling, hurtling around her orbs. She was lost to me in this form. Jimmie, for his part, took on the countenance of Mercury, the messenger-god of Jupiter, the god of games, of commerce, and storytelling. Like all of the Roman Gods, he was barely clothed and seemed strange beside us, hardly armoured for war. He pointed his staff half-heartedly at Knight Five like he wasn't about to give up his point. CYL laughed at him. She alone, kept her form. She, as I've decided temporarily to treat her as such, roared tremendously and took Jimmie's Rook and hid it in her mouth. Then she took The Map and shook it wildly, and with a BANG it all flew apart. I wondered how many times she'd done that before in the history of the Universe! Eventually everything settled back into a rhythm and my companions' original countenances which were dear to me returned also. I was greatly relieved. I could see that all three of them enjoyed the game, but I had watched with trepidation.

"So, which way do we go," I said, unable to think of anything to rival their positions. But apparently it was enough as CYL, Ms. Lin, and Jimmie all smiled at me with great affection. In the end CYL inferred that I should trust The Map. And despite everything I had just seen I was inclined to do so, even though I wasn't sure how, I mean, not even knowing how to do that. CYL drew a vague line up and around and thru several glens, around points of light and the blackest of nights. I asked her if she was avoiding something. She looked at me, and said she couldn't do that. That she was just looking at wind and draft.

"If you mean with this map if there is something you can avoid, you can't do that."

"Do you have another one," I asked.

"No, we don't."

"Are you going to go with us, CYL," I asked, almost plaintively.

"Hardly, my dear. I have important things to do here. But if you need me, I'll be near. Remember, trust yourself, and The Map."

I went over and showed the vague line which CYL had drawn to the Velvet. He said, "Hummpff," or emitted some exhaust which sounded like "Hummpff." The point being that he already knew that, or didn't care much about our planning. I don't ever remember the real Elvis being so headstrong with his manager. I hope we get there.

It was time to go. The Velvet was playing another record, *"Well, it's one for the money. two for the show, three to get ready..."* I could tell he was anxious to complete the lyrics to "Blue Suede Shoes," his way, and after we said our goodbyes to each other, he jumped into the air like a cat.

5.

The Cloud Of Doubt And Depression

~ We all hated to leave CYL behind. He or she, as I was uncertain again, blew kisses to us, all the way to the next orbit. Ms. Lin wiped a tear from her eye and looked into the greyness in front of us. Jimmie was looking at The Map and every now and then he would say, "How about that!" All in all I had no idea if I was steering us in the right direction, or if the Velvet was cooperating, but Jimmie didn't object to our course, and he had The Map to begin with.

I looked behind us to see if we left any jet trails. I've always wondered where those things come from. I think there's a lot of conspiracy theories on that, too. And I may be contributing to them right now. Sure enough, behind us there was a bubble bath of Joy Dish Soap almost a mile long. I've always been accused of using too much of it. I don't know how the people who track these things will explain this one. I decided to look straight ahead after that.

Ms. Lin was looking through a small telescope on her console. I thought it was the neatest thing. So, when she said, "Uh oh," I thought the lens cap had fallen off and disappeared somewhere under the table. I offered to look for it.

"Look for what?" was all Ms. Lin said, and it appeared to be more serious than that.

"We're entering a Cloud of Doubt and Depression."

"We are?" I said.

"Yes. Jimmie. Hard left, quickly."

But the attraction of this nuisance was greater than Jimmie's ability to avoid it. I also remembered CYL's admonition that we may not be able to avoid anything at all.

"It's the unknown, Vick. Hold on!"

I thought about my office at Nike. How I'd be going out for tea about now. Making small talk with everyone at their cubicles, inquiring how their efforts to form a union was going. All of that was known. It wasn't something that was know, known. I just repeated it every day. It was comforting, in a way. Everything about this adventure is unknown. At the very least, unlikely. And things seem to happen right on top of each other. There doesn't seem to be a break where we just stare out the window for days. I always thought that's what it would be like. But, no, now it's The Cloud of Doubt and Depression.

"I don't imagine Jimmie can do anything about it?"

In fact, Jimmie had disappeared.

The unknown plays a big part in every story. In most stories the unknown is a specific thing, like who poisoned Aunt Ethel, but in this one the unknown is much more productive. In fact, there isn't much known about any of this. So, for Ms. Lin to say, "We've entered the unknown," which is exactly what she said next, it must really stand out. I wondered how long we'd be in here.

"It's hard to say," Ms. Lin said. "Maybe a day, maybe a week. It could be a year. It's hard to say with these things. You get sucked into it and there just doesn't seem to be any way out."

"Can't we just drive thru the wall of it and that way get out."

"It doesn't seem to work that way. It doesn't really seem to have a wall. Not really. We just have to hope we come out the other side. Jimmie's working on it."

Just then Jimmie "appeared," and announced that he had put the Thistle Blanket on the Velvet to keep it from compressing.

"I wouldn't go outside without gloves."

I wondered if we should inform CYL, already. The Velvet was doing his best, playing, "Don't Be Cruel," at full volume, but the darkness was worse than soot, and there didn't seem to be any space to work in at all.

"That's the thing," Ms. Lin said. "You feel as if space itself has collapsed. You feel very alone. But, I know what CYL would do."

"What's that," I said, as calmly as I could.

"She'd lay down on a stack and pretend she was a cylinder. I've seen her do it. Don't you think we should try it."

Just then a man in a bus went by. He said, "hello," and in the face of everything else that was confusing he appeared to waver.

"We really should," I said.

I didn't know what or who to pretend I was. But we all became very quiet. The darkness roiled and the Velvet shook. It sounded like hammers and voices were trying to get in. I breathed very deeply. I'd seen that done a lot in yogurt commercials. Before long I was on my way to Montana in The Warrior. Ms. Lin, Piedmont, and Leonard were with me. Ms. Lin laid the map from my glove box out in front of us, the other one, the one that had Montana on it, with its thick red lines which really were the interstates. Ms. Lin concentrated and spread her fingers out like they were the threads of a guitar. Towns with names like Madrid and Ceres lay at the end of them. We were all the way to Iowa, already. Some kids on their bikes waved at us. I noticed that one of them had a girl's Schwinn. I commented that at that rate we'd never get there. Ms. Lin looked at me. In Wyoming, we turned up into pleasant hills where horses ran beside us like we were a train. The thip, thip, thip of corn rows was replaced with ranches with big tubs of water. Blacksmith vans were on the road with us with their ancient arts, on their way to cavalries, maybe. The Warrior kept an eye on them. It seemed like we were driving all night. I was anxious to see if Montana really was the Big Sky Country. When I saw a sign that said, 'Montana, 10 feet ahead,' I was determined to get there. An antelope was grazing by a stream. The atlas said to look out for sugar beets. I fastened my seatbelt.

6.
Another Time, The Other Side

~ I couldn't believe it. We were out.

"How did we get out?" I said.
Ms. Lin was looking in her telescope, again, and Jimmie was nowhere to be found.
"Oh that! You were magnificent, Vick."
"I was!"
From that time on I began to believe I could do it. Whatever I had to do. I don't know why. I don't know if it was because I believed in myself, or because I had company, or because I was playing loose with facts. But we were on the other side. I felt for my token. It was still stuck on my tackle vest, and seemed smoother than before. I also had my lariat and my hat. I thought of the Masked Man of Infinity, how jumbled he was upon Rozinante yet keeping his appliances about him. I thought of him and hoped he was well.
The days went on. If nothing else the Velvet was smooth in his ability to hold an audience. We were implacably sewing the stars together, much like we sewed the stores together in our venture into Downtown Floss.
One day at the controls I asked Ms. Lin about her past, about her real home, and about the Universe. I pressed her at great length for I had been curious from the beginning about our relationship. She was generous and told me all about her neighborhood, about her friends, and where she went to school. Too much to repeat here, and some things may have been confidential. "We lived in The Map.", she said. Then she said we should see her friend, Messaline, by all means. So, she said to The Map, "Messaline."
"Is she far from here," I said, not really knowing what far meant.

"That's up to The Map!" she said, almost delighted to have our fortune told by somebody else. In fact, it seemed like no time before the Velvet was docking on a reef of some sort in the middle of what looked like an emerald sea. Being an earth sign I had a feeling this chapter was not going to be about me.

"Messaline!" "Messaline!"

When Princess Talim was young (Here I am breaking my rule about confidentiality) The Map was in its infancy. I had no idea about her concept of time, so that could have been yesterday for all I knew. But I got the impression that a lot of things were still molten and not formed yet. There was a lot of leeway as to how things were going to go. Even color was still unassigned, and gender, and friendship. And, of course, Schedules. Princess Talim and Messaline bubbled up together. They lived almost a mile apart, a ridiculous number in the universe, and couldn't help but see each other in the span of a day. They were immediately drawn to each other. It was magnetic. And they stuck to each other for all of their childhood. But circumstances separated them as things became more complex and the forming of things actually created fissures in the world. Talim fell thru one fissure, and Messaline fell thru another. But their regard for each other was immutable. In each of their lives new fissures came. It was like they were dropping down and down through several wonderlands and every now and then the warren burst through and they were connected, again. It's possible that's where we are right now.

"Messaline!"   "Messaline!"   Burst forth from my co-pilot's seam. "Messaline?"

Deep in the Emerald Sea I couldn't hear a thing but the water was suddenly unrested, and the reeds along the sides rustled and began whispering to each other. "In our hollows send word down that the girl is here from The Tudor Crown. Send it down, send it down."
"That, too?" I said.
"It was one of them."

After a while I said, "How long does it take for the word to get there."
Ms. Lin said, "She's probably considering who else is around."
In fact, someone said, "He looks very puny," and jumped off a lily pad and upon the ground.

In a repeat of encountering CYL, Ms. Lin rushed forward and kissed Messaline. It just seemed to be longer. Then they shared a thousand things. Jimmie came to my rescue and we went off to tinker with the Velvet if we could get away with it.

After a few centuries were covered in their conversation their embrace fell slowly away and I heard Ms. Messaline say, "But if you've gotten this far there must be something to it."

"The Reverend agrees. He gave him the parable."

"The one about the trout?"

Suddenly they both broke out laughing and pantomimed with great gesticulations The Reverend going thru his big book.

But that cleared up and I was sure, in fact, that The Reverend had a special place in their hearts. He just wasn't around to hear them giggle.

Messaline said, "Did you understand it, Mr. Prey?" before we were even formally, or in any proper way, introduced.

"I'm sorry. Messaline, this is Vick Prey, the Private Investigator I told you about. Vick, this is Messaline."

"Very nice to make your acquaintance," I said, as expansively as I could. "I don't know if you have anything you could add to our quest. We already have a footman, a badge, a lariat, a hat, and a map. I suppose I could fit something into another pocket."

"But you didn't answer my question." she said. "If you do you can take that."

Then, these two giggled and flew off.

"How long before we beep the horn," I said to Jimmie.

"What horn?"

"Oh, right. This isn't The Warrior. I'm sorry you missed that part, Jimmie."

"I was on the roof."

"Unbelievable."

Ms. Lin returned and brushed by me.

7.
The Fan Cleaner

~ Now we were on our way and I had no trouble adjusting to my routine, again. I had also taken up the habit of announcing, "Vroom, Vroom," in even the quietest of times. I don't know if I was trying to make up for it, the quiet, or if I was just being annoying. I think it was the second possibility, actually.

Ms. Lin, however, took it as a symptom of an underlying problem. She was probably right but I couldn't imagine taking the time to go over my childhood also, to get to the bottom of it. But now Ms. Lin was on heightened alert for these "outbursts."

"I think you need your fans cleaned," finally, she said.

I had any number of responses rolling around in my head so she could pick whatever she wanted. "What?" "Fans?" "Now!"

Soon, of course, there was a sign in the universe, *Fan Cleaner, Just Ahead.* The Velvet began to de-accelerate, and we landed on a pod which looked like a chanterelle mushroom. There really was barely room for us to land.

"Is this place inhabited?" I said. Of course, it was inhabited, as all things are. In this case our new seer emerged from what looked like a mechanic's garage and waved profusely. "I'm over here!"

Once again Ms. Lin hopscotched over to yet another acquaintance and put her arm around him, hugging him tightly. He blushed profusely.

"Hello," he said to me. All of these dwellers in outer space seem to be very polite. Far from the image which had been implied in several Star Trek episodes. And forget about Dr. Who. If it hadn't been for Rose I don't think I would have enjoyed it at all. The "Alien" we now encountered had a huge bag with him which he didn't seem to be struggling with but which clinked and clanged, loudly, like there were spokes or shards or at the very least a lot of impressive metal parts in it. I was a little alarmed by that as it was me he was about to have a look at.

"My name is Phil. I also fix clocks. Do you have one with you."

"No, I don't. And I don't think there's one in the Velvet, either. What's in the bag."

"I don't think there's anything in there. I just carry it around and predators leave me alone. I think it's part of evolution."

"Well, where does the noise come from."

"Beats me. Like I say, I think it's part of evolution. Maybe for bags. So, if you don't have any clocks, do you have a problem with your fans."

"I didn't even know I had any fans, until Ms. Lin brought it up."

"We all have fans. Do you make odd noises."

"Well, yes, I guess so."

"Then you have a fan problem. Come over here and let me have a look at you."

I went over, reluctantly. Actually, Ms. Lin pushed me.

"How long have you been doing this," I said.

"About 300 years. My father was a fan cleaner. His father was a fan cleaner. I really like to fix clocks but it's hard to get people to see the point to it out here. But fans you have to have cleaned, even if you have The Map. You do have The Map, don't you?"

I quickly looked at Ms. Lin. I thought The Map was a secret.

Now Ms. Lin blushed profusely. Nothing out here is done in small measure.

"Phil knows about The Map. He actually had a large part in the design of it. I wanted you to meet him. He's very important, and special."

I gave in to Phil, and he patted and pulled, and something went "BOING!," then settled into the back of my jacket.

"What was that?" I said, worried that I had acquired something heavy that would hold us back.

"Oh, nothing. Just some old straps and a few bar notes which were in the way. I think you'll do better now."

I thanked him profusely. I also asked him if it would be ok to have a piece of his mushroom.

"We all should!" he said.

When we got back in the Velvet I said, "Vroom, Vroom."

8.
The Trial To Clear Everything Else Up

~ The Extraordinary Testimony Of Danny Myers

"Danny, because of your extraordinary testimony here today and because nobody here really seems to be afraid of you, I'm going to order the transcription of these proceedings be sent to my chambers immediately." "So, can I go home now." "Of course not. I have to read it first."

~ Thru our open vent windows the Velvet let the universe pour in. Ms. Lin was whirling like a dervish, something which she does every morning, and Jimmie was crouching and trying to dance like a Cossack. He fell over several times but always rolled back up and started kicking again, yelling, "Hey, Hey, Hey." I thought he was amusing. I wasn't about to try to do it myself. I was saving my energy. Periodically The Map would go out, like it was adjusting to danger. That's the only thing I could make of it. I asked Jimmie about it, and he said, "Hey, Hey, Hey." The glow of the belt of Orion was visible now. I looked at it thru the big window on the Velvet's nose. It reminded me of the Aurora Borealis and I wondered whatever happened to that back in Port Radium. The show here sizzled moderately at its distance. On the console an inscription appeared, "The Dragon's Fountain of Tears." Evidently the Elvis Velvet was trying to come up with something new. That never ends, regardless of age.

In front of this glow, actually within reach of a few minutes of us, a hubbub was brewing. I was sure we were invited to it or we wouldn't be on course for it.

"What's that," I said, to our dancers.

"Oh that. It's The Trial. I wouldn't worry about it. It's just a formality," they said, in unison.

"Been practicing, eh!" I shot back at them. "So who's on trial?"

It wasn't long before the Bailiff, a gentleman in a red vest, who kept saying, "God Bless," led me down the aisle as all sorts of conveyances arrived outside. Thru the window I noticed a familiar figure. It was Hoss. I was sure of it! He had Ross's trumpet slung across his back and was directing traffic and kept saying, "Out you go, Amigo," to friend and foe alike. An imposing figure in a bottle-green Twingo said, "I'm Italian," to which Hoss replied, "You, too." Someone inside, observing this exchange, said, "They got Andrea Camilleri. How'd they get him." The person in the pew beside him said, "They should have got Helen Carlson. She can write." "I like John Dalton." "He's too dark." "You miss the point." "Still, Helen Carlson, she can write." And we were past them, on my way to the dock.

I was hoping this was a purifying ritual as I've heard they can be very good when you're embarking on a game changer. But, alas, I was to learn it was the final check before everybody committed to me. Looking back at the aisle in the center of the courtroom I wondered if witnesses for the defense and prosecution had their own sides. I was to learn that they could be anywhere. The judge was a large fellow from Kern, California. He used to be an evangelist according to Ms. Lin, and his name was Willard Van Fossen. I wondered if it was the same Reverend Willard Van Fossen The Warrior and I met when we passed thru Kern Valley. I was willing to bet it was. I didn't go up when he called for believers to come forward and receive salvation that night. I was hoping he didn't remember that. At any rate he seemed like a fair individual back then so I wasn't worried.

Soon, we all got to our tables. Ms. Lin was beside me at the defendant's table, along with our attorney. His name was Carl. I had no idea if he was any good. It turned out he was like wet wood. We couldn't get him to light for nothing.

Elena Garro was the first witness on the stand. "I like her writing very much," I said to Ms. Lin. "She's very obtuse."

"I feel we are a soulmate."
"Don't you mean plural, Ms. Garro."
"No, I do not."

"That wasn't too bad."

Then the Prosecution called Dr. Ziegler, all the way from Yellowknife, in the Northwest Territories.

"Uh, oh."
"What's the matter, here."
"She knows a lot about me."
"Well, I'm sure she'll be very professional in her remarks. A lot of that is regulated, you know."

"He has very narrow ear canals."

"D'oh!! I hope that doesn't count against me! Why doesn't Carl say something."
"It might. I don't think Carl can see the importance in it. But the jury might. Thun is quick. You'll need good hearing."
"I want to rebut. How do I do that."
"Do you have narrow ear canals?"
"Yes."
"Then don't bother rebutting. You can't rebut facts."
"But I can hear just fine."
"That's subjective. And it's an opinion. Neither one counts here unless it comes from an authority, like Mr. Camilleri. We'll just have to see who's next."
This was going badly. A lot of jurors were already shaking their heads. Some of them actually looked at me and mouthed, "tch-tch-tch," however it's spelled, but they meant it.
Andrea Camilleri was next. I think he had to get back to his new novel and couldn't be detained long. I didn't know if he was on my side. Carl looked at him quizzically.
The judge asked him to present his credentials.
"I've written several novels, a theatre guide, and a play. I'm still working on the play, but it's really very good. My novels, for which I am very well

known, center upon a police department in the town of Vigata, Italy, which I made up. Salvo Montalbano is the Chief Inspector and holds sway over his men. Unfortunately, there are no women in his department, although in other jurisdictions there are women officers and often their exploits come up. One in particular, Laoura, caught my protagonist off guard, and affected him greatly. Aside from in an official capacity there are several other female protagonists in the story lines, Paola The Red, Mikayla, and of course, Ingrid, who is not a policewoman either, but who aids him wonderfully on several occasions."

"I see. So, you are an authority on affairs of the heart, alibis, triangles, red herrings, chases at 30 mph, that sort of thing."

"I've got it down, yes."

"Mr. Camilleri, are you aware that Mr. Prey has appropriated some of your lines. I believe he's given you credit, but how do you feel about your lines being filler in somebody else's novella."

"As long as he doesn't use the good ones it's ok with me. So far I don't think he has."

"Of all your characters who does Mr. Prey remind you of."

"Probably Catarella."

"Could you describe this Catarella for the court."

"He's a minor cog in our wheel. He has very poor writing skills, and when he does write things down it's on small, tiny pieces of paper, and it's mostly gibberish. He has no control over doors and they constantly fly open from him and crash against the wall. He's loyal to a T, and exasperates callers effectively. By the time they get to me they're screaming and I just hang up."

"What's your new novel about."

"Catarella. In this one he gets kidnapped and our department falls apart. His importance finally sees the light of day."

"Thank you, Mr. Camilleri, and good luck with the play."

"That didn't go too badly."
"How many of his books did you buy."
"All of them."

Next up was the head of refreshments from the Desert Grove.

"This should be ok," I said. "I think we got along very well."
"He ordered 12 triangle sandwiches, plus his, and didn't leave a tip."
"That's not fair. I didn't even pay for them," I objected, loudly, over the advice from Carl.

There was a gasp from the courtroom. My admission was sinking me. Was I cheap, in addition to being virtually deaf.

A yellow green haze came thru the windows and started vibrating.
"Egads, what's that," I said to Ms. Lin. "I mean, who uses colors like that."
"Thun does. He's near."
The next witness was the owner of the corral where I encountered The Miller Gang. I had no idea how to read him. I was actually interested in who he was because he could have left a light on and I wanted to mention that to him.
"He left the corral a mess, a total mess. There were pole axes everywhere, and Mexican shot gun shells, and gum wrappers, and lowgrade motor oil, and tooth picks. It was a real mess. And then he disappeared, didn't explain his actions at all, didn't tell anybody where he was going, poof, just disappeared, like that."
Carl jumped up and said, "Your Honor, it would take the strength of a mule for my client to pull the trigger of that implement of destruction."
I looked on the table and saw that Carl was reading scripts from the Three Stooges. This one was entitled, "Disorder In The Court."
"Carl, I don't think your client is charged with actually shooting anybody. This is about character. Can you address that."
"I'm not prepared to do that."
"Then, sit down, Carl."

"Ms. Lin, I hope a surprise witness pops up and has something good to say about me. This isn't going well."
"The Prosecution calls, Ms. Ray Lin."
"Ms. Lin!!!???"
"I just think that there might be another way to do this."
"I don't understand."
"I don't either."

"State your name and your relationship to the defendant."
"I am the Princess of The Bar In The Deep Blue Sea." Also, Planet M. In their regard I am called Princess TALIM. My street name is Ms. Lin. I prefer to be called that one."
"Very well, Ms. Lin. How long have you known the defendant?"
"4 days."
"And during that time how have you found him."
"I have found him to be Handsome, Funny, and Wise."

"And yet today you stand in opposition to his fulfilling his task. Why is that, Ms. Lin."

There was silence.

"Your Honor."

"I'm on it Carl. Ms. Lin you really have to say something."

"I'm afraid he won't be understood."

"He won't be understood? By whom, Ms. Lin, by Thun."

"By Thun?" Ms. Lin said in a measured voice.

Uh, oh. Here comes the other side of Ms. Lin.

"Thun has no soul. He has an army but it's never clear how many there are. He has many spies. He relies on confusion. He lives in a hut on Clurostan. He has no wives. He has no intimate friends. He trusts no one. He has incredibly bad breath. He's fairly stupid. He eats alone. No one knows what he eats, but there's never any trash. That's his only good point. No, I'm not concerned he won't be understood by Thun."

"Then, by whom, Ms. Lin."

"By **YOU.**"

You need to imagine a great interruption in the proceedings. Including Carl jumping up and saying, "I was right."

Several journalists ran out of the room for the bank of phones. Then they ran back in and opened up their computers.

Ms. Lin was spent. She collapsed in my arms and I forced our way thru the throng. We were going back to the Velvet regardless of their decision. We were going on to Orion. We were going to confront Thun and free Gim even if we had to do it alone. At the very least, we were going to change his color scheme.

9.
The Coalition Forms

~ "Do you feel better."
"Are we back in the Velvet?"
"Yes, we are. You were magnificent." It was my turn to say that.
"But, their decision. I may have spoiled it."
"I doubt it. If you did there's quite a formation behind us that must be lost."
Ms. Lin got up and looked in the sideview mirror.
"Oh, Vick! They believed in you!"
"No, they believed in you."

I don't know what Thun thought, to see this ragtag force approaching his domain. But, it didn't matter. I only hoped that CYL was tuned in because I had no idea what I was going to say to him, either.

10.
The Battle

~ "You Brought A V.P. To Defeat Me!"

Ms. Lin was right about Thun's breath. Luckily he was focusing on my new hat and it blew over us. Meanwhile the Chalice of The Path Of Kings was overflowing. We were all lined up now, Carl, Willard, the little girl from the bridge, with all the tokens I never really talked at any length about. Around us now there were bursts of light, starbursts, starlight. Beautiful portraits of the sun by Van Gogh and water by Turner were hung dramatically salon style. There was one of Messaline, but this was unsigned. "Does this go on forever," I said, to Ms. Lin. "You mean, beautiful paintings of intriguing women!" "Yeah, I was thinking of that." "No." An asteroid came by and took them all away. Thun shifted and laughed at me. I looked at the remains of his reading interests which were strewn about. *The Death Of A Cozy Wrestler,* which appeared to be a mystery. A book of poems by Mellarme. A crossword puzzle which was half completed, a big question mark drawn over the clue, 'The Prettiest Stamps Are Uruguay's.' I didn't get it either. It had four letters. A strange selection, *Good Behavior,* by Donald Westlake. A little book by Willem Elsschot called, *Cheese,* and a limited edition of, *Nightmares of an Ether-*

Drinker, by Jean Lorraine. On another shelf was a photographic meditation on the "harsh, yet beautiful terrain of Iceland," called, *Island Mountain Glacier*. This was by Anika Steppe. In a paper bag were books of fantasy and poetry. *The Guardians of Rathswave*, by Liz Proctor, *Beyond Metaphor*, by Daniel Reinhold, and, *Elm Branches*, a book of poems by Gary French. I was stretched to the limit to recollect these last authors, but could imagine them in their small rooms, sifting through a thousand words for one line, one moment, one flight of relief. What did all this have to do with Thun. I thought this very strange.

There was too much coming at me. The little girl from the bridge was collecting tokens, and I knew if I gave her mine, I wouldn't get it back again, this time.

"This is it?"

"Yes, it is," said Ms. Lin.

I looked up and down the line. Jimmie gave me a count of our numbers and I kept turning the paper over and around, hoping for a better figure. My forces were waiting for word from me. Given what I'd been led to believe was expected of me, I didn't think, "Charge," would suffice. Suddenly, I felt terribly alone, and I was sure that this is what Ms. Lin meant from the beginning when she said, "Oh, no, you'll be quite alone." I turned and asked her if it was. She said, "Almost."

Suddenly, someone else was coming! Bright as the star of Venus. This person wasn't coming in a straight line. More wandering about from planet to planet. We all cocked our heads. Carl yelled, "This way!" Whoever it was, it looked like they were riding a horse and were jumbled upon him. At last this person pulled up to our line. Yes! It was my correspondent, Miguel de Cervantes, in his heart's role as The Romantic Clothier, Don Quixote de La Mancha. And he was upon Rozinante. I couldn't believe it. Jimmie said, "Ooouuuu, I like that!" Ms. Lin ran up to him and gave him a kiss, and DQ blushed profusely.

After he regained his lead, The Ingenious Squire smiled at Ms. Lin in gratitude, then he leaned over to me and whispered, "I didn't miss anything, did I?" almost falling completely off Rozinante in the process. "No, you didn't. I see you got my clue about the open door!"

"You mean the one you veiled so deeply in your effusive letter to the editor I had to have Sancho dig it out. Yes, I got it. A pity he chose to stay behind. It appears he's found someone else in the kitchen, and Keith Richards went with him. But here we are, lad. And I'm fresh as a daisy."

I knew we were close to the end, now. An outline upon a banner flew by.

(DQ engages Thun. The Night Train To Georgia arrives. I open the cask where Gim had been imprisoned)

I turned back to Thun. He was certainly a contrast.

"Who's that?" Don said, looking hazily at Thun.

I watched Rozinante paw at The Path of Kings. Back in Floss a spray of shooting stars showed up over the car wash. Susan DeNio was just pulling out. "Wow," she said! It was going to be a fortunate night.

"Well, that's Thun," I said, hopeful now, yet not knowing what registered with DQ. It's possible his new sense of freedom would obscure his view, if anything more were needed to do that.

But, Thun errored. For at that exact moment he chose to call his armies to the fore. And as he waved his big arms in a soft circular motion, which soon developed into a big draft, verily he looked like a big windmill. Especially to Don Quixote, who upon seeing him in this form grew alarmed, then animated, then aggrieved, then shouted to him in a thrilling voice, "So, there you are, You Giant, You!"

Thun, not understanding a word of what DQ was getting at, increased his wave. That was too bad. For now, in the stars of heaven, on The Path of Kings, The Illustrious Don Quixote de La Mancha announced in a very firm voice, "Now I have you." And then, as Thun continued to wave madly for he had very large armies, indeed, the Great Pen Of The Age straightened the pot upon his head, flipped down his visor for the last time, actually it fell down, raised his lance to rest upon Rozinante's ear, and shouted in a very loud voice to his companion, "FOR DULCINEA, ADVANCE, ROZINANTE, ADVANCE!!!" and rushed into his enchantment. Whereupon DQ picked Thun off as clean as a blueberry on a Michigan morning.

Everyone threw their hats up in the air, and Ms. Lin said, "Well, that was something!" And even the armies of Thun cheered as the two combatants disappeared into the fog.

Then a ship arrived. It was The Night Train To Georgia, just as the outline said. I don't know where Glim stores all these things. But, he got out with Hew.

This time I did say, "You missed it."

"Just as well," Glim said. "I'm sure I would have bitten Thun and ended up being quarantined. You do remember your concern in the Passageway that I could be a danger to somebody. Don't you!"

I smiled at him.

At that point, Hew rushed over to Ms. Lin.

"Are you ok, Sis."

Ms. Lin thought that was quite endearing and gave Piedmont Red a big kiss.

The only thing left now for me to do was to free Gim from the cask which Thun had imprisoned her in. Both armies laid down their arms now, and were mingling with one another, laughing, and taking selfies. I was alone.

It occurred to me that THIS was the point Ms. Lin had been referring to all along when she said, "Oh no, you'll be quite alone." Right now. This is the last thing I came to do. I just wanted to say, "Open Sesame," to the cask, and get it over with. But, I knew that wasn't enough, after all we'd been thru. Besides, I tried it under my breath and it didn't work. And then, in some ceiling of clouds that parted like a whim, I heard CYL say to me, "Is that all you have to say, Darling Boy. Is that all you have within!"

No, it wasn't.

For this exhibit I opened up another vault, of repeated observations, mostly, which in other places never fit in but which were, nonetheless, objects of my affection. And so, to the cask, and to everyone present, in my effort to free Gim this is what I said.

The Ocean comes in midnight waves.
There are several publications which will tell you
what time they come, and with what force.
What they don't tell you is what they're doing there.
Consider the no good hunting dog.
The fawn and him laying in the sun.
Bob always wanted a Challenger R/T Scat Pack 1320,
but he couldn't have one.
So, he called his dog, 'Scat,' instead.
After about a week of, "Here. Scat," Scat disappeared.
The Cuban film, *NADA*. "Momma, where are the singers from,
and their charming songs, momma. I want to meet them."
Daisy, Mrs. Bouquet's sister, admonishing Onslow,
"It's bad luck not to buy something from a gypsy."
Advice at a Ohio car jumping event, Dec 30, 2013,
"Drive at the ramp as fast as you can and hope for the best."
If I give you two minutes to tell me what art is,
and you only take one, have you underestimated it?
Linda talking down a monk who was selling amulets,
November 25, 2014 in NYC. "That'll be $60 dollars."
"I don't have $60 dollars." "Ok, $40 dollars, $20 dollars,
whatever you have." "I only have $2 dollars."

"Ok, two dollars."
There's a sign on the freeway
on Dequindre and Delong,
says, 'If your situation isn't working,
let Tasha turn it on.'
To have the sun delayed, and never
enter a room straight, is part of incarceration.
A crime, unless the criminal admits it himself,
cannot be proven.
Humility/Character. Commit yourself to something
which cannot be completed in your lifetime.
Peggy March. CeeLo Green would have liked her.
He would have turned his chair around immediately
to look at her.
Larry singing to Colleen, "To be honest with someone
else's heart is as good as it can get."
Colleen, "Larry, you been holding out on me."
Myself to Ms. Lin, "Is it really, Mars!"
The poetry of Gerard Manley Hopkins.
Lightning Hopkins. "Don't even stop at a red light."
Secrets are hard to share in a community that can
read minds. Children have to make up their
own language, which they then warble to each other,
much to the dismay of their parents.
Somewhere there may be a mirror planet where color
is reused. It's possible we're not going that way.
In the hum I detected a whistle.
I wondered if a train was picking people up,
and dropping them off, even out here.
There are only some things we can't go back. But,
yes, you can see the past. If you want to.
What is encryption, to light.
"I've encrypted the lock. I've
ordered my dark stars to swoop."
I shot back at Thun,

"Your dark stars are in love."

At that last part, which must have been a very good observation, the door to the cask began to open. It looked like the jaws of a shark were opening up. A crazy outline of sideways teeth unclenching. And then, when the whole mouth was open, Gim stepped out. She had a sparkler in her right hand, and with her left hand she waved a warm greeting to all of us. Whatever hats had been caught earlier on their way down were now thrown back up in the air, again. Then Gim came over to me and gave me a kiss on my forehead where the Reverend Chicory D. Possum had assaulted me.

"Thank you, Mr. Prey. I knew you could do it."

Of course, I blushed profusely.

11.
My Last Notes

~ I couldn't believe it was over.

But it was.

I took off my badge, my hat, and my lariat and put them in a rather large envelope, on which I wrote, "My Unlikely Adventure." I felt like the little tree at The Retreat, naked now of any fruit which had been upon it. I looked around for The Map and saw that it was sailing off with my envelope in the direction of CYL's gas station. I wondered who on Earth they would land on next.

In my last notes, Gim and Glim returned to The Bar In The Deep Blue Sea, and led their flock back to M. Gim uncloaked it, and luckily, for everyone, and the world, the fabric was still intact.

Hoss and Ross opened a coffee house at Floss Inc., and Hoss became a beloved poet.

Washington married Century and they both became champions.

The Great Spool escaped.

Port Radium glowed in the haze of the Aurora Borealis and length of night over the winter above Yellowknife. Dr. Sharon Ziegler opened a Japanese Restaurant and called it the Midnight Diner. Someone pointed out that that was already used elsewhere but hers was only open from 4 – 7, in the afternoon.   Landline and E. F. Kiseljak came there every day, and spoke Japanese.

It turned out there actually was a sequel to the movie, *WILLSEYVILLE!* And Colleen had her little girl in Harlan's house. Three days later, Harlan showed up with Myrr and his two friends from Colorado. Larry let them in. Colleen was in the living room, in the bed from the lot model, which she insisted on keeping. Her babe was in her arms, and when she introduced the child to them, Frank and Goldie looked at each other...

"'Peaches???'"

Hew returned to Earth to traipse and sing. One day he came upon The Warrior, who had gone off on his own and was wedged under a Eucalyptus tree, out of gas, and disconsolate as could be. Hew promised to save him and showed him a cylinder of gas that said, 'Forever yours, from CYL.' Then Hew opened the door and found a puppy inside, who was shivering in the front seat. Hew said, "How about if I call you, *'Leonardo!'*" and he gave him some broth and a very big treat, out of a bag that said, 'Phil,' on it, which made very loud noises on the seat.

In my absence my office at Nike got all plastered over with sticky notes and looked like a tree. Factorus flew in the window, which I HAD left open, and started to read John Dalton's, *The Concrete Sea*.

Not long after The Illustrious One and Thun disappeared into the fog, Thun, in fact, fell off. It appeared that Don Quixote's lance had wound up in Thun's lanyard rather than in him, and once it disentangled from that Thun tumbled to the ground, further on the path. To DQ, what he looked down upon now was no longer a Giant but a person in distress. He helped Thun up immediately, as the Code of Chivalry would have him do, and put him on Rozinante to sit behind him and ride with him into Eternity. Of course, they were the oddest couple you've ever seen. Don talking to Thun about Dulcinea's beauty and Thun objecting with his bad breath. Until recently they were still together.

Ms. Lin and I went off to populate the stars. After all, there are new ones discovered every day, so it's not entirely improbable. I never did understand The Reverend's parable, but I think we got out of this pretty good.

And Jimmie.

Ah! Jimmie.

Jimmie opened a Lone Star Beer Distributorship on Solar System XRZ, and lived to the age of 403.

T H E   E N D

Part Two

Some Things
That Occurred To
Valentine
After Four Days

Rebalancing

A lot of things have happened to Valentine Odey since he rescued GIM in the classic novella, *The Envelope.* Exactly what happened in the unlikely circumstance that he had rescued GIM was splintering lightly away. It was relegated to a feeling of soft completion and that was about it. Valentine Odey was still employed by The Nike Corporation on Earth where he was tasked with solving puzzles about population graphics and what Nike should do about it, and Factorus, the Crow, was still in his window. Valentine called Factorus, Factorus, in lieu of all the facts that he, Valentine, was supposed to have at his fingertips. Valentine also kept a bag of peanuts in his desk and lobbed them at Factorus, who easily picked them off, like a sleek boxer. Factorus was there now, in the window, parading back and forth on the window sill, still peeved at Valentine's absence. Factorus was very beautiful. One of the questions we were left with at the end of the classic novella, The Envelope, was the real nature of Thun, the bad guy, who was last seen being whisked away on the tip of Don Quixote's lance. It seemed odd that in Thun's dark lair he had been surrounded by books of fantasy and poetry, first edition books from an old bookshop, half completed crossword puzzles in which "the prettiest stamps are Uruguay's," travel guides about Iceland, and an obscure array of other books about cheese and indecision. Curious about 'Exchange,' and undoubtedly questioning GIM about it. But, for what reason. Only for his employer? Valentine Odey, aka Vick Prey, The Private Investigator, In Truth He Would Like To Be A Poet, never questioned this imbalance until he began to dream again.

PORTFIRO

For Linda, and not just because she said, "I love it!"

Thun had had it. If he had to listen one more time to how pretty Dulcinea del Toboso was he was going to throw up. But Don Quixote was in front and therefore controlled the situation. And, as always, there were parts of Don's dissertations which appealed to him. "She is fairer, and more elusive, than the Dust of Equinon, and darker, than the Smoky Furor of Neptune. Ah, Thun, such things can't help but propel us, and in our peaceful slumber by night disturb the sheets around us. I don't imagine you've heard that before, have you?"

A message was intercepted by Sky Command. But they didn't know what to make of it.

Valentine must come back/Stop
Thun jumped off/Stop
The Odds will be tilted/Stop
Bring donuts/Stop

The message was signed by Carl.

Valentine stretched his arms out to his sides and touched each wall of his office. He worried if he ever got a larger office this routine would be disrupted. Valentine liked regularity. He rather disliked chance. With his morning exercise complete he felt refreshed. Actually, something larger was sustaining him, he just couldn't put his finger on it. A copy of *The Necklace*, by Guy de Maupassant, which he vaguely recalled consulting somewhere lay open on his desk. Everything else around him was in perfect disorder. All his stacks of mysteries and treatises about philosophical differences were teetering on the brink of disaster. Valentine stretched and yawned and ruffled in the cool breeze that came thru the open window, past Factorus, and onto him. Valentine hailed Factorus heartily, and thinking little of it said imploringly, "Oh, Factorus, where have you been!" keen that one of them should explain their

138

absence, and he should explain his absence, as though only he could explain his absence, and that Valentine hadn't been gone at all.

Thru Valentine's open window the vast grey dawn was pouring in. On the Comet channel on the little tv in his corner they were playing another version of Godzilla. He expected fire to come out of Godzilla's mouth any minute, and when it did he would turn it off. Valentine was afraid of fire ever since his house burned down when he was a kid. On the PBS channel they were hosting a dramatic presentation of a Korean folktale. Immediately he prepared some popcorn and got some butter, and sat down with Factorus to look at it. The narrator began his narration in front of the play.

~ "We enter a peninsula which is beautiful in its pink flowers. It's like the earth said, here, here I will have pink flowers. Chunhyang is running thru them. She throws herself upon Mongryong's halter, trying desperately to stop him from going to Seoul without her. Chunhyang screams at Mongryong not to leave her but he breaks free and ultimately his donkey trots at a fast pace. It is the pace of obligation. Here comes the new Governor, and of course he has an eye for Chunhyang, the courtesan's daughter. She rebuffs him. She says there can only be one for her. The Governor's order to execute Chunhyang reaches Mongryong who has graduated at the top of his class and is now the King's Emissary. Now here comes Mongryong, the Emissary to the King, running to save Chunhyang. He is in time, and disguises himself in poor clothing yet insists that he is a nobleman and should be allowed into the Governor's birthday upon this day of Chunhyang's execution. He's laughed at, not knowing his true identity, and the Governor challenges him to write a poem of any meaning. He writes a great poem in a beautiful hand, but it is a poem of warning. The other noblemen are alarmed and seek to flee this apparition. But the King's Men have arrived, having been sent for by Mongryong when he first learned of Chunhyang's fate, and they beat the greedy noblemen with sticks and arrest the unjust Governor immediately. Mongryong assumes the position of Governor and has Chunhyang brought before him. With the brim of his hat down he asks Chunhyang if she will reconsider her decision. She says, No. That there can only be one for her. Mongryong has his aide take to her the jade ring she gave him on his leaving. She looks at the ring as Mongryong raises the brim of his hat. Chunhyang cries out sharply and can't be held back. She runs and presses herself to the Emissary to the King, and the storyteller flicks his wrist and opens his fan, as a sign that love has crashed thru everything." ~

"Did you see that, Factorus!" Valentine almost flew out of his chair, so enamoured was he with the connection of Force and great poetry. Factorus, for his part, said nothing, but observed Valentine.

Valentine opened his door and looked out into the long dim hallway. There was no one in it. His door was covered with sticky notes and looked like a tree. Or a bear had come by and shook himself vigorously. Valentine looked both ways for a bear and then closed the door quickly before he could reply to any of them.

Valentine was tired after this walk around his room. He decided to rest before everyone came to see him. So, he sat down in his chair, which hardly fit into his office, where all his mysteries and treatises about philosophical differences were piled up around him, and put his head on the empty bag of peanuts which barely fit into the rest of it. And, of course, it wasn't long before he was asleep, and Valentine Odey was once again far away.

The Beginning

I was just closing, *The Necklace,* and looking forward to, *Why Me,* another wonderful book by Donald Westlake, when there was a knock at my door. Thank God. But it wasn't so much a knock, as a paw. A rather large pawing which alarmed me. Just so they know I was in here I said, "Who is it?"

The only response I got was more pawing. I was afraid my door might soon have to be replaced. Rather tepidly I said again, "Who is it?" This was followed by additional pawing which alarmed me worse. But I had been armed by good writing, so I went ahead and said, "Would you like to come in."

This brought about something which resembled a rattle in a big bottle. It reminded me of my old Hudson idling at the curb. I always liked my Hudson, and I think that's why I said, "Well, then, you should!"

Th door opened like it had no choice. It didn't crash against the wall or anything like that. It just stepped back from whoever was there. It was a Cat. A very large Cat.

At this point Factorus said,

140

"PORTFIRO !!!"

I looked at Factorus, and then the Cat, and then back to Factorus.

"You can talk!"

"Of course I can."

"But, I never knew that."

"You were content to lob peanuts at me. I think that arrangement suited both of us, but now it may not. Besides, don't you have someone at the door."

I turned around and "PORTFIRO" was still there. I was hoping he had the wrong office. But, he took a soft step forward in my doorway and turned his big fat head to the left, and then the right. He looked very fierce, with creases narrowing along his cheekbones to a tight mouth, and whiskers which were feeling out for any obstacles he couldn't smell or see or feel on the bottom of his big feet. I smiled at him and he looked at me with cold, umber eyes. There was no warmth at all in them. But I was lit up enough for both of us. As it appeared that Factorus had recognized him I hoped he would help out.

"Factorus, what do you think."

"I think he wants something!"

"What is it."

"I can't tell you that. It would cheapen it."

"Do you know what it is."

"Yes. But you do, too. And you know where it is. You may be the only person who knows where it is."

I took a little time out to look at Portfiro. His umber color eyes moved slowly from Factorus to me and back to Factorus.

"Well, what do you suggest," I said to Factorus.

"I would tell him you'll help him find it."

"Or he eats me."

"Pretty much."

The lights came on my Hudson.

"What do you propose we do now."

"We get on Portfiro's back, well you do. I'll ride on your head, and thru the window we go. It's always open."

A Canvas Painted Over, Lightly

I turned back to the employee of the Devious System. He laughed at me in my suit. I was afraid that would happen. My puffy pants, my token which was hardly fearsome and smoother now than ever before, my signature hat, and my lariat. I felt they had all served their purposes, as fleeting as that had been, and I was left bare like the branch on the small tree at the Retreat. A pleasant voice resumed beside me, "Who's that?" Don said, as he looked out hazily at Thun.

Some things are coming back to me from my earlier nap. In fact, I'm remembering I had one. But at the same time, someone put me back on the easel and began to paint me over, lightly.

Dufy, Kupka, And Rouault

Portfiro was surprisingly soft. Factorus's feet upon my head was not. And he kept saying, "WHEEEEE." I was worried how this must look from the parking lot. The outer walls of my office, which I'd never seen before, were growing smaller and smaller in the distance and eventually we disappeared. Now it was all dark. Portfiro strode thru it, faithful to whichever way I leaned. For a while that was almost circular as I was trying to stay on. But in time I found my balance and we were straight on after that. You can imagine the breadth and width of it, even though it was unheard of. Portfiro's long legs exploded before him, and I could hear the faintest expelling of breath. Portfiro seems without tire. For his part Factorus is hammering my head into the ground with his bouncing, and filling my ears up with his incessant cawing. It sounds very much like he's repeating a parable of some sort into the void. I have no idea who **he's** talking to. Every now and then he changes up and says, "Get out of our way!!!" I don't ever remember him acting like this on my window sill.

Three round men appeared to us, out of the vale of gloom. Dufy, Kupka, and Rouault, painting in their rooms. Take this way, Dufy said, and his colors were awkward and spare. I could feel them being applied and I aged and almost fell right there. Kupka said, "NO", and swung his brush and a circle encircled me and connected me to Portfiro's skin and locked me in and Factorus fell to one knee. Then Rouault laughed, and his colors laughed, as bright as they could be, and lit up our way as though it were day and we disappeared with a "thip" over two big ships and a sign that said, "Bombay."

The Tudor Crown

"Does Portfiro talk."

"No. He's new to this. He might have something to say later."

"I'm sure he's also very busy. Maybe we should take a break."

"Would you like to stop at The Tudor Crown?"

"I think that's a good idea. I'm getting a little hungry. I hope they have sandwiches."

"We'll ask. Portfiro. The Tudor Crown, por favor!"

A manager, by the name of Munch, greeted us at the door. Initially, it appeared he was addressing Factorus. "Say, look here, boy, this a high class club. How bout you fix that faucet, rub-a-dub-dub. You outta here before the clientele come I'll take care of you and then some." Apparently he thought we were the plumbers. When he noticed that Factorus had no hands, he turned his attention to Portfiro. But all this time it was the stage that Portfiro was looking at, with the Rose Color Swan. Factorus, who became a manager himself, said, "He'll fix that, but how bout you let him sit up at those drums, fill up a little time, get the whole place hum." The house manager said, "Well, ok," then turning to Portfiro he said, "You gotta name." Factorus said, "His name is Dutch." The manager said, "Ok, Dutch, why don't you go head put some honey in my cup. Just don't get too comfortable, make me send Larry up. You can play, right?" Factorus said, "He can play." And I'm thinking, this should be good. Either way I don't think Larry wants to go up.

The stage with the Rose Color Swan stuck out like a big tongue. Actually, that's exactly what it was. A big tongue lolling around in the universe, scooping up space junk like the Rose Color Swan. Portfiro jumped up on it and pulled the Rose Color Swan over to the drums, a sure sign that *"Nights in The Gardens Of Spain"* might be on the playlist, in the absence of jasmine and citrus trees. But Portfiro had something else in mind. He aimed the biggest drum ahead of them, past Munch, and The Tudor Crown, and began to pound on it. He pounded at first with confidence, but not with ardor. The Rose Color Swan pointed this out to him. She pointed out that Mecca was worth it, that Rome was worth it, that Jerusalem was worth it, that Love was worth it, and he should play with ardor. He did. Portfiro pounded with ardor past Munch and The Tudor Crown into the chum of the universe.

The Flood

With Portfiro pounding incessantly a crack appeared and opened wider to accommodate us. It was a flood. Factorus and I jumped on Portfiro and we took off. But not before Factorus yelled at Munch, "The River is wise." Now we would follow the flood, the flood of Portfiro's incessant drumming.

The Ferryman

Soon, we saw a ferryman and asked him for a fee if he would ferry us on this path which seemed to flow endlessly. "Of course!" he said, and we got in his boat, which consisted of several industrial drums tied together with pennants and ropes. I was a little leery of our commitment until he said, "Watch out for the Geminids. They're early this year," and they pinged off the drums and provided us light as we sailed on Portfiro's river of drumbeats that night.

Into the darkness, into the sea, we went across this way, and back across three. They all had names. The sea of Hate, the sea of Jealousy, the sea of Fear.

"Where do they empty into," I said.

"There and Here," the ferryman said, and he pushed into the water with a very big stick and we slid over them without taking a sip."

Portfiro stood in the front so we had to look over him, with his big tail swishing and fat like the alarm bell ringing on a feral cat. His eyes were umber, I've said that before, and you could crawl around to the front, if you wanted, and look into them.

As it was, Factorus hid under him, out of the siege of the Geminids.

I asked the ferryman if he had a favorite star, if one was a snob, or if one in particular was more helpful in his job.

"They're all helpful. You just have to know how to read them. They're like hours that haven't been filled yet. You ever heard the one about Kelle, who made a little cough!"

The Envelope, again. Egads, I hope not.

I laughed.

"I hope we're going the right way. I'm supposed to know that, you know. Don't tell them that I have no idea what they're talking about."

"Oh, I think you do. Something will open up, and you'll know. You didn't get any messages lately, did you?"

"What was that!"

The Walk Of The Mandarins

"This is as far as I go"

Our boat slowed. "From here you'll have to walk."

The Geminids had subsided. I was hoping we'd learn something from the ferryman, other than just being ferried. He laughed like someone much bigger than he. And laughed and laughed.

From there the water subsided, revealing Portfiro's drumbeats once more. The ferryman gave us each a hat, and waved his own, and the Geminids resumed their shower over him on his way back.

The hats the ferryman gave us resembled something from the Ming dynasty. We looked like Mandarin officials.

The walk of the Mandarins was supposed to be straight and pompous. We hopped, or at least I did, to break that up, from one beat to the next. The beats looked like oval pavers from Home Depot for the patio. Only ours were all in a wavy row, going off across the street, into the neighbor's yard, thru his front door and out the back. There was no end to them. On the back of our hats there was a braid which swished like Portfiro's tail. Soon we met an official who said he had to read us a story and he also had a braid on the back of his hat. Factorus flapped, and Portfiro rattled and opened his mouth, but the official insisted, so we each sat upon our paver and listened to the official prat.

"This is the story of a writer who lives alone with his cat. The writer's name is Tomeris. He doesn't go out. He just looks out his window and comes up with stuff. This is back on Earth, of course."

(Which didn't seem that far back to me.)

"Ya ready."

"Tomeris has a door in the middle of the room where he writes, which is in addition to the door to get in the room. On either side of this door, the one in the middle of the room, there is a desk. He starts off in the morning on the right side of his room, which would be on the right side of this door which is in the middle of the room, where he has a window and he can see his neighbor's house and the house across the street. Here a lot of what he writes revolves around what his neighbors do, and he develops characters who go in and out, but who pretty much stay in their own area, which is marked by a fence, and then a sidewalk, and then a smaller patch of lawn and then the street. So, going in and out becomes a theme. He tries to write about how his neighbors are different when they go in, or when they come out. He notices for one thing that they usually carry something in more than they carry out. So, he likes to write about that. He has his characters work with whatever he sees his neighbors bring into the house. So, people are preparing garlic, or peeling things for dinner, or talking about what happened when they were outside. Sometimes they go out in their yard and take things with them. He tries to see if it is the same things they brought in, so his characters won't be confused. On this side of the door which is in the middle of the room he doesn't like his characters to get carried away. One day a little girl brings out a book which has a picture of a Princess on it riding a tiger. He doesn't remember this book having been brought in so he's flummoxed by that."

Factorus had to say something.

"You may have mistaken us for another group. Possibly one that's on an author tour. I can't see where a writer of the description you are painting has anything to do with us. Plus, my hat is very tight. Maybe you were expecting a lovable bird like a sparrow, but this thing is giving me such a headache."

"I'm sorry about that. You must have a very big brain. I would offer you my hat, but even it may be too small."

"Well, since you put it that way you should probably go on."

"Very well."

"At night Tomeris gets up and goes thru the door in the middle of the room, which I have told you about, to the other side of the room. On this side of the room he sits in a blue chair and gets out a clean sheet of paper. Over here he likes to write in Arabic, or in French. This is always the confusing side of the room for him because over here he has to make everything up. The window on this side of the room opens up to the left side of the house where there is a pond, and a dogwood tree, and a spot for the moon. Our writer imagines there is a beautiful girl in the moon who comes to him. He imagines she is a Caliph's daughter, dressed in beautiful green raiment with long wool leggings that bunch up on her calves and she has on earrings which droop down with globes of youth and fortune and love."

All three of us looked at the moon.

"On the night in question the sky is clear and the moon is entirely visible. Tomeris believes he sees the Caliph's Daughter, again. She is alone, sitting on a piece of marble, and her head is down like she is contemplating sadness, or something like that. Suddenly a small cloud turns her face to him. The cloud dissipates and she looks at him so clearly he forgets everything. In a way she gets up and summons horses who whiny and billow in the moonlight. Her earrings jingle. Wildly. She's coming for him. He's sure of it! She fractures in the dogwood and catches on the face of the pond. Her globes of youth and fortune and love pound on his window pane. He throws open this window and her scent of amber rushes in. So this is what she smells like. Tom runs back to his desk and writes madly. He doesn't want to miss anything. But his pencil falls from his soft hand. His skin folds into stripes, and his papers blow in the wind. It's no use. He's already turning. The Princess comes to his blue chair and looks deeply into his heart. And satisfied that he's a beast she's on him."

"In the morning the middle door is open and Tomeris is gone."

"He's gone," said Portfiro.

"He's gone."

The Emerald Sea

"Well, that was something."

The official said, "You're welcome," and collected our hats. Then he drove off on his Segway.

I think he missed the point.

The best of times could be before us or they could be on the bottom of our feet all along and leaving their tracks. I think a petal that opens up in a new year has not been a petal before. Its freshness is without parallel. It's heart without mouth. The point is, Portfiro opened up like a petal in a new year. It was very demonstrative, and without guard. Maybe he didn't think we'd notice. But even Factorus looked at him. Portfiro turns his head away from us and stares into space, one of the great lines of the 21st Century.

"He's trying to hunt, Valentine." His lovely, umber eyes taking in the void we haven't looked in yet.

Just then the pavers gave out and tumbled like a stack of bricks, and we tumbled down, and down, into something which looked like an Emerald Sea.

Messaline

Deep in the wash of the Emerald Sea
Alone in her home lived Messaline.
On this day she was surprised
when a ton of bricks landed by her side.
She also had a butler, whose name was Cron.
She always imagined that someday Cron
would say, I'm sorry, My Lady, but
there's someone here to see you,
But on this day he did,
But today that's exactly what he did say.
For not far from the bricks and the pavers, rue,
Valentine, Factorus and Portfiro
had landed, too.

"Is this it," Factorus said.

"It might be. It seems familiar. It's possible I've been here before."

"How do you suppose WE got here."

"A fissure opened up. I think that's how it works. But, where's Portfiro?"

In fact, Portfiro wasn't far away. Portfiro had landed like a cat, soft and mysterious and curious, like that. And not wanting to rattle or cause a scene Portfiro sat on the last beat, and saw Messaline.

"This way, Sir," said Cron, and he opened the door which was between the left side and the right side of the Moor. "I think you'll find that she's been expecting you. She may have been hoping you look more like her, but I'm only the butler. This way, Sir."

Down a corridor fit for a deer, Cron said, "My lady, Portfiro is here."

Messaline turned like a slippery thing, with gills and reeds and slippery things. She looked at her suitor and made her eyes like a raft, to see he was clothed in fur and class.

"Well, aren't we a pair!!!" she said at last.

Portfiro approached her, his feet hardly clapped, and he roared with his rattle which made her laugh.

The Outline

There's no easy way to say this. The outline I had been working on entered my mind; Portfiro meets Messaline, they walk. They meet the man with the wick in his nose, who alarms them. Rozinante and The Ingenious Nobleman appear, to ply him.

"Do you know who I am."

"Yes."

"Are you afraid of me."

"No!"

I'm not sure if this exchange came at the beginning or the end. It doesn't matter, really. For I had no idea who Portfiro was, anyway.

Portfiro and Messaline walk along the Emerald Sea. She asked him which Knight was he.

He said he was the 13th Knight. The Knight of Couplets, but he was late, so he got left out.

"Well, I don't think that was fair."

"You don't."

"Of course not," said Messaline, with her hand stroking his back.

"Nor I," said Portfiro, purring lightly.

Messaline ran ahead.

"What do you do, Portfiro."

"I like to read, mostly, but I have another job which harrows me."

Why could he not catch up easily.

"What do YOU do."

"I live in the sea, and the sea, sometimes, lives in me."

"Could I live in the sea."

"If you did that you would have to marry me!!"

Coaxed, Portfiro told Messaline about pressing things, about the metre of Mozart, and other things he had been studying. Messaline told him about water, and its metre, and other things she had been studying. There was no edge that either had in discussing things. The moon above them hung from the spoon like honey.

"You know that I was exchanged, to be in this form," Portfiro said.

"I figured that."

"I could exchange you."

"But wouldn't that exchange us."

"She's not making this easy," I said to Factorus.

"Nor is he."

A sound of hooves approached Portfiro, and a man with a wick in his nose surprised him. "I'm here to alarm you. The odds have been tilted. And Rozinante and the Ingenious Nobleman are here to ply you."

Portfiro was suddenly tired.

Other voices intervened.

"You seen Jeannette."

"Lemme see, Jeannette. She the one with the blue hair and the Silver Fendi Handbag."

"No man, she the one has, Jeannette, tattoo in a real nice cursive top of her chest. A business card. You know."

"Oh, yeah. Jeannette. Nope, haven't seen her. I do, you want me to tell her call home."

"I want you to interrupt her vacation."

"Oh sure, I'm gonna do that. So, who was I thinking of."

"Not on my ship. Probably a fantasy."

"No, it didn't seem like that."

I felt like our transmission was being confused with another one.

Then Hew curls his large hand around a pair of spotted containers from the Luna Pier Kitchen and pulls them slowly to him. Maybe he could be saying, "Red, The young lady is betting, Red."

Egads, this is getting serious. I hope we can hold this together.

Messaline and Thun walk by the water's edge.

"What do you want from me," says Messaline.

"I want to know how you can love desperately."

PEEKO, THE ACCOUNTANT

This is for my accountant, Paul Stearns, a lovely man, who really doesn't deserve this.

Deadly Is The Deadly Night

Several years have passed. Years in another time. For in Valentine's world Time is but a Player, no greater than a Lark, or any note of such a bird, or any line, including a very thin one. This later part is an affront to Time which considers itself the ruler of all events. But Valentine doesn't care much for affronts except the front door of his office which he likes to keep clear of sticky notes. Inside his office there are tall towers of mysteries and tomes of philosophical differences, all of which are teetering on the brink of disaster. Valentine is constantly adjusting them to keep that from happening. And having restored order, at least for a minute, he attacks the next book on his list. In this case, this morning, on January 22 in the year 20.. he is reading a novel by Dr. I. Will Pullem, a dentist in Rockford, Illinois, who pulls teeth by day and writes novels by night. The title of this one is, *Deadly Is The Deadly Night.* It's about a dentist who has been unfairly compensated by Medicare, in fact, nothing, and so goes looking for the Examiner who returned his bill. He also takes with him some chloroform, a little cup to spit water from, and a drill. It goes on for a hundred pages which Valentine has consumed half of. *Deadly Is The Deadly Night.* It's a self-published thriller.

It so happens that on occasion Valentine has to have his hair cut. Today is that day. And when that happens he puts a very big marker into the book he is reading, in this case, *Deadly Is The Deadly Night*, and announces to Factorus that he has to go get his hair cut.

"Take over for me," he says.

Which is exactly what Factorus does. He opens up the drawer in Valentine's desk upon Valentine's leaving and frees a fat package of peanuts with his beautiful beak. Then he finds something shiny to put it on, like the cover of Confederacy Of Dunces, or Napoleon Crosses The Rubicon, and skewers the package with great heart. After which, he lobs several peanuts up into the air and immediately goes flapping all over the office to catch them. Then he walks over the spreadsheets on Valentine's desk, and leaves marks that adjusts the populations of Hong Kong, and Budapest. And when that's done, and he's very satisfied with that, he tells people who knock on the door, the real one, "I'm busy right now, I may go to the zoo." That usually does it. All this takes time, and is quite exhausting. So, when he's done he hops up on the window sill and puddles like a sack and goes to sleep until Valentine comes back.

The Fresh Start Barber Shop

Valentine always goes to the Fresh Start Barbershop on Delavan Avenue in Buffalo, NY, for his haircut. It doesn't matter that he doesn't live in Buffalo, NY, or anywhere near it, he likes to go there. Ron is waiting, usually out front, talking to his wife in her car. Valentine announces, "You got time!" barely breaking stride. Ron looks up, and tells his wife he'll see her later.

Valentine enters the shop and is pleased to see that he has it all to himself. At least temporarily. Valentine hops up in his favorite chair and awaits Ron. He makes a mental note to ask Ron if he has any more of his cards. *'Need A Cut, Call Ron.'* There's a drawing of a crow on it, which Ron said he did himself. Valentine got out his little notebook and wrote in it, "Ask Ron where he saw the crow." He thought it looked like Factorus.

Ron comes in. Valentine has been trying to figure Ron out for some time. Like, where is he from. He has it narrowed down to, two blocks away, Detroit, or Thailand. This is a consuming project for Valentine. Ron remembers Valentine from before. He says, "My guy," which is very pleasing to Valentine. Ron throws a sheet around Valentine, brushes his ears with the shaving brush and says, "No. 2," taking a guess, to which Valentine swishes his hand around under the sheet and says, "Let's do a seven today!" Ron says, "Ok." Valentine, unrequested, tells Ron all about his week, how he's been to Mars and back, and Pluto, and the lost civilizations of Greece, and Toledo. Ron clears his throat and spits into something Valentine doesn't want to know about. Valentine pauses, and when he has his thoughts back together he says, "Oh, yeah, Toledo."

On this day, Peeko, the accountant, comes in and sits in the chair next to Valentine, to be attended to by Umar, the other barber in Ron's shop. Peeko was welcomed heartily.

Now the shop is humming. Valentine was whirring in his chair. Peeko was whirring in his chair. Ron was whirring, and Umar was whirring, and the two electric razors above their heads were whirring. The whole place got hum. Valentine is very sensitive to hums. He basically falls into a category of hum susceptible. And it wasn't long before he fell into a very big crevasse. And in there he slid out his chair, and out the door, with Peeko running right behind him, into a Uber, and out of there.

The Conversation In The Uber

"Where are we going," Peeko said, as the Uber rocketed away from the curb.

"We're going to Ron's house. I want to see what he eats. I'm trying to figure out where he's from."

"Did you put his address in the app."

"I'm uncertain what it is, actually. We may have to ask our Uber driver."

"You ask him."

The Uber driver looked at them in the rearview mirror. He looked like a dentist.

"I don't suppose you've noticed that our destination is left blank. We were wondering if you had any idea where Ron wanders off to in the evening."

"Who's Ron. He doesn't work for Medicare, does he."

"I don't think so. I hadn't thought about that. That's a very unusual concern for you to have. This isn't a second job for you, by the way, is it," Valentine said, now concerned that he had been caught up in the evil plan of the dentist in, *Deadly Is The Deadly Night.*

Peeko, beside Valentine, was lost in space. The Uber driver kept an eye on him, and the three of them together began their quest.

The Palace

At last they arrived at a Palace. It resembled a Temple and was entirely made of gold. In the yard there was a little Buddha with a silver cross around his neck. The Buddha was picking at it and trying to look down over his fat jowls at the design of it. Otherwise he looked very happy, and serene. Ron's wife was in the second floor window. At first she narrowed her eyes trying to see if Ron was in the Uber. She could have picked him up and this seemed like an unnecessary expense. I'm sure Peeko would agree with her and he probably couldn't wait to say something.

One of the things that Valentine lacked was newspapers. Let alone a social media account. If it didn't come in a book form he was not included. So, he didn't know that ICE was everywhere, or that they were behind the golden door, and were already going through the refrigerator. The chance that Valentine's method of detection had been adopted by the government would be so astounding that he couldn't believe it even if he could get the door open, which he couldn't.

The Uber driver was now sure that there was a connection here to the Medicare Office and that Peeko was the Examiner. As Valentine and Peeko were beating on the golden door the Uber driver quietly got out of his Honda and approached them with his little cup to spit water from, his bottle of chloroform, and his drill.

Meanwhile, ICE had located several chillies, fourteen lbs of pork in a bobblehead doll of Reggie Jackson, a mason jar full of curry, and a fork which had weird writings on it. It all pointed to Thailand.

Having reached the golden door, the Uber driver jumped on Peeko and was drilling him. Peeko was screaming, Valentine was screaming, and Ron's wife fell out of the window and landed right on the Uber driver's head. ICE came out and said, "Who is this."

"Why this is Ron," Valentine said, "The barber who lives there."

"Who are you."

"I'm Valentine."

"What are you doing here."

The whirring in the barber shop came to a stop. Valentine woke up, and Ron said, "That's it, Pop."

THE TUNNELS

This is for the veil that all writers are looking for.

The Arrival

"Aye," the Captain said. "This is the entrance, what's left of it. I doan know exactly what happened to it."

Valentine Odey stepped off the Ferry to Fair Isle and looked around for cameras, grips, constables, costume designers, possibly Sara O'Donnell, the likenesses of Jimmy Perez and Tosh, and the specter of Arthur McCall.

They weren't there, of course. It was the reason he was here. Having dozed off in front of his little tv in the middle of an episode of Shetland he had booked the ferry in the hopes of recovering an ending. The sky was grey, as it should be, and a wind was whipping southeast in hopes of joining the Atlantic Sea. Out of sight below Valentine a tunnel stretched from sea to shining sea.

On the outside of his door back at his office the sticky notes were piling up. The assumption was, as it always was, that Valentine was working on a case. That was true. But not a case that involved the fortunes of Nike, exactly. Once again it was a case that involved the fortunes of Valentine, like happiness, salvation, oddness, good writing. A train whistled in the distance like a water owl somewhere over the North Sea. Valentine adjusted his P-Coat and traipsed forward without hesitating.

"I'll need to check with your forensics people," Valentine barked at the Captain, "Before I see my lodging."

"Aye," the Captain said, "You'll need to do that." And the two of them walked off in the wind and the rain that clacked.

The Eye Of Reckoning

Having seen what forensics had and deciding on his own that this would be a difficult case Valentine was taken to his room at the Eye of Reckoning, a B&B. There, a note had been placed on his pillow. "Beware of Meddling." Valentine rushed down to the desk immediately.

"Excuse me, but could you tell me who made up my room this morning."

"I believe that was Asha, Sir."

"Asha???!!! Asha Israni???"

"She's only temporary until the beginning of the next season."

"Still, I need to question her. This is unexpected. But, I can't let fame upset my apple cart."

"I'll ask her to meet you in the Lounge, Mr. V. She's from Glascow. There I doan think they allow fighting."

The Lounge

The Lounge in The Eye Of Reckoning was quite extensive. There were several people in it, and fiddles, and bag pipes, and Irish Setters, and a sea of red and blue sweaters. Asha approached me in a tunnel which looked like a hallway. She was dressed in a black blouse and a black skirt. Her hair was tied back, a little too severely, I thought, possibly a ruse. All of this in addition to her 9 inch stratosphere shoes. A maid?

"Mr. Odey?"

"It's Detective Inspector. Actually, it's Valentine. Actually, I can't believe it's you."

"If this has anything to do with the note I had nothing to do with it."

"How are you aware there's a note."

"Manuel told me."

"Is he the desk clerk?"

"Yes, I think you were just talking to him."

"Please do not leave the island, Ms. A. I may have to speak with you again."

The sea wouldn't stop undulating. Surrounded by the sea. Undulating like it's breathing. Like blood is coming into the heart, Fair Isle, and exiting.

Valentine One And Two Debate The Outcome

Valentine sat under a Saracen tree and thought about the outcome.

"Every case has two doors, possibly three. One will complete the case, and one will lead to nowhere but will appear to be the right one."

"The language," he thought, "has a lot to do with it."

"It seems rough and tumbled. Like a quarry where the ground is dry and all the stones are sorted and rumbled. Think, Montalbano, where do the waters come from."

"Asha speaks sweetly and her words shed from her mouth completely. If she's one of them I doan know if I can assign that completely."

"I'm sure it's the door, or one of them."

"Oh, Fair Isle, where is the understanding, if your words are all garbled in a tin and few of them are left standing."

"Oh, Fair Isle, it's about understanding."

"Aye, this is what you need to do, then. You need to understand where the waters come from."

The Whirlwind

Dr. Arquoa eyed Valentine with his poker face.

"I can't say that anyone is actually dead, Detective Inspector."

"The tunnels have collapsed. It doesn't look good, atall, Sir." That was the Captain.

"Who was in them?"

"Aye, that's the point, Sir. We don't know that."

"At what time did this happen."

"Tosh was talking to your counterpart, DI Perez. It was about 9 o'clock, Sir. The tunnels collapsed."

"So, were they in them."

"No, Sir. They were here in the Eye Of Reckoning."

"And yet they were in them."

"So, it appears, Sir."

"Can you take me to the scene."

"We're in it."

"That's true."

"I think, Captain, it has to do with that note."

"Beware of Meddling."

"That one."

"Aye, that one."

"Bring Asha back to me. I think she knows more than she told me."

"Aye, she's Indian, Sir."

"I don't think that has anything to do with it."

"Aye, I'll get her."

"How soon do you want her, Sir."

"Right now!"

"Aye, you would, Sir."

DI Valentine Cracks The Case

When Asha was brought back to see Valentine she knew the jig was up.

"Ms. Israni, where did you get those dark eyes."

"Inspector?"

"Your eyes, mum. They're not just any charcoal, are they."

Asha blinked rapidly, but she couldn't hide the evidence she had been fearing he would see.

Valentine looked into them. ("These are the tunnels where the waters come from!")

"They're Char-Kole, correct. Only used by artists, and only found in the deepest sea. That's where the entrance is, isn't it, to the tunnels that have appeared to collapse, but are as plain as they can be. And you were afraid of meddling because you love Jimmy. Isn't that it, Marie!"

THE BLACK BEAR

This is with love for families caught up with addiction. The hardest things are unanswerable, even with dreams.

There is a Cherokee clan who chose to leave the world of man behind and live in the Smokey Mountains with the black bears. Some people in the mountains think there are descendants of that clan who live today in the mountain forest as Black Bears, not just with them. They also believe that if a Black Bear of that clan is wounded in battle with another bear, or is damaged by a hunter, or by a personal disaster, that there is a mysterious lake they will make a long journey to go to, and when they get there they will plunge into its cool refreshing waters and swim to the opposite shore. And when they go up upon the opposite shore they will be completely healed of all their wounds.

Valentine read this brochure from the North Carolina Backwoods Society and put it on his desk. Immediately he wanted to find that lake. He had been thinking of himself as a Black Bear for some time, with spinners and hanks of hair and flesh hanging from him like regret. Something that happened before he was assigned the job of addressing population puzzles and what Nike should do about it. Valentine closed his door and got on a bus for North Carolina.

The ride was long and winding. There were stops but you didn't have to get off. You could stay in your seat the whole way. Through plain and unusual landscape, the bus hummed. The bus had a driving hum to it. A persistent, flat source that road in the undercarriage beneath Valentine.

Valentine wrote as they passed reflecting buildings that the windows on the bus looked like a pastel of sheetrock and intricacies of psychology. He also wrote that the bus looked like a transatlantic liner.

Valentine put his Marble Memo Pad back in his pocket and returned to the North Carolina Backwoods Society brochure.

'The Cherokee Ani Tsa'gu hi clan chose to follow the Black Bear and leave the human world of struggle and hunger behind and live with the Black Bears in their abundant forest. All cultures and faiths derive from the telling of supernatural occurrences, it is a way to unite the natural world we live in with the supernatural world we have difficulty in understanding and explaining. There's always an element of truth or reality in most myths and legends, as it forms the character, culture and history of people and should not be regarded as exaggeration or fairy tales. Our lives in the world consist of more than merely the organic. Myths and legends are what we have evolved from as a species; it is what has made us the people we are today.'

Debbie looked out her window in the den. It was summer. A time of traveling and a young black bear walked right by her window, in her sight, in her yard. It was like he had waited for her to look out for him. He was heading south, for North Carolina.

For Valentine the smell of diesel was always the smell of departure. The bus had an African Queen smell to it, of dark cabs and slurry rivers, and mystery.

The pretty girl who sat down next to Valentine in Harrisburg said, "Where are you going!" Valentine said he was going to find a lake in North Carolina. She asked him if it was a special lake and Valentine said that it was. She said that when she was young her parents took her to a lake where the water was so clear you could see the bottom of it.

"What was on the bottom of it," Valentine asked, wondering if he had already been directed where to look.

"I don't know that. We were water skiing!"

Valentine persisted. "But if it was a special lake to you it must have been something about the water, don't you think."

"Of course! When I stayed up it was like magic water, and when I fell down I was very disappointed in it."

The pretty girl got off at Hazelton. When she was leaving she turned and asked him the name of the lake he was going to. He said, "Black Bear Lake." She smiled and got off the bus.

Valentine got out his notebook, again. He wrote that the darkness inside the bus was similar to the darkness outside the bus. And that the bus occasionally had to back up, which surprised him, therefore they appeared to be washing back and forth, that people got off, and that people got on. Valentine writes mechanical, and also fearless in the day.

The bus door opened and closed. A terrible air horn released like a whippoorwill, and Valentine was left in Cherokee, N. C. with his Marble Memo Pad and his expectations. I don't know what his expectations were, exactly. A sign that said, 'Recovery Lake, Black Bears, This Way.' I don't think it works that cleanly. But Valentine was hopeful.

A marine diving equipment store employee told him he would need professional deep sea diving equipment for such a lake as he was describing. So, he would have to go out of there with a big bubble on his head and a long hose which would connect to a tank in a boat on the surface. Valentine tried to imagine if Black Bears have tanks and all this apparatus in their quest. "Seems like a lot of professionalism is needed in this project," he said. The employee agreed that that was the case and went to assemble the boxes.

And so, Valentine found a big lake which was off the beaten path and started to unravel his equipment. He was sure that to find the answer to recovery he would have to go very deep, right down to the very bed of the lake and prod around, like for bear tracks, or scat, or something like that. The valves hissed, the bubble tipped, the boat he rented almost flipped, but at last he plopped into the water. And down and down he went. I don't know what else he expected.

When he got to the bottom he found a path. It was beaten and worn down and washed over with tracks. He dragged his hose and followed it, like a feral cat, on the hunt for something cold and delicious. But it wasn't exactly like that. It was warm. His body filled with a feeling of comfort. Still, it's not as easy as it seems to recover from wounds or follow dreams. There were two signs ahead. The arrow on one pointed to, "The Surface." The other pointed to, "The Bed." This was the dilemma of Recovery Lake. Valentine didn't know if it was all a fake.

But the young black bear emerged from the trees and ran for it.

KEEP THAT MUMBLE JUMBLE DOWN

"Keep that Mumble Jumble down," shot out of the mouth of Coronel T. Booker Brown.

For my beautiful red accordion.

Valentine had returned to the club and was on the stage playing his accordion and singing to the Rose Color Swan. He was lost in the quiver of Lady of Spain, and was just about to say, "I Adore You."

For reasons unknown to Valentine his dream began to break apart to the disdain of the commentary of Coronel T. Booker Brown and in some part to his own need to be accepted. And so he prepared some white toast on which he put ground cinnamon. Coronel T. Booker Brown looked at him, quizzically. Valentine was soon saying up into minute dreams, bubbles of the original one he started with, that "trays of silverware were falling down, spilling out forks upon the ground." This got the attention of Coronel T. Booker Brown, and he held his hand up to his crew to be quiet. "Let this thing brew."

By this time Valentine had turned into a hurricane of words and the Lady of Spain had turned into a coquettish Moor, a morning moon which he observed out his window before dawn. Coronel was disappointed in this because he was rarely up at that time but he observed Valentine and saw something of the owl in him, too. Therefore he continued to hold his hand to his crew.

Valentine stumbled, and reverted with his accordion to the metre and lyrics on his music stand.

Lady of Spain, I adore you
Right from the night I first saw you
My heart has been yearning for you
What else could any heart do?
Lady of Spain, I'm appealing
Why should my lips be concealing
All that my eyes are revealing?
Lady of Spain, I love you.

Night in Madrid, blue and tender
Spanish moon makes silver splendor
Music throbbing, plaintive sobbing notes of a guitar
While ardent caballeros serenade:

Lady of Spain, I adore you
Right from the night I first saw you
My heart has been yearning for you
What else could any heart do?
Lady of Spain, I'm appealing
Why should my lips be concealing
All that my eyes are revealing?
Lady of Spain, I love you.

Coronel looked at Valentine with some regret. Not because he didn't enjoy this, but because of what was expected from Coronel. After all, people in the club talked to one another, and wait to see who Coronel talks to. So, he could smile, like Stellan Skarsgard in the magnificent Netflix series, *River,* and continue to say, "Keep that mumble jumble down," or he could break out and applaud Valentine with his hands. And Valentine for his part could continue to play in his manner or he could see the hand that Coronel was dealt and take his accordion off and punch in the microphone about street tough caballeros, Spanish doubloons, government concealment, throbbing heads, swollen lips, and children yearning for love, in a cadence that lifted Coronel up.

The silence in the club was deafening. Stellan Skarsgard, in his capacity as Inspector, stood apart, waiting for one of them to fall.

THE PARK

A shopping fantasy.

In a dream which he almost missed because of a lack of activity, Valentine Odey pulled into the parking lot of the Super Duper Supermarket. The chain had long gone out of business, so long that the number of cars at any time was limited. In Valentine's mind it was more like a beautiful park. The grey asphalt was pocked. Permanently scarred by the sun and the weight of oil which had dropped. Valentine turned his car off in the semi-light and the dark.

Six lengths away from Valentine there was a girl in a black SUV which had also parked. She was looking thru her windshield, and may have been listening to the radio or streaming something on her device. Her gaze was so intent that Valentine thought she could turn dark into light. Valentine began thinking of all sorts of ways he could meet her, six lengths away, and they were the only people left on earth at that time in the park.

For her part the girl was unaware of him. She was looking at the trees. The brown leaves. Something like Proust came to her mind. "Aged peasant hands, waving in warm October." She smiled. Even they had love on their mind.

Valentine got out of his car and took a bouquet of flowers over to her door and ran back. The girl opened her door and took the flowers in and smelled them. They were cinnamon. "Only a true heart could make this spice," she said to herself, thrice.

Beneath the park there were tracks where the coal train went by with a crunch and a crack. Valentine didn't like that. He thought it was wounding her. But she turned and laughed. But in truth she thought it was an extension of him going away every day to burn in the cauldron and shrink in the blast.

Valentine rummaged thru his glove compartment, looking for something. He located it behind a pair of Winchester Sunglasses and a hat. He looked at them before he took out the map. It was folded to Montana with a note on it that said, "SUGAR BEETS, LOOK OUT FOR THAT." Valentine opened it entirely and flapped it in the direction of the girl. He thought that innocently enough it would show her that he wanted to go out with her without having to ask. She, however, smiled, and put her headphones back on and lowered the seat against her back. Even so, Valentine could hear Leon Bridges singing, "River," to her as a rain blanketed their windows and covered their view of each other.

When the rain stopped the girl with the gray eyes was gone, and Valentine was left alone again in his beautiful park.

COPIES 10 CENTS

For Tom Matthews, without whose poetry Valentine could not have dreamed this. And for the Summer Palace Press, who published Tom's poetry.

Arthur Doyle in the 21st Century knocked on a door that said Copies 10 Cents.

Once a year Arthur Doyle knocks on a door that says, "Copies 10 Cents." The door is weathered and old and vines have grown up around it and over it. Yet Arthur comes each year to have copies made of old friends. No one else sees the door for what Arthur does. Arthur does not look like Valentine at all. Arthur looks like a king. For the occasion upon which he knocks on the door he wears a crown. It is bejeweled with jewelry he got at the Salvation Army and equipped with forks that look like peaks and fits him perfectly.

Arthur knocks on the door and waits. No one ever comes to the door. The door is weathered and old and vines have grown up around it and over it. Arthur calls out in a Middle Age voice, "But, I need copies to be made of Lancelot, and Galahad, and Bors." But no one ever answers the door. Inflation and the age of the door, possibly, and change, has overcome the ability of the door to provide these copies, let alone for 10 cents. Of course, there's no path worn to the door, as no one else sees it for what Arthur does. It has no window. In fact, the sign may have been stolen from somewhere else years ago and placed here. But still Arthur comes to the door. He knocks on the door.

In time Arthur died. The door continued to age, and vines grew up around it and over it. One day three knights came to the door and asked where Arthur was. The door had no response. Each knight took a turn knocking on the door, in various knightly ways, just to be fair, or to be sure. But the door had no response. So, the knights got back in their car and went back to England.

VALENTINE DREAMED HE HAD ALL THE MONEY IN THE WORLD

This is for all the metal and ink and paint in the world, and all the artists who, over money, choose them.

Valentine dreamed he had all the money in the world. Not just a lot of it, all of it. The first thing he did was tell everyone they would have to come to his house to get any of it.

Immediately every phone started to ring.

People wanted to know if he lived there. His conditions seemed unreasonable and they wanted to let him know that. It would be impossible, callers from the Congo said, to expect them to come to his house for their money. But Valentine stuck to his guns. He didn't own any but everyone thought he surely must have a great deal of them.

Letters started coming to his house, as every address got one, asking in this way if he lived there. But his terms were clear, you had to come to his house to get any money. You didn't have to have a good reason to get it. NO, you just had to come to his house.

Soon, it became clear that NOBODY knew where Valentine lived. The world effectively ground to a halt. Even the space flights were discontinued. Great banners were flown all over the Earth, "Where Do You Live." But eventually they fell, out of money, too.

TV stations ceased, social media grew bored, the meetings of world leaders seemed pointless, transportation stopped, and nobody watched the Final Four.

Bigger signs grew up, like, **WHERE DO YOU LIVE**, and printers and their ink became powerful.

Columnists wrote, "Without Valentine, How Will We Survive."

But artisans and Anselm Kiefer thrived.

'RENT A WHITE MAN'

This is for my dentist, Dr. Richard McCutcheon, and Cindy, his assistant, who are always understanding of my problems.

Valentine dreamed that he didn't have enough money. This was a sequel to the dream in which he had acquired all the money in the world. Obviously, something happened.

The response to his ad which he posted on a telephone pole was immediate.

"What do you mean by that," was the first reply he got, from someone who sounded very indignant. Valentine composed a scathing letter and sent it back to her, with a note that he wouldn't be cleaning her yard. A lot of other responses followed from people in the neighborhood, who had no idea who Valentine was, and almost all of them had bad grammar, which Valentine threw out in a huff. He certainly wasn't going to spend his extra time with employers who had bad grammar. Suppose it got back to Nike. But finally one stood out, the grammar was very good, and Valentine decided to go see her.

"How much do you cost," the woman said, who was disappointed in her Japanese gardener. Also in Hank, Pedro, DJ Ding Dong, and Curly. Whoever that was. Valentine had no idea what any of them did.

"Well, I don't come cheap," Valentine said. "You have to feed me, too."

"How much do you eat."

"That depends."

"On what."

"On whether I'm expected to work in the house, or the field, if you have one."

"Well, you're very picky. I simply need my shutters cleaned, and my rugs shaken. So, I guess it involves a little of both. Should I be looking at your teeth."

"I don't have any."

"Egads, you didn't mention that on your poster!"

"I didn't think I had to."

"Well, how are you going to eat."

"I have dentures."

"Yikes, you're not going to take them out, are you."

"Probably not."

"Then can you start on Monday."

"My other job requires me to be there from 9-5. I also have a crow. He needs to eat, too."

"You never told me that! This is becoming very expensive. What does HE eat."

"Peanuts."

"In that case I think I can afford both of you. Is he white."

"He's black. He's a crow."

"Well, I'm black."

"I know that."

"You don't have any prejudice, do you."

"No, Ma'am, not unless you can't spell. In which case I'm out of here."

"I was a very good speller in school."

"I can tell that."

"So, can you start on Monday. Shall we say, 7-9, am."

"I'll probably be in my suit. Is that alright."

"I suppose. What shall I call you."

"Valentine."

"Oh, I like that."

"What shall I call you."

"Mrs. Pertle."

"Well, Mrs. Pertle, get ready, because you have just rented a white man."

"I hope I'm not disappointed."

THE MAN WHO DIED IN HIS SLEEP

For my Uncle Harvey who gave me a book of Dylan Thomas's Poetry to remember my dad.

Valentine had a vivid dream that in heaven, or hell, at McDonald's, old men gathered around a table and talked about how they died. One had been run over by a car, another cut down by a Kalashnikov, a third by fire, another had fallen out of a tree. One had been murdered in broad daylight, another had picked the wrong fight, a third had volunteered to remove an alligator from his neighbor's yard, another in a game of chance had turned over the duplicate of a similar card. All of these were told with great gesticulations, and as close as ghosts could get, to animation.

The man on the end, who was Valentine, said that as it turned out he died in his sleep. Everyone turned to him and said, "Ahh."

Then they all returned to their stories of their death. Valentine went outside. He had nothing to talk about. He no longer felt, "lucky." He was ostracized, even in death.

Soon, he ran across Gabriel who was cleaning his trumpet.

"Can I help you," Gabriel said. "You seem upset."

"I'm here without a scratch," he said. "I have nothing to account for in my passing. Nothing that's of interest or in conversation, everlasting."

Gabriel, who had heard everything before, said,

"But, how do you think I get my breath! These notes are simply meant to reflect, the happiest of times as well as regret. The one you picked up I surely held as long as all the rest."

"Is that what I should tell them."

"Valentine, you died in a dream. Who knows what you were doing in there, or if you were sliding in with your cleats. Go hang out with Dylan, come up with stuff, like, 'Through the green fuse drives the flower.' Tell them that this is what interrupted the hour."

BETRAYAL

This is for Detective William R. Sperger, Joan Ellis, and Dr. John Williams, who are members of a cult which will go unnamed.

Valentine dreamed that he was picked up by FOO, the Forces of Order, and placed in a fookr.

"I think you've made a mistake," he said. "I can't imagine what I've done wrong."

"Think about it. You've exceeded the number of dreams which are allowed in a week in Fooloo."

"What fooloo."

"If you mean, "What's Fooloo," it's a mucus between consciousness and sleep."

"Well, that's a lot of crap."

"On the contrary, actually it's a delightful place, kind of like maple syrup. It's basically a place where things get fogged, and dreams are forgotten."

"Is there any way that I can just wake up and forget this one."

"No can do. We've also had a call that you keep a copy of Confederacy of Dunces in your office drawer, in lieu of extra peanuts. Of course, you know that that book was banned by all employers in 2053."

"Who called."

"I can't tell you that."

"Let me guess. Is he black."

"Color has no angle in Fooloo."

"How about where he called from."

"Please sit down in your fookr. We're almost to the station."

"FACTOR US"

AMERICAN PIE

This is with fond regard for C. I. Baxter, who has an endearing curiosity about Education, and Fort Wayne, IN.

On the little tv in his little office Valentine dreamed that he watched the tide of people wash back and forth across the Rio Grande. In fact, back and forth across all of Latin America. As his task was to resolve population puzzles and decide what Nike should do about it he could see that smugglers and the US Government were making his life difficult.

So, immediately, Valentine got on the phone and called the Pentagon. He told the receptionist that this shifting of feet and hearts was messing up his charts, and that even the smallest part, without care, without manner, without a leader's heart, could upset the apple cart. The receptionist transferred this information to her superior, that the Smallest Part, an organization deep in the shadows of the heartland, probably in Fort Wayne, Indiana, was planning to take over the government. The superior transferred this information to the WH, that refugees from El Salvador had stolen all the apples and El Salvador was the last refuge for apples and that the refugees were needed back there to pick them, and Pete Buttigieg was leading them. The President went on Valentine's little tv and announced that a plot to steal every piece of the American Apple Pie had been discovered and he didn't want any part of it so the refugees could stay.

Valentine could not understand this logic at all. He also could not understand how this guy got to be the President.

DR. BHALLA

Dr. Bhalla is a delightful, calming force who wears a blue cone upon his head in surgery which looks like cotton candy. And for the wonderful night nurses at Cayuga Med and Strong Memorial. Unfortunately, no one is safe from Valentine's pen. And this includes the ambulance that came to get him.

One day Valentine dreamed that Dr. Bhalla decided that not enough blood was getting to Valentine's brain, which may account for the presence of sentences without power, sentences trailing off, or always having to explain.

"You need surgery soon," he said, "if we're to get anywhere in your head."

And so a day was scheduled and Valentine said goodbye to Factorus.

"Where you going this time, Boss," Factorus exclaimed. "You going on a bus, or a horse, or a train?"

Valentine was touched, that Factorus asked about his health, in his vague way, and not about the location of his bag of peanuts. Not that Factorus hadn't looked.

"Don't Move. Don't Breathe. Don't Swallow."

"Don't Move. Don't Breathe. Don't Swallow."

"Don't move. Don't Breathe. Don't Swallow."

"You can breathe now."

Dr. Bhalla swung his great crane around and surveyed the room.

Valentine lay there and thought about Shackleton encountering ice. The only thing warm about that scenario was Kate Newmann writing about him with affection a hundred years later.

Dr. Bhalla focused his apparatus and moved his copy of *Metamorphosis* out of his way. Dr. Bhalla looked like an Indian God, possibly Krishna. He pulled his levers and the apparatus upon which he excelled looked very much like a chariot.

"Uncover his pelvis," he boomed.

Several red canals flowed in cumulous red clouds as the Mars probe sets off for a vast terrain.   Across Valentine's brow, a recording exclaimed, "Don't Move. Don't Breathe. Don't Swallow."

The human parts of the apparatus scurried about, asking each other about the weekend, and what shifts they were on in March, all of this to take their mind away from the horror of the job, to route a needle into Valentine's brain, where God knows what is going on there, or if any of them, after Valentine gets done with THEM, will ever be the same.

THE ART OF WRITING

This is for everyone who has an extensive library.

Vonnegut showed that writing could survive the Dresden firestorm. Now writing was in the crosshairs again. It began with an opinion in the Seattle Times that cursive slowed things down. Valentine Odey threw the paper across his office like he didn't want to touch it. Factorus ducked. This wasn't the first time he had ducked. Factorus had become very good at ducking, the more Valentine read things.

"Boss, You're going to have a stroke you keep reading stuff like that."

Valentine, however, had gone off to bed.

Before long, Anglena, Valentine's Fortuneteller, laid out the cards and began to turn them over, pairing one with another, and looking up at Valentine. She smiled, and Valentine thought of other fellows who had been in here, or women, for that matter, who looked at Anglena lustfully. He wanted to grab them by their shouldersr and tell them to get out. Then he would sit down supplicantly and ask Anglena to look at his hand. Outside, the morning was thick with fog. A train ground thru the fog like a persistent washing machine. Looking out onto the world Anglena laid out the cards and began to turn them over, pairing one with another and looking up at Valentine. She smiled, and Valentine was relieved to be there. Nothing was written between them.

THE BLACK EYE

The Greta Garbo dream.

Valentine lives on the edge of technology. An edge which he defined himself. For example, he has installed over his face a black eye, a device so devious that he cannot be reached by social media.

When Valentine goes down the street, outside of Nike's hub of sheep, he is avoided at all cost, he is the lion of a jungle lost. He buys his paper from Mr. Sills, who runs a bodega by Hanford Mills, and takes it to a public bench where he scours the personals for the perfect wench.

But none would be so perfectly sorry to leave their number for one so starry. The warning is now even in Facebook Ads, that they would end up hungry, or sad. For Valentine is like one who behind his black eye, and paper, has only dreams in which he is clad.

THE CONFEDERATE BILL

The soft scuttle of Richmond and the violins that play within her, leave a patch of gray fading, indeterminantly. And the wave of blue that comes down the street now gathering speed.

This is a dangerous dream. But Valentine had it. It's hard to escape the past, and just when you think you did, it sweetly calls down the path.

In 2065 the United States Congress passed a law that life by craft was dangerous and that in particular all statues bore the possibility of becoming alive and should therefore be destroyed. This was many years after George Floyd. A number of muddled bills had been passed for him, but this one was intended to square things.

Valentine dreamed that he went to Richmond to find where they put all the Confederate Statues. He wanted to ride back to Mississippi with Robert E. Lee. Not because he, Valentine, has a helpful opinion about that war, or race, but because he liked art, and horses, and trips, and anyone with grey hair. After a pleasant drive down I95 he got to Richmond and located the General and Traveller, which they had laid up in a shed on the campus of the University of Richmond next to some sprinklers. Valentine broke in and smacked the General right in the nose and said, "Ya ready." Then he got up on Traveller right behind the General, and Traveller kicked the rest of that shed open and off they went.

It was 4 o'clock in the morning and Fall Break. The growth of over three hundred years had emboldened the trees on campus and they spread out over the majestic grounds, the cut sidewalks and the blue lights and hid the three, along with Factorus, who wasn't going to be left out of this one. Traveller clopped along the walks and over the handsome quad and softly into the gracious Virginia breeze. There was no disfavor between anything.

In the air ahead a ton of articles swirled around them. Forks and knives, and Articles of Confederation, and a thousand rebellious things. Valentine regretted sorely that there was no one on campus to see it, although they may have seen nothing at all. Just a vestige of 4000 lbs galloping. Anglena continued to lay out the cards and Valentine saw the way to the woods light up before him, with knights traveling in them, shielded by accident, knights of all the wars in history, who had come to see how this one turned out.

Our Four Horsemen (that includes the horse) rode past the art school where the administration had posted a poster on the door that said, "Divisions will heal and so will dreams." Below that the Adjunct Instructors who were on strike had posted a summary of their lives, "They're not all dreams. Not all dreams." And below all of it the Black Union on campus had written, "Black is Beautiful." Factorus, who was getting dizzy reading all this stuff, sided with the Black Union.

In the Rose Tavern, where they stopped, with Invisible Ink, every three letters Thomas Lane wrote nine, and eight. "Which way do we go," said Valentine, worried that The General himself might have forgotten that by now. Thomas Lane furtively drew a map with a line on it that curved all over the place and looked a lot like the letters nine and eight. One loop went along the Lincoln Parkway, then south along the Mississippi River where two boys were fishing. Another loop, the one that was closed like a 8 went thru Georgia, and Arkansas, and up thru Ohio. Valentine thought that one was too confusing. So they took the other one which was shaped like a nine. Factorus, who was holding on to Traveller's tail took a meclizine pill and closed up like a black centurion.

The semester ended and another began. In our collection of knights, which was mentioned above, Confederate Boys were moving north through North Carolina with their magnolia scented letters matting in their pockets. Our boys were riding south along the Mississippi River where they saw a Colonel out in the field picking cotton. "You missed one," Valentine said. And the Colonel went back into the field to get the forgotten cotton ball. Valentine said to Mr. Lee, "See. All you had to do was share the load a little bit and everybody get along just fine. Eventually everybody be ridin on the Robert E. Lee, not just you and me."

Factorus opened his eyes and coughed. Sometimes, Valentine's logic was off.

For his part, The General was worried about P. T. Beauregard who he'd appointed to defend Vicksburg.

"We have to find him before he gets melted into a traffic light or a juice machine." Factorus took another meclizine pill and drifted off. Valentine drifted also. This time he thought about the music that had an effect on him when he was growing up. He thought about the Vandellas, and Martha singing in her grandfather's Metropolitan Church in Detroit, and John Lee Hooker enunciating, "BOOM, BOOM," to his wide-eyed audience at Wayne State University. He thought about Iris DeMent years later singing in her own church in Iowa, taking her daughter on tour with her in NY, her red shoes keeping time under a piano that was on fire. He thought about wolves howling down old mountains and the mountains howling back at them. He thought about working in the guard shack with Ruben Gilliam from Enoree, South Carolina, Redwoods swaying on their majestic block in Southern Oregon, and mountain lions in the Sacramento Mountains of South Central, New Mexico, roaring at the brains of tourists. He thought about young men and women on a street corner in Little Rock, Arkansas, making up their own language and challenging each other to say it, and trails coming out of Dodge, Kansas, how they are probably littered with the hums of cowboys who didn't know what else to do with them. He thought about the musician with her hat down on the pavement in Spring Hill, Florida, singing her heart out. He thought about the falcon hovering over all of them, away from her training, hidden by the sun. All these things he thought are what's right in the world.

But divisions had taken over the world. And Tributes were unable to adapt. It was understandable that Congress had to act.

Our company was on the doorstep of Vicksburg. A mechanic who was probably successful if only because he looked like Abraham Lincoln told them that Beauregard was scheduled to be melted down at 3 o'clock. Jean Basquiat popped up from underneath a car and said he'd like to see that. Then Traveller reared up and bolted out of that garage with Valentine and Factrous and Robert E. Lee, and now Jean Basquiat.

At Sotheby's in New York, an Auctioneer held up a genuine confederate bill that was supposedly signed by Robert E. Lee and reluctantly by Jean-Michel Basquiat, which saved General Beauregard from the melting block. And the proceeds bought a park. Which is where all the statues went, and even the Left said they looked majestic, as long as they were shown in the amber streetlight, when the kids were asleep, after dark.

THE AMERICAN DREAM

This is for the ladder industry, if that's what it's come to.

Valentine and Factorus peered over the fence.

"I hope this ladder can hold both of us."

"You're the only one hanging on."

"I understand your separating us, caging us, disrespecting us, but what I fault you for is not understanding us. We want The American Dream. We still believe in it. It's a real thing for us."

"What's she saying???" Valentine begged of Factorus.

"She wants access to the merry-go-round."

"Those things are dangerous."

"So are knives in the hands of gang members, and empty bowls for dinner."

"We should let her use our ladder."

"I think that makes us accomplices to a crime."

"Because it slips down her side of the fence?"

"Because you slip it down her side of the fence, and probably because you make a big sign to go with it that says, 'HEY, YOU CAN USE OUR LADDER.'"

At that point the ladder tips over the wall and slides down the other side, with Valentine on it.

The woman starts climbing the ladder, leaving Valentine behind.

Valentine, who has just become the newest citizen of Mexico, is alarmed.

"Hey. What about me!"

Factorus flapping above the wall, clearly sees the new writing on it.

"You're almost there, my new angel. Pay no attention to that man behind the curtain. Our future awaits us!"

THE ROMAN SANDALS

This is for Bakersfield, for reasons known only to Valentine.

One day, after Valentine had cleared his desk and properly laid his head down on it, Factorus dared him to jump off a cliff. Valentine hadn't had a flying dream in some time and didn't know if this was going to be one of them, or if Factorus had had it. But in this dream Factorus was adamant. And so it was that on Monday they took a train across the continent to the seaport of Acapulco on Mexico's West Coast. Valentine really didn't need to provide a marketing plan to Nike for the trip as they thought he had retired several years ago.

"It's beautiful here," Valentine said upon arrival. "Have you been here before, Factorus?"

"Only in passing," replied his ingenious friend. Valentine reflected that Factorus was so clever, and wished he could write like him.

The following day it rained. Valentine waved this off as a minor delay. "This will give us time to buy nice swimsuits and get something to eat." To Valentine this sounded like a full day. Factorus had no need of a swimsuit but he was hungry, and hunger was always a full day. Halfway thru a taco order with Mexican Coke (real sugar) Valentine agreed with Merle Haggard that Roman Sandals had no place in their noble experiment, and kicked them off. The left one hit the cook in the head and knocked him out cold. Valentine was then detained and forced to work his shift, which extended into the next day. Factorus ordered a burrito and went back to the hotel to wait for Valentine. On the third day the sun was out and a fire raged in Valentine's belly from having eaten several hundred tacos which he had prepared himself over the past two days. He was ready for anything that involved water.

Valentine threw the shutters open on their floor and shouted, "Hey, Factorus, look at this!" And outside on the streets of Acapulco tourists were queuing up to see The Cliff Divers of La Quebrada. "They're waiting for us, my friend. And what a display we'll give them. Are you ready."

Factorus flapped his wings and cawed in support of his boss. He always found that that appealed to Valentine.

After the delay with the tacos Valentine was now on a roll. He couldn't believe so many people came to see him. "Nothing rides justice like the truth," he cried as he put on his swimsuit and fashioned its little string into a bow tie. Out in the hallway Merle Haggard was checking in to Room 319 with a view of the cliffs. He was wearing Roman Sandals, and a cumulous cloud hung in the hallway where Merle had been.

Valentine opened his door and was assailed by a cloud of Blueberry Kush. "My God," he cried, "I've been chloroformed."

Valentine was now in a dream within a dream. The clambake which had assailed him in the hallway enveloped him in his bed.

On his porch, Merle watched Factorus swoop and dive in the air streams that fell off the back of La Quebrada. "Bravo!" he cried, while Valentine dove for pearls. Somehow he thought they just lay there on the bottom of the ocean waiting for him to pick them up.

COUNCIL AT STANDING
ROCK

Valentine and Factorus in a dream circle at Standing Rock.

When LaDonna Brave Bull Allard tells you
"Our Camps will be here Forever"
The names roll off her tongue
The Iowa, The Sioux, The Delaware, The Wyandotte,
And you see them standing tall in Mother Earth's setting sun.

When LaDonna Brave Bull Allard tells you
"Our Camps will be here Forever"
It's because their soul was kissed
And they will always be here despite you read
That they disappeared in the country's mist.

When LaDonna Brave Bull Allard tells you
"Our Camps will be here Forever"
Walmart comes to fill out their tree
And one more custom is taken away
But the young brave never leaves.

When LaDonna Brave Bull Allard tells you

"Our Camps will be here Forever"

She means the heart, the feet, and the lungs,
And all those old men getting ready
sitting there beating drums.

THE ANCIENT WIND

Dream Flooders.

Charlotte. August 27, 2013. Charlotte was a hound dog. She did catch a rabbit once, and she was a friend of mine. Other than the time she ran away from her previous owner and lived at the SPCA, unclaimed, she lived on our hill. In all her years she only bit one person and she was sorry about that. When she went blind we affectionately called her one of the Blind Boys of Alabama. When she died we buried her so she was facing that way. She was a good dog and there isn't a day that goes by that we don't think of her.

Lily. September 22, 2013. Lily was a alley cat. A sweet alley cat, who never howled, like Charlotte. Lily lived on what was available outside. When she came to live with us she had to get used to what was available inside. For a while that was a shock. But she got over it. The older she got the more she liked to be outside, again. Her favorite place to be all day was the hedgerow. But then it was the driveway, and then it was on the big rock in the garden by the front porch. She was making her way back to us as her circle was closing. She probably thought we wouldn't notice it, but we knew. Now it's quiet. Outside, somewhere in town, the leaves rustle in an alley. I bet that's what she thought she was in, in the hedgerow.

TWILIGHT ZONE

Remembering Hal's Deli on Aurora Street, in Ithaca, NY. One of Rod Serling's haunts.

Valentine peered into the abyss.

Everything had been cleared out of the restaurant. The counter, the stools, the white Formica, the small tables, the class pictures of Cornell Graduates, the newspapers, the ashtrays, the diners. Everything was gone. It just looked like a big, hollow place.

A figure stood in the grey well where the horseshoe counter used to be and appeared to be pouring over a manuscript for a new show. His thick black hair swayed like the Forest at Ghent. His mouth moved in time with his pen. All the episodes, and all he meant.

And on the window outside there was a sign that said,

SPACE FOR RENT

The person I saw invited me in. I put my hands to my chest and tilted my head, "Meee!!" I said.

"Yes, you. Get in here, quick."

And so I did.

"You got any ideas. We don't have much Time."

"How can you think in here. It's dark, and eerily quiet and all those people out there are paying no attention to us for a start."

"They will if you come up with something. Look into the chasm, Valentine, and find it."

"I was thinking of a courtroom scene in space where the Internet goes on trial for Mischief against Our Kind."

"Forget about 'Our Kind.' Tell me about the trial."

"Well, we get Edgar Allan Poe for the Prosecutor. He's very unkempt, of course. But, we have him swing a processor around in front of the jury. It's very big and the jurors are petrified it's going to land on them. Poe is screaming about its corridors of deceit and despair, and pointing vigorously at all the ports, and then he smashes the processor on the floor and says, 'There, There.'"

"Is that it."

"Not entirely. Edgar is sweating profusely and he shouts loudly, 'THERE, THERE, tear off its thin alloy sides. There, THERE, is the beating of its Tell-Tale

Heart.' Then the Bailiff grabs him and takes him away in handcuffs. What do you think."

"I like the ending. A nice twist of fate. You can stay in for one more."

"Ok. We're in a newsroom. There's this guy, name Crossmore, or Chris Moore. He buys a week's subscription to the Chicago Tribune and calls in to complain because he's only getting the news one day at a time. So, for him we make it seven days at a time, up front. But then his girlfriend gets killed in a drive-by at a club on day 7 and he wants to go back. We negotiate with some Gaming Board that Philip Dick dreamed up. Chris gets two days and his girlfriend is saved."

"You're wearing me out, Valentine. I like it! What's next."

"Ok, well, ..."

And this goes on until the sign blows off and all of Valentine's ideas are happily spent.

HARRY RINE DE YOUNG IN THE CLUB

Valentine's boyhood preacher at Redford Presbyterian, relates a meeting of the Apostles at which Jesus explains a situation to them. It has a lasting effect on Valentine.

The Plumber was a drummer
From nine to six
Boy's so cool
He coulda played at Ric's.

The Singer come on
To jabber with a fella,
Something about LOVE
And some dude name Othella.

Over in the corner
Homeboys talkin skip,
Got their own conversation
About Shake's money clip.

The Singer says, "HEY, from A – Z
We all hooked up
To the same
Currency.

Music so sweet
Don't you forget,
John Dillinger liked money
But he loved Billie Frechette."

CAPTAIN MARK NEIL

For my first cousin, once removed, which may not be far enough for him! I'll have to ask him.

Valentine doesn't have a lot of fast friends. That he has friends at all is usually not in a way that they know about. Valentine looks for friends to further his ambitions. His ambitions in his dreams are expansive. They usually involve things far away, past in circuitous ways the carotid artery in his neck which is blocked. He has to be careful he doesn't hit that. Sometimes Factorus clamps his feet around his carotid artery and Valentine yells at him. Factorus has a carotid artery, too, but it's very hard to get at. Valentine has tried.

Valentine summed it up to Factorus, "A dog would like nothing better than to have a dog friend."

"So," replied Factorus, feeling somewhat hurt, "It's a species thing. Nothing personal."

"It's a species thing. Nothing personal."

Finding friends can happen at any time. After their little chat, Valentine decided to keep his eyes open.

In his latest expansive dream he went to Bed Bath & Beyond to purchase a pillow for his office. There, he unbelievably spied a member of his species, albeit another alien probably from a district in Mars, dressed up as the Assistant Store Manager. Valentine immediately assigned him the rank of Captain and discretely saluted him. Mark Neil, for his part, kept an eye on Valentine, while successfully hiding his identity from everybody else beneath his dark horn rimmed glasses.

Valentine watches the District Captain navigate the narrow aisles of the store with his clicker which he points at a row of towels. It's obvious to Valentine what he's really doing. He's counting Daleks, or at the very least keeping track of them. Valentine immediately considered Mark a friend. In time, on more visits to the store, Valentine could see that Mark was really talking to them, and that his clicker was really a matter muter that allowed information to be sent back and forth between them without being heard. This was eye opening for Valentine. Therefore, their relationship deepened.

As the number of pillows and towels in Valentine's office piled up and his visits to the store increased, Valentine's outlook on life swelled in a positive way in the face of real friendship. On a bad weather day the Daleks would yell, "Fire, Fire," and Mark would move them. Valentine would have done the same thing.

"Exterminate, Exterminate." "Maximum Power." "Fire, Fire, Fire."

On one trip to the store which was on a particularly frightful night the Daleks were exerting influence on a row of bath mats.

"Exterminate, Exterminate." "Maximum Power." "Fire, Fire, Fire." But Captain Neil knew just what to do to keep the galactic weal from unwinding.

When Mark was transferred the magic stopped. The towels were no longer Daleks, and the bath mats were only mats.

Valentine had to hold himself back as Capt. Mark Neil took off for Mars. Mark had been transferred "home."

There was no intrigue in the aisle or combat. After that Valentine would sit on the window sill and talk about silk and cotton with Factorus.

THE BIG SOUND

This is for my old neighborhood. Telegraph to 5 Points, and 6 Mile to Grand River.

Valentine was at least 20,000 Leagues Beneath The Sea. It was a very deep sleep in which a man in a Produce Truck, who looked very much like Jules Verne, was coming closer to him in Valentine's old neighborhood.

And soon there was a sound that came out of the man's mouth that for Valentine was very profound.

"W A T E R M E L O N

I H A V E W A T E R M E L O N."

Of course, the man had a lot of other things. Like carrots, and lettuce, and broccoli, and tomatoes. Potatoes and beets and things that look like tornadoes. But, WATERMELON was the sound, the ringing endorsement of everything out of the ground. The sweet, wet hound, of summer, of company, and sitting around. It was also Valentine's first real memory of Melody, which he was revisiting. The Produce Man with his big sound.

Today, Julius Verne and his six children perform another service for the community. They drive a truck thru the neighborhood and pick up all the plastic that people don't know what to do about.

And Julius sings in a clear operatic sound.

"A L L P L A S T I C. I H A V E A L L P L A S T I C."

And everyone, not knowing what watermelon is, come rushing out.

Then Jules goes back to Atlantic City and loads up his submarine and takes all the plastic to the bottom of the sea. Thru the very big glass in his hull he clucks his tongue and shakes his head at the mass he is forming. He instructs his crew to surround it. They throw a net around it and pull it tight, so not even a particle can escape which fish might bite. And out of the sea after centuries, an island arises which crunches to feet. Up, up, and away, into the heavens it goes. One day God sits on it on a day in which he has a fever and it becomes a molten mass, on which there is a house, a boy and a ceramics class. Then God creates a truck and a band to play to go around the neighborhood and a singer for this day. It turns out the singer is Notorious B.I.G. And Valentine dreams he sings like a bird to all of his felons of which Valentine is one,

"I H A V E F R U I T F O R Y O U.

I H A V E W A T E R M E L O N."

THE LINE

Formerly Called, An Irrational Fear Of Socialism.

One day Valentine found himself in a dream in a line to dream. It was very disconcerting. Behind the window which everyone in line had to go up to there was an element which, from his distance, looked like The Tributary. But when Valentine got to the front of the line, he found that it wasn't The Tributary at all but a Meatgrinder. And instead of helping you go off in all directions as The Tributary is supposed to do it ground everyone into a big pile.

"This is very disturbing," Valentine said.

"Just get in," a programmed module grasped at him, and it was all Valentine could do not to become part of the line which had been the line in front of him.

CASTING CALL

Valentine went up to God.

Of course, Valentine had an outtake with him, which is

kind of like takeout only a little more spherical.

"I want to be this guy, it's perfect for me."

Are you sure, God said.

Yes, I'm sure of it. I've read the script.

How much of it did you read.

Quite a bit.

THE HIGHWAYMEN

Strangely, One of Valentine's favorite dreams.

Valentine dreamed he went out to get a cup of coffee. The machine he had in mind was 250 miles away. He left Factorus in charge and went to get it.

"Factorus, remember, don't let anybody in. Tell them anything you want, just don't let them in. I don't want to have to explain you when I get back."

Factorus, who was already in Valentine's seat, was not at all insulted by this last remark. In fact, he was diligently working on his lines and was pleased that Valentine would have to explain himself when he got back.

Valentine got in his Plymouth Duster and started out for a row of machines along the Pennsylvania Turnpike, which he had stopped at once before. He held out hope that they had not been upgraded, that the cups didn't have those silly holders on them, and that the lids didn't have those unhelpful vents and fog lights. Other than that, he couldn't wait.

Factorus dressed to the nines like he was a diplomat from Ethiopia and spun in Valentine's chair, and then amongst Valentine's stacks of poetry and mystery and tomes of philosophical differences he began reciting Wallace Stevens to the confusion of the 3rd floor at Nike Headquarters. "Complacencies of the peignoir, and late coffee and oranges in a sunny chair, and the green freedom of a cockatoo..." Factorus swung upon the chair, Valentine's chair, and imagined the green freedom of a cockatoo. Others gathered at his door, Valentine's door, and imagined also.

Valentine continued on for a very long ways. He put his tape of Diana Ross and The Supremes in his cassette player and opened his window. "Stop, In The Name Of Love," blasted into the lane beside him. Valentine wasn't a very good singer so he simply put his upright left hand upright out the window to emphasize what Diana was getting at. Several drivers honked at Valentine and gave him all sorts of signals with their hands which he tried to duplicate, but he wasn't very good at that, either. Rather, he opened his mouth wide and bared his dentures at them, "STOP, in the name of LOVE, before you break my heart." WAAH, WAAH, WAAH.

In the distance, way in the distance, a cockatoo swung upon a perch and imagined he was sitting in a chair. He was listening to himself singing on his perch, and he had a cup of coffee which he pretended to hold and slurp.

FOREIGN DREAMS

For Bob Dylan.

In the gallery in question there are two pictures of the Palazzo Hotel in Venice, Italy. One says, 'The Palazzo Eleanora Duse, Venice, by Walter Sickert. A somewhat shabby air consistent with the artist's interest in the less conservatively picturesque.'

The second one says, 'The Palazzo Dorio, by Monet, in which the famed actress Eleanora Duse kept an apartment.'

I couldn't decide which one I liked better.

GHOSTTOWN

This is for Douglas Anne Munson, if only as brief as her stay here. The crime, was her cancer.

The vehicle in which I am riding is humming like an ashram. If the woman I am with asks me to be involved in pot boiled crime I may have to decline. She looks at me in the mirror and smiles.

We pass by a hotel in which Mercedes Lambert is writing Ghosttown, her sequel to Dogtown and Soultown, and writing to Lucas Crown about her circumstances. She's having a hard time of it. She thinks of Lupe as she made her. "She had on a black miniskirt, a screaming pink stretch top that bared her midriff, several large rhinestone bracelets and a pair of white go-go boots," standing in the shade of a pepper tree. She tells Lucas that she's thinking of going to the Czech Republic to teach English as a second language, give up her lawyer ways. She makes Lupe sassy, treats her kindly, overall, thru three books. Now she wonders if Lupe is really who she is. After all those plots, all those lines, left standing in the shade of a pepper tree.

I'm worried, again, that somewhere in this there's going to be a crime. I hope it's not one that she expects me to figure out.

Mercedes laughed and smiled at my reflection.

MY BED IS NOT THE SAME SIZE AS YOUR BED

The Scene: Confederate Memorial Hospital In Shreveport, LA.

"What's he saying."

"Something about the size of beds."

"But, exactly, what is he saying?"

"'My bed is not the same size as your bed.'"

"Egads, another Dreamcatcher. Who picked him up."

"Bossier City. He was talking incoherently and insisted on seeing The Reverend."

"He said, 'The Reverend!'"

"It appears so."

"Did he also mention 'The Relationship.'"

"No, he didn't."

"Then he's only gotten so far. The Reverend is always at the beginning."

An earlier scene: Several girls running up a staircase, catching their breath.

"Did you see that!!!"

"I know, I couldn't believe it."

A man, beat up, lying in the street.

Members of FOO, the Forces Of Order, scoop him up and put him in a fookr. The first scene returns.

"Do you think he's dangerous, Doctor."

"No more than the others. I don't think he got that far."

"But as far as thoughts of The Reverend. There's danger enough in that."

"If that's all it is, it's manageable. Was there any sign of the girl?"

"A line opened up but quickly closed when we got there. It might have been her."

"That's where the danger is! Put him in the Round Table Complex. And for heaven's sake don't let him fall asleep, he may get away."

"Why do you think he's here, Doctor."

"For the same reason the rest of them are."

Valentine was watching Comet tv on the little tv set up in his room on the 3rd floor. He was watching The Truman Story, with Jim Carrey, who got all tangled up in the mast of his little boat in a swirling sea. Valentine sat on the edge of his bed yelling at Jim to cut the rope and get away, and when he did Valentine was exhilarated and fell back, himself, into his own exhausting sea.

HOOP UP YOUR PEONIES

This is for my daughter, Delevan. I hope I haven't embarrassed her tooo much, and for the graduating class of 2013.

One day Valentine dreamed he was invited to give the Commencement Address for Tompkins Cortland Community College, The Nursing Program. Valentine looked in the mirror and saw evidence of decline, therefore he decided to accept the invitation.

Immediately he began to research "Commencement Addresses," on U Tube. He was surprised to see that they were broken down by conference. The SEC, The Big 10, Big 12, Big Sky, Ivy League, Horizon League, and so on. Also by, Predominantly Black, Predominantly White, Some Hispanic, Spicy Asian (My Favorite), Possibly Native American (subject to check), by gender, Coed, Male Only, Female Only, Line 10, Mars, No Mars. And finally, denominational. Catholic, Evangelical, Protestant, Zen, Hasidic, Baptist, Southern Baptist, Real Southern Baptist, Atheist (probably the Ivy League), and Woodsman Clear Cut. Valentine saw this embarrassment of riches as either prosperity or despair. He just knew he had his work cut out for him. Then there was the matter of style, which was separate from content.

He tried to remember his own commencement and realized he missed it. He thought of a short story by Philip Dick, *We Can Remember It For You Wholesale,* in which a memory you wished you had could be implanted in your brain for a small fee. Valentine looked at the invitation again to see if he was being paid for this. He wasn't. This would not be something he knew by heart. This would have to be something that came from The Heart. Already his was beating loudly.

And so in the end Valentine drew his inspiration not from the great speeches online but in part from a gardening manual he got in the mail. It said, "How to hoop up your peonies." This released a flood of gibberish in Valentine's brain, which he could barely keep from falling off as he pulled scraps toward him at his desk. Only half of it was contained. But it was enough. And so with confidence, if not with reason, Valentine approached the podium on that fateful day, which happened to be the 23rd of May, 2013.

"Graduates!"

"Parents and Benefactors."

"Pets, Trees, and Friends of the lawns of this great institution,"

"The advice I have for you today arrived recently in the mail. As I felt it was a little sketchy, I've blown most of it up into a proportion which I hope is large enough for this occasion. Here it is:"

"In your job ahead, the world will depend on you to clean up their act. I don't think I need to tell you every implement you'll need to do that. Trowels would be good. You may need to give them a Latin name in the operating room if you show them to the patient. Same with the pitchforks. String will be string, and a few things will be needed which go ding. But I'm sure you can figure all that out, or an assistant with experience will gladly show you. What you will not be shown is why I'm here. I'm here to pump you up. Page One of the manual:"

"When your name is called today and you can't believe it's you,

Hoop Up Your Peonies."

"When the little tag on the end of your diploma says, 'Return to the Bookstore, too,"

Hoop Up Your Peonies."

"When you wonder if you put oil in your car when you got here,

Hoop Up Your Peonies."

"When your first patient stares at you,

Hoop Up Your Peonies."

"When you regret that you've never taken time to go to the zoo,

Hoop Up Your Peonies."

"When you are sad, or glad, or mad,

Hoop up Your Peonies."

"When the hospital you apply to doesn't have Crew,

Hoop Up Your Peonies."

"When life seems ruined and you wonder if you ruined it,

Hoop Up Your Peonies."

"When your heart is broken because there's nothing more you can do,

Hoop Up Your Peonies."

"When you miss your dog more than your parents,

Hoop Up Your Peonies."

"Parents. When your daughter says she wants to be your son,

Hoop Up Your Peonies."

"When everything seems to be dragging you down and that sun is just not coming around,

Hoop Up Your Peonies."

"When the little boy and the little girl in the Waiting Room need a hug from you,

Hoop Up Your Peonies."

"Tomorrow, if you find yourself in a pandemic that you didn't ask for,

You have to pursue. You know what to do."

"And finally, Class of 2013, when you leave here, if the security deposit you got is all you got,

Hoop Up Your Peonies."

Valentine isn't done yet, even though he should be, if he had any sense of timing.

"There is one more thing, for those of you who haven't left yet. A poem by Arthur Hugh Clough, who was a clerk in the British Education office in the 1800's and a devoted assistant to Florence Nightingale."

"Here it is!"

"'Say Not The Struggle Nought Availeth.' A poem by Arthur Hugh Clough, a fragment, which I've adapted for our heroes and heroines today and in their days to come."

"' ... And, but for you. Possess the field. For while the tired waves, vainly breaking, Seem here no painful inch to gain, Far back through creeks and inlets making, Comes silent, flooding in, the main. And not by eastern windows only, When daylight comes, comes in the light, In front the sun climbs slow, how slowly. Possess the field, though it were night.'"

"Good Luck, and keep an eye out for me."

A DAY IN THE STEELE MAGNOLIA LIBRARY

For the homeless.

Darlene set her bag down and selected a
bag of candy from somewhere deep inside the bowels of it.
The individual cellophane wrappers crinkled and rustled loudly
as she opened them. She apologized.
She certainly didn't want to be asked to leave.
I smiled and told her not to worry about it.
"We'll make our own rules!"
I dreamed I had all my notes spread out on our table.
Darlene said it looked like I was writing a book.
It did look like that, I thought, the way I had the pages set out.
She asked me what it was all about.
I told her I didn't know but that it didn't have any violence,
to speak of, or swearing, or smoking in it, or sex, for that matter.
She said, "What kind of book is that!!!???"
I told her I wasn't sure but that maybe she'll be in it.
Her reply, "I'm only here on Tuesdays and Thursdays,"
captured my style perfectly and my heart.
Darlene was the most interesting person I met that day
in the Steele Magnolia Library.

THE WHITE RABBIT

In the end, for the cast.

Valentine stood at his office window. He looked out over the parking lot
where Factorus was sitting on his Ford Galaxy. Everything about the block
looked in place which pleased Valentine. Even a paper bag which that
morning had hung up in the Maple tree didn't offend his sense of order,
which surprised him. So, it seemed that everything was right in the Universe,

or in as much of it as he knew about. He waved warmly at Factorus, who had turned to look into the past. Coming up that road, still in the distance, but clearly coming now, was an object coated in cinnamon that was buried and soft, which soon would be coming by Nike's trough. Valentine watched its progress with alarm. He would certainly call Security if it stopped here! But it didn't stop there. It did however slow down when it came by the Maple tree where the bag was hanging off. In a very big seat he could see a young man looking back, at an unusual dog who had irregular angles and hound ears which flapped, and beside the boy a very pretty girl with long blonde hair and silver rings in several stacks was gesticulating wildly and scanning intently everyone they passed.

"KEEP LOOKING!"   "KEEP LOOKING!"

she said, like a zippy drum beat pat, which all of them did, especially the RV, which hopped and danced in front of all the Nike employees.

"Well, that was something," Valentine said. "There should probably be a law against that."

But, instead, there was a knock at his door. The real one. It was David, who worked in the mailroom.

"Hey, Mr. V. You sleeping!"

"That's good, Dave. Do you have something for me."

"It's a letter. It's not from anyone here. I'm sure of that." It smelled like asteroids.

Valentine tore it open immediately.

Inside there was very regal looking stationery, embossed with a falcon. The letter said, "My Dangerous Darling, I may be leaving," and the envelope was bleeding.

Out his window our cast was disappearing over some pine trees. Holding up his pants our Unsettled Squire ran out of his office

SCREAM

ING.

Part Three

The Kenworth

Diaries

Valentine Is Retired.
It Was Forced.

Upon running out of his office screaming, Valentine Odey tripped on the balustrade of the 3rd floor and went tumbling down the stairs, one set after another, until he reached the grande entryway of Nike, Incorporated. There he landed under the Maple tree at the feet of Autry, the astonished security guard from Guatemala. Large portions and remoste brigades of space soon followed in Valentine's brain, outside the knowledge and safety of Dr. Tarun Bhalla and his All-Star Train.

On the way to the hospital Valentine looked up at the ceiling in the "Church." There was a beautiful painting of a Bear running through the mist of a Great Pond. In his innocence Valentine wondered how the parishioners got up there to paint it. Ladders was his first thought, then scaffolding, then a trapeze. Valentine had to be careful because he could go off on a tangent and lose the whole dream. But it was comforting, and he wanted to touch the bear regardless of the admonition he had given the children in the story about The Envelope. Outside, a gibbous moon was traversing the beautiful windows below the ceiling, first thru the canes, then the crows, and then the masts of the big frigate looking ships. Ricky galloped with his sticks, wildly, like everything was coming to some sort of conclusion. A large and varied obstruction came over Valentine and blocked out the light of the moon. It was The Congregation who had recently come out of a swoon. Several of them poked at him like he was the Pillsbury Dough Boy. "Stop that!" he said. "Oh, stop that, you Loon!"

Autry, who had insisted on accompanying Valentine to the hospital clamored into the ambulance beside him. Valentine noticed him and took his hands.

"Gene, thank goodness you're here. I can't wait to tell you about Ms. Lin. Besides that fact, we have to go after her, you know. In time I'll tell you everything. Did you bring your horse?"

"Mr. V, you've had a big fall and I'm afraid you're not right in the head. You know I don't have a horse."

"Of course, you have a horse, Gene. How else will you confound me."

"Name's Autry,

Not Gene."

DOWN IN SAN BENITO

The beginning of things that happened to Valentine after he was fired.

Valentine's Shoes.

A caravan has just left Villahermosa, Mexico on its way to Guatemala

"Are we there yet," an elderly man offered from his stretcher, in a dry, pale voice. His bearers panted and said, "No, Senor, not yet."

The saguaros cactus spines occasionally caught his feet and Valentine Odey, which is pronounced O Day if you needed to know that, said, "Ouch!!!" to no one in particular. A rattlesnake slinked by and rattled something in Spanish. It sounded very much like, "Hissssay." Valentine said, "What was that."

The oil derricks of Villahermosa tracked our caravan as it snaked south, their masts intubating the earth, the earth gasping for air, for a return of its solitude. The economy for the caravan presented itself on the surface, and the bearers of Valentine picked up small pieces of refuse. The caravan itself barely scratched the surface of the resident's awareness, of Villahermosa. All these things are part of the desert.

The Caravan came to rest at the top of Guatemala in the parking lot of the Salesian Monastery in San Benito. It was really a Mission and not a monastery, but Valentine preferred it to be a monastery. Valentine was unceremoniously dumped on a porch next to the office. A Pinata which resembled a President of the United States was sitting on a swing across from him. "Are you Lincoln," Valentine said without the benefit of his glasses. The Pinata said, "Of course not," and picked up a piece of candy which had fallen out of his head onto his lap. "Where did everyone go." "COVID. They went to wash their hands." "I was hoping we were away from that." "Well, you were wrong. What's your name by the way." "Valentine. What's yours." "Yatta, Yatta, Yatta. I'm a comedian." "That's funny. You'd tell me if you were Lincoln, wouldn't you." "Trust me, I'm not Lincoln."

The Pinata observed Valentine like a seven foot sunflower observing a child. The rows in their garden included a pot of geraniums, a bicycle, and a cat. "Who's the cat?" Valentine said, with a hopeful voice. "That's KR. Kyle Rodriguez. He bites, so I'd watch out for him if I were you." KR looked at Valentine and extended his claws like he was in a gym and was looking at a new piece of equipment. Valentine looked in his duffle bag to see if he had a book about animal psychology, specifically, cats, in there. He had all sorts of mysteries and a biography about Adlai Stevenson but no books about Mayan cats. Valentine decided to go to the library, first, if this was to be his new home, before petting Kyle Rodriguez.

In his mind Valentine was always trying to adjust the situation.

~ Over the scales and over the trees,
clothed in mail and impervious things,
I rode up to a castle wall.
which looked very much like a shopping mall.

"Who goes there," is what I expected to hear
from a Sentinel in camden and gwelph upon the drear.
But, a speaker cooed, at me and all,
'Hey, there, Boy, we have Big, and Tall.'

I raised my visor
which fell back down unfortunately with a dink.
"I am here to claim the fair Sirine," I said,
"Where is she, anyway, my good and just Queen."

The Store Queen, whose name was really, Larry,
told the Trumpeter whose name was Morse,
'O, Morse, Blast this guy with all your force, O
knock him good, Morse, off his big fat horse.'

But the Trumpeter thought that I was cute
So, he played something instead from, Hot Pursuit,
And I got down and danced
upon the Green and clinked and clanked.

Then the bridge unwound
and with the chains clinking came slowly down.
And I, looking variously like an English Lord or a Hound,
road upon Ginger into Tarry Town ~

But the true situation remained implacable and was not in the branches of his mind, of course, but in the furniture on the porch, and the nature of the porch. Still, Valentine wanted to preserve the progress which he believed he had made. Progress which inspired him and helped him understand the situation, even though he was mistaken.

"I don't imagine you have anything in there I could write with, do you," he said to the Pinata who was now growing in importance. "I've thought of something that has momentarily sustained me."

"No, I don't."

"I was afraid of that. And now it is gone. Something about a horse. I don't know which way this is going to go without one."

"The Spaniards got them. I think they took them all back to Alhambra."

"And yet this feels like a horse."

"It's **Florette**'s rocker, which is shaped like a horse. It's her comfort food. Probably not a good idea for you to get too comfortable in it."

A sparkly eclipse came over Valentine's side of the porch.

"WHO'S THAT ROTISSERIE CHICKEN SITTIN ON MY ROCKER."

KR ran for it. The porch tilted unforgiven toward the eclipse.

"I'M GONNA PLUCK ME SOME FEATHERS, AND THEN I'M GONNA HIT YOU RIGHT IN THE HEAD, LINCOLN."

Valentine said, "I knew it!"

The Pinata swayed on its swing dislodging several more pieces of candy, which this time fell to the porch. Florette scooped them up and then reached for Valentine. The Pinata seemed to be coming apart from both physical and mental whacks, which is how Valentine felt about his own life.

"Stop, Woman. I've been brought here as part of an act of mercy. This happened after I fell down a flight of stairs in a book which nobody bought. Do you like to read books?"

A caramel which appeared to contain quikrete was gluing Florette's teeth together, and threw her off balance on the porch. Her blouse billowed in the moonlight as she curtsied and descended into Valentine's lap. "Were you a star in this book which nobody bought."

Valentine contracted like an accordion. "I tried to be, but the setting was like a Shakespearean sawmill with secrets in the carriage. I was lucky to make it out alive."

Florette sighed in that she wished she could have been there.

Valentine sighed, also. Most of the mysteries he had in his duffle bag started off better than this. His ability to sift and find gold, or at least to elaborate on what was in the pan was disappearing into the mist along with the tribe he was researching and wanted to belong to. Even the air was quiet with no crows in it. With all the strength he had left he raised up Florette and screamed at the top of his rocker,

"WHY AM I HERE."

The sun that disappeared over Mauritania rose in San Benito. Father Pedro Morales opened the window of his room and welcomed the sun in. The sun then advanced thru his room into the kitchen and sat down for breakfast. Breakfast consisted of quesadillas, honey and toast, and a glass of milk. A painting of an emaciated Christ hung over the table, but the sun didn't feel bad because the sun is here for the whole length of time, in which, because of the population's love for Him, He was well fed. The coconut trees outside the window of Father Pedro Morales's room shook their pointy braids at the tourists in the lens of another warm day. The broken-hearted melody that had left Mauritania was being reformed in the song of morning in San Benito.

"Be a palm to your enemy. Let the blows they give you propel you to sway in their wind."

Father Pedro's pen faltered in his hand, not from age as he was a young man but from the obsessive, compulsive disorder that was his Cross as he composed the sermon for Sunday. The sun had moved on from the kitchen to the sacristy and flickered in the flame of the Harboring Hope candle which always burned until dawn. Father Pedro got up and blew it out, and went back to his sermon, and wrote, "Darkness is wary of even the smallest light, because it is sincere." Then he felt bad about the candle which had given him such inspiration and relit it even though the sun was content with the dawn it had brought.

Father Pedro reevaluated his line, as he was destined to always do, and asked himself whether it was darkness or light which the congregation would hear to be sincere. The thought that it could be darkness disturbed him.

Father Pedro has three books on his table. The Holy Bible, the King James Version, which is bound in red cloth, a copy of Platero and I, by Juan Ramon Jimenez, and a very thick tome about Mayan Religious beliefs. He draws from each of these for his sermon, and from his observations of the sun.

Father Pedro was more a missionary than a priest, of course. But he was still relied upon to provide the Sunday sermon, and to arrange for something to eat. Sister Maria Farquez is the mission cook. She's very petite and sweet and everything she cooks she cooks without meat. Father Pedro talked to her about this. He felt if she could just slip in some chipped beef it might improve attendance. But Sister Maria put down her petite foot and doubled the guacamole. The truth is she had responded to a missionary ad in the Hazard, Kentucky Herald and thought she was going to Benin, which isn't far from Mauritania. So, it was rice, beans, and yams on Sunday, Tortilla scoops with guacamole on Monday, and coconuts the rest of the week. Father Pedro looked at the adzuki beans in the refrigerator.

"A change from Pinto beans," Sister Maria said.

Father Pedro put his mask on and went out into the parking lot. A man was interfering with the children who were trying to play baseball. Father Pedro had never seen the man before. The man looked disheveled and out of place. "But, I can hit like a rock," he kept stammering, pleading for a turn at bat. The Pinata on the porch thought he was a riot and laughed so hard he almost exploded. Valentine sat down on a rock and threw some kid's glove, which he had appropriated, onto the ground. "But, I'm good at it," he said. Father Pedro went over to him and addressed him honestly.

("Are you crazy") "Can I help, you, Senor?"

"I may have been brought here to play baseball," the new man stammered. "But these indians won't let me."

"I see!" Father Pedro said. "But have you shown them your papers. That way they can see who they're dealing with. I'm sure they will let you play if you can do that."

"That's a good idea, Father. I'm not sure what papers you're talking about. But even if I did I probably left them in my office and I have no idea where that is. I was also kidnapped, you know."

"Well, this is certainly complicated. How about if we let the children continue their game and you and I have a chat in MY office. Do you like Pinto beans."

Sister Maria Farquez was armed. Father Pedro frowned on it, but the kids thought she was very cool. It was a Colt 45, and she had it in a holster that swiveled when Valentine came in to her kitchen.

The moon is a collector of objects. Like secrets, glances, car fare, and romances. Each of these things is kept in a separate jar and buried on the far side where the wild things are. This is where they ferment, and foment, and are labeled as scones and where the wild things eat them thru their mouth and their nose.

In the barrio Carmen turned to her husband.

"Autry. Where did you leave Mr. V."

"At the orphanage. On the porch. I should probably go back this morning and see if he got adopted."

"You mean go back and get him. Is nobody going to adopt him. He's too old and too opinionated. That man is gonna start a revolution in some poor country someday. I'm surprised they let you cross over the border with him."

"He was asleep. I told them he was a rich man, and he would come back and reward them. But you're right. I should go look for him. He could be anywhere by now."

The moon flipped over to the far side, and though it was faint and appeared to be wiggling and Carmen and Autry Ramos had no idea it was alive and giggling.

Sister Maria could tell an adverb when she saw one. And out the little window over her little stove she could see a stranger coming who wasn't "quite" there. Maria swiveled her holster and turned the burners on and waited for Valentine and father Pedro to come in. When he did so she could tell that he was odd. Not just because he came in first without caution, but because he smiled at her like she was beautiful. Actually, Valentine was smiling at her holster. It reminded him of another one he had come across in the States.

"Excuse me, ma'am, but are you Rio Margie Marie?!?"

"No, Senor, I am not."

"You're sure about that."

"I feel I would know."

"It was just a thought. Do you have anything to eat."

"Do you like beans."

"What do you put on them."

"More beans. It comes in a bowl."

"Sister Maria, this is Mr. Valentine Odey. He's visiting us from California."

"New York."

"Oh right, New York. But I thought you lived in California."

"It was temporary. I was getting my teeth fixed."

"Well, if they fixed them you could sit down at this table which I have made for you!" said Sister Maria Farquez, interested.

Valentine took his baseball cap off and fluffed it in the air.

"The first meal I've had since The Crossing. They wouldn't even give me a sucker."

'Well I don't think that was fair."

"Nor I. Are you sure you're not Rio Margie Marie."

Sister Maria could tell that this Rio person was an important source in the past for Valentine.

"Come sit down, Mr. Valentine and I'll dish up the best beans you've ever had."

Father Pedro smiled and thought he should leave these two alone.

"Would you like some tomato sauce, too."

"Would I!"

Valentine was disposing of the last pinto bean in its sauce and swirled his soft tortilla around the bowl.

Swirling is a bad thing for Valentine to do, as his mind starts swirling, too. The pretty girl beside him in the red jumpsuit didn't help matters. Valentine was past the far side of the moon and on his way to Mars.

"I don't think the attendants will tell us much, you know," he said to her, "As I'm sure a lot of what they do is secret. Did you bring your decoder?"

"My what!"

"Your decoder. Mine is pretty old but I'm glad I kept it. You can use it if we get in a jam and I'm detained."

"I get off in Chicago."

"Oh."

"Oh, what?"

"Oh. Thank you. I was starving."

"Well, of course, you're welcome. Are you going to be staying here at the Mission."

"That's uncertain. I'll probably be collected by Autry today. He's from San Benito, you know, and I believe he's seeing if his family will let me stay with them."

"There's always room here if they don't."

Valentine disembarked from the Space-X Capsule and thought it looked like Barcelona.

Autry started out with the porch, but the porch was giving up nothing. The Pinata shook his head from side to side which created a Starburst avalanche. Florette was arranging her hoop skirt and the geranium was potted. Autry went looking for Father Pedro. Father Pedro was working on his sermon. He wondered what Christ was working on as he walked thru the desert. "The days went on, devoid of all that was good or interesting, that went into nights. I thought of leaving Capernaum for home. Going back to my office." Wait. Christ had an office? I didn't even think he had a chair. "Acapello. Broken hearted melody. Van Snyder. Lord Huron. The man who lives forever." Father Pedro was falling into his normal abyss. Consulting notes which had nothing to do with the situation, hoping a spark would light. And then taking forever to sift thru the ashes. Autry found him somewhere on the Nile, talking to John. "Have you seen a scraggly fellow with bad teeth and a watch." "You mean Valentine." "Yeah, him!" "Try the kitchen."

"Hey, Sister, what's cookin," was the sound of Autry and a familiar one to Sister Maria as he came into her kitchen. Over in the corner, of the middle of the room, sat Valentine with his bowl and a minty old broom.

"I've been put to work to earn my keep," Valentine said, to ward off any exclamations about him. 'So, you can just continue to address Sweet Maria."

"There you are!!!" Autry exclaimed, none the less, "I've been looking for you!"

"Oddy is in my care now, since apparently he was abandoned."

"He who has been abandoned, and slighted, and robbed," shouted Valentine, to expand on Sister Maria's defense.

"He's now sleeping in the Laundry Room until he's mentally recovered."

"Well, that might be awhile. 'Oddy?'"

"It's pronounced A h d d y. He's no longer Irish."

"I'm Bulgarian now, and Sister Maria and I are engaged."

"Oddy, shut up. Let me handle this."

Valentine stood up and cried,

"Women and cats, if you compulsion use, The pleasure which they die for will refuse."

"My God, Oddy, what's that about."

"Sister Maria, you have to give Valentine back to me now before Thomas Chatterton consumes him. He really will go on and on if you let him."

"Save me, Sister Maria, from what I suspect will be a large brood of demanding children and a heroic spouse. I'll never fit in. But with you I am filling up, like with ethel gas."

"Oh, isn't he strange!"

Father Pedro came in, saw that he had fallen into a trap and left immediately.

Carmen Ramos opened the door and smiled broadly at Valentine. A number of young children clung to her and gaped at him, also. Valentine said, "I knew it."

Dinner was wonderful, although Valentine missed Maria's beans, and after that the children asked him if he would read them a book. Valentine looked in his bag for something appropriate. He always liked Bank Shot, by Donald Westlake, but it might be too unbelievable. Westlake would laugh at that. Stealing a whole bank, not just robbing it. And then, where to put it. Valentine put it back, reluctantly. His Polish favorite, Z. Miloszewski, and the State Prosecutor, Teodor Szacki, was way too long, and Inspector Imanishi Investigates too obscure, everything by Philip Dick too crazy, even for Valentine, and, unfortunately, City Trap, by the Master, John Dalton, too dark. That left Adlai Stevenson. And Valentine pulled him out of his bag slowly, ending with a flourish.

The large brood gasped and cheered. Adlai Stevenson, His Life and Legacy, A Biography by Porter McKeever.

"Have you heard of him," Valentine asked.

"No," the chorus replied.

"Well, we'll have to take care of that."

More cheers. Aren't kids wonderful.

Valentine didn't know where to start. In time he would get to the candidate's eloquent choice of words. Adlai was a politician. A Democrat. Although his wit wasn't as good as Bob Dole's he was also funny.

Valentine explained with great gesticulations that Adlai was a friend of the working class, and that he would rather sit under a tree and regard the beauty of a field in Illinois than ride in a grand car. This presented some difficulty as the kids would rather ride in a grand car. But Valentine's gesticulations persuaded them that Adlai Stevenson was a great man.

"What happened to this man, Sir."

"He lost," Valentine replied. "But that's where you come in! You will have to take up the mantle of Adlai Stevenson."

More cheers. Valentine thought of having children.

Valentine regretted that Factorus was not there to see his transformation. Factorus was a Crow who lodged on his window sill back at Nike where Valentine had worked and been tasked with solving puzzles about population graphics and what Nike should do about it. Valentine called Factorus, Factorus, in lieu of all the facts that he, Valentine, was supposed to have at his fingertips. Valentine kept a bag of peanuts on his desk there and lobbed them at Factorus, who easily picked them off, like a sleek boxer. As a middle manager Valentine was always worried about the shifting of feet and hearts. In desiring that everything stay the same Valentine was not a very creative manager, and he gave very little thought to the role of children. His transformation now was to make children part of a bigger heart. Therefore, he wished that Factorus was there to see him start.

"Do you have any peanuts."

"We have pecans."

"With shells?"

"Without."

"It's not the same. But thank you, I may not need them, anyway." Then Valentine went on a rant about the beauty of Guatemala. The Mayan mysteries and the palm trees and the roots under them that tied everything up neatly. All of them watched him wave and heard him lovingly out, which pleased Valentine.

"And now It's time for bed. Even politicians need their rest. Off with all of you. Except for you, Mr. Odey."

"Apparently, it's Oddy now."

"Whatever."

In the quiet that remained Carmen, who was really born in Paris, said, "That was lofty talk, Senor Valentine. I know you didn't make it up but to repeat it in South America to the children may be confusing, or even dangerous. The goal here is to get out."

"But the goal here should be to stay."

"To do what? It's difficult enough to eat. To eat safely is even more difficult. And the mission is falling down around the Father. There's no cathedral or even chapel big enough to bring us in. No, Senor Oddy, it's better to chance it at The Crossing. Autry explained to me what you used to do, and I'm sorry if we mess up your charts but we have to think of a better purpose for our time than going to Walmart."

Valentine regretted his charts. If he ever saw Factorus again he would complain bitterly. He looked out the window. Of course it was empty of crows at this time of night, especially the one he was looking for.

Florette told Father Pedro that Valentine had asked her to marry him.

Under what circumstances was this?" Father Pedro asked, rather surprised.

"It was on the porch when he first arrived. We were embracing on my rocker in front of the Pinata. I was worried he might be a Sicario, although he looks like somebody who sells shoes, so I said, 'Shoot me, and I will die with you.' But then I decided to get up."

"I have to tell you, Florette, that this conflicts with certain things our guest told me about his relationship with Sister Maria."

"He's not to be trusted, Father, nor is she. I've made my case and I'd like to be married this Sunday."

"I'll get back to you."

Father Pedro asked Valentine to come in.

"Valentine, Florette told me that you had an intimate encounter with her on the porch. Do you have a gun."

"Are you telling me I need to be armed. I haven't even proposed a revolution yet."

"No, I'm concerned you have made it appear that way, to get out of a proposal that occurred to Florette."

"Maybe Sister Maria should sit in on this."

"I'll go get her."

In Father Pedro's absence Valentine put his hands on his hips and threw his head back. He hurt his neck.

"Oddy, what have you done now."

"Florette told Father Pedro that I have a gun. But I don't even have a very good aim."

"I never said you actually had a gun. The question was, did you or did you not propose to Florette."

"Where was this, Oddy."

"On the porch. I proposed as politely as I could that she get off me. I probably would have said anything to see Kyle Rodriguez again. But even Socrates made an apology. So, I guess I could."

"This sounds like a misunderstanding. I'll speak with Florette. But you have to admit, Valentine, that we don't know a lot about you."

Father Pedro went to look for Florette and found her on the porch. She was looking thru Pinata's pectorals for a Kit Kat Bar.

"God, Pinata, everything in here is melted. We gotta get you in the shade more. Hi, Rev. Did you talk to the Stranger."

"I've spoken to him, Florette, and I think this is a big misunderstanding."

"So he's trying to get out of it, huh."

"He said that he has a big respect for you but it didn't involve marriage and he apologizes if you misunderstood him."

"He apologized."

"Pretty much. So, can we just forget the whole thing because I gotta get back to my sermon."

"If you'll make my tragedy part of your sermon I'll forget it."

"Deal."

Father Pedro went back to the office, trying to think if there was anything in his three resources that could mend this fence.

Father Pedro Morales tried not to show favoritism with his parishioners or any of the team in the bunks. And he tried to extend this courtesy to his Three Resources of material. *Platero and I* was the youngest but its wisdom was maybe the oldest. The Mayan Philosophy spirited him off into a magical realm, and the King James Version of The Bible, with its red cloth cover was his rock. Now he set all three before him and asked them who wanted to speak to him first.

"In our Maya heritage the village is the center of the World and is held up at each of its four pillars by one of the gods. This can be Dangerous, or this can be Strong. K'uh, the Devine life source of existence sits by the entrance and lets us in. If one of the gods gets bored and moves there could be an earthquake."

"In my Father's House here are many Mansions. If it were not so I would have told you." How often are we hung up by the meaning of 'Many Mansions.' Does this mean that there's room for all of us. That there's always room in the Inn. Or does it mean that there are many ways to be with God. Or there are many ways to love God. Does it mean God moves around a lot. We always dwell on the first part. But what about the second part. "If it were not so I would have told you." I have to tell you that this has always been the star's part for me. "If it were not so I would have told you." We have an Honest God. We can trust God. He, in the big hat, might leave some room open for us to decide what is being talked about, but you can trust Him, or Her. It might not always be good news, but you have the reliability of Trust. "If it were not so I would have told you."

In *Platero and I* there is a chapter called The Little Girl. All of these chapters are short, and therefore with power. "The little girl was Platero's delight. As soon as he saw her coming toward him among the lilacs in her little white dress and her rice-straw bonnet, calling him in a finicky little voice: "Platero, Plateri-llo!" the little donkey would try to break his rope, and would leap just like a child and bray excitedly.

She in blind confidence would pass once and again under him, kick him softly, and put her hand, a candid lily, in his big rosy mouth lined with big yellow teeth; or holding his ears, which he placed within her reach, and she would call him all the affectionate variations of his name: "Platero! Plateron! Platerillo! Platerucho!"

In the long days that the little girl in her crib sailed downriver toward death, no one remembered Platero. She, in feverish delirium, called him plaintively: "Plateri-llo!" And to the dark, sigh filled house would come the distant, doleful call of her friend."

Valentine was invited by the Ramos's oldest boy, Carlos, to play ball with his friends. Valentine almost wept at this opportunity.

"Can I hit?"

"You can come up to bat."

Carlos was 13. An awkward age but one where a boy was starting to feel his prowess. "We have girls on the team, too, he said. You'll like Rene. She plays second.

"What will I play?" Valentine asked.

Probably First, if you're a good scooper. A lot of the throws are short."

"Geology was one of my favorite subjects in college."

"Ok."

Carlos played Centerfield and yelled in encouragement in Spanish and French. Manny played third and shortstop. He wore gloves on both hands to respect each position and threw one off when he knew which way the ball was going. Rene guarded second. Preacher was in left. Washington in right with his rocket arm. And Rosy, a disabled girl with a padded Russian winter hat for a catcher's mitt, was the catcher. The average age was 12. Valentine was now 75.

Father Pedro was the Pitcher. Valentine said, "Show me what you got." And he stood there like Ted Williams with his bat resting on his left shoulder and his feet spread apart. This wasn't softball. The Rev threw it by him and Florette in the stands, yelled, "Hit it, Val!" which was too late. The stranger adjusted his stance, looked hard at the pitcher, and whistled lowly, "tweet, tweet." But even this wasn't enough and he was almost out. Florette was losing confidence. The Pinata was laughing, and Valentine hit it out of the park. From then on he was a Mayan God.

Sunday came and Carmen was busy getting everyone dressed, including Valentine.

"Where did you get those shoes," she said.

"They were given to me when I retired. Actually I had them on at the time and they told me I could keep them."

"Well, we're going to retire THEM right now. Here, put these gaucho boots on."

"But they have weird designs. Won't this bring unnecessary attention to me."

"I need to get reports where you're at, so we don't lose you. So attention is good."

"Carlos, get your brothers moving. If we're not there first we won't have a pew to sit in. I'm tired of the aisle. Autry, where are our daughters."

"They're putting ribbons in their hair. Mr. Oddy gave them quite a few."

"I got them at the stable. I hope the horses don't mind."

"Ok, we all ready?"

"I have a coin which I'd like to put in the offering basket. Do you have an envelope?"

"Just toss it in."

"That sounds so pedantic. I thought we were Catholics."

"We're Mayans. Last one there gets sacrificed. You ready."

Valentine got in the car.

"Is this a Hudson."

"Yes, it is.'

"Then we might all fit. My God, what's that thing on the floor."

"It's a enema kit. Honore's goat is clogged up. We're going to drop it off."

"Do we have any goats."

"No, but it's still useful."

Valentine was very quiet for the rest of the ride.

Father Pedro Morales was feeling his age. He was all of 33. He wondered if he was worthy. His obsessive-compulsive disorder was commanding the stage as he took his place behind the thin podium.

"Welcome to the day the Lord made, and what a fine day it is!"

"AMEN," loudly rang out in the small chapel. And a window which had been propped open fell down with a bang on two pigeons who were trying to raise a family. Sister Maria ran over to them and petted them, and blew upon them. After a while the two pigeons got back up on the ledge and stared disappointed at the window. Father Pedro put his first index card on the bottom and started over.

"Good Morning. Rene, could you go outside and tell the people out there that I said, good morning."

"Sure thing, Rev."

"And the rest of you can say hello to each other and write your names on your envelopes while we wait for Rene to get back."

"Hello, how are you," Valentine said to an elderly congregant behind him, "I'm the First Baseman."

Rene came back and everybody put their pencils away.

"This is the day that the Lord made, and everything that goes on today is His doing. I'm just the vessel that the water gets poured out of. But all of you have brought the water to me at one time or another. Can you imagine my problem trying to sift through water to determine what to say, But here we are. We need a new building. Not just of a physical kind but a spiritual kind. Both are ongoing. The first part we don't seem to have a lot of control over, in our fiscal straits, but the second part we do. Love and kindness doesn't cost money. It might cost time. It might cost pride. But it doesn't cost money. The pillars of our community watch the respect we give to each other. Otherwise they get the idea in their heads that we can be fooled. So I encourage you to go to your neighbor's house, even in these times, and even if you have to stand outside in your mask, and bring honor to them with your interest in them. Bring hope to them with your honesty, and bring food to them with your love. Other than that it's really hot in here with that window closed so we're done for today. Go in Peace. And may the Lord be with you. Somebody feed the donkey."

"Amen."

"That was it!" Valentine said. "Where was the offering basket. What about my coin," the stranger asked Carmen.

"There's a can you can put it in by the door. The clink is supposed to please to the gods. If you put paper money in they get suspicious."

"We didn't sing either. I was hoping we could break out with Hold on –
I'm Coming, by Sam & Dave. I don't know if it was intended to be a spiritual,
but it had a lot of energy in 1966."

"I don't know if the walls could stand it. They're all about to fall down.
That's why the Father Pedro keeps everything short. Plus he has this writing
problem."

"Father," Florette said, grabbing the Father's frock. "I don't remember my
name being mentioned."

"It was implied, Florette, and was the reason for the tour."

"Well, I'm not good with riddles, but if you say I was implied then I'll
accept it. There certainly were some beautiful parts to it."

"Autry and I just like getting out," Carmen said. "Do you like the cake"

Valentine turned his thoughts to sweet Maria, whom he had almost
forgotten about.

"Where is that vixen, anyway."

"Hi, Oddy. Remember me."

It was a long time since Valentine had been in a village or small town. At
Nike he had lived in a complex of halls and cubicles which resembled a small
town, but it wasn't the same. His number of acquaintances was very small as
he didn't like to go out in the hall. If it wasn't for Factorus he might have
gone completely mad.

Now he was out for a Sunday ride in San Benito on the bike. The sun was
departing from its mission in San Benito, withdrawing from the sacristy and
the ballfield and beginning its big sweep to Indonesia, where it will be
welcome with open arms. The moon, meanwhile, is already in Jakarta in the
windows of lovers, above the sill and beneath the shade, listening to all the
sweet lies they say. All of these conversations and the moon will soon be
pushed around to San Benito, to be resumed. Valentine waved to all of them
and wished them well, and continued on his way.

Valentine felt for his phone in his pocket. It wasn't there, of course. It was
back in his office at Nike, ringing on his desk, next to someone new, on Zoom.
Valentine wondered if he left his window open, but even if he did it was
probably closed by now. New occupant with new rules. Immediately Valentine
thought of Factorus, The Crow who lodged on his window sill at Nike, to catch
peanuts which Valentine tossed to him. This was a heavy memory, and
brought a lump to Valentine's throat. "Oh, Factorus, where are you now."

Valentine laughed, if Factorus could only see his new shoes.

He swung his gaucho boots out to the side and pedaled wildly ahead. Above Valentine the air was short and several birds of prey were discussing events that appealed to them. But none of it appealed to Valentine. He was earthbound, for today, and the immediate future.

"Where are you going, Oddy?"

"I'm going out of town to the Ruins to see what's behind the False Door."

"I don't see why that's so important., Oddy," Maria told him. "I'm really worried about your brain. You need to focus on something simple." But Valentine was determined, and was on his way.

Every village has dogs. A pack of them approached Valentine and he clapped. "You can come with me if you want but at some point you have to go back." Disappointed the leader gave a bark and they went looking for their own bone to uncover in the jungle hearth.

Then the trees intervened, offering to shade him and help him breathe. But to them he also declined. I will go as I go and intermittently appreciate your soul.

Then the air, offering breeze, but this he declined, too. It would take away from others the refreshment that they need.

When at last he reached the place where the Ruins were he parked and stood respectfully back. They were magnificent. He sat in a lawn chair and wondered how the Mayans did this without any evidence of wheels or bulldozer tracks. He thought his own life resembled this one, with stone upon heavy stone laid up in the past, and he didn't know how he got here either. So they were even.

Valentine began his search for the False Door. There was a recess in the back which he speculated was either the bathroom or the False Door. He concluded it was the False Door because there was no gender sign beside it. Either that or the Mayans were more enlightened than he thought. The sign that was on the door, however, said, 'You get one question.' "I guess this is to keep pilgrims from lingering, going over every question they have in their heads," Valentine said. A voice from inside the door said, "Thank you for asking. Next person."

Valentine felt cheated. But after all he was just an offering at the door and it looked like he wasn't getting in. But then the door said, "Do you want a peek." To which Valentine of course said, "YES!" Then the False Door opened to a feminine chamber of beautiful craft. In the corner Valentine saw the wheelbarrows, and whinnied and laughed. "I knew it!" he said and slipped out of the chamber like a cat.

"Excuse me, Senor, but are you alright," Senorita Z exclaimed, as she lined her students up behind her and told them not to complain. "But teacher, he is a funny man. He sounds like a horse. He looks like a horse."

"Enough of that!"

"Oh, sir, don't cry. You know how children are. But is there a reason you are whinnying at the False Door. Are you trying to contact someone who has passed. Perhaps the horse of a Queen. Are you related to the deceased. Do you fear for a horse that is suffering who you would like to see released."

"NOOOOOOO. I've found out how we got here and how each of us in our lives has managed to get stacked!"

"Oh, you mean the wheelbarrows."

And Valentine went back to town, downcast. He should have asked about the meaning of life with his one question. He missed it. Maybe something had been learned, but another opportunity passed.

"Do you think Adlai Stevenson ever stayed here."

'In San Benito?"

"Yeah."

The Pinata shrugged which created a far rustle of peppermint patties. "If he did he enjoyed a lot of peace and quiet. I don't think he had family here."

"We should create a family for him. That can be our mission."

"We already have a Mission."

"A fan club then. What we need is a Adlai Stevenson Fan Club."

"Oh, sure. Poor Guatemalans going to rally around a dead US politician who lost the big election, twice. Wait a minute, they might."

"His speeches will live on in the barrio, and on the ballfield, and in Sister Maria's kitchen. We'll create a movement."

"Who will we be against. If it's the government ours isn't so forgiving."

"We will be for things. For the good things. Adlai will lead us."

"Oh, Good Grief, I'm going to have to load up for this one."

Under the porch Kyle Rodriguez extended his nails and smiled like Kelly Anne Conway.

Down in San Benito
Where the Sun is on the line
Carmen is in the living room singing,

"I heard it through the grapevine."

She has her broom up by
Her mouth and swishes with her skirt
Around the room with Gladys Knight
And Autry's muddy dirt.

"Ooh-Ooh I heard I through it the grapevine
Not much longer would you be mine
I'm just about to lose my mind
Honey, honey yeah."

Carmen singing to the picture of Christ
From her very core
As she passes by His place of Honor
Over the pile of shoes by the big front door.
"I'm just about to lose my mind
Yeah, yeah."

Valentine in his room out of sight feels that something is amiss in the forest which will delay dinner. But Carmen has entranced him.

"People say, 'You hear from what you see,
Not, not, not, from what you hear.'
I can't help but being confused
If it's true won't you tell me Dear?"

"Ooh-Ooh I heard I through the grapevine
Not much longer would you be mine
Ooh-Ooh, I heard it through the grapevine
And I'm just about to lose my mind
Honey, honey yeah."

Carmen's skirt brushes against his door and Valentine feels a tingle go up his spine. Something is amiss in the forest alright and Valentine is going to bed without dinner tonight.

The mission is being taken over by developers, going to gentrify the area, call it the Mission District. Get everyone come down from San Francisco to relocate. This is the news that Carmen was trying, unsuccessfully, to sweep under the rug. News that included the ballfield, the chapel, the dormitory, the kitchen, and the porch. Unless something got in the way of it. Valentine called the first meeting of the Adlai E. Stevenson Fan Club to order.

The first meeting of the Adlai Stevenson Fan Club to promote good things and the fields of Illinois took place at Home Plate on the Carlos Merida Ballfield, next to the dormitory for kids who were displaced one way or the other. The whole vulnerable team was there, with all their borrowed gear, gathered around their First Baseman. Valentine has his shirt off and is showing the team his tattoo. *Power In A Few Can Never Replace The Strength In Many.* It's a very long tattoo and goes under his armpit.

Where's Rosy?"

"She had an appointment. Manny's pushing her, so he'll be late, too."

Valentine put on Rosy's padded winter hat, pulled out *Adlai Stevenson, His Life And legacy,* from his duffle bag and started reading to the San Benito Mission Rats.

"This is Adlai."

'I believe the people are wise and just.'

"But now the carpetbaggers have taken over," Valentine added to Adlai. "And all the things you are used to are for sale. Now is the time to abide by things they cannot sell, and see where that takes us."

The Stranger was mixing Adlai with his own rhetoric. Adlai had the advantage.

"What page are you on, Sir."

"The page of history."

"And what page are we on."

"That's for you to decide, Carlos."

"In the Popol Vuh it says when one of the gods shifts his burden it causes an earthquake."

"Good, Preacher. You're getting it!"

"How bout me, Sir. Can I get it."

"Of course, you can, Washington. And you've got the arm to prove it."

"Love is on second!"

"Rene, Love is second to none. You go, girl."

Valentine looks at the book in his hands and gets wound back up with Adlai.

'What counts is not just what we are against, but when we are for. Who leads us is less important than what leads us – what convictions, what courage, what faith – win or lose,' Valentine patiently presented.

231

But soon Valentine was anxious to hurry up the point and began jumping up and down like a shopping cart. "Kids, here it is. **YOU ARE THE THIRSTY ONES.** Backpackers into the wilderness. Winsome Reclaimers of the Planet. Storers of Justice. Wild orchids on the sides of hills. Pamphlets strewn on the barricades. You are the pencils and brushes. Viva Liberté, Kids, VIVA, VIVA THE ART OF JEAN BASQUIAT."

"My God, Oddy, what are you talking about!"

The Stranger wiped his brow like a fish monger in the wet market at Wuhan. His dark countenance receded and a lightness appeared on his face. He had an idea.

"My Sweet Maria, that's it."

"What's it. Oddy, I think your brain has exploded."

"The walls. All these walls. We have to re-use them. They're about to come tumbling down anyway. It's time to boost them."

"My God, it's too late," Maria cried. "Somebody go get the Father, and the Pinata, and maybe Florette, too."

On a cot in the Dormitory Valentine was being tended to by the Father, the Pinata, and Florette, who had carried him in.

Valentine was quite feverish and all his connections to reality were lost. He was hallucinating about honor, and duty, and country. He imagined he was General MacArthur addressing the graduating class at West Point. On the table beside him a poem called 'The Failings Of The Marksman' which the General might not actually approve of was fluttering to get his attention. The dedication said, For the vulnerability and fabrications of old age, and for the wonderful Night Nurses at Cayuga Med and Strong Memorial Hospitals.

Sweet Maria read to him.

~ The passive sweet boy turned the corner on the street.

The Marksman fired at him and missed by 20 feet.

The passive, sweet boy stirred in his sleep.

The passive sweet boy thought the air was like milk and honey inside a bottle.

The Marksman thought the air was a disturbance and rested his stock upon the bottle.

The passive, sweet boy reached out to swat it.

The passive sweet boy thought in flat indigo colors.

The Marksman mistook him for a mystic over whom Van Morrison hovered.

The passive sweet boy lay watchful loosely in his covers.

The passive sweet boy carried his copy of La Belle Dame sans Merci.

The Marksman followed him in his sight.

Valentine began to weep.

The passive sweet boy looked down to regard a local flower.

The Marksman took out his revolver and flicked his ashes upon the tower.

Valentine thrashed on his cot and complained that everything tasted sour.

The passive sweet boy kissed his mother and arranged her sheets.

The Marksman fired again and missed by 14 feet.

Valentine screamed and gnashed his teeth.

The passive sweet boy was hidden in the sun.

The Marksman waited for the sun to go behind a tree.

Valentine tried to reach out of the dormitory and move the tree and sweated profusely.

The passive sweet boy began to hum as though he were a honey bee.

The Marksman cupped his ears and missed him, the flower, the book, the tree, and everything.

Valentine relaxed and found a spot in Florette's arms where he could rest comfortably ~

"Do you think we should take him to the Dispensary, Father."

"I think the medicine he requires is already working. But I can't say what will come of it." The Pinata, however, had an idea about that, and began stocking up on Clark Bars.

"Why are you going to do that!!!?" Sweet Maria asked, of Valentine, who had been discharged and was back in the kitchen resting.

Valentine had just told Maria that the team was going to go on a mission to get The Alamo.

Sweet Maria shrunk down in her chair and pulled her 45 out from under her.

"Go on," she said, disappointed that her efforts had come to this.

"Because the people are just and wise, which Adlai pointed out to me. I know it sounds crazy, but the Ruins and The Alamo are from a quarry right around here, right down to the false door to trick tourists. I checked, yesterday, even though I didn't know what I was doing at the time. But today with Adlai's help and our crumbling monastery in mind I got it. The Spaniards took our stones to Texas! Stole them right out from under the Mayan's nose and we're going to go get em back. Bring em home where they belong, to San Benito. And then we're going to build a beautiful chapel, and a ballfield and a real nice rock fence around that so Kyle Rodriguez can sit on it and scare the crap out of our opponents. We'll be the pride of Guatemala and those developers can go to Honduras, see how that works out with The Military."

Maria was exhausted. She made a note to finish reading The Trial, which she had begun in high school.

"Did you tell the Father about this."

"I told him that material has been donated by the US Government. He's all for it."

"How about Texas."

"Ted Cruz, who is Texas, is for anything that takes the attention away from him until Dallas warms up. Besides, with this pandemic the gift shop is closed and nobody remembers The Alamo, anymore. So, we're going to go get it, and relocate it where it will be appreciated."

"Oddy, have you given any thought to how you're going to get it here."

"Me and Carmen are working on that. I think it has something to do with Hudsons."

The line of Hudsons that approached the border below San Antonio was a sight. All the guards came out to look at it.

"It looks like a sea of turtles."

"That's probably why they changed the model."

"Are they coming here?!!! Maybe they're part of the parade."

The parade of course was the Battle of Flowers on the streets of San Antonio. A wonderful event, part of Fiesta San Antonio in the spring, to celebrate the return of flowers and the fun of shoes.

Valentine leaned his head out the first Hudson and greeted the border guard.

"Hasta Luego! What a beautiful day, eh."

"Excuse me, Senor, but what is this parade that you have going."

"We're part of the Big One. We brought our own float. We promise to go home afterwards."

"Well, I'm going to take a count and the same number better be back here by dark."

"Oh, we will be."

"Do you have anything in your trunks."

"Wheelbarrows"

"Well, that's ok. As long as it's not people."

"Hasta Luego, eh."

"What does Hastra Luego men, anyway," Valentine asked Carmen.

"See you later."

Maria was in charge of registering the San Benito entry. She put on a hat that looked like she'd been to the Kentucky Derby and pulled back the flap on a big tent.

"Hi, Darlin. You here to register."

"I guess."

"So tell me how big it is and what your theme is."

"It's a porch, basically. Part of our Mission. If we left it it was going to get gentrified, with tea sets and Jardine's. It's about 10 x 20 ft and has a donkey on it, and a disabled girl, on a rocker that looks like a horse,, and a Pinata. And Valentine, who has some issues I'd rather not go into, and a cat. That's about it. Oh, a bike, and a geranium, that's potted. Our theme is salvation."

"Does it have a proper skirt around it."

"Oh, yeah. And Valentine does, too."

"How does it move. Do you have a car pulling it."

"We have a Hudson, but it will be busy. Autry and Florette are going to be under it, instead, coaxing the four pillars to keep up. It's Mayan powered."

"Perfect! I'll tell the Mayor."

"You should tell him to bring all his men to the parade, keep their eye on the float. They'll have less things to worry about after that."

"So, what's the name of your float."

"'Platero and I.' We borrowed that from Juan Ramon Jimenez but I don't think he'll mind."

"Well, it's getting late. So, you should probably get your ass over there and get in line."

"Thank you, Mrs. ...."

"Pertle. Eleanor Pertle. I used to know somebody name Valentine!"

"What did he do for you."

"He washed my shutters and cleaned my rugs, and then he went to work somewhere 9-5. He was a little odd, big on spelling, but I didn't mind."

"I think it's the same one."

Flash mobs appear to celebrate something. Usually one celebrant starts to play something, or sing, and then a child approaches them and joins in, with something like a oboe, or a clarinet. People stop, they get out their own oboes, and the celebration takes off from there.

In our case the doors of the Hudsons opened in the air like a row of apertures of old cameras and adjusted to the silence surrounding Historic Alamo. Father Pedro Morales got out and crossed himself, and crossed himself again just to be sure he got the angles right and knelt on the broken ground outside the reception area. On the ramparts of the fortress Jim Bowie peered over the wall.

"That you, Father."

"It is, Jim."

"We've been defending this a long time, Father."

"It's your defense we long for, Jim, the defense of Freedom, Liberty and Happiness. It's your defense we want, and the stones."

"You got Valentine with you."

"He's with the Sheriff. They won't be coming here."

"Those Hudsons big enough for all of us."

"Big enough for you, and Davy, at least, if he's up yet. The rest will fit. We're been waiting a long time, Jim."

"So have we, Reverend. Time's are changin. It will be nice to be Wanted again, which is probably what's going to happen after this. I'll open the door."

Autry and Florette were struggling mightily in addition to the Four Pillars to keep up. Rosy was hugging Platero and telling him she loved him. Platero was nuzzling her back and steadying the rocking horse she was strapped to. The tassel swishing at the end of Platero's tail was pissing Kyle Rodriguez off. Pinata was throwing candy to the crowd and diminishing, but laughing nonetheless. Valentine was sitting on his bike and grinning like the potted plant. All of this showed up on cell phones all around the world as the perfect picture of something that wasn't right. Danny Ocean in Hollywood said, "This looks like a heist." But it was too late to avoid that.

A low row of black plastic, which Valentine could never understand the purpose of, but which seemed to be required, encircled the dismantling site. Flags, and sleeping bags were folded up with care, and every stone was labeled and every note was there, and it was the case that not a thing was left behind, or forgotten, or really could be traced. The Father said a prayer, a benediction of sort, and Jim Bowie and Davy Crockett gave a mighty snort.

The Hudsons were packed and on their way. The Alamo Bell was on a roof in plain sight. Carmen was driving and Maria was riding shotgun with her 45 on her hip. The only thing left for Valentine to do was to draw the attention of the sheriff away from the wheelbarrows which were left to pay tribute. This is where Valentine used his ruse. This is what he was meant to do. This is why he got off his bike, put down his potted plant, hiked up his skirt, which he did, stuck out his feet, and this is why he yelled loudly in San Antonio's Festival of Flowers, "San Antonio,"

"LOOK AT MY SHOES."

MENTIONS

Thanks to Counselor Cynthia Grant Bowman, who bartered her copy of Adlai Stevenson's biography with me for a draft of my work. It's her fault.

Thanks to Norman Whitfield and Barrett Strong for writing the lyrics to I Heard It Through The Grapevine, and to Gladys Knight & The Pips who sang it to me.

Thanks to Adlai Stevenson, and Juan Ramon Jimenez. It's possible they didn't know each other.

And thanks to all my extended Michigan relatives who were kind to my mom and dad in my wandering absence.

BIG
BOY

Valentine is moved.

Valentine surveyed the state of his cell in the Bexar County Jail. He was sure any complaint of his about the Feng Sui of its arrangement would fall on deaf ears. Guest No. 327393 and his cellmate were in their county issued pink jumpsuits. Frank looked better in his. Still, the physical arrangement was difficult to appreciate. The mental aspect of his confinement was not under review. Not yet.

"What are you in for, Frank."

"Shoplifting. You."

"Pretty much the same. 'Cept we got the whole shop. So, it's probably Grand Larceny."

"You need a lawyer."

"You got a lawyer."

"No. I thought if you got one we could share."

"Do you have a phone."

"No. I thought if you had one we could share that, too."

"Have you ever had a pink jumpsuit before."

"Actually, this one is mine. I brought it with me to save the county money."

"Where do you buy pink jumpsuits."

"At the Big 'N Tall."

Valentine tried to think where he'd heard that before, but it only momentarily thru him off.

"Why do you think we're in here together, Frank."

"I was just told to see if I could get you to talk."

"They specifically picked you to see if you could get me to snitch."

"Pretty much."

"I don't think you're supposed to be so upfront about that, Frank."

"I never said I was good at it."

"Well, you're terrible at it."

"Can you give me anything."

"My loyalty to my gang is irrevocable, Frank. I might let you beat me at checkers, but that's it."

Valentine and Frank look around for a checker board. Their hunt is interrupted by an annoying screech of metal as their cell door is unbolted.

"Let's go, Red. You've been bailed out."

"May I ask by whom."

"Says he's a member of the Crow Nation. Calls himself Fly By Night. He looks a little sketchy to me. Pack your things."

"I believe my things are baked on me."

"Then let's get moving, we need the space."

"What about me!"

"Sorry, Frank, the crow said only one Whiteman at a time."

"But I'm not white."

Valentine, who was already enamoured with the nickname, Red, said, "You're not. What are you, Frank."

"I'm Asian."

"What's your last name."

"Guam."

"I'll be darn."

"Well, Sheriff, you better tell Fly By Night we have company. Let's go, Frank."

And Red Odey, which is pronounced O Day if you needed to know that, Frank Guam, and Fly By Night left by the front door.

"Why they call you Red, anyway."

"You mean the guard. Probably told I'm the pinko, Communisss, stole The Alamo."

"Well, did you."

"Nice try, Frank Guam."

Red turned to the member of the Crow Nation.

"Did you set new coordinates, yet, 'Fly By Night.'"

Fly By Night, who was of course was Factorus, the crow who prospered in Valentine's open window at Nike, was hesitant to talk in the presence of Frank and therefore just grunted.

"Frank, this is Factorus. At Nike we used to sit together on my window sill and talk about silk and cotton.   Factorus, this is Frank, an Asian plant who's supposed to get me to tell him where the Alamo went.   So, are we comfortable with each other now."

"I guess, boss. I just have to make room in the transformer."

"Where did you leave it."

"In the library, in the travel section."

Valentine's reading selection tended to drive his narrative. So, this choice pleased him.

Fly by Night took Frank Guam over to the travel section in the San Antonio Public Library to show him the transformer.

"I put it right here, behind 'Montana.' It's all folded up like a toy. It's disguised as a transformer. Pretty good, huh."

Frank Guam shrugged and spotted a catalog about Polynesia with a pretty face on it.

"Can we check this stuff out."

Meanwhile, The Communist was devouring Delmore Schwartz in the poetry section which was empty except for a cutout of Amanda Gorman beckoning people to come in.

"Maybe, but you have to have it back in two weeks. You'll probably have to mail it."

Valentine embraced Amanda Gorman and screamed wildly, "'Let us go casing the bars with the eyes of a Mongol Horseman.'"

"We won't be here."

"I thought that was very rude of them to kick us out of the library."

"We couldn't even get the transformer out."

"Some kid is probably on his way to Mars as we speak. We'll have to find an alternative means of transportation."

Our boys were sitting at the counter in a truck stop off an exit of I10. The waitress taking the order of a trucker next to them said, "You want a shower with that."

"We should get a shower," Fly By Night said.

"We don't even have enough for this meal. We start runnin I don't want to be caught in some shower."

"Yeah," Frank said, "That would be worse than being caught with our pants down. We wouldn't even have them on."

"Frank, what do you have wound around you under your jumpsuit."

"I got the cutout. We needed a feminine side, besides she's a poet."

"Besides which that and this meal is going to land us back in the masculine side of Sheriff Salazar's jail."

"You fellas ready to pay."

Red looked at the waitress in front of them, whose name was Darlene.

"Darlene, that fella next to us who just went off to have his bath offered us a ride and we'd like to pay for his meal, and ours, when he gets back. I can't remember which truck he said to put our grip in."

"You mean, Bubba."

"Oh, yeah, Bubba."

"It's the Kenworth with the red and white cab. He has a confederate flag in a snowball on the dash. It's probably running."

"Thank you, Darlene. We'll be back."

Semi's, in general terms, are beasts. They're broncos which have been tamed with paint, and chrome, and places they've seen. And in the parking lot of a truck stop they purr and growl next to each other like a drone of restless bees. The smell of diesel and departure coats them, and the fog and drizzle of rain and night bloats them. Our boys ran amongst them looking for the Queen.

"Frank, climb up on that one and see if there's a snow cone on the dash."

"It's not a Kenworth, it's a Mack."

"How do you know that."

"I used to drive one."

"You never told us that."

"You never asked."

"Then you get to drive."

"Where do I sit," Fly By Night asked.

Out of the dark, where darkness lay, they found the Kenworth in the very last bay. Factorus got in first, then Red, then Amanda and Frank, and as far as their arrangement that's the way it stayed.

On the 3rd of April Bubba was singing in the shower as his Kenworth pulled away.

Far above San Antonio Valentine said, "I wonder what's in the back."

"It's heavy," said Frank, "I can tell you that."

"We should probably check boss."

"So pull over, Frank, in that oil patch."

The boys got out. A sign said, 'Welcome to Muskogee, OK, The Place Where Squares Can Have A Ball,' and there was a big picture of Merle Haggard smoking a joint.

"When did that happen."

"Times have changed, Boss. Merle always regretted that song."

"Well, I didn't. It was very catchy. I hope he didn't change the lyrics, too."

"There's a lot of money in cannabis, Red, something you should think about."

"What I'm thinking about now is what are we hauling. How do we open this jetpack."

Rain was coming and the wind was whistling "White Lightning is the greatest thrill of all."

Clink and Crack, and the back door opened, to a Prized Bull Buffalo, the Greatest Animal of the Plains, of them all.

Fly By Night, for reasons of his own, took off his hat.

"What's that," Valentine said.

"That's a buffalo," Frank said. "Maybe he has to go out,"

"You take him out!"

The buffalo, meanwhile, was in no hurry to go out. He had a stall set up for him in the middle of the back, with sage brush and straw and a buffalo doll, and other things that buffaloes like.

"Hey, Brother, you wanna step out a minute, stretch your legs," Fly By Night coaxed, and cooed.

Valentine said he was going to wait in the cab with Amanda Gorman. which Frank had sat up between them. "I'm going to try to explain this to her before she gets freaked out."

"Frank, you got any oats or nuts under your jumpsuit."

"Come on, Big Boy, this is where it's at," Factorus said to the buffalo, empty handed.

And, eventually, curious, Big Boy clopped down the bed of the truck and walked down the plank which Factorus had set out. He looked around and sniffed the air with his magnificent brown snout.

FBN went over to Big Boy and gave him his hand to sniff. Unfortunately FBN's hand had no scent because he was a mirage in this form. Factorus knew that and told Frank to turn around.

"Oh, no, you don't!"

"Frank, turn around, it's not like that."

And with Frank turned around to study Merle, Factorus turned into a crow and got on Big Boy's back.

Big Boy lit up like he was the star bull in the rodeo show and flew by Amanda Gorman who wasn't buying anything Valentine was telling her.

"Now what," Frank said. 'I knew I shouldn't have turned my back."

Valentine looked out over the wide expanse of Oklahoma and shrugged.

"They may be picking up where they left off. We'll just have to wait, and hope they miss us."

Initially when Valentine retired, he thought about robbing banks. He had composed a note which he would use. It said, "This is a hold-up. Half dollars, only. No die packs." He put the note in the inside pocket of his gray sports jacket for safe keeping and sent it to the cleaners by mistake after wearing it for 30 years at Nike. When he got it back the note said, "No Half Dollars. Only die packs." Evidently it had been dry cleaned. Because it didn't have the pizazz that he intended. It was a long way from then to watching a buffalo stamp off wildly across a prairie with a crow on his head, but Valentine thought this beast had gotten away with something that was unfiltered. He looked admiringly at him as he disappeared over a rise on the flat earth.

"Well, Frank, if we wait here any longer the posse's going to find us. Let's go."

So, Frank buttoned up the back of the trailer and off they went. Red put his elbow out the passenger side window, and said, "Anyway, that's better."

In Salinas, KS, a state trooper pulled up alongside them and asked if they wouldn't mind he looked in the back of their truck. "We're looking for a prize bull." Valentine showed him the inside of the trailer and said, "So, are we." The trooper thought he was a bounty hunter, all set up for when he found the bounty and tipped his smokey bear hat at Valentine and Frank. When he'd gone they pulled Amanda back up from under the seat. "That was close."

A million years ago the American Steppes were covered with buffalo. Different colored people gazed at them and squeezed in where they could. Then the weather killed the people but it couldn't kill the buffalo. Then the no color people came with their guns. They didn't have 4 x 4's, or pickups or golf carts, but they did have horses and on them they rode and shot down the brown tide, or tricked them into running off cliffs, which was called 'driving.' The colored people who were left were rounded up and put on reservations and told not to complain, but they missed the buffalo. The way they had taken the buffalo was sparing and for need, and with reverence and awe. Their lips were sewn shut from disbelief that this respect was lost. It was more difficult to find this respect than to oppose it and it didn't make sense in the end to fight it. So Chief Joseph said, "Looking Glass is dead. From where the sun now stands I will fight no more forever."

A semi commands respect on the road. Especially one with an Asian, a Black Girl, and a Communist sitting in the cab. You have to look up to them regardless of what you might think. And in this case you also have a black poet sitting across from a snow cone with a confederate flag in it, both of them waving according to the rhythm of their road. With Amanda beside him our Communist thought about reading his work before an admiring audience and digging into their psyche deeply with mild and wild gesticulations. So deep that he bumped into somebody from his past. She had friends with her, too. And they were all jumbled up and flying in a balloon. Red grabbed his head and shook it. Half of them fell out on the floor and started to climb back up the gearshift. One of them had a lance.

"What was in that salad, Frank."

"Mushrooms. Fly By Night left them with us. I think they're portobellas."

"No they're not."

A blonde who had reached the 8 ball at the top of the gear shift looked at Red and threw some shade at Amanda.

"Frank, we better pull over."

"You need some dressing."

I need to be tied up."

Valentine went back to his writing. He was trying to work on literary devices, like foreshadowing.

'Looking out the window, the cell phone kept going off.'

Valentine decided not to share this with Amanda. In fact, everything he'd been writing for the last half hour was balled up on the floor of the cab.

"Where are we, Frank."

"Colorado. The Rockies are coming up."

"Maybe the thin air will aerate my brain. I'm not coming up with anything."

"Why do you have to come up with anything?"

"Because it's important, Frank. I'm trying to make an impression on Amanda.."

"She's a cutout."

"She's more than that, Frank. She's an idea. A beacon. A beacon in a harbor. A harbor I've never been in. She has style, Frank. Not that loosey goosey stuff I come up with. And besides, who's on that phone, anyway."

"It's Bubba's phone, so I suspect it's Bubba."

"Tell him we're in Shreveport, on our way to Disney World."

"You tell him!"

But Valentine had gone back to his writing.

"We should check if Bubba keeps any food in that kitchenette behind us. I mean real food, not road kill."

Valentine took Amanda with him and went into the pantry and kitchenette.

"Look at all this stuff, Amanda. If you ever wondered what Coast to Coast, Straight Thru, looks like, here it is. Grits, Hush Puppies, Aunt Jemima syrup, flapjacks from McDonalds, a mix of jerky rolls, Wonder Bread, regular mustard, Pepsi with no ice, something that looks like a squirrel, and corn nuts."

Amanda looked like a line just wasn't working out. Like Magnolia buds had fallen on a bee and smothered him.

"He didn't have any peanut butter?"

"No, and he didn't have any umeboshi dressing, either."

"Is that a crack."

"Why are you people so sensitive."

"Sensitive? Last time you ever heard a trucker ask for umeboshi dressing."

"They don't have trucks in Japan, or the Philippines."

"I don't think they have truck stops."

"How do they eat."

"They wrap it up before they leave home, like you're supposed to."

"Is that a crack about my country."

"Your country. What country do you think I live in."

"You live in Texas."

"So, what kind of sandwich is this."

"It's a Log Jam. Jerky rolls on wonder bread with regular mustard. It's an open faced sandwich."

"I don't think Bubba eats open faced sandwiches."

"You talked to him on the phone, didn't you."

"I apologized. I told him we had to go see your mother."

"What did he say."

"He said she better send you back soon or he was going to break every bone in her son's body."

"He said that."

"He also asked about Big Boy."

"What did you tell him."

"I told him Big Boy had gone on ahead."

"What did he think about that."

"He really got mad. He sounded like a lion in a jangle."

"We better hide the truck."

"I did even better. I hid the phone."

"Was he still talking."

"Yeah. I wouldn't open the glove compartment if I was you."

"Where's Amanda?"

"She's taking a nap."

"I wonder what kind of world's in Amanda's dreams."

"Probably the same one we're in. She just flies around in it in different directions."

"We should get a newspaper. I want to see how Shohei Ohtani is doing."

"Pull in to a rest stop. Bubba left some change in the door."

"What did you get."

"The Denver Post."

"Who's in it."

"Big Boy."

"You're kidding. Front Page!"

"Front Page."

"What'd it say"'

"He's in a circus. Got an act with a crow. 'Barbarian Mammal and His Manager.'"

"Our Boys!"

"I'll wake up Amanda."

Circuses are about the broad spread of ground the Tent is on, and being entertained by Big acts. Carnivals are about narrow ways and a world of feats and dubious facts. Fairs and Amusement Parks are somewhere in between with the addition of cotton candy. But intrinsically in all of them there's a need to be fooled. To be taken out of our everyday world and introduced to one that seems beyond us. In carnivals the Fat Lady says, "I can't breathe." In the circus the Fat Lady says, "Give me a squeeze!"

"What's that."

"It's a Log Jam. You want it."

"Hell no."

"Red, how can Amanda be speaking."

"Because both of us had that salad. You can actually make her say anything you want."

"Amanda, I don't want you to say anything. I just want you to think sweet thoughts until this unfortunate circumstance passes thru us."

"Here's one, Frank."

Snow's so deep
Sheep can't go anywhere
Happy to see Norm come over.

"What's that!"

"It's a haiku. I'm trying to get to the point. Not use so many words."

"You should go back to words. Lots of them."

"Words are our hearts' emotion. The number of them doesn't make them stronger."

"I didn't do that. Did you, Red."

"She's on her own. Maybe I'll let her talk to Bubba."

"Trust your GPS. Go to your friends."

"That looks like the Carrier Dome. Are we in Syracuse."

"No, we're in Commerce City, Colorado. That's the Big Tent. We've temporarily reached our destination, along with that gas station we just left."

"You took long enough. I had to use the Setters"

"I suspect they both have 'Closed' signs on them now, so it doesn't matter."

"Are we leaving Amanda with the truck."

"Of course not. I don't want her to be an incentive for some dubious group like the Patriot Front to steal it. I won't let that happen."

At that moment a Trapeze flew by our gang and the artist scooped up Amanda right out of Frank's arms. The crowd roared and Amanda's eyes fluttered like cardboard.

Then the elephants pranced around the ring and the barker cried, "Look at that, Look at that," in his big pants and gold bling.

"Where's Big Boy."

They're probably saving him for last. After all he is 'The Barbarian.'

Off to the side, outside the ring, there was a hallway of marvelous things. And in one of the rooms there was a lectern and chairs, and a sign that said, "Tall Tales Are Told Here And Real Poets Are Spared."

Red felt drawn to it. Both parts, if he could only come up with something.

But Red didn't have time as suddenly there was a roar in the Big Tent.

"Let's go, Frank."

Out in the Ring the Barbarian Mammal had appeared with his manager.

Big Boy was resplendent in his red armour suit right down to his silver dreck boots. He came out in a screen of smoke and dust like Herman Munster emerging from the dungeon in a Black and White Tux.

The kids were screaming, the adults were screaming, and even the circus lights were screaming in the relentless room.

Factorus in his berth was perched upside down on Big Boy. The Strong Man stepped back, looked at Big Boy and Factorus and said, "I can't lift that!"

And above them all Amanda was swinging like a Jaguar who in this case was all black, out from her stand and gracefully back.

And then the tether snapped.

It was like the air was sucked out of the tent. As quiet as a tenant who couldn't pay his rent. The Jaguar batted at the air and the Strong Man rushed from where he sat. Everyone was dropping in despair. It was like The Wallendas in Detroit and you were there. Frank and Red looked on helplessly. But Factorus flew like a bat from his seat and saved Amanda from falling a hundred feet. They looked like the perfect He & She, and landed on Big Boy as softly as a flea.

And then the Tent exploded instead. Everyone hollered and clapped and Death defeated, slunk out the back.

"Well that was something," Valentine offered after they had all squeezed back into the Kenworth. The original seating arrangement was tight. Frank driving, then Amanda, then Red, and then Factorus, who was wearing a crow feather and preferred again to be called 'Fly By Night.' The Kenworth struggled as Big Boy was safely in his shack, munching on hay and blueberries and reading all about himself in the Denver Post.

On their way out of Colorado our gang was approached by the Love Has Won Group, who told them their leader has much better stories and descriptions of roles. They were now snaking up Wyoming toward the land of sugar beets. The Kenworth kept going.

"Do you think we're saving the planet, Red."
"I think we better hope the planet saves us."
"Frank, what do you believe in."
"I pay attention to the gas gauge, if that's what you mean."
"I'm trying to stretch it. Like, Big. What are we here for. That sort of thing."
"Other than making money."
"Since that's the one area we can't compete in, yeah, other than making money."
"See, that's the thing, Red. The power of money clouds the issue."
"Ok, so let's say you have all the money in the world, what's left. What do you believe in."

"Security fences, Rottweilers, maybe a Pitbull, but not one of those sweet ones! Guards, laser beams, spotlights, armament, walkie talkies, burner phones, 5G."
"Do you ever go out."
"Sure, in a plated car."

"There doesn't seem to be a lot of depth to that, Frank."

"I'm enjoying it!"

"Ok, so you don't have ALL the money in the world. Just a little bit over the bills. Do you have a underlayment beneath your flooring."

"What."

"Do you have a base. Something you can walk on."

"You're getting around to Karl Marx, again, aren't you. You really did steal the Alamo, didn't you, Red."

"I'm trying to develop a new way of thinking, Frank, a philosophy, to sustain me, that's all."

"You mean like Betty White or Schopenhauer."

"Schopenhauer! No, just something that sustains ME, maybe the earth also. I was hoping you had some Asian Advice could help me out."

Factorus turned to look at his comrade from the Nike Wars.

"Boss, you're getting worse."

"I have something," Frank said.

"What."

"A well aimed spear is worth three."

"That doesn't sound Asian."

"It's from a fortune cookie."

"After readying the every emotion, there is understanding entering the realm."

" Red looking around, "Who said that."

"Guess."

"Sometimes traveling to a new place leads to great transformation," offered Fly By Night.

"OK, fellas, I get it. It's not easy. I was just curious."

Valentine looked out over Wyoming. It seemed to be occupied with beauty. It didn't seem to be plagued by doubt. The sun was drawing the colors of the desert to it. The pensive mountain ledges reminded him wonderfully of Greta Thunberg with her braided yellow hair wrapped snugly around her. They turned up into pleasant hills where horses ran beside them like they were a train. River canyons were replaced with ranches with big tubs of water. A Horseman rode by and tipped his hat at them. He seemed to be untamed, also, and Amanda waved at him. Leaving Wyoming they were anxious to see if Montana really was the Big Sky Country. When they saw a sign that said, 'Montana, 10 feet ahead,' our anxious row was determined to get there. An antelope was grazing by a stream. A thumbed copy of *The Envelope* fell to the floor. A passage said to look out for sugar beets, and they all fastened their seatbelts.

Outside of Moiese, Montana, in a meadow minding his own business Big Boy was captured by a band of wild Indians. Valentine threw his hands up, also.

Fly By Night, however, smiled, and ran to them with tears in his eyes. Chief Carotid Artery embraced him, and said "Who are you," in a language no one else could understand.

"I am a Crow. The Crows and Flatheads are generally on good terms. I hope you accept me."

"Sure, but who are the cotton balls. And that unusual totem."

"Oh, there's Frank, whose ancestors walked across to here from Asia many summers ago. And the other one's name is, Red, so that's good, no. The totem is Amanda. She's a poet and a storyteller."

"The tribe will decide if that's true. For now all of you are our prisoners. According to the treaty which is hidden under the ugly rock which the tourists leave alone we can take up to five a year. It's part of our beliefs. We can also use the Kenworth and the Buffalo. Follow me."

A Flathead brave jumped up in the cab of the Kenworth and started it up.

"Frank, what did that gas gauge say, anyway."

"Empty."

"I command the Kenworth to stay," Valentine intoned in a rather officious voice, and the Kenworth sputtered to a stop.

"That might have worked in 1850, Cotton Ball, but not today. You have no power, and it's out of gas. Leave it, Micky. We'll bring the tanker over later. Time to go. 'Empty.' That's a good one, Cotton Ball."

At the other end of the meadow, which really wasn't that far from where they were captured, Valentine was assigned a tent with Frank, and Amanda and Factorus were taken away.

"Well this is another fine mess you got me into."

"Me! It was you that had this idea. We should have washed dishes for a month and let Bubba whistle in his Kenworth instead of the shower."

"I grew rather fond of that ghost ship. I wonder where they put it."

"It's probably gassed up by now."

"I know."

Of course, a new plan involving escape was formulating in Valentine's brain, but it kept bumping into three obstacles. Factorus, Amanda, and Big Boy. Marines leave no one behind, although Valentine had been in the Army.

"Red, I think we should just wait this out. It's not like they're going to boil us and eat us."

"I don't think."

"You're probably right, Frank. I mean we're still in America. There are a ton of other outlets. Plus, Chief 'Carotid Artery.' He's got to be careful."

"Who do you think gave him that name. It sounds like a page in a textbook."

"Probably his doctor. Mine calls me 'Heart Attack.' It's how they remember things."

"Well, we should be respectful. Can I have the top bunk."

"Where do you see bunks."

"Sorry. It's just a habit when I'm in a new place."

"We'll call him Art, confidentially to each other, of course, unless it slips out. You take that corner, I'll take this one."

The cutout of Amanda was set up in the center of camp until her power could be explained, because Chief Carotid Artery was sure she had some.

She couldn't help be the center of attention in a camp that was laid out like a orange with all the segments leading to her.

Chief Carotid Artery sat down in front of her cross legged and studied her. Amanda kept a journal and visited many places secretly. After a while Amanda smiled and could be heard without the benefit of mushrooms.

"This is the story of the House of Pete Plain."

"What's Art doing."

"He's nodding."

Red and Frank peeked out of their tent. The coast did not look clear at all. In fact, a Grandmother by the name of Pleasant Hemlock Grove said, "Get back in there."

"In the spring of 2006," Amanda began,
"The forecast on the weather channel
said Intermittent Rain
and the other channel said Hurricane.

Easy pick, Pete said, in Binghamton, NY.
That's where Pete lived, on the
Susquehanna River."

"The Iroquois!" Art put in context for the children. Art's own African and
Moor roots delighting in Amanda telling a story.

The Totem continued.

"Out in Ohio
in the NW Grange,
then down in Louisiana
some more of the same,
a storm picked up
that couldn't be tamed.
It had a lot of water
and it had a name
on the tip of its tongue, which was
'The House of Pete Plain.'"

"Hoo Hoo, Hoo Hoo!" Amanda said, mimicking a wise ole owl.

"HOO HOO, HOO HOO, responded the Flathead braves."

Amanda continued.

"The thunder and lightning
was something to see
but mostly it was just the
relentless pounding at sea."

"The river was doing a backstroke,
looking at Kathy Young singing about a
Thousand Stars In The Sky,
and trying to get her to look at the river.

"The Innocents, who were accompanying Kathy,
sang, 'It rained and it rained
On the House of Pete Plain
The water in the river

Was the reason to blame.'""

"But the river didn't look at it that way.
I don't think Kathy did either.
It's hard to imagine a river
in a bad light in a good song.
The river was just picking up confluence,
& logs, & cars, a lot of odds & ends
that people had left in their yards."

The tribal members who had brought their children to listen to the story praised the Chief, who got the totem to talk, plus it was a story about a Great River. Amanda explains that Pete's in his house listening to the rain, listening to Kathy on one of his records and the water is coming in Pete's window, straight in.

"Pete has his feet up. He doesn't want to miss a word of Kathy.   He's like Ahab, the Whale Chaser holding on to a beautiful vision."

The delighted children now regarding Pete as a Whale Chaser, in addition to having a cool house.

Amanda has her hands moving around now.

"Out in Ohio
in the NW Grange,
then down in Louisiana
some more of the same,
a storm picked up
that couldn't be tamed.
It had a lot of water
and it had a name
on the tip of its tongue, which was
'The House of Pete Plain.'
The Sheriff came down in his motorboat,
said, 'You better get out, Pete,
while you can still float.
We have Wind and Earth in the Convention Center.
I'll take you there
I think you better.'"

"But Pete rose up
like a Appalachian Bear,
(and all the Indian children rose up I swear)
and pointed to his walls like an old oak tree
and this is what he said to me,"

"Pete said,"

"Them's my pictures
Them's my books
I'm gonna ride 'em til the river
Let's us both off the hook.
You can put me on a horse
You can put me out to Sea
I got Wind and The Earth in the heart of me."

"The Sheriff didn't know
if Pete was a model.
He just shook his head and
hit the throttle.
It was probably a good thing that he did
because shortly after that a big wind came by
and took that house right off at its mast
and the House of Pete Plain, and Pete,
and Kathy Young and The Innocents
went floating down the American version of the Seine,
which is in France."

"Today if you go down to the Susquehanna River
in the Land of our Brothers and Sisters, the Iroquois,
pick a warm day in June
when a Thousand Stars are coming out
under a Crescent Moon.
And if you listen to the night
And hold each other tight
you might hear Pete trying to explain
why he's out there ridin in the
House of Pete Plain".

"Hey, Hey." Amanda singing with the braves.

""It rained and it rained
on the House of Pete Plain.
The water in the river denied any blame.
The Thunder and Lightning
was something to see
but mostly it was just the
relentless pounding at sea.
The Sheriff tried to get Pete to see
That in one more minute his house would leave.
But Pete had his own idea about that."

"What was his idea about that, kids!   What did Pete say."

"Pete said,
Them's my pictures
Them's my books
I'm gonna ride 'em til the river
Let's us both off the hook
You can put me on a horse
You can put me out to Sea
I got Wind and the Earth
In the heart of me."

"HEY, HEY."

Factorus slipped a note under Valentine's tent.

"Don't worry, boss. Everything's going to be alright. I have to accompany
several braves on a purifying mission. There's supposed to be a hot springs
around here somewhere and we're going to look for it. We also might go by
the National Bison Range and see if we can find Big Boy a girlfriend. I know
that sounds like rustling, but it has a different sound to them. Still it might fall
under the five a year rule. Evidently you can mix and match. I really built you
up with Chief Carotid Artery. He's meeting with the Council later today, so
keep your shirt on. Don't worry about Amanda. Almost everybody in the tribe
has signed her cutout, so she'd be like a passport if we ever get out of here."

Sincerely yours,

Factorus, newly minted The Crow Changer, alias Fly By Night

"He does have very nice handwriting.   Maybe we should write a Constitution."

"Maybe we should look in the one we got. I'm sure it favors us."
"That includes me, too, right."
Pleasant Hemlock Grove appeared in the flap.
"Art wants to see you."
Frank and Valentine looked at each other, disappointed.
"I thought that was between us!"
Our revolutionaries walked in single file behind Pleasant Hemlock Grove, between the lodges and the fires, around the community center, and across a glen to a house made of bricks and forested. Pleasant Hemlock Grove wished them well and said, "Good luck. You can go in."
The interior was like a series of chambers, representing the moon and the sun and the stars. In the very last chamber Art was sitting next to a pool of water listening to Van Morrison.
"'Into The Mystic,' Boys. That bloke's an Indian. Trust me. Have a seat."
A good author would describe the seats in detail but they were essentially lawn chairs.
"The Crow holds you fellas in high regard. In other words, I'm of a mind not to send you to the salt mines. But as much as I believe the Crow you have to prove yourself to me."
"You have white men in salt mines."
"We don't, but the Wyandotte do, outside Detroit. It's a theory that QAnon amazingly missed. But lately it's become difficult to get "workers" there with covid and all. Anyway, it looks like you'll miss it as long as you can prove yourself."
"Chief, I'm Asian, you know, so I wouldn't qualify, anyway."
"Nice try, Frank. You been here long enough, you're white."
"So, what do we have to do, Art, to prove ourselves and keep Detroit out of it."
"You have to prove to me in a way that we all can agree, officially, that the relationship of the Buffalo to me is more than just a conspiracy. I don't care how you do it. Just keep Alex Jones out of it."
"Do you have a library we can start with."

"No. I mean yes, we do. But you can start with Big Boy. He'll provide all the material you require. The rest is up to you. You have 48 hours. Don't forget to fold up the lawn chair on your way out."

Back in their tent Frank and Red assessed their situation.

"Frank you seemed to know that Big Boy was a buffalo. So what else do you know about them."

"They're big and hairy."

"I don't think that's what the Chief is looking for. And Google isn't helpful, either. Frank, we just have to observe the only specimen we got and come up with something. Maybe we only come up with intuition but we've got to come up with something. I'm not supposed to even be around salt."

"Micky told me Big Boy still sleeps in the Kenworth at night. He's a Taurus and they're real homebodies. Micky says he watches movie marathons featuring John Travolta and curls up in his blanket."

"Then we'll camp outside the Kenworth and pick up in the morning like real cowboys. We'll pretend we're mending fences but we'll be keeping an eye on Big Boy. If it's the last thing we do at least it will be fun."

"I'm with ya, Red."

The problem with this resolution is big Boy wasn't in the Kenworth that night. Something stronger than the attraction of John Travolta or his blanket had drawn him to the top of a bluff a block away. A storm was brewin in Big Boy, spit and spewin foretellin some ruin, as a female led by Factorus under the moonlight was coming over a pretty rise. Big Boy could see the apprehension in her equally pretty eyes, and as a Taurean he would erase that fear on one side or the other of sunrise.

Frank and Valentine were camped out next to the vacant Kenworth. "Makes you wonder what he's doing in there all alone, doesn't it, Red. I mean watching movies all night. Maybe he's watching Midnight Diner on Netflix. The episodes with Marilyn will keep him up."

Chief Carotid Artery also saw what was coming, and he knew there would be an immediate consequence to taking Little Flower. In the morning when the Territorial Deputy showed up, he didn't try to avoid it.

"Yes, Harold, we took it. We have the right, under about ten thousand treaties, and in particular the one under that ugly rock over there."

The Deputy who was understanding but went by the book stared at the cutout of Amanda Gorman.

"Still, Art, I have to arrest you as the leader of the tribe, for theft from a national park. You'll have your day in court in two days."

I would like to have Frank Guam and Red Odey represent me on this. They're from out of state.

Do they have authority to practice law on the Flathead Reservation.

"No, but neither does the USA.

"OK, I'll compromise."

"OK, I'll let you."

Big Boy showed Little flower his Kenworth. He nudged open the bay doors and watched as her eyes lit up.

"At night they put in fresh straw and some cantaloupes. And on the TV I can get both Netflix AND Acorn. Closing the doors is a little tricky but if we leave them open we can see the moon."

"Oh, Earl, you've thought of everything."

"His name is Earl?"

Frank and Valentine were taking turns digging up the ugly rock.

"Red, I hope there's something exculpatory in here because this is a lot of work."

"The Truth is work, Frank. Lies are easy."

SNunk

"I think we hit something."

Sure enough our boys had hit the mark. Bound by reeds and rolled up in bark. The treaty from 1876 itself was stuffed into a little treasure chest and Frank and Valentine sat down to go over it.

Meanwhile Earl and Little Flower were grazing in the meadow. Earl suddenly took to running. Up and down the dale and back again. Hard running. Thundering running. Little Flower flared her nostrils at him. His big wooly coat fluffed up and he looked like a whole herd. He was one with the earth and the meadow and the sun. The Chief looked on from a distance and was a part of this canvas, also. Red blinked and took a mental picture of it.

Valentine's brain is like a vault. Very little gets in or out of it, unless he knows about it. He does not have a streaming mind. He has to work at it. Frank, on the other hand, has that Asian thing going and his mind is more like a widescreen. But like the Indian in a foreign context, he's been schooled to disregard relationships which are clear but not mighty. So Valentine started to read the Treaty, and Frank got out his fortunate spear, and between them a blossom took shape that might get them out of here.

"What do you find most interesting about this Treaty, Frank."
"That it was written in 1876."
"Why is that."
"Because the United States House of Representatives outlawed the drafting of any more treaties in 1871."

"How do you know that."
'I was a History Major."
"Then it's a plant. Somebody made it up. Who would do that?"
"Harold."
"Did you read that in a history book, too."
"No. I read it in his eyes. He has government eyes, but occasionally they're grey, like a wolf. He stays hidden, so it's hard to observe them."

Harold smoothed the pleats in his Dickies and coughed into his Covid mask.
"I think I'll check the ear plug on that female, make sure I got the Number right before I file my report."
"I hope everybody's been practicing safe distancing, he said."
Art watched Big Boy grow quiet with his coal eyes fixed on Harold.
"You should take your own advice, Harold. Maybe make up a number and get in your Land Rover while it's still within running distance."
Big Boy lowered his head. He had already decided if Harold touched Little Flower he was going to deck him.
Factorus flew by and said, "It's 42, Harold. The number is 42."
Art said, "It's 42, Harold."
A Sky Writer over Moiese said, *"It's 42, Harold."*
Harold said, "It's probably 42, because that one's missing."
Nobody in the tribe disliked Harold, really. He just had a hearing issue.

The parade of tribal chieftains making their way up the grey steps of the Magistrate's Office in Moiese was very colorful. Rivalries were put aside for the benefit of supporting Art. Shoshone and Arapaho with their ankle straps whisking in their walk. Navaho braves with their turquoise rings and dark eyes. Comanche with their yelp barely beneath the surface. And on and on. All of them dancing into the Hall of Justice.

Frank and Valentine were supervising the delivery of crates of documents to present in their case. Crates and crates. At one point Frank stopped and asked Valentine if he knew what was in them.

"Do you mean in what order things are in."

"No, I mean what the hell is all this stuff. I thought you said we were going to talk from the heart. This looks like congestive heart failure."

"It's all reference material in case we need to refer to it. Basically it's to impress the Prosecution. It's not what's in there, but what might be in there. That's why I want the Comanches up front. Where's Big Boy.'

In fact, Big Boy was walking up the ramp with Little Flower.

"Are we getting married, Earl?" Little Flower said.
"If that's what you'd like, My Dear," Big Boy replied.

The evidence was overwhelming.

Art was brought in by Pleasant Hemlock Grove who gave the Magistrate the evil eye. Micky was outside wedging the Kenworth into the parking lot.

"Hear ye, Hear ye, the Honorable Willard Van Fossen, otherwise known as Bill, is presiding. If you're not already up, get up."

"Thank you, Colin, but you should probably tone that a little bit. Ok, we're here today for the charge against the Chief here of the Flathead Tribe for theft by deception of a buffalo. How do you plead, Art."

"There was no deception, Bill, we just took it."

"But where did you get the idea that you could do that. Certainly not in the Treaty under the ugly rock, even though we've never seen it."

"Objection, your Honor."

"Who are you."

"I'm the co-counsel for the defense."

"And I object, you Honor."

"Who are you."

"I'm the other counsel for the defense."

"Do either of you have a degree."

"Does Upholstery count."

"I don't think so. Chief, are you sure you want these two to represent you."

"Sure, why not."

"I don't know, it just seems like there's a lot on the line here."

"I have faith in the buffalo."

"You're an odd duck, Art, but I'll allow it."

"The Defense calls Ms. Amanda Gorman."

"Wait a minute, the Prosecution goes first."

"Thank you, your Honor. The Prosecution calls Ms. Amanda Gorman."

"Excuse me, Counselor, but do you have a degree."

"I do, your Honor. From Harvard."

"I'll allow it, anyway. Will somebody help Ms. Gorman get on the stand."

"Ms. Gorman, my name is Jim. I represent the United States Government in this case. Let's begin with, what is your relationship to the defendant."

"We share a power."

"And what is that power."

"It can only be explained to someone who already understands it."

"But doesn't that defeat the purpose of conversation."

"I don't think we have anything to talk about."

"Your Honor, permission to treat Ms. Gorman as a hostile witness."

"I'll tell you what, Jim. I think you better stop while you're still above ground. I don't think it's going to get better."

"I have just one question, your Honor."

"Go ahead, Jim. Dig it."

"Ms. Gorman, do you think Chief Carotid Artery is capable of deception."

"Everything is a matter of deception. How we see it brings out its reality."

"Told ja, Jim."

"Would you give us an example Ms. Gorman."

"Sure. See that couple over there in the evidence box. You probably see brown faces with horns and a weight problem. But they see each other as how the Disney movie always turns out. A good writer is capable of deception. Deception is just a part of character."

Red jumped up.

"The Defense rests, your Honor!"

"Which one are you."

"I'm Valentine."

"Do you have the upholstery degree."

"No, he does."

Then, sit down.

The courtroom giggled and a three year old blew bubbles at the Prosecution. Willard got red in the face. The tribal contingent looked at him sympathetically.

Finally, Frank helped Amanda down from the stand.

"Jim, do you have any other witnesses."

"Actually, I think the defendant already confessed, your Honor."

"So, that's it."

"Pretty much."

"Alright, I'm hesitant, but does the defense have anything to say."

"Yes, we have a lot, your Honor.'

"Which one are you."

"I'm the Asian."

"You're the one with the upholstery degree."

"From Hofstra, your Honor."

"Ok, go ahead."

The defense calls Micky Foot to the witness stand."

"It's Two Foot."

"Ok, Micky, where do you work."

"I work at Sure Shyft Transmission in Moiese Where Crow Rides Are Advertised. That's a jingle we have. It doesn't make sense to me, either."

"Ok. Have you ever seen the evidence over there packed in to the evidence box."

"Yes, I have."

"And where was that."

"I was asked to drive the Kenworth back to the Holding Area, which is what we call the area where we live, and the Evidence was asleep in the trailer compartment."

"Would you point out the Evidence you're referring to."

"Right over there. It's Big Boy."

"O, Earl, they're talking about you!"

"And what did you learn about 'Big Boy.'"

"I learned that he was very well mannered but lonely. He kept chewing on his doll."

"And when you brought him to this Holding Area did you notice a change in his demeanor."

"No, he was still polite, but lonely."

"Do you think Mr. Odey here or myself were responsible for his loneliness."

"Objection, your Honor, speculation and irrevelant."

"Oh Stick it, Jim. You're getting on my nerves. Objection overruled. The witness will answer the question."

"No, it's just the nature of the buffalo after all he's been through."

"So, when you heard that Fly By Night and others were taking Big Boy to the National Bison Reserve to find company you didn't find that unusual."

"You mean did I think they were going on a raid, or something."

"Yes, a Raid. To take something that didn't belong to them."

"I don't think so. It would be hard to take something that didn't belong to us in the first place. In fact they left a Thank You note which the kids had drawn hearts on."

"Is that so. And what else was written on this Thank You note."

"Your Honor, I'm going to have a fit if you allow this drivel to go on."

"Have it, Jim. I'm interested to see if you use saliva or if you just clunk up. This is an unusual line of questioning but I'll allow it. Go ahead, Mr. Guam."

"Thank you, your Honor. Micky, about the note."

"It was about our respect for the Refuge. It said, 'You can come and get Little Flower back anytime.'"

"Thank you, Micky. That's all I have your Honor."

At that point if it had any sense the defense would rest, but Val got up, instead.

"Your Honor, if it may please the court."

"Sure, why not," Williard said.

"Your Honor, the Defense calls Harold to the stand."

"Hi Judge."

"Hi, Harold. Are you ready."

"I'm confident in my report."

"I'm sure it's very handsome. Ok, let's get to it, Counselor."

"Could you explain to the court the nature of your employment for the past 10 years."

"I am the Regional Deputy for Code Enforcement for Wildlife Management in Northwestern Montana."

"So, you're a zoning officer."

"Pretty much."

"Do you work for the Flathead Indian Reservation or the tribal members therein."

"Good Gracious, no. I work for the Government."

"But you have a great deal of contact with the tribe in your day to day rounds. Would that be accurate."

"We run across each other. I spend a considerable time in the office going over maps."

"Maps?"

"Yes, I like maps."

"We'll go back to that."

"Harold, are you familiar with the phrase Crystal Blue Persuasion."

"If it's in the vending machine I haven't had it yet.'

"Actually it's a song. Would you like me to sing it for you."

"Your Honor, I've tried to be understanding, but this tact by the defense is making my gout act up."

"Jim, we've been to about every part of your body, now. Is there anything else we're missing. I understand this train is on a new track for you. but The Shondells are a favorite of mine. I'll allow some leeway, but be careful Mr. Odey, you better be good."

"Thank you, your Honor, and if you could instruct the courtroom gallery to back me up that would be helpful."

"OK, Here we go."

"Harold."

~ *"Look over yonder*
What do you see?
The sun is a-rising
Most definitely
A new day is coming (ooh, ooh)
People are changing
Ain't it beautiful? (ooh, ooh)
Crystal blue persuasion
Better get ready to see the light
Love, love is the answer (ooh, ooh)
And that's all right
So don't you give up now (ooh, ooh)
So easy to find
Just look to your soul (your soul)
And open your mind
Crystal blue persuasion, hmm, hmm
It's a new vibration
Crystal blue persuasion
Crystal
Blue persuasion
Maybe tomorrow
When he, or she, looks down
On every green field (ooh, ooh)
And every town

All of the children
And every nation
There'll be peace and good brotherhood
Crystal blue persuasion, yeah
Crystal blue persuasion, aah-aah
Crystal blue persuasion, aah-aah
(Crystal blue persuasion, aah-aah)"

"How'd I do, Harold."

"I don't see what it has to do with me."

"See, that's the thing. If we think of ourselves separately it probably doesn't. Some poets even think that beneath it all the desire of oblivion runs."

"But, going back to your maps, Harold, are there buried treasures in them?"

"Oh yes, I like to look for them."

"Do you sometimes bury them."

"What do you mean," Harold said, becoming pale.

"Because when Frank and I uncovered the paper under the ugly rock we noticed it wasn't a treaty at all, but an observation. In part, somebody wrote, *'This entirely is the Land of the Buffalo and their Spiritual Twin, the Indian. There are no boundaries between Them. Their Bond is like the wind. It connects them but doesn't smother them. A knife cannot cut them and meteorologists cannot predict them. As long as prairies run the Buffalo and the Indian are One.'*

"You wrote this, didn't you, Harold! All those days riding around, and looking at your maps. You hid it under the ugly rock because you were afraid of your feelings being dug up. But the times are changing, Harold, and people like you are more in demand. Therefore, to everyone here the defense submits the Treaty of 1876 as our evidence. It is the Plaintiff's own Crystal Blue Persuasion." The Gallery cheered for Harold.

"Your Honor, I give up, Jim said."

Colin smiled, the Judge said, "We're done here," and with a magnanimous wave from Art, Frank and Red were free to go.

MENTIONS

Thanks to all the cultures I've offended here. It's not easy being obsessive, and in truth I hold all of them, including my own, in high regard.

Thanks to Amanda Gorman who is an inspiration. I hope I reflected her in an appropriate way. This is fiction, but she's real.

Thanks to Tommy James, Eddie Gray, and Mike Vale for their composition of Crystal Blue Persuasion, which I copied almost intact, and thanks to Tommy James and The Shondells for singing it.

Thanks to our real American Landscape. My God, isn't it spectacular.

Thanks to my characters, who went on to great things.

Frank took the cutout back to the San Antonio Library and apologized, and went on to become a reference librarian.

Big Boy and Little Flower started a whole new generation of free roaming Buffalo who are causing endless problems for the Wildlife Service.

Pleasant Hemlock Grove was elected to the United States House of Representatives where she scares the hell out of Marjorie Taylor Greene.

Chief Carotid Artery had his surgery and is doing well.

Darlene married Bubba and bought the Diner.

The Kenworth was shipped off to a Museum in Broken Arrow, Oklahoma, and became the subject of an e-book.

Factorus, alias Fly By Night, the Crow Changer, stayed behind to become a beloved medicine man on the Flathead Reservation and parted ways with Valentine!

And Valentine. Ah, Valentine. The Redman from Transylvania. The last that was seen of him he was boarding a liner for Europe thinking it was a Greyhound Bus.

The
LINER

We're all crossing something. In this case it's water. Valentine is now on his own on a perilous deck. The past haunts him, the present is confusing, and the future is stacked. This is for the next generation of poets and artists. I hope you can work with the material that my generation has left you. I hope we **haven't** screwed it up. This is another chapter about Valentine which he can't take back.

Valentine was out on deck. He was sitting on a bench and trying to stick his feet in the water. The fact that he was on the third deck didn't seem to bother him. He kept saying, "S t r e t c h," and when a passing shower got his feet wet he said, "See."

The Dolphin & Seal was on her fourth crossing of the summer season out of Astoria, Oregon, bound for Limerick, Ireland. From there Valentine would trek across the Continent to Transylvania to look for a pocket watch which his ancestor had left behind and which had been described at great length in a passage in the man's diary.

A door opened to a cabin. It opened a very small amount, and the long legs of a woman in a blue negligee parted in the wind. "Egads," Valentine said. And in the rocking of the boat, the blare of a horn, a few screams, and a banner that flew by promoting the Isle of Waterloo, Valentine also said, "Well, this is new."

Shirley Bogdonovich returned to her mirror. The rolling of the ship made her curls bounce like a slinky. She dabbed rouge on her cheeks to at least weight that down. And then she smeared her lips with a big wide swath of purple lipstick. She was going for the vampire look.

Next to Shirley on her makeup table was a copy of Stories by Ivan Turgenev. He was Russian, but it was close enough.

The Captain of the Dolphin & Seal was exasperated on deck, exclaiming "It's nothing to worry about, it's really not much," as the old girl, not Shirley, rolled and pitched. Valentine sat without a care in his Fruit of The Loom underwear. He thought he was alone, until all this started. "A person can't even have a thought anymore," he said, like he had paused in traffic with one, and was beeped to go ahead.

Before this happened he had been working on a poem. It was called, *The Cheshire Cat*. Of course it began with, "Who are YOU." Valentine had come up with several lines to accompany this question, but in the end he just said, "But how do I know you're even a cat," which he rhymed with bat, and scat.

Having completed it he put it in a folder titled, Chapter 3 or 4, which was getting quite fat. By now the Captain had relaxed and sat down beside Valentine.

"Are you enjoying the ride," he said, trying to butter up Valentine after the rolling had momentarily stopped. "Would you like to join me at my table for some leftovers and pop."

"I'm sorry but I'm probably not dressed for it, plus I'm busy composing. Would you please go away."

And so, The Captain exited. He, obviously, wasn't going to be a big part in this story, at least to begin with.

Valentine placed *The Cheshire Cat* under Shirley's cabin door. On the other side Shirley extracted it quietly from beneath the door and took it to her make-up table to examine it closely. Her negligee rustled lightly as she made her way over, the resumed pitch of the Dolphin & Seal holding her back, and

Valentine's lines reassembling in the interim. Even after this they would be reassembled.

On one favorable roll she made it and sat down before her oval mirror with its pleasant veneer and red velvet sash. When she read, "Who are YOU," she said, "At last," and this would be the beginning of an extraordinary relationship. Each night for the rest of the cruise Valentine Odey, which is pronounced O Day, if you needed to know that, would sit on the third deck of the Dolphin & Seal in his Fruit Of the Loom underwear and compose poems for Shirley Bogdonovich.

On the Second Night Valentine composed The Red Bird

For The Red Bird

Outside my window
there is no lark
nothing to herald me
at the morning's start.
But a red bird awakens
and begins to sing
"Over here I have
time, and for what you really need,
everything."
I arrange all my files
and my pencils, too,
comb my hair
fold my cuffs
sit down on my chair
and come up with stuff.

Valentine tip toed over to the cabin door. It was very late as it was a clear night and there were a lot of walkers that had to disperse. But they had and Valentine after waiting patiently was able to put his poem in place without changing one verse.

For her part Shirley read it and put it in a cup. The fact is, really, she gobbled it up.

Valentine looked out the porthole in his room. Above him the third deck seemed to loom. In more than one way he was afraid of it. For thirty years his task at Nike had been to keep hearts on track, and now his might be dangling. The distance from his blue deck chair to Shirley's door was 15 beats. He had counted them. Room for error. It would help if he could see Shirley fully, in an evening dress with a scabbard and sword, perhaps.

Next, The Scabbard and Sword

loss
hope
humour
good times
transmissions
light of candles
faces of cards
love
loyalty
money
Iron
confusion
Iron is the muted one, and makes up for it by its strength. But even in the ironman
there is mutability if he's heated up enough.

Shirley laughed and put the menu for dinner on the Dolphin & Seal under the door with a match. Valentine, who didn't smoke, was at a loss.

"The balmy days gave way to nights." Valentine immediately crossed that off. What he was missing was feedback.   Other than that mysterious match. Of course, he could knock. But that seemed so slack. Especially in his underwear. One of the cleaning crew asked him to pick his feet up.
"Excuse me, monsieur, but did you forget your shoes."
Valentine was amazed that he didn't mention the absence of anything else. Valentine looked closely to see if he was blind. Apparently, he was. He had, however, run his duster into Valentine's toes and could tell the difference. Valentine took a liking to him. "Master Craftsman, what is your name."
"Eh, mon nom?"
"Are you French Canadian."

"Si, right away."

"What?"

"What."

"I was asking if you are from Quebec"

"My name is Robes Pierre."

Valentine almost dropped his underpants.

"I know there's no such thing as can't, but I thought you were dead."

"Si.   Right away."

After Valentine had managed to screw up the charts of a major corporation, repurpose the Alamo, and defend the honor of a bond in court, he was hoping for a reprieve. A long cruise away from trying to save people. Now he has run into the author of the French Revolution, no less.   That events this time would be led by a blind man seemed logical to him as he had already offended about every other condition and color.   It was the blind man's turn.

"Well, Robes, we're going to need a spy if we're to be successful and I think I have the perfect candidate. You may have already cleaned her room, and know more about her than I do. But if we're going to work together you have to share. So, whatever she's left about that you could get your hands on might be important for our cause.   Can you recall anything important or bulky, like a bomb. We could use that.

"Eh."

"Robes, you fox you.   This is not the time to play coy with me.   This is not the time for gambling. Besides, I have to work on a poem for Shirley. We should talk later about our plans."

The Muffler Bill

When Jerry Hiniker put his plastic bag down to
pay his muffler bill
people starting throwing trash in it.
When he was done he had
A flash card set to get LGBTQ right
Maria Muldaur's lipstick blot, in three places,
The key to Eric Wisniewski's garage in Detroit

and half of Mary Chapin Carpenter's apple in there.
I often wonder how this ended up
when he got home.

Shirley looked at this and shook her head. She may have fallen for the wrong poet. "I mean, what is he thinking." Nonetheless, she put a thank you note under her door, this time on a napkin.

"The man in the blue chair. What can you tell me about him," Shirley said to Robes who was looking for a bomb under her bed.

"He's very bold, Madame."
Shirley regarded this revelation. Shirley Bogdonovich was born in Hungary where she had a little store and plans. This might have explained her love of the sea, and everything, including ideas, with a grand swath to them. The bolder the better.
"But why doesn't he wear clothes."
"He doesn't wear clothes?"
It occurred to Shirley that this would be difficult.

Things settled down from there into a routine. Valentine composed poems for Shirley, and Robes continued his search for a bomb under her bed. Valentine forgot about saving anyone and concentrated on seducing Shirley Bogdonovich. Shirley worked on her replies, hoping the nail would hit the head.

I Took The Moon For A Walk Today.
For Ms. Bogdonovich

I took the moon for a walk today
It was very silver looking and grey
I tied it to a string
And wrapped that around my favorite ring.
But tonight when night came
My ring grew even more round
Like it was empathizing without the sun around
And the moon fell off upon the ground.
So will you come with me

And we'll walk upon the sea
To each of us we'll tie a string
And look for silverings.

To which Shirley replied, "By the way, I didn't think Robespierre was a very nice guy."

After that Valentine told Robes his name was Kenny. Kenny was now young and debonair.

"I can see!" He said.

To which Valentine said, "It goes with it."

Kenny was transferred to the Dining Room. It appeared his speech had improved, also. I fact, he now spoke 21 languages, plus French, and was in demand. Valentine was left to himself to try to please Shirley.

"Well. that didn't work out," he mumbled and shuffled the pages of his narrative. It's not easy being a writer. He also started to wear clothes.

The new deck hand brought him a bowl of fruit, and a glass of orange juice.

"What's YOUR name," Valentine said.

"My name is Curtis. Is there anything else I can get for you."

Valentine said, "Yeah. An Acroball pen, medium, black." Thanks to Shirley he was going to reinvent himself, again.

"I'll see what I can do."

Curtis was very sharply dressed and liked to do the Mambo. At least that's what he told Valentine when he was pressed. He grew up in Haiti and his father was a permanent guest, of the state. He had evidently led a parade demanding higher pay. Valentine's ears perked up. Was it possible Robes had not gone far away.

"And your mother."

"She has a girlfriend. And my brother is gay."

"How does that go over in Haiti."

"Like a bailout after numerous catastrophes."

"Well, Curtis, I need assistance in a matter of the heart. I'd ask your mom but she might steal it for herself. Occasionally would you mind delivering something for me, for which I will pay. I usually leave it under the door but you can deliver it in person, if you like. You can tell her it's from Mr. Odey."

"When do I start."

"Right away!"

Curtis brought a silver tray with a white cloth to Valentine's deck chair.
"What's that."
"Something appropriate to make a delivery on."
"You have a high regard for me, Curtis. I'm not sure that I deserve that.
But I appreciate your thoughtfulness."
Valentine seems to have mellowed. It probably won't last long. But for
now he's taciturn and paying attention to circumstances.

"Would you be so kind as to take this to Ms. Bogdonovich, Curtis. It's
early but I think she'll be looking for you."
"Madame, I have the pleasure of presenting you a note from Mr. Odey."
"Thank you, Curtis. And would you please wait to take my thanks back in
the same way, on a white cloth on a silver tray."
Shirley went over to her make-up table. This time she put on crimson
lipstick, and read again in *The Envelope*, "Her face is like a painting by Renoir
with faintly colored lips." She combed her long grey hair and opened up the
note on the silver tray.

Anglena's Fortunes

Anglena laid down a set which
didn't look good. Hermits and Knives.
I couldn't imagine what I'd gotten into.
She said, "Do you want me to tell you the bad
as well as the good."
Already I'm looking at an arrangement
that doesn't look good.
"Sure," I said.
She said I have a natural interest in people
and that I didn't have to force it.
As she fished thru the cards,
the Wands, the Hermits, the Cups,
I looked at her lips which I didn't think
were part of my fortune.
Today when I drove by
I saw that Readings were $20.00,

a Holiday Special.
I thought about her
in her parlor,
telling somebody else
their fortune.

Shirley wrote back that fortune often has knives but not all of them are sharp.

Immediately, Valentine tried to work that in.

Valentine invited Curtis to sit with him on deck so they could discuss the world. Curtis didn't know if this would be appropriate but Valentine told him that he, Valentine, was on very good terms with the Captain.

"Curtis, what is the purpose of people."

"I'd say to preserve our seed as well as sow it so in the time of the Dark Shawl it can be hidden in the back of a voodoo doll."

"What!"

"It's the same thing as saying we all need to come to our senses. Tear down fences. Love each other even if meetings are coincidences. I just put it a little differently."

"Can I use the voodoo part with Shirley."

"No can do. I think you're better off with your approach, Valentine. You're a dreamer. I'm a pragmatist. I'm worried about getting set up in a carnival range to get picked off right behind the ducks. You're worried about the ducks."

"I guess you're right. I am worried. AI coming down the track. Things like that."

"You worried with AI in town there will be nothing for billions of us to do?"

"I'm worried the algorithms won't be able to keep up."

"Once again, you're worried about the ducks."

Valentine looked around and wanted to tell Curtis about his background in "accounting," how he had been shaped by keeping track of parts, but he thought he'd embarrassed himself enough already.

In a break from Valentine, Shirley went back to the detective novel she brought with her which she had intended to read in the first place. Ngaio Marsh's Wonderful *Night At The Vulcan.*

~ The alley was quiet now. Without moving she took stock of herself. Something thrummed inside her head and the tips of her fingers tingled but she no longer felt as if she were going to faint. The brandy glowed at the core of her being, sending out ripples of comfort. She tried to think what she should do. There was a church, back in the Strand: she ought to know its name. One could sleep there, she had been told, and perhaps there would be soup. That would leave two and fourpence for tomorrow: all she had. She lifted her suitcase-it was heavier than she remembered-and walked to the end of the alleyway. Half a dozen raindrops plopped into a puddle. People hurried along the footpath with upward glances and opened their umbrellas. As she hesitated, the rain came down suddenly and decisively. She turned towards the front of the theatre and at first thought it was shut. Then she noticed that one of the plate-glass doors was ajar.

She pushed it open and went in. ~

Shirley always wanted to act in the theatre, or to appear in a movie in one. 'The Vulcan' sounded like a good start. She noticed that the plate glass on her mirror was ajar, and leaned over to go in. There was a scramble going on behind it, everyone running around, looking for their role, for their assistant, for their clothes. Shirley hid behind a curtain in front of a big window that was closed. It was stifling hot. She reached down to open the window. The maize and wheat of a field swatted against it along with a morning from her past. She bent down to open a window in her store in Pecs. Suddenly the Director yelled, "Hey, can you act." Reluctantly, she came back.

The wind seemed to be rapping at the window. In this case, it was Curtis at the door.

"Madame, I have another missile from Valentine. He's hopeful it will cause a spark."

"Thank you Curtis. I'll leave my response on the white tray by the shuffle board park."

Someday Marrakesh, For Ms. Bogdonovich

On the day when Arthur died he was carried back to the door which had appeared in a dream. From his bed with his attendant beside him explaining how to work his phone he saw a new sign that said, 3-D PRINTING, PRESS HERE. Arthur reached up and pressed it. The old door was immediately replaced with two doors which were titanium and had wonderful colors on them and pennants and pictures of trumpets and horses in armour. Arthur, who looked young again and very regal with his crown of forks and spoons and a thousand royal things knocked on both doors with great anticipation. The doors open up to a courtyard in which children are wheeling hoops of brass with a stick and they are laughing and running, and horses are being outfitted with banners and pawing the ground, and dogs are barking and people are laughing and going about their business. And inside the door are Lancelot and Galahad and Bors. Of course, they are preparing for adventures, themselves, and young girls who would like to be on the horses with them run up with lockets of hair and envelopes to be opened and smelled when they get to Crete and Marrakesh. Arthur steps thru the titanium doors and the Heralds on the ramparts of the old house give a tremendous blast which rocks the wooden siding and frightens Arthur. He puts his hand up to stop them, worried about the horse's ears more than his own. Then he steps forward to speak.

"Children of my age. Pages, Colors, and Marvelous Things. Rejoice in being old enough that we've been printed again."

The note of thanks which Shirley left on the white tray was mildly scented with a floral brocade on the border.

"If you keep this up they'll think we're counterrevolutionaries!"

Curtis and Valentine were sitting on the third deck watching a Magnavox roll by. Bob Dole was addressing a group of senior activists in Russell, Kansas.

"I don't want us to lose a generation of ingenuity just because of an economic crisis"

"What'd he say?"
"He said you should get a job."

"What! I'm 98 years old for Chrissake. What do you mean, get a job."
"It's about time you became part of the solution, not part of the problem."
"What the hell are you talking about. I'm 98 years old."
"You consume as much as a 75 year old."
"All I eat is peanut butter and applesauce."
"Yeah, but it takes lights, heat, company, and a lot of valuable resources to do it."
"You should eat peanut butter. Besides, is this a leap year."
"A leap year! What the hell are YOU talking about."

"He should have been the President," Valentine said.
"Which one are you talking about."
"Bob Dole. He had a sense of humor, which is what we could have used."
"Maybe you need to show Shirley that YOU have a sense of humor."
'Maybe I will, but I don't want to be the President."

Reluctantly, Curtis knocked on Shirley's door with a big orange nose and a green hat.

Josef and Kristine

When Josef Red Bird tried to rob the first Bulgarian Bank
he was confronted by the teller.
"You have to fill out a withdrawal slip, first," she said.
"Are you kidding me."
"No, I am not."
"Since when."
"It's a new rule. Kind of like fees."
"Do I have to put an account number on it."
"Actually, yes you do."
"Well, that's crazy. I don't even know anybody's account number."
"Would you like to open one yourself."
"You know, I don't think I have time."
"Actually, it doesn't take long at all."
"What's your name."
"Kristine."
"Is there a minimum."
"Yes. You have to put in 50 lev to start."
"I don't know if I have 50 lev, that's why I'm here."

"How much do you have."

"Let me see."

"Do you have 50 lev."

"I have 53."

"Oh, good. So, give me 50. You should be thinking about what color checks you want, because sometimes that takes people a long time to decide."

"What colors are there."

"Red, and Green."

"That's it!"

"Can you imagine how long it would take if there were more colors than that."

"I have a red car."

"Oooohh! I love red."

"Would you like to see it."

"I get off at 3."

"I'll come by the drive-thru window."

"You're funny!"

Shirley thought Valentine was the funniest thing.

But soon it was back to basics. Valentine got out a piece of paper and wrote in big block letters, and mountains appeared, down the streets and thru the town he was interested in. He wrote in cursive, and dancing appeared. A pretty woman appeared in the town square who began dancing to ward off the coronavirus. Val dotted his eyes forcefully and drums were beating incessantly to accompany her. He swirled his capital S's and an orator appeared, to admonish with a rough flourish, "A set part is not forever. Rust will get it, or the heart." Valentine wanted the orator to go away.

Exasperated, Valentine wrote a scathing trilogy to Shirley. In the first part he protested that she had entrapped him, forged his name upon her card and then skipped out on him. All of this, of course, was untrue.

In the second part he asked for forgiveness. He likened himself to an Iron Horse which had been drawn out on the Plains and was running out of gas, or coal, or wood, or steam.

In the third part he proposed that they meet.

For this occasion, Shirley wore a Red Mask, a black satin dress which opened in the front and a flowing black train. Valentine was assisted by Curtis who picked out his clothes. "These shoes look like gunboats, Curtis. What were you planning to do with them, anyway."

On the deck of the Dolphin & Seal they danced La Pizzica, a healing dance to pave the way to health and clarity, not necessarily youth in their age, but still their castanets raged.

Then Shirley danced around Valentine like a soft dervish, throwing her arms up and out to the melting sun. Valentine tap danced in place like the keys of a typewriter. Curtis beat incessantly on his drums. They seemed to have the evening on the run.

In the morning at 5:43 am a bomb went off under Shirley's bed.

MENTIONS

Thanks again to my characters who went on to great things.

Curtis became the President of Haiti.
Kenny was hired by the State Department.
The Captain ran to the bridge to save the ship.

And Valentine was in bed with Shirley.

An Astonishing Thing

A time when every creature's Tao was astonishing.

I'VE BEEN PENETRATED!"

Valentine Odey, which is pronounced O Day if you needed to know that, was busy pulling the last piece of shrapnel out of Shirley Bogdonovich while at the same time providing information to an AT&T operator with a sexy Chinese voice who had reached out to him to exchange his flip phone to the 5G Network.

"This isn't going to allow your military to listen in on my calls is it."

"Of course not, Sir. I don't think they would be getting anything, anyway, from what I see in these transcripts."

"AHA. I knew it. I **don't** suppose you have the call I made to Arabia on a particularly vulnerable night."

"Yes, we do. Looks like you struck out on that one."

"I'VE BEEN PENETRATED!"

"Egads, what was that."

"It's just Ms. Bogdonovich. We've had some difficulty with our bed."

"Well, my name is Miss Lu. Just let me know if I can be any help."

"Valentine, who are you talking to?"

"Miss Lu. She has offered the full support of the Government of China if we need it. I suppose I'll have to redo my ending to The Liner. I forgot to mention the position we were in and in my haste to get to the barn I summarily implied we had been blown into the sea and washed up back in Astoria. I tried to make up for it in The Mentions, but who reads that. I'll let you in on a secret. Curtis becomes the President of Haiti and Kenny is hired by the State Department. They don't know that yet. Do you think I should go back and redo the ending, or should we just push on from here."

"What's the chance anyone bought The Liner."

"That might be in our favor. We go on from here!"

"Is that shrapnel worth anything."

"Not even for fishing lures."

"Are we married?"

"I suppose I should clarify that. I don't think The Captain knew what he was doing."

"You mean we're not married."

"It's complicated. Even going from Astoria, Oregon to Limerick, Ireland is complicated."

"I'm glad we're still alive."

"I'm glad you're feeling better."

"Valentine, do you know if Curtis is engaged. Maybe I could be a First Lady."

"I'll check."

The Dolphin & Seal limped into her berth in Limerick, Ireland where she would be pampered and entertained by the cast of Riverdance. Shirley disembarked on Curtis's arm, Kenny was on his way to an interview, the Captain was waving to everyone in his cabin Whites, and Valentine was making arrangements to get to Transylvania on his phone.

"Hello, Avis, I need something which will get me to Transylvania. I'll be looking for a watch and may end up in the most rugged of places so it will have to be sturdy. A tank? I hadn't considered that. Is this the Chinese military? Miss Lu, is that you."

Valentine saw Shirley being steadied by Curtis and hailed her across the shamrock on the dock.

"Shirley. Curtis has a gunboat. Just sayin."

Shirley turned and blew a kiss to her bard.

"Good luck, my sweet Valentine. I hope you find out what time it is."

And that was the end of that.

"Miss Lu, are you still there."

"What is this thing."

"It's a Studebaker."

"Is there any steel left in the mill."

"For other models, possibly, but this is the Champion Coupe, blue, 1950. There's another one just like it in Havana. We had a call from a Miss Lu. She said you'd take it."

"That fox. She's getting in all my henhouses. But only if you have two sets of keys. I'm not going to be responsible for her negligence. They lost Taiwan, I'm sure she'll lose my keys."

"She's waiting in the car. Not in the car. But on the GPS she asked to be installed. Have a nice trip."

Valentine approached the Studebaker with a wary eye.

"I hope we get along," he said. "You have a very nice patina. Do you mind if I get in."

The Avis Desk looked out the window at Valentine in the lot talking to the Studebaker.

"Another nutter from the States, Erin. How far did he say he was going."

"He didn't know. He was thinking 20 miles. He left his American Express Credit Card, which is expired. I'm sure we won't see him again. Finally, we get rid of that Studebaker."

"Ok, where are you, Miss Lu."

"I'm hiding in the closet."

"If you're referring to this small structure on the dash, that says Model 3200, I hardly think it provides enough room. How tall are you, anyway."

"I'm 4 ft 8. How tall are you."

"Well, at one time I was 6 ft 1. I think currently I'm 5 9. I seem to be drying up. I hope you keep an eye on me."

"I will."

"I should probably turn this on. I'm just curious, Miss Lu. Is there any way to turn you off."

"I don't think so. Ooh, it looks like you've run into the Avis sign. Unfortunate for you, Mr. O. Do you want me to explain to Ewan what happened."

"I think it's Erin. Why would they put a sign on the side of the building. You should use that in my defense. Anyway, you have such confidence in me. It seems that every heroine I encounter has confidence in me. Why is that."

"It's a fault we have. We start from the top. I'll tap in to Ewan's phone. Wait here"

Valentine put the Studebaker into reverse and disengaged from the Avis waiting area.

"I can't believe they gave me a stick shift," he mumbled out of reach of Miss Lu's ears.

"You're in the clear, they said you could go. Something about they'd rather demolish the building. You must have impressed them."

Valentine Odey fished in his pocket for the key.

"I was trying to hide it in case they asked for it back. Hold on, Miss Lu, I'm going to see what this baby can do."

Michel and Erin watched as the Studebaker ascended into the air over the town of Limerick.

Some kid over Germany was playing Mississippi Fred McDowell on his radio and interfering with Valentine Odey's transmission. Fred's propulsive, locomotive style driving Ms. Lu crazy.

"Turn left, turn right, no, go straight. Back up. Recalibrating, turn around. Shake it. Bake it. Goodbye Mr. O. I'm out of this kind of range."

"Hi this is Petra. I'll be taking over for Miss Lu. Are you the one in the car that looks like the nose of a football, are you."

"Jadwiga, from Poland, how are you. I'll be advising you from here."

"Mr. Odey, I am Alina. We are now over Central Romania. Please fasten your seatbelt if you overlooked that for the past 2000 miles. Put your gearshift in a secure position and prepare for landing. The weather this morning is 23 degrees Celsius, which is about 74 degrees in Astoria. Tanya will be waiting for you."

Mississippi Fred McDowell kept the bass note pounding with his thumb as Valentine descended into Transylvania.

The football had a dizzying fall. Way beyond the end zone, way beyond Fall. In its finale the thundering splat of 4000 lbs of sheet metal and lead came to rest outside a castle, in a flower bed, and Valentine got out.

"I'm back," our hero said, "Is anybody home."

The prettiest little girl came out and touched the Studebaker on the nose.

"What's this," she said, and thumped it anyway, with a bright red rose.

"It's my car," Valentine said, rather indignant that after two thousand miles, not to mention the flat, it had been banged on the nose by a girl who wasn't much bigger than a cat.

"You seem very bright," Valentine said. "I hope you realize I've come a long way. Do you have a name, or should I just call you Mae, or Soo, or Hoo although that name may not actually apply to you."

"My name is Tanya," she said. "My Aunt says that at the very least I'm a pest, but that most of the time I'm the best. Why are you here. You're not at all like the rest."

"But, you're the only one I met."

The gargoyles of the Lion Dogs on the face of the castle barked at Valentine. He was very taken back by this and wished he could examine them. But they were too high up and cemented in place. When Valentine continued to squint at them they rained down insults and strained. It didn't seem like a very welcoming place.

"Oh, don't bother about them," Tanya said. "I mean, it's not like their leash is going to break."

"Actually, I was thinking I should get back in my Studebaker and go on."

"To where? Tanya said. "Everything past here is mired in mud and imperceptible space. You've reached the right place. You just have to stand your ground."

Valentine always wanted a set of Dunlop Tires. He had no idea if that would be advisable, or if it would make whatever car he had at the time run better. He'd never even seen a Dunlop tire. But he had a Dunlop golf ball once and was fond of it. He also saw a billboard once for Dunlop Tires. He felt if he had Dunlop Tires he could really stand his ground.

The 12 watt bulb in the stairwell provided very little light.

"I can hardly see at all," Valentine complained.

"It will be better when we get in the yard. There will be natural light and LED fixtures to warm you."

"How will I be called."

"Whatever I name you."

"His name is Vilnius."

Immediately everybody wanted to claim me.

The days went on and turned to years. Vilnius grew as strong as an oak in the forest. But Tanya grew, too. And one day he looked at her and certain emotions came unglued.

"How old am I he said."

"You are twenty-seven rings and all of them new!"

"But how old was I when I came here."

"That was a different age. Not one we add to."

"How old are you."

"I'm seventeen rings. And all of them are new.

Vilnius was new, alright. Everything before existed in a vacuum. The Studebaker sat in the castle yard and was revered as the vehicle that brought the seed from outer space. The lease agreement in the glove box was regarded as his manuscript. Twelve guards were assigned to read the lease on a rotating basis. Each of them had their own interpretation of it, and they presented their interpretations on Friday afternoons at 3 o'clock. Everyone looked forward to it. At the end of the interpretation, no matter what it was, everyone jumped up and said, "Yeah!"

"We should get on my Pterosaur and go flying," Tanya said. Vilnius, who was newly admiring Tanya, thought that was a good idea.

Vilnius held Tanya tight as the Pterosaur flew to great heights and then swooped over Transylvania. Small hills and valleys stretched out before Vilnius and stirred him. Tanya leaned in to him and kissed him. The Pterosaur leveled off and they floated in light covering. The clouds shielded their activities as Vilnius and Tanya entered the Bronze Age. Silver and Gold was a long way off and was hardly on their minds at the moment.

"Pterosaur, take us to the Hill of Time," commanded Tanya, and Vilnius sat up like a line.

"Where's that," he said, and Tanya sat up before him.

"It's where the Hands are. We have to let them set us before this fire slips away."

"It can go away that quick."

"In Time it can go away. I don't want that to happen."

"Ok."

Vilnius was an agreeable sort. He also hadn't entered the age of Doubt yet so he didn't really understand what Tanya was saying. Tanya was on the edge of that age and drew Vilnius close to her.

The Pterosaur charged into the night, as it was night now, and flew like a lightning bolt thru it.

The little hand and the big hand were sitting under a tree. "On the face of it," the big hand said, "You will never catch up with me."

"On the face of it,' the little hand said, "You can't get ahead without me."

289

"Let's play Rock, Paper, Scissors to settle this."

The big hand, of course, threw down Scissors, and the little hand threw down rock. Ordinarily Rock would win, but the tree they were sitting under choose paper and covered them. So when Tanya and Vilnius got there, their fate had already been decided, as neither hand had won so neither one could tie them.

"We'll just have to see how it goes," Tanya said, and they got on the Pterosaur and went back to the castle.

There wasn't a King of this castle. The position had been vacant since the Revolution but the children still liked to play like they could be one. After all they lived in a castle. Vilnius was at the age to be a Prince if you could be that, too. Tanya, of course, was already of the age to be a Princess , and long before their flight on the Pterosaur she waited in the wings, not necessarily for Valentine but for whoever it was that was suitable to show up. Suitable for Tanya as she was very particular, and whatever she did, she liked to do herself.

And now from the rampart she watched Valentine walk across the yard.

Only she knew that he was, 'Valentine,' of course. She wondered if even he remembered that. He seemed like a amiable duck, in line with whatever row he found himself in. He didn't seem like a valiant Prince at all. For some reason Tanya didn't count this against him. The thing that appealed to her was his affection for dogs, particularly old ones, who would bark if he opened a door halfway across the castle away. Now George was barking, as V walked across the yard to announce his name.

"GEORGE!"

And this would go on almost every day.

Of course, George lived in the Studebaker. It's possible they made it spacious just for dogs like George. He preferred the front seat, on the passenger side, of course. The Studebaker hadn't been started up in years. Valentine, or Vilnius, was tempted to do that, but it wasn't easy to start up a monument, or go anywhere with all the bleachers set up around it. So, Vilnius would just sit in it with George and pretend they were going somewhere. George was blind so Vilnius could get away with anything. "Look out for that boxcar, George," but George knew he wasn't the one driving. You couldn't fool George. Almost anything.

Tanya was in a play. Her part was Emile Brossard, a columnist for the Resistance. In real life Emile wrote articles daily. The hardest part was usually where to start. Today Tanya was interviewing Vilnius, about where he got his heart. The Elders said if there was ever to be another King he would have to have a heart.

The stage was adjacent to the Studebaker Exhibit, so the bleachers could be used. The set was like the kitchen in Death Of A Salesman. Very sparse. A steel table, a sink and counter, some cupboards, and chairs, a box of Rice Krispies and some milk.

Tanya, as Emile, is sitting at the table. Vilnius gets out of the Studebaker and comes onto the stage.

"Hi Tanya!"

"It's Emile," she whispers, and holds up a cue card.

"Oh, right."

"Can you tell me where you've been tonight."

"I had business. An appointment. It didn't take long. I'm surprised you would feel that wasn't alright."

"My job is to ask questions. I meant nothing by it."

"Perhaps I was late. That's why you asked."

"No, I'm interested in what makes you happy. Wherever you were must make you happy."

"It provides. I contribute to the common weal."

"And what is this business you're in."

"Writing."

"About what. Maybe we have something in common."

"George."

"George! Certainly you mean more than that."

"Not really. I write about adventures. He's full of them if you take the time to listen to him."

"Are you full of adventures, too. Because I'd like to listen to you."

"Sometimes I feel I have someone else in me. He may be full of adventures."

"Is he on one now."

"It's possible. But I'm not sure what it's about. I guess it takes time to come out."

"I understand you took Tanya to the Hill of Time."

"I was trying to find something."

"You mean, recapture something. Something which you had in the past."

"I didn't lose anything."

"And yet you were trying to find it."

"You're confusing me. It's a watch. But it isn't mine. It belonged to someone in my line. He left it here."

"In your line. That's a strange way to talk. What does this watch look like."

"It's shaped like a heart."

"And what are you supposed to do if you find it."

"I haven't thought about that. Wind it, maybe."

"Wind it! Doesn't that mean that something again will start."

"I don't know. I'll have to ask George."

"Or maybe we should start over from the start."

Biff came in and said he didn't make the basketball team.
Disappointments were piling up for Valentine.

In the next scene, Emile Brossard and Vilnius return to the Hill of Time to try to work things out.

In an effort to recreate the Hill of Time on their small set the design squad for the Castle Theatre has gone to great lengths.

"Higher, it has to be HIGHER," the crew chief said. This is not a pocket watch, this is the HILL OF TIME."

"Have you ever been there," Tanya said, annoyed that it was taking so long to assemble the Hill of Time.

"I haven't been there, but I imagine it's very high."

"Actually it's 47 feet, Tanya said. According to the Hands that's the perfect number to go sledding. I don't think we have to go that high for our purpose. Couldn't you just post a sign that says 47 ft., and put an up arrow on it."

"Ok, but no sleds."

"That won't be necessary. Thank you."

Vilnius made a note that actors and stage hands sometimes fight. Not something he would be good at. He would stay in sales.

Finally, Emile and Vilnius were standing on top of the Hill Of Time. They could almost see out of the castle but their effort to find the watch was fruitless. This scene was either not destined to go very well, or it was poorly written.

"Doesn't it seem odd," Vilnius said, "That we're portraying Time as stationary."

"Time doesn't go anywhere," Tanya said. "We do."

"OH!" Valentine said."
And he immediately forgot about the watch.

The Hill of Time was taken down and now the play was delayed because of rain.

One day George left the castle. This is not in the play but it's important. Nobody knew where he went. He was gone for an entire month. A month of cold and snow, and dark, and coyotes. Each of these things was a marauding predator, but they didn't get George. It was said that he hid out on the Hill of Time, that the Hands petted him and kept him warm, and pointed out to him where to get food and water. Nobody could prove that, but there wasn't anywhere else to go that had kindness to it. The Hands were kind even though they had a daunting job to do. When George came back it was like his Tao was complete. He had had his adventure.

Emile was sitting in the Studebaker, in the back, waiting for the rain to stop. The Elders were conferring off stage. Despite Vilnius's new lack of interest they were sure that whoever had the ticker had the time to be their King. So, when the rain stopped they decided to form a Search Party and search everyone in the realm, and generally take the place apart.

No one had the watch. The castle had been entirely picked over. Emile reported it as so thorough, "The Hounds have been up here working with their glasswork."

Vilnius felt bad for Tanya that nothing had come of her reporting that resembled art. Even the stage was left in disarray around the Studebaker like a pile of cards and serving trays.

This was a castle that wasn't ok.

But then the Studebaker started up like a roar in the room, and a little boy whose name was Moliere said, "What about George, doesn't he play a part," and under his fur matted by running they found the heart.

MENTIONS

This story was for George, the only real character in it, whose actual last quarters were hardly fit for a King, but who completed his Tao without complaining. George was a beloved, old dog, and I like to think right now he's running menacingly through the rain.

APE SHIT

Valentine is taken to a hideout for his safety, and others.

The man who returned to 'The Barber's Pearl' complained that his fortune cookie had no fortune in it and waved his receipt at the counter girl, I guess, to prove that he deserved one. Chief Carotid Artery deftly removed an arrow from his quiver and patiently strung his bow.

"Egads," Valentine said. "What are you going to do with that."

But it was too late and the arrow whizzed along the menu screen and split the complainant's face.

Valentine woke up sweating profusely, and asked for a mirror to look into, just in case.

The roar in the room came out of the patient's mouth in 9C. Valentine Odey, which is pronounced O Day if you needed to know that, sat up in a sea of attachments and said, "Where am I?"

A very pretty nurse who looked like Adele said, "You're in a coma."

"Well, how do I get out of it," replied Valentine who figured all the things attached to him was the coma.

In addition to all these things there were several people surrounding Valentine. One of them was Shirley, who looked perfectly healthy.

"I was on top," she said, proud of herself. "You've been out of it for two months. Where have you been."

"I've been to Anina and back again, apparently. Did you ever get married to Curtis."

Their conversation was interrupted by an Indian who looked like he'd been walking around in an abandoned coal mine in W. Virginia.

"You can't buffalo me. I know you're ok. They need the bed. You should get out of it. Factorus told me to give you this."

"What is it."

"It's a bag of peanuts. Let's go."

Chief Carotid Artery wheeled Valentine out of 9C and into a very long corridor which was lined with well wishers.

'Who are these people," Valentine said, as he reached out to grab a blonde.

"They're your characters. They missed you."

"Where are we going."

"We're going to a hideout so they can have some peace."

"That doesn't sound like they missed me."

"They've always had an odd way of expressing themselves. This is no different."

"So where are we going."

"We're going to a Crypto mining plant."

"But I don't understand anything about that stuff."

"Either do your characters. You'll be safe there and so will they. Fasten your seatbelt."

"I bet the guard won't let us in."

"Oh, he will. There's something about a Kenworth running at you at 80 miles an hour. They let you in."

A facility that looked like a repurposed insane asylum was perched on top of a hill. The forest around it was rather pleasant and green. Obviously the beneficiary of carbon offsets purchased by the Monkey Business Mining operation sitting on top of it. The guard at the gate jumped up and down and crazily waved his arms at the approaching intruder. The Kenworth blew it's horn back at him and crashed through the cow gate.

B A M. And for good measure, Toot, Toot.

Valentine was tempted to say, "I'm home," but he'd used that before. So, he just swung the cab door open and fell out.

Chief Carotid Artery ran around the Kenworth and picked Valentine up.

"Are you ok, Valentine. What were you thinking." "I was thinking that a star's entrance is everything. I was also sitting on my bag of peanuts and was worried that I had damaged them so I hastily got off them and accidentally opened the door before I realized we were here. My medication has probably spoiled my senses. My God, this place looks like a Gulag. Are you sure this isn't an elaborate plot which Bubba has hatched to get his truck back. I don't remember seeing him in the corridor."

"Bubba is back in Texas. He couldn't get off. But Darlene was there. She was passing out the crab cakes. Here comes the guard."

"I'll handle it. I've dealt with his type before."

The guard, who also looked like Bubba, kept saying, "What the, what the..." until Valentine helped him out.

"What the Hell."

"What the shit."

"What the fuck."

And waited patiently while the guard pondered his options.

"What the fuck."

"Good choice," Valentine said. "Now, where's the bunkhouse. Actually, where's the bathroom, first. Unless there's one in the bunkhouse, which would make sense."
"What the shit."
"Now you're backtracking. And you were doing so good."
The guard, who had neither holster, or gun, or pepper spray, or back up squinted at Valentine. And then he noticed Chief Carotid Artery in full Flathead Indian gear with a stack of feathers sticking out of his headband, and a bag of arrows on his back.
"What the hell."
"If you mean the Flathead Tribe doesn't even live around here you're right. This is Iroquois land. We're simply on location for a film we're considering making. Maybe you can be in it."
"So, you don't want it back."
"Not yet. But we're going to keep that on the table. Now, I shan't ask again about that bathroom."
The guard pointed to a building that had a big B on it.

"So, that's the bathroom."
"No, that's the hive. The bathroom is over there under H. Sometimes I switch the letters. Nobody seems to mind."
"Is your name, Bubba."
"No, it's Merle. I should get back to the guard shack. Are they expecting you?"
"We have a reservation," CCA said, to which even Valentine blinked.
"Well, that's ok then," Merle said, but cast a disapproving glance at the Kenworth.
"He seemed like a nice enough fellow."
"Most of them are, Art. Guard shacks are humbling places. After a while you just want to give out suckers."
Valentine followed The Chief who pushed open the large glass door to Bldg B with confidence. A vast empty hallway greeted them. And yet there was a hum, which greatly distracted Valentine.
"That sounds like a choir of quail, Chief, or a whole room is being disciplined. Where do you expect it's coming from."
"From the walls. Thick as Tribal pea soup."

"You guys make pea soup."

"Sure we do. What do you think you were eating in Montana."

"I thought it was porridge."

"Well, it wasn't. You've got to keep your nationalities straight."

HHHHHHHHHHHHHHHHHHHMMMMMMMMMMMMMMMM.

"Jesus, that's annoying. And I don't see picks, or shovels, or assay offices, or big hats. Or posters saying, 'Go West.' Are we there yet."

"This is a new age, Valentine. Old time mining is out, just like your 'porridge.' Algorithms are the new dirt. Currency of the mind is in. Everybody trying to get on the Block, get on the ledger. It's kind of like Amway. You hope the pyramid keeps growing. If people stop washing their clothes it's over."

HHHHHHHHHHHHHHHHHHHMMMMMMMMMMMMMMMM.

"Is there anybody in this mine?"

At that moment three of them walked up to our boys.

"Can we help you, Mates."

Three large square pegs hovered over our two round holes.

"We were looking for the loo."

"We don't take time to do that in this building. It's H you want."

The fellow who was speaking was very brutish looking and the two acquaintances he had with him were even more brutish looking. Valentine was tempted to say, "You're very brutish looking." The two brutish acquaintances took a threatening step toward Valentine. Without fanfare Chief Carotid Artery stepped in their way. His right hand disappeared over his shoulder into his quiver. Even with over a hundred years since anyone in his tribe considered this, he didn't hesitate and would have slain them if he had to.

Algorithms are like tarot cards. When you flip one over and it says, "This is the card of Death," you back away from the computer.

"Hey, Hey. No offense, mates. We just have to be careful who's in here."

"Well, I'm sure Merle has already entered us into his log by now. If you know we're here I suspect your boss does also. I suggest you call him, or her, which I hope is the case, and learn that we have an authorization code to be here. In other words, we were expected. Put that arrow back, Art, it's making me nervous."

The Big Brute listened intently to a cup which was attached to his hair and dangled in front of his nose. A sheen of Brylcreem dripped down the mobile wire into the receiver on the cup and garbled all the instructions he was receiving from somewhere in the Hive, as a result of which our boys were escorted to a nice room to stay in, instead of the back door which dropped off into the lake. In fact, their room was in an annex that was connected to Bldg H. Valentine was relieved. The Chief laid out a blanket and Valentine laid out his clothes.

"How long will we be here, Art," he asked, looking at the two pairs of socks in the middle of the bed.

"Until you can come up with something that makes sense. This may be your last chance. Don't squander it, Valentine."

In the back of the plant, besides the lake, there was a track, on which trains with long columns of coal had long complained, an evening parade which pleased Valentine, who listened to it rumble in the valley before coming here, at sunset under his home on the hill beneath the shade. But that daily train was gone now and the Power Station it went to was now a crypto mining plant.

There were several things that baffled Valentine, starting with women. And ending with crypto currency. He had relied so long on spellcheck that he was astounded when he typed it in and nothing happened. It was accepted. He felt like he had fallen into a well. And no explanation of this well could get him out of it. It seemed counter intuitive, like putting the wastebasket on the left side under the sink instead of the right. So, when the Chief told him where they were going he said, "It serves me right, I've denied a Father of his Son, and now I have to pay for what I have done." Art said, "What the hell are you talking about."

After Valentine had located his copy of Emergency Poems by Nicanor Parra to where he could find it in the dark, they went to look for the cafeteria.

"Are you sure they have one, Chief."

"I don't think Door Dash is coming out here, Val. Somebody's feedin these people. And it isn't Darlene."

Val and Art cut across the yard in time to see Merle switching the Letters on the buildings, again. The 20 ft ladder he was on looked like Lew Archer's 'Ivory Grin' with several teeth missing. Merle sheepishly grinned as he tried to navigate the ones that were left.

"Now what."

"'C.'"

"Let's take it."

Behind them Merle fell over in the yard and spilled a whole can of other letters.

In 'C' there turned out to be a row of vending machines, so it was close, and a study hall. Aisles of student desks and tuna fish sandwiches as far as the eye could see. But there was one table and at that table our boys sat down next to 'Lucia Berlin.'

"Hi, fellas. Did you get your tuna fish sandwiches yet. You gotta get that fish oil working if you're going to figure this shit out." Lucia was looking at a programming manual that had 400 pages in it. Jackson Browne was singing 'These Days' on the school intercom. And the study hall was humming.

"Where do you get the manual."

"They're in the desks. But you should get the tuna sandwich first. They run out of that. What's your names anyway." Valentine could see that everybody else had name tags on, but that didn't mean he was going to give up that easily.

"Are you the librarian."

"No, I'm the Cleaning Lady. My name is Dólares. I'm really a sculptor and a set designer. But I'm very fond of Lucia Berlin. I'm also waiting for everybody to get the hell out of here so I can clean up. Are you the Lone Ranger, because I'd like to see that silver bullet."

"I'm not the Lone Ranger."

"And I'm not Tonto," Art said.

"But you've shown up in the nick of time. Think about it."

"Valentine thought about it."

"Who's the boss around here."

"Driller. His real name is Ed. Like in E.D. He smokes a pipe. I mean who smokes a pipe. No offense to the Chief, here, but who the hell smokes a pipe. Maybe he thinks he's a pirate."

"You seem very angry."

"You seem very new. But Ranger John Reed will catch on. I put revolutionary notes in the margins of the manuals I can get a hold of. Keep your eye out. But you better go get your sandwiches before the Monitors get nervous."

Above Valentine, Art, and Lucia glass eyeballs flew around monitoring the student's progress like they were in one of Harry Potter's halls.

"We're all part of the application. I'm in Room 12. Come see me later if you're still here. Bring Merle."

"That was intense," Valentine said.

Valentine and the Chief debated how to approach Merle.

"I think we should just walk right up to the guard shack and egg it. He'll come out."

"I think I should just politely ask him to come out. I'll even put my hands up."

In the end they walked over to the guard shack and in unison, said, "Help, my foot's caught."

Merle peeked his head out of his little window and saw two figures grappling with a bear trap. He immediately got his pliers and rushed out.

"Pliers??? Man, this is a bear trap. We need a Jaws of Life, or you got one dead Indian on your hands."

Merle went back inside the guard shack and got the Jaws of Life which was still in the box it came in along with the instructions for assembly. He had tried to put it together himself when it got there but he couldn't get the holes to line up. So, Valentine, Art and Merle were all wrestling with the parts to the Jaws of Life. In the end Merle said, "Hey, you're not in a bear trap at all!"

But now Merle's thighs were being extended in opposite directions by a feature of the Jaws which had come to life. Art and Valentine struggled to adjust him. They were all three squiggling around in front of the guard shack. Merle was screaming, "Put 3 into 5, I'm sure of it." But the holes continued to have their own system, and Merle continued to be extended.

At last there was a high whiney "darn," and Merle disembarked.

"That's one feature I can do without," he said, vigorously rubbing his pelvis. "What did you guys want, anyway."

"There's a meeting tonight in 12. We were just trying to get your attention. Dólares said to bring you."

"You might have to carry me, unless we can find a horse."

It was a pleasant day at the crypto plant. The sun was fizzing away another umpteen trillion gallons of fuel and the fans on the computers were soaking up most of it. The leaves on the trees were burning their lovely Christmas red and green colors, or yellow. Three stick figures in this arrangement made their way to Room 12. The little hands on the sign at the guard shack said, 'I'll be back at 9 am.'

Dólares opened her door after Merle gave the secret knock. It was like, knock knock, and Dólares says, "Who's there." "Merle." "Merle who." "Merle from the guard shack." "Ok, Comon in."

Lucia Berlin was sitting on a couch with Frankie Freeport, a black transgender stripper from Gary, Indiana. Frankie brushed her hand in the air, like, "Who is this."

"Frankie, this is the Documentary Crew I told you about."

"They don't look like good film to me. Maybe the Chief, but this other cabrón looks a little sketchy."

Valentine looked at Art, suspiciously. "You in on something here, Art"

"I may have had a conversation with Dólares. She was in the hospital for depression. About her job. We got to talking about what would make her feel better."

"And what would make her feel better."

"We're going to rob the bank," Dólares said, with the authority of a moviegoer.

"That makes sense. You don't need me to do that."

"We need you to write it up, make sense of our ideals, or at least be accurate so the company isn't the only one plundering. Art said you can make sense out of anything."

"Art I'll deal with later. But if this involves a Flight from Montgomery you gotta leave the Kenworth out of it. I'm not going to have him loaded up and be chased all around the country by law enforcement. We already have a State Trooper from Salinas, Kansas looking for us."

Dismissing this concern Frankie said, "Maybe we rehearse in the truck, but we don't load it up. Smells like Buffalo in there anyway."

"Could I talk to you, Art."

The hallway was like a tube, in which the incessant hum from within the walls annoyed our country rubes. In the yard the leaves were swirling around in their doom and the lake brooded with its grey hood in another time of evil and good.

"Well, here's another fine mess you got me into."

"That's Factorus's job. I'm just filling in. This is another story. Merle, Dólares, Frankie, and Driller, whoever he is. You think you need more help than this."

"I'm thinking the Honorable Congresswoman from Montana might come in handy."

"She might be busy with Marjorie."

"Then get her, too."

"I don't think Marjorie is vaccinated."

"We might not be vaccinated. I've lost track how that's supposed to work. Just call Pleasant Hemlock Grove and see if she can get away with Marjorie. Tell them we're going to rearrange the currency of the World. Emphasize, WORLD. They haven't been in Washington long, but long enough to know where their maize is buttered."

Valentine and Art gave the secret knock to get back in the room. Dólares was knitting a protest sign that said, 'THAT'S BULLSHIT.' Frankie was holding her bolt of yarn and smoking a cigarette. The other Frank in the room was Frank Bug, a security pro from Temple Beth-El in Hudson, Florida. He kept tapping the walls with a tuning fork and said, "I got a G Flat."

"Who's the other black cat on your lap."

"That's Fidel."

"Ok, so, help is on the way. We're getting the government involved so Driller will think twice about disappearing us. I think. But until help arrives we have to have a plan."

"A plan for what," Frankie Freeport interjected. "You guys might be in over my head. Are we seriously gonna get something to eat out of this or not. We got brothers and sisters gettin all sorts of free stuff out in Oakland and we sittin here in a cleaning woman's crib making plans we don't even have enough to feed a cat. No offense, little black cat. I might just go find me another stage where some straight folks can appreciate me."

"Frankie, Frankie, you're the Distraction," Dólarez cried. "Without you there's no yellow light." Merle got up and blocked the door. Frankie could have swiped him aside if she wanted to but in truth she was flattered. She owned the room. Why would she leave it.

"Art, make the call. This room is not going to outdraw any heist movie that I've seen. I can't even write a script around it. No offense, Lucia, but this cast sucks."

Frankie took offense.

"Say hey, Mr. Coma, you the one woke up and got us this far. Nobody else dreamin this stuff up. You gotta dream us out of it. Without offending everybody, starting with me."

Outside, in the distance, way in the distance, like barely audible in the distance, a train whistle was blaring. In a carriage car two figures were seated across from each other.

"Do you think I should wear feathers in <u>my</u> hair."

The Honorable Pleasant Hemlock Grove looked hard at the Honorable Representative from Georgia.

"Marjorie, if you wore feathers in your hair, some constituent in your district is liable to shoot you and upon getting closer regret he couldn't take you home for dinner. No, I wouldn't advise it."

Well, I've never been to New York before, and I just want to look good."

"You'll look good. This is not the Big Apple, Marjorie. It's more like a orchard. Just don't point that gun of yours at my brother."

The coal train chugged north. The seal of the House of Representatives which was affixed to the carriage car came undone and bounced off somewhere into Pennsylvania. As a result after Hazelton nobody lined the tracks to see them and Marjorie grew concerned. But all the little fracking rigs in the dark appeared to be small towns saluting her as she went by so she sat back and smiled at her honorable friend from Montana.

"Is your brother cute."

"He looks like a sunset and walks like a tree.   If that helps. He's also a friend of Mr. Odey who used to work for Nike."

"The missiles!"

'No, Marjorie, the shoes."

They came out on the other side of the world. Daylight. Forests, far north of the New York-Pennsylvania line. The coal train with its little carriage car was approaching a valley beneath a roost where our hero in his prime cut his lawn and read Proust, also more recently Guillermo Rosales and Elisa Shua Dusapin, to boot.   A recent storm had tipped the tracks so the carriage car went by and almost lost its hat. "Ohhh," Marjorie said, "What was that."

And on this new slant, Pleasant Hemlock Grove relaxed, and said, "We're getting closer to the plant." Unlike the Cedar, Fir, Juniper, and Larch of her own District, this one seemed denser, more serious, but still, trees. The way she was brought up they were called Standing Company. So she looked out on them with affection even though they were not soft. The leaves from the Oaks and Maples mounded on the tracks and crunched beneath their iron feet. This was Iroquois Confederacy Land, and the Mohawks among them were the Keepers of The Eastern Door. Fierce fighters, they would later become iron and steel construction workers. Fearless of heights. Builders of Skyscrapers. Pleasant Hemlock Grove thought of the broad claim her Nation had in many ways, to America, and sat up straight across from Marjorie.

"What bank are we talkin about."

"The bank of computers," Art said. "And all that crypto shit they got locked up in them. Blocks and chains and ledgers and a lot of very heavy stuff."

Valentine, whose knowledge was limited to excel spread sheets, and even that reluctantly, tried to process this news.

"How do we get all that stuff out. How do they get all that stuff out."

"They suck up about a balillion kilowatts of municipal electricity and have a whole zoo of monkeys cranking away in the walls on a big treadmill that Hewlett Packard built. And the head ape is holed up in an office next to Driller in the tower. They feed him bananas and cool whip and all the monkeys want to be like him so they crank out algorithms until they solve a puzzle they didn't even know they're working on. Then they get to be the big ape until the next guy succeeds. It might be difficult because he's a real ape, and they're not really monkeys, but it's hard to control ambition."

"And this is our brave new currency."

"With a big ▲ and a picture of the ape on it."

Art continued.

"The problem is it's currency for a very limited world. Dólares wants to spread it out, speed it up. That's why we're here. Other than you get to write some fuzzy stuff about it. We just have to figure a way to get in the walls. Frank Bug is working on it. Christmas is just around the corner."

"I think Frank Bug is Jewish."

"All he has to do is get us in there. We'll do the bagging."

There was a ding on Merle's phone.

"Egads, somebody's here. After hours dinging is likely to bring ED out. Who's going to carry me back to the shack."

Reps. Grove and Greene were waiting patiently by the clock. "9 am, my eye," Marjorie said. "I'm not standing here all night in the dark. This place looks like someplace Jim Jordan goes on vacation. Do you even think he owns a suitcoat."

Our Documentary crew came running up in time to see Ed approaching the members of the House of Representatives.

Ed told the three Brutes to take a hike.

"Boar Pants!!!"

"Plessy!!!"

"You guys know each other," Valentine gasped, and set Merle down.

"Plessy!!!"

"Boar Pants!!!"

"Uncle Ed?"

"Caro!!!"

Majorie looked at Merle.

"Nah."

Valentine shook his head but no other characters fell out. Or scenarios. He was speechless.

Merle turned his sign over to say 'Open.'

The trees were confused. The lake was confused. The Ape in the tower was confused. On a scale of 1-10, it was Frankie Freeport they should be worried about. But we're not there yet.

"Who's the big ape," Plessy said, as Ed closed the door to his office and Abner spooned his cool whip on the other side of 4" of plexiglass.

"That's Abner. He's the face of this whole irritating experience. His face is on more crypto than you can shake a stick at. But don't shake a stick at him. He gets annoyed. He prefers it when I play "Goodnight, Sweetheart," by the Spaniels.

"That was our song!"

"It was the only CD I kept. Those were the days, Plessy. Me running the Big Dig in Butte, and you coming to the IHS dance. Now I'm here because they need someone with credentials so they can throw off the Common Council, think they got a real wild west mine right in their tight little neighborhood. They get CNN up here every month to do a story. Never occurs to them we don't have any picks, or shovels, or assay offices, or signs that say, 'Go West.' All we got are those goddamn signs that say, 'THAT'S BULLSHIT.' I think Dólares is behind it but Abner likes her so I can't get rid of her. She's from Cuba, you know. Do they have any apes in Cuba. I don't know that. She knits all those signs. As soon as I find out who's helping her I'm going to crack down. I think it's Frankie Freeport. I haven't slept in a month with that goddamn hum. Can you hear it. It never stops. It's in the walls. The employees are in the walls, too. We play everything by The Monkees to keep them entertained in there. Plus it soothes Abner, too. This is the most annoying place, Plessy. If we're backing up the world's stability, the world is a nervous wreck."

Driller put his head in Plessy's lap and blubbered. His pipe fell on the floor and the Jamaica Rum tobacco spilled out. He liked to think he was a pirate.

"So, what's the plan."

"It's simple. We wait til the Exchange has got a Hot Wallet then we pick it. Frank Bug has found the weak spot in their program. It's a B Flat. We just got to distract all their monkeys so we can do the picking."

"Pleasant Hemlock Grove is already distracting your Uncle Ed."

"I know."

Showtime.

Frankie Freeport walkin down the hall, soaking up stares like denatured alcohol. Raising up her arms like Joel Osteen she exposes all the monkeys in their Levi jeans. Merle's on point, he's Bucky Phillips on the run, another ghost ridin 'round with 23 guns. Valentine and Caro are bringing up the rear, drumming on drums and hollering, "Look over here." And in this magician trick where they saw the woman in half, Frank Bug redirects the flow and all that crypto shit goes off to a food bank in Buffalo. In Dólares's room Frankie's cigarette is igniting the ball of yarn which will soon send the castle up like an old country barn. All the monkeys, freed from their posts, run for the Kenworth to head for the coast. The Brutes are armed and trying to get in to put a stop once and for all to all this crackle and spin. But Merle with his 23 guns and the Jaws of Life stands and repels them. At the end of the hall just out of sight there's a little hatch door that goes into the night. Dólares is waiting in her little submarine which gleams in the lake under the whoosh in the trees and the little coal train. "Hurry," she yells to everyone. To Valentine and Frankie and Frank, and Plessy and Caro, and the little black cat who is long and narrow. And to Driller, most of all, after all, who is hauling his chest, of coins and tobacco and rum for the rest. The castle is burning, "Where's Merle," Caro cried. "It's too late," said Dólares, "He'll always be on our side." And as they left for Cuba by canals and ways they all looked up at the smoke and the haze. And what should they see, no not Santa and his reindeer, but something just as odd and equally queer. It was the big Ape holding Marjorie above the blaze, in the tower by the lake that the Ice Age made. And as the submarine submerged into a literary nook Marjorie cried out,

"HOW DO I LOOK!"

MENTIONS

Straight away, thanks to Big JD, who let me use his social media handle in a cameo appearance in this story. The job of a good writer is to steal material, but in this case I asked permission. It's not 'Driller,' but you're close. Thanks, John!

And thanks to Stiller Zusman, whose long tray of black olives on her table became part of the end of it.

THE DEEPLINE

(ANOTHER SHORT STORY BY G. N. PRICE)

It's a new year. Covid is gone and all the masks are now fouling the oceans of the world. A Shark is swimming off Brazil with a mask on his snout, says, EAT MORE PIZZA. The author is sitting on a porch in Ecuador with his mask on. He has no idea the crisis is over. A submarine comes by and a tall figure holding a black cat asks him if he knows where Cuba is. "You passed it," he says, and goes back to his book.

"Hmpff." "A submarine," the author said. "Who ever thought of that." He turned his attention back to his miniature book, but soon his mind went back to the submarine.

"Hey, wait a minute," he said. "I know that cat." And he ran to the ocean and dived in.

The clunking on the hull was getting to Valentine.
"Another fine mess we didn't tie down. Who wants to go out there and see what it is."
Frankie Freeport, who was sipping a Margarita said, "I don't do water."
The Chief was looking at treasure maps with Uncle Ed. He was also looking at his sister who was a treasure for him. Dólares was working on a vest that said, "Good luck," for Simon Cowell, in case he showed up, which wasn't likely. Besides, the stage was empty. Bug went over to mumble in a corner and light a minora. He had to be reminded that oxygen was at a premium in their circumstances. "How'm I suppose to read this manual about sub steering if I can't see it." Pleasant Hemlock Grove was writing a letter to Congress about how nothing in this submarine fit, and the Author was twirling on the propeller like Barli the Ice Bear on a spit.

I've listened to the hunters' spiel
And caught some words as I came near them.
It seems they always want to sell
A bearskin coat. Should I then fear them?
Except for me, no bear's around

And me, I need to wear one too
Unless there's someone who can lend
A coat to them, that leaves – guess who?

From the title by the same name, by Ida Bohatta, a series that entertains the author, as his feet turn into fins.

"HELP!!! HELP!!!" he gargled to a Sturgeon and Walleye who were on their way to Lake Superior in Michigan.

"Don't touch it, Phil," the Sturgeon said. "You don't know where it's been."

After 10 days at sea the submarine approached a wreck off the coast of Kuala Lumpur. Some kids were diving into it looking for ash trays they could sell to tourists. Believe it or not ashtrays were considered artifacts in the year 2073. And if you could find one with a Winston in it, it was gold.

"Well, Lucia Berlin, we got this far, now what do you suggest," which was Valentine exercising his critical race theory as the only white man there who wasn't on a spit, or named Boar Pants, or chanting in a unintelligible dialect. And then a singer walked into the control room and invited everyone to the 'Bird's Nest.'

The 'Bird's Nest' was in the middle of the sub. Kind of like a birthing room for hope and faith. Kind of like a club. You could bring in coffee and cake and everyone who came in had some connection to the lake.

Dólares spread out a little rug and said, "I'm sorry I forgot to introduce you, everyone this is my Reflector. We all got one and in my case she's Ronnie Spector."

Valentine said, "I was hoping for Rachel Nagy, but I don't think she ever got beyond the Detroit River."

Then Ronnie sang and in her mouth she brought branches to the nest, and feathers from other birds and pieces of eight from Driller's treasure chest. She sang like a dream, "Be My Baby, Nowww," to everyone's beating breast.

To Valentine the Chief said, "This one's going differently, my friend. Are you telling this or has someone else taken over your fate."

Valentine looked at Bug. He was wearing glasses and had one lens held in by a piece of scotch tape.

"It's possible."

And such were the circumstances for our crew as the sub rocked and leaned and rested in a cover of algae and green on a rim of the South China Sea. The DEEPLINE, which was named for a deep line that Dólares noticed on her 40th birthday, bleated its diesel engine and little smelly bubbles interrupted a wedding ceremony.

As several large rocks were chucked in their direction Valentine yelled, "DIVE, DIVE!," to no one in particular.

Everything that led to the sea was in their way. Balls, thick Styrofoam packaging for the delivery of band saws, refrigerators, with their doors closed almost floating, refrigerators with their doors open, with onion dip, expired, bloating, pork chop containers, pork chops, First Editions, Revised editions, Working Boy editions, Anonymous Editions, rubber duckies, plaques, fish on plaques, lies written on the plaques with fish on them, phone numbers on matchbook covers, phonebooks, phones. Everything that led to the sea. One way or another. It was getting to where there was no room for the sea.

After a period of reasoning Valentine yelled. "Periscope up," in the hope that that would reverse things. A very long periscope popped out of the sea and examined the surface for the existence, of anything. A large freighter carrying mascara was on the way to Panama and a wiffle ball was lapping toward Thailand.

Back in the club Neil Young was holding out for ½ of 2 cents on Spotify and Joni Mitchell was singing, "It's life's illusions I recall." Revolt was in the air the DEEPLINE had left.

"I think we need to draw up a list of observations to the World before it's too late," Valentine chapped, and closed up the arms to the periscope with a thunderous clap.

Valentine is back in the club
In this case The Bird's Nest
And a microphone is fixed between the wings
Of a rose color swan.
It's not one of those microphones
That you take out and hold
With your pinky stuck out.
You have to talk to it
Make it shout.
This a man of the street
Thinking about depth
And what to do about it.
The man walks up to the stage
Looks how it's set up
It's set up about his knees
And he curls up
He sees the steps where you step up,
Where you put the people on notice

That you're going to address them.
But in his case he jumps
In a bound and grabs the microphone
Like Janis Joplin is mad at somebody.
A growl comes out of his mouth
And alarms the crew of the DEEPLINE
So much so that they hold their breath
And Valentine uses it.
Dólares's DEEPLINE is now
The TIEFGANG, a German sub
On the prowl of the face of the South China Sea
But not just there as its little nose is
Pointed to the South and North and
The West and East. Valentine is
On the air broadcasting.
"These are the observations of
The Radical Crew of The TIEFGANG."
And the sea roiled on its coils and chummed
Dizzily.

"The ocean is not a hole," began Valentine. "Well, it is, but it's not your hole, it's not a hole that you made. It's a well that we fell into at the dawn of time. It took us a long time to get out of it and we were hardly recognizable when we did. To get back to our original forms it has taken an even longer time, and we're not there yet. Part of getting back to our original forms is to have respect for the hole we crawled out of, which is the ocean. In English TIEFGANG is DEEPLINE, in Spanish it's Linea profunda. And in Choctaw it's actually a movement, a swipe of the arm. If you're Choctaw you get it. We of the TIEFGANG will swipe our arms at you if you don't get it. The ocean is not a dump. Treat it with respect. Dig your own hole for your crap. Better yet, figure out how to have less crap. This is the First Observation of the Radical Crew of The TIEFGANG."

"And now I invite our brother, Frank Bug from Temple Beth-El in Hudson, Florida to come up and provide our Second Observation. He's a computer security expert. Let's go Frank."

"In case you didn't get that I'm a Jew. A Rabbi to be exact. I hold my congregation and my glasses together with scotch tape. Because scotch tape does a good job. Everybody should put scotch tape on their glasses if it helps them see better. Because a lot of you can't see shit. You got nice glasses but bad eyes. Glasses can't fix bad eyes. Glasses fixes bad vision. Once things get in there you got to have the right kind of eye to interpret what you think you see. You look at me what do you see. If you see a Jew too cheap to buy new glasses we got a problem. If you see a funny little guy uses scotch tape to keep the lenses in his glasses we're making progress. Keep it simple. We're all trying to make it on low wages. This is the Second Observation of the Radical Crew of the TIEFGANG."

"And now I invite our sister, Frankie Freeport, to come up and provide our next Observation. You go girl."

"I'm a Trans. You might not know that since I'm so good lookin. I'm also black, and I'm a stripper. They call me Sweet Onion, the Midnight Clipper. I have a lot of layers, and you do, too. Whether you're straight or crooked or pale or pink everybody has their own way how they set up their kitchen sink. God does, too, but we do the dishes. And all of you have my very best wishes." Frankie wiggled and stretched in her very best thong. "Have you ever seen one of these things wet. The last time I was I couldn't even make rent. This is the Third observation of the Radical Crew of the TIEFGANG."

"OK, Driller, come on up here with your white privilege."

"Arrrh, I follow that Husky Doubloon. Flowers in their lapels. I'm a florist from Constantinople. Ignatius Reilly and I are selling hot dogs on Constantinople Street, a short distance from Burma Jones' cumulous cloud. Ignatius and I are concerned about the breakdown of Medieval Society and the ascendancy of bad taste. If it weren't for cheese dip the lack of theology and geometry in society might be it Unlike the purposeful weight of Ignatius, inflated by Dr. Nut, I encourage you not to fall for everything that falls in your lap in dreams. One day when I was dreaming my hair caught fire.

"SHIRLEY CREIGHTON!!!"

I said. Then I patted himself around my head until the flames went out and I could go back to bed. This is the Fourth Observation from the Radical Crew of the TIEFGANG."

"Plessy, if you have anything left from scurrying into the tunnel with the others to save your lives, now's the time to say it."

"I'm trying to reconcile Boar Pants' dream with our relationship's revival, actually. I understand the deeper we go the more pressure we're under. The peril which has been brought up by my flight attendant is one of reading. The *Confederacy of Dunces* isn't going to solve things. Nor is Gary, The Working Boy. Paco Taibo may be more appropriate in our situation, with his hammer and heart, or Valentine's own flowery summations. The stage is important at any rate. The accommodations from which we say things. Not all of us own. When we surface from this one I hope we remember some of it. To exit we will use the same funnel we took to get here, but that's only because we came here together. That's not always the case. On every stage, traveling on every plain, or for whatever distance it's not only how well we play, but how well we fit our co-star. It cannot be an exaggeration in that case to say that you play with your heart. I assume that's what my friend was trying to get at. This is the Fifth Observation of the Radical Tribe of the TIEFGANG."

"Chief, could you put your bow on this."

Sure, Mate. But it's just something I've been saving. When I was a boy I drew a picture of a crow on a chalk bed in Montana in a place called River Go. I got down and covered it with leaves from a great tree and put berries on it and snow. And then I ate the crow. It tasted like a snow cone from the white man's fair. I expanded with sleek black wings and long brown hair. My skin was softened from the clay that rested on the bank, and I was red as the bed in the soft red river's tow. I flew over tall mountains and plains below and saw the strength and humility of the Buffalo.. This was my first Vision, but is the longest one I hold. That Strength and Understanding can sometimes come from eating crow. Otherwise, don't mess with me. This is the Sixth Observation of the Radical Crew of The TIEFGANG."

In some compartment Dólares was sobbing. Worried that this was unreal, or real. Worried that all the sets would have to come down, that not even this time was sealed. What will happen when the cork explodes. Dólares grabbed the microphone. "Calling all over the Earth," she said, "Calling all students studying in Perth. Do you think that only the rich have ethics. Do you think that only they set the bar. How do you know when a story is over. Do you think it's only when you're not in charge. In every writer's window, slightly beneath the shade, there's a Kenworth loaded with sentences whooshing in the glade. Look at what you have and preserve it. Where do we go from here. How do we appreciate the labyrinth of an eye. That's not just for God but for all of us to decide. This is the Last Observation of the Radical Crew of the TIEFGANG. We should go now."

The TIEFGANG surfaced in a canal outside of Paris for Dólares and Fidel and Frank and Frankie to depart. They were the norm. Water trickled down the rungs. Frank looked up from his lens and said, "That's ok, Frankie, I'll shelter you from the storm." The propeller was empty. The author had dropped off in the Aegean Sea. Chief Carotid Artery, Pleasant Hemlock Grove, and Driller got off on an ice flow to walk across the Bering Straits and start over. Valentine sat alone on the deck in a lawn chair. He was unaware of an object coming at him from a great distance at tremendous speed. There was once a man who ran toward disappointment, was pursued by unease, and as everyone else grew to succeed he lived on the brink of reality and dreams. The sky overhead was so blue it was like it could swallow him up. And just when he was worried about changing his stationery it did.

THE END

About the Author

The author lives in two houses. One is with his beautiful wife, Linda, who rescued him a long time ago. This one's on a hill in NY, which faces Michigan. The other house is in his head, which has shutters on some days, and beautiful sunsets on others. It's important, I'm sure, that he can never see the sunrise. In the MPs his nickname was Nails, which doesn't seem to fit. His favorite author is John Dalton, English Noir Master. That might not seem to fit either, but it's his book.

This book, in its entirety, was written in both houses.

Mentions

In addition to my wife I'm grateful to our son, Ned, who is the poet on the stoop, and our daughter, Delevan, who continues to surprise me. Also to Maggie, our granddaughter who is a delightful UFO, and our grandson, Elijah, who is beside me. And to everyone who has accepted my drafts and been kind. In the end I've used 107,000 words, all of whom I suspect are surprised to be next to each other. I'm not good with outlines, or research, or turning on a faucet. This was intended to be respite for the reader, really. In the end I leave my hero to be picked up, literally, by an old flame. After all that's the way it started, so that's the way it ends. For your relationships there are reasons that probably go back a long way why you're next to each other. Don't fritter away the story by overly trying to sketch it out. Hoping to agree on an outline first is like trying to find a phone book. They ain't no more, and the numbers don't work anyway.

G. N. Price
Danby, NY
June 2022